THE
EMPRESARIO'S WIFE

THE
EMPRESARIO'S
WIFE

*The Woman at the Center
of the Texas Revolution*

A NOVEL BY BARBARA H. SEEBER

**BOLD
STORY
PRESS**

CHEVY CHASE, MARYLAND

Bold Story Press, Chevy Chase, MD 20815
www.boldstorypress.com

This is a work of historical fiction. The narrative
is a product of the author's imagination and
characters, events, and places are used fictitiously.

First edition: October 2024

Library of Congress Control Number: 2024919275

ISBN: 978-1-954805-91-0 (paperback)
ISBN: 978-1-954805-65-1 (e-book)

Cover design by Michelle Bushneff
Maps on pages xvi and xvii by Carl Mehler
Interior design by KP Books
Author photo by David Beacom
Maps on pages 1, 183, 247, and 311 are used
courtesy of David Rumsey Map Collection, David
Rumsey Map Center, Stanford Libraries

Printed in the United States of America
10 9 8 7 6 5 4 3 2 1

But the effect of her being on those around her was incalculably diffusive: for the growing good of the world is partly dependent on unhistoric acts; and that things are not so ill with you and me as they might have been, is half owing to the number who lived faithfully a hidden life, and rest in unvisited tombs.

—George Eliot, *Middlemarch*

For my parents, who taught me to love history,
and my aunt, Mary Ella Hurt,
who taught me so much Texas history

PREFACE

For much of our past, the story of America was revealed through battles, through the men who fought them, the adventurers, and the explorers. Much of America was not yet America. The western and southwestern parts of the continent were wild, untamed, even unclaimed. Part of that southwestern area was called Mexico and ruled by Spain. After independence from Spain in 1821, Mexico was dominated by a dictator-general named Antonio López de Santa Anna.

Americans came into that Mexican nation as early as the 1820s, lured by Mexican officials with land grants for settling and civilizing those vast stretches. From the 1820s into the 1830s, these Americans were called *empresarios*, loosely meaning "land agents." More businessmen than adventurers, they were men who could make things happen, with the power to award land to settlers for mere pennies per acre when it was selling for a great deal more in the United States.

The first of these empresarios in northern Mexico was Moses Austin in 1820 and then his son Stephen F. Austin in 1821. They were followed by Stephen Austin's fellow Missourian and friend Green DeWitt in 1825. They received land grants of hundreds of thousands of acres to bring in families who would populate the rough reaches of northern Mexico, a land made risky and dangerous by hostile Indians, including the Comanche, the Karankawa, and others. To the empresarios—those visionaries who hoped to get rich selling cheap land to Americans fleeing the economic woes of the 1820s in the US—Mexico looked like a golden opportunity. In many ways, after a few years, it would be.

Mostly it was men who traveled into this treacherous land, men who welcomed the prospect, along with a few women who didn't. Or perhaps those women had the sense to know there was plenty to fear. Sarah Seely DeWitt was one of those women. Sarah supported her husband and his venture, even selling her own land in Missouri to help finance the expedition, and brought four of their five children. She left an easier and more prosperous life in Missouri. Imbued with the American spirit, she was following the lead of her parents, who had sold land in Virginia after the American Revolution to settle in Missouri, which was then the frontier.

Today, Sarah DeWitt's story is largely lost. She settled with her family in Gonzales, Texas, and is buried in the DeWitt family cemetery there. Sarah was the first married Anglo woman to secure a land grant from Mexico in her own name. She is remembered for making, with her children, the "Come and Take It" flag. It flew in the first battle of the Texas Revolution on October 2, 1835, as they sought independence from Mexico. (That same flag was probably also carried aloft, some months later, by the volunteers who left Gonzales to fight at the famous battle of the Alamo in 1836.) But little has been written about the life of Sarah DeWitt as one of the first women on the Texas frontier living through those turbulent and pivotal times.

The Texas Revolution started on DeWitt land and led to one of the most significant annexations of land in US history. Ultimately it yielded territory, along with the 1846 Mexican War and associated treaties, that reached all the way to the Pacific Ocean. Yet Sarah's story, from her journey to Texas with her empresario husband in 1826 until her death in Texas in 1854, remains largely unknown.

Green DeWitt's role as a founding empresario appears in history books. As a Texas middle schooler, I learned about him in history class, though Sarah's role was never mentioned.

Sarah is the empresario's wife. While this book is a work of fiction, Sarah and the other principal characters' stories are based on the lives of settlers in or near the DeWitt colony in Coahuila y Tejas, Mexico, in the nineteenth century—before it became Texas. These historical figures and the events they took part in are true to the history of the time, 1826-1836, and drawn from records leading up to the Texas Revolution. Once the capital of the colony, Gonzales is today a bustling south Texas town of some 7,500 citizens located between San Antonio and Houston. Travelers heading east or west into Gonzales on Highway 90-A travel along Sarah Seely DeWitt Drive, the main thoroughfare.

The desire and curiosity to learn "from whence we came" abides in all of us. My mother and grandmother led me to understand that the lives of our forebears, even many generations removed, continue to touch ours—that the past *is* closer than we think. They also helped me appreciate, in our age of global travel, the terrible heartache of leaving home and family with scant hope of laying eyes on loved ones ever again. Because my parents were divorced when I was very young, and I did not often see my father until after college, I learned about my connection to Sarah and Green DeWitt as an adult. Imagine my surprise, after studying Texas history, to learn that Green DeWitt was my paternal grandfather, six generations back, and his wife, Sarah Seely DeWitt, my great-great-great-great grandmother.

As I pursued a career as a writer and journalist, I began to think more about Sarah. She burrowed into my head, though she sometimes felt more like a thorn in my side. I dreamed of her. Eventually, I found portraits of her and Green in the Gonzales Museum. (Gonzalans are very proud of their history as the "Lexington of Texas.") That image of her piqued my curiosity, and I embarked on her trail. I ordered obscure books and found that almost all the information was about men and battles. I talked to local researchers. One of them, Dorcas Baumgartner, also had relatives in the DeWitt colony and provided a wealth of information. Another local historian, Tom Lindley, a friend dating back to elementary school, supplied me with maps and pointed me toward important articles published in *The Quarterly of the Texas Historical Association* (later known as *The Southwestern Historical Quarterly*) and elsewhere. My mother gave me Texas history books. I engaged my father on every anecdote and bit of family history he could recall. My aunt, Mary Ella Hurt, past president of the Gonzales Historical Association and a tireless supporter of my efforts, took me to all the relevant Gonzales historical sites, including the location of the DeWitt home on the Guadalupe River. Though nothing remained, the supposed home site of Sarah and Green thrilled me and gave me chills. The hair on the back of my neck stood up as I walked those paths. With Sarah whispering in my ear, I began to write.

That was just the beginning. The challenges of writing and publishing a first novel are daunting. My aunt and my son, Jason, urged me on. My editor and colleague from National Geographic Society, Barbara Brownell Grogan, shepherded me through. And Sarah was always there, a soft voice in my dreams and nightmares, a presence as solid and compelling as her headstone in the DeWitt cemetery. She enlivened my imagination and taught me what historical novelist Hilary Mantel has so succinctly written: "The dead are not dead. The past is not past." It lies just back there, twisting and turning, making us what we are today.

CONTENTS

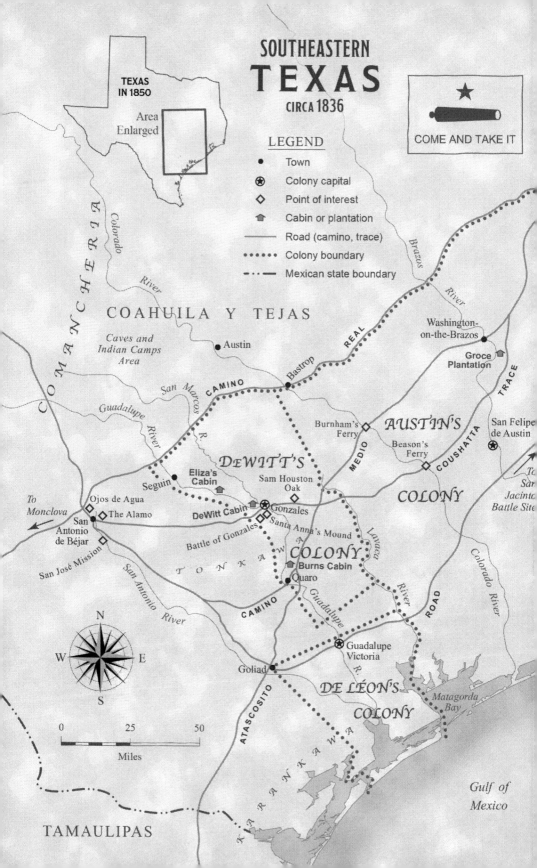

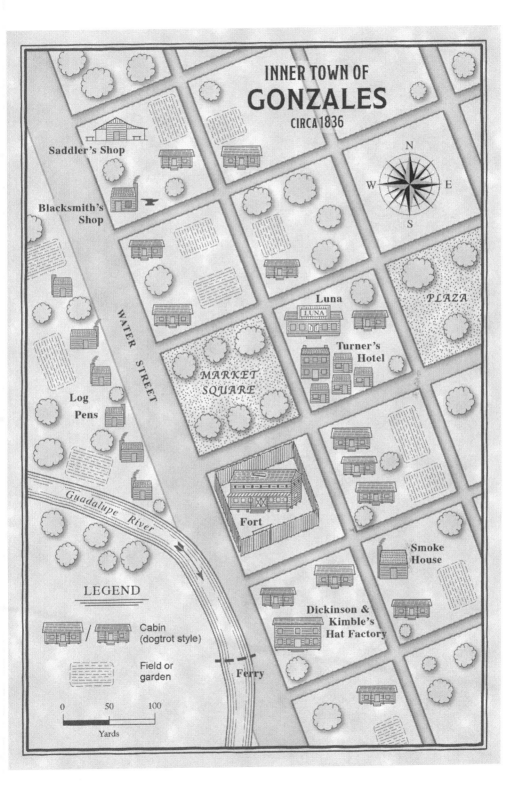

PART I
OJOS DE AGUA

Coahuila y Tejas, North from the Gulf of Mexico
1827–1828

In the beginning were those glassy pools of bright blue-green. Shining like eyes of the earth, they stared from limestone basins. The sweet clear water, fed by bubbling springs, beckoned all to stop and drink and, in the deeper ones, even to swim. Long before there was a land called Texas or a village called Gonzales or San Antonio de Béjar, the *ojos de agua* glimmered in the rock face like jewels. Watering hole to dire wolves and mastodons; camp-site to the Karankawa and Comanche; central point on the Camino Real. The pools lured Franciscan friars and Spanish explorers and American empresarios who came seeking their fortunes and—all too often—lost their lives.

That almost happened to me. I wasn't seeking my fortune. I was seeking a pleasant day in a life I could barely make sense of. But the *ojos* lured me too. A siren's song. I didn't die there. I lived. Dangled my fingers in the water, drank from the pools, and lived to tell the tale.

GETTING THERE

The day is warm for December. The state of Coahuila y Tejas offers, at least, balmy days instead of the winter chill of Missouri. The children, excited about getting underway once more, chatter and sing to the rhythm of the oxcart wheels. Crammed into this little cart, they thrill to new adventures and unpredictable days even though we are months into it. Eveline and Naomi point at trees and flowers they've never seen before; C. C. longs to catch sight of a snake wriggling through the waist-high grass. I gaze through the side rails of the cart, little Clinton asleep against me as we bump and sway around the stumps cleared to make the road, many higher than the axles of the squeaking wheels. Mile after mile, ragged cactus with blood-red fruit and barren stretches of dusty track and dry ruts replace the sunlit expanse of the blue Gulf of Mexico.

The cart driver, Eugenio, bounces along in the creaking cart, its two wooden wheels taller than a man. His face lined and his stature small, he charts our path, carrying the *Americano Anglos* and the

Mexicano Tejanos along the Camino Real, the La Bahía Road, and the unnamed red dirt trail we follow.

I scan the sky, a blaze of cloudless blue. An eagle flaps out of an island of oaks and rises above us. Suddenly the huge bird dives, then soars again, grasping a long snake in its powerful talons, the very image on the Mexican flag. Watching it merge with the horizon, I recall some wild man on the Gulf, ranting about the flag and the eagle on the flag, the emblem of the Great Spirit: "Flying, *volando* before explorers, *como usted*, *Señor* Explorer, *Señor* Empresario DeWitt, to guide, to dee-rect your course."

Green smiling, pleased at the wild man's words, ensnared by his own vision. My husband, Señor Empresario Green DeWitt, leader of the exploration into his new world.

In the midday glare, two specks rise behind us. Mustangs? Indian ponies? I make out riders. The cart driver hears, sees them too, and turns twice to look over his shoulder, keeping the oxen at their deliberate pace as the horsemen close the distance.

I lean forward. "Eugenio . . . back there?"

A dark look. He pounds the air with his flattened hand: "*Señora*, down, down, *bajo . . .*"

The gesture is unmistakable. I fall across the children. Twelve-year-old Naomi looks at me with terror in her eyes as C. C. and Eveline huddle, snuggling in close. I cover Clinton, all four of them, with my body, arms extended. The riders chant something over and over again, the words at first indecipherable. Then I make out the chant: "*La-dro-nes . . . la-dro-nes del nor-te.*"

La-dro-nes, la-dro-nes lodges in my brain like a bug in a chicken's craw. Who are they? What are they calling us?

Four horsemen thunder up around both sides of the cart. The horses' eyes are fierce, nostrils flaring, their breathing a snorting, rolling blow. The riders lash them faster, faster. One stares straight at me, nosing his horse in to grab at me. Leering through rotten teeth, he brandishes his pistol, waving it at C. C.'s mop of blond curls. Eveline's shrieks and Clinton's wails merge with the pounding hoofbeats. The ground shakes. Grinning, he lifts his pistol and points it at me. The others begin shooting through the sides of the cart, into the tall wheels, into the air. I count four, five, six shots. Finding a pole in the floor of the cart, I swing at the pistol aimed at me. He laughs, shoots into the air, and wheels away as the riders gallop ahead. Clouds of dust rise, then settle on us. They fire six, seven more shots. I taste the grit between my teeth as the riders gallop away.

Abruptly, the wagon ahead halts amid the dust, the riders now out of sight. Eugenio brings our cart to a stop. I pull myself up, hugging, reassuring the children—now sitting bolt upright—and brace for what I might find in the men's wagon.

Ramrod straight in the wagon, Green looks wary beside Will, holding the reins, but no more disturbed than he has for months.

"It's nothing, really nothing, Sarah. Stopped to adjust our load a bit after that little chase." Impatience shows in his ice-blue eyes.

"Nothing? Nothing? They *shot* at me, at the children, pointed a pistol straight at C. C.!"

"Hotheads, Sarah," Will observes in his even-tempered way as he moves to the back of the wagon to check the load.

A dark stain is growing on Green's sleeve. I gesture at his arm . . . at bullet holes in the side of the wagon.

"Warning shots, Sarah. One grazed my arm. A scratch. Poultice'll fix it."

"They kept shouting *la-dro-nes del norte*. What did they mean?"

"They're calling us thieves. They're still worried I'm going to claim some of Empresario De León's grant. We're passing through Guadalupe Victoria, *his* territory. Point taken. Soon we'll be in Empresario DeWitt's colony. *My* territory. Get back in the cart."

Beside the wagon, Will shifts and pushes the trunks and cases back into position. Finding a clean cloth, he douses it with a splash of whiskey. Will knows what to do when no one else does. Which, at this moment, is to bandage Green's arm and remain his unruffled self.

Swallowing hard, shaking, I start back to the oxcart. *All these months*, I think, *even this mad ambush is just prelude after the perilous prelude down the Mississippi, across the Gulf, into the harbor of Matagorda Bay; after the months spent at the waystation on the coast waiting for Green to negotiate with Mexican officials while Indians, covered in alligator grease, watched from canoes; and food supplies ran shorter and shorter by the day; until the Mexican emissaries bade us depart De León's territory with-out delay and proceed north at once. Constant peril. And they proceed as if it were "nothing, really nothing, Sarah," just swatting at flies.*

Green and Will side by side. Blue-eyed, silver-tongued, smooth-talking Green conjures the future from thin air, while wily, cool-hand Will puts his energy into the here and now. Green pushes the boundaries; Will tends them. And after these long months since departing St. Louis, I am still an onlooker, a doubter, struggling to follow Green's lead, to share his life. More than ever before—the out-of-the-blue, chanting riders just another of the threats coming at us—I feel the weight of it. For Green, for all of us. The magnitude of the mistake. Yes, it seems more like a mistake every day.

"Momma . . . ?" Naomi searches my face as I climb back into the cart. My stalwart, trying to remain steady as she hugs her baby brother close.

"Poppa and Will are fine." Four pairs of eyes stare, nodding tentatively, trying to believe me.

"But Momma, why were those men shooting at us?" Eveline asks. Clinton sucks his thumb. C. C. and Naomi stare, waiting for me to answer the question.

I shrug and shake my head. "They want us to get out of their territory," I say, knowing that explains little.

"So they wanted to scare us," Eveline says with sudden clarity.

"Yes, dear, yes. But they're gone now. And we'll soon be in our own territory, Poppa's new colony."

"Are you scared, Momma?" C. C. asks.

I smile at him for always knowing how I feel. "We must be brave. You were all very brave." C. C. gives me a seven-year-old's sweet look and pats my hand.

We are moving again, Eugenio coaxing the oxen back onto the track, deeper, deeper into the interior. This final leg will bring us smack dab into it. With our pile of goods, far too little money, and a scattering of people, we are to begin. Green will have his colony, and the children and I will have the life he has set for us. Green's colony, the DeWitt colony. The name is strange to my ears. That's the idea, the future we are to believe in. I want to, for him, for all of us.

6

Ahead, Green sits with shotgun cocked, scanning the brush beyond. Will heads the wagon toward a crossroads. On a tree an arrow points north to Quaro. He prods the oxen forward, following the Guadalupe River.

And I dream backward . . .

From the oxcart, the children and I watch the shimmering blue waters of the Gulf recede as we travel north into the wilds of Mexico. No, back, all the way back to St. Louis. Disappearing behind us, my mother, father, sisters, and daughter Eliza wave from the wharf; the waters of the wide Mississippi slosh, slapping loudly against the schooner's sides. Eliza's handkerchief flutters until I can no longer make out the white spot in the distance. The goodbyes are as fresh as yesterday, though now months past. I blink away a tear. Eliza, our eldest, will come to us after her final year at school.

St. Louis: Eliza and my mother and aunts and sisters baking and embroidering, harnessing the horses, banging out tunes on the piano, gathering for Sunday services. Cousins and nieces and nephews visiting when Green was away running for sheriff or stumping across Missouri to win a legislative seat. In the bosom of my family, bringing up our babes, championing my distant hero, glorying in my life.

My life before Green caught Texas fever, and Destiny moved in with us, before the distance between us grew palpable, like the long stretches in this vast, unsettled land.

I want to say to Green: "I can't seem to get those days back. Oh, yes, I once looked forward to crawling beneath the covers to hold you, to share my life with yours. But now your dream is my nightmare. I long for the days when I counted myself a lucky woman and ours a happy marriage, before you tugged me over a treacherous line."

I shudder at that cold January day when he burst in the door waving a piece of paper. A copy of the notice he'd placed in newspapers in St. Louis, Louisville, Nashville, and New Orleans. The words still swim before me:

"To Men of Industry, Capital or Enterprize: . . . a grant in the Province of Texas, State of Coahuila . . . attractions so fine . . . for a trifling remuneration only. . . ."

The day our lives changed.

"You will be repaid a thousandfold, Sarah, a thousandfold."

The words echo in my head, the words Green repeated again and again as he urged the sale of my property to finance his venture. Is our past together a bulwark adequate to withstand what lies ahead?

"¿*El empresario, está bien . . . no le molestaron al empresario?*" Eugenio breaks into my thoughts, his sympathetic eyes searching my face.

"He's all right. *Está bien.*" I can't say more. I can't say that my enterprising husband *seems* all right but in truth is possessed. Driven by a sense that life is short and legacy long. Destiny, his sometimes impish, sometimes fortuitous angel flies ahead, hovers above him, and leads him on. His muse is a part of our marriage and life now.

Destiny reassures him that the handful of settlers we bring can multiply. In a few short years, Destiny envisions four hundred families, the minimum requirement to fulfill his empresario agreement. Destiny whispers the number that will earn him the prize, thousands of acres. A tract "bigger than the state of Rhode Island," he often reminds me.

And now Green has hardly more than three years to accomplish it, according to his contract with the Mexicans. *Set to expire in 1831*, I remind Destiny, *with most of 1827 already behind us.*

Remember his dreams, Destiny comes back at me. *They captured your heart.*

Yes, a lifetime ago.

The cart lurches around a bend, the oxen quickening their pace as the road veers east.

"*Ya, Señora, ya vamos para la casa de sus amigos.* Your freends' howse," Eugenio struggles in English, trying to reassure me.

"*Muy bien, por fin*, at last."

He twists toward me. "¿*Señora, tiene hambre?* Hungry?"

I hesitate. In response, Eugenio pops a morsel into his mouth and then holds out his palm, offering something drawn from his serape. I look closely into his hand, up into his ragged, three-toothed grin, and back into his gritty palm. An oily smell rises from its contents. Looking closer, I see eyes on stems and the pointed crook of grasshopper legs. Fried grasshoppers.

"*Gracias, no.*" I shake my head to reject the offer.

Eugenio insists. "Good," he says, summoning his best English. "Good for *estómago*," patting his caved-in frame where a stomach might have been. "Eat, *come*," he tries again in both Spanish and English to make me understand.

I watch for low-hanging limbs as the wagon enters another thicket. The long mesquite thorns are treacherous. As we emerge from the thicket, C. C. lets loose a horned toad in my lap.

The lizardy creature scrambles up my arm, beady eyes bulging. I pluck the toad from my shoulder, its pale throat pulsing in and out in regular puffs. C. C. collapses in laughter across me—his giggles slowing only when I drop the small brown thing back into his hands.

"You ought to make him walk." Eveline curls her lip in sisterly distaste.

"*Señora, no se preocupe*, no worry," Eugenio calls back to me. "No hurt you."

"Eugenio says the horned toad won't hurt us." I smooth Eveline's strawberry blonde hair and hold her hands, which have disposed of any number of C. C.'s creatures in the salty waters of the Gulf of Mexico. "But the sun will burn you. So put on your bonnet, Redbird."

"Momma, Momma, look, a '5' on that tree." Eveline points to a crooked number on a big live oak.

"At last. Just five miles to Quaro." In the trackless prairie, the marker is utterly welcome. "Yes, yes, the Burns told us to look for that. We'll soon come to Irish Creek and follow it to their place."

"Momma, do they have a house?"

"I hope so. They left the coast to build one."

Eveline tosses her head with a ten-year-old's impatience. She doesn't complain, but I feel her yearning for a roof over our heads.

The high prairie rises in clumps and mottes of scrub post oak and thorny mesquite, the arboreal equivalent of C. C.'s horned toad. The scrawny trees, which offer no shade, are said to have an especially long taproot to sustain them through the worst dry spells. Those who've traveled this stretch from the Gulf inland always mention the mesquites starting along here, where the land turns from loamy black earth to iron-rich, rock-red clay. A landscape like none I've ever seen, made stranger still by the mesquites, their dark lichen-covered bark, tiny leaves, and brittle rattling pods, smelling amazingly of honey.

I search the horizon. The smoke columns to the east, surely sent by the treacherous Comanche, are lost now in the bright southern light that washes out all but the deepest colors. Blue and gold. Cloudless sky and winter grass, the road a red line.

Alongside us, the Guadalupe River twists closer now, thronged with trees, a pretty ribbon flowing and curling all the way to the Gulf. From the road, the river appears and disappears. Adjusting the brims of the children's hats, I stare beyond C. C.'s blond curls to the clear water below. Sunfish dart in schools, and what looks like a swarm of bees skims the surface of the water. No, it is the bees' shadows on the water. I crane forward. At the top of a huge cypress, the bees buzz in and out. A bee tree.

Four heads loll back now in exhaustion. I lean back too, against the quilts. The shaggy willows, cinnamon-brown river cypresses, and the dark trunks of the walnut trees draw me in. I look for a sign that this place will be good for us. Do bees portend something? *Long life*, I pray.

At the top of a rise, a herd of mustangs comes into view. The horses form a line and then, as our noisy cart and wagon approach, dance off to the east. Necks arched and tails flying, they disappear into this vast land that seems to flatten everything back into prairie.

ON IRISH CREEK

Blanco, fat and white as lard, squawks from a fence post. I recognize him from afar and hear his boisterous cock-a-doodle-doo as the wagon pulls in sight of the Burns's house. The rooster's crow soothes the cackling hen yard, orchestrating a little symphony, one that Green could have written himself. A hymn to claiming territory and protecting his flock.

In the distance, Molly Burns scatters corn to the chickens as if the settlement of the West depends on it. Acquired in New Orleans, Molly's beloved Blanco, along with the pretty Rhode Island Reds now clucking around her feet, required a trade of her best hat. She believes civilization travels in seed stocks and barnyards. She chops weeds, plants neat rows, fences plots with brush, and cares for her brood, her days a tradition as inspiring as the acquisition of land to some brave hearts. Her settler's heart is exactly what the DeWitt colony needs.

Molly looks up and starts toward the gate. Behind her, Creed comes from the creek, motioning for their girls to follow. The procession of them, like a family of possums heading single file on their path, makes me smile. *Thank you, Lord, for these dear friends.*

Lithe as a cat, Molly is at my side when the cart pulls to a stop. "Oh, my dear Sarah, my dear Sarah."

She hugs me tightly while her girls lift C. C. and Clinton into the air and whirl Naomi and Eveline down from the cart. Blanco crows from his post.

Creed, jocular as ever, steps up to Green. "So, it's our empresario, our esteemed leader." He pumps Green's hand. "The very one who's dreamed up our future for us," he says, giving Green his due and taking his measure at the same time. "And his crack deputy," Creed hails Will, who is unfolding his long frame from the wagon.

As handsome as he is good-natured, Creed's graying curls and jutting jaw make me think of one of those busts of Greek philosophers. But his philosophy is neither scholarly nor academic. Despite a deceptively gruff exterior, Creed is a human tuning fork. Put him in a group, and pretty soon everyone is singing the same note: enjoy life and promote harmony. Having fought in the War of 1812 as a youth, he seems to have had enough conflict to last a lifetime.

Creed's glance lights on the bullet holes in the wagon.

"Had a little incident back down the road," Green says in explanation. "The gang of the estimable Empresario Martín De León, no doubt. He doesn't like me passing through his territory."

"Our Tejano neighbor to the south, who thinks part of *our* colony belongs to him," Creed snorts. "So did the grandee De León run you down? He's a good deal more exalted in his own eyes than in anyone else's—puffed up, they say."

"I think we settled that difference. But he wanted me to know that I'm not one of his favorites. Waited for us to pass through Guadalupe Victoria—so he could send a little reminder to move on quickly."

"Glad you're none the worse for wear," Creed pronounces.

I cast a dubious look at Green, now wearing a jacket to cover his bandaged arm, wondering if he will acknowledge the whole story.

Molly hustles us out of the gathering darkness into the house as Eugenio shyly hands me a leaf of fleshy aloe vera, cracked open to release the gel.

"*Gracias, muchas gracias.*" I follow his lead, smoothing some onto Eveline, next to me, and across my own nose. Before I can say more, Eugenio moves away, reaches into his pocket, and pulls out what I recognize as a peyote button.

He looks at me as he pops it into his mouth. "Eugenio fly like the eagle." He flashes a grin and disappears into the woods.

Molly shakes her head in admiration as I join her in the house. "Getting shot at—you must be beside yourself."

"Colonel Dauntless shouldered it. I must as well."

"I see that gentlemanly knot at his throat is still in place. He does have a fine way about him. Never knew a man to wear a bow tie, summer or winter, rain or shine. Negotiates it all, even the fiery Mexican empresario De León."

"Yes, give him a speech to deliver or a cause to consider . . ." I start and stop.

Molly sits me down by the fire. "How in tarnation are ye managing now? Staying calm, I mean. Unless you're just plain tuckered out. Life's changed a heap since St. Louis! You never wanted for a thing, and now ye haven't had enough flour to make biscuits in a month of Sundays!"

I laugh, then consider her question. "Maybe it comes from being in the middle of Momma's brood. The first thing I learned was to sit still, 'cause three pairs of eyes were watchin' to see if I was bad, and three pairs of eyes were watchin' to see if I was good."

"I'll swan." Molly laughs too, moving to the hearth to stir a black pot bubbling with squirrel and venison stew. "Growin' up in the middle turned *me* into a faintheart."

"It's true nothing rolls off you, Molly. But that's a mark of your sensitive nature."

Molly shivers, draping her shawl closer over her shoulders. A lass when she married Creed, then a young widower with three little girls, Molly seems worn by our journey, her apple-cheek face thinner and those laughing Irish eyes wary of all. I shiver too, fearing how this place will change us. Letting the fire mesmerize and warm me, I stare into it for a long moment before pulling myself back to the present.

"So, what has happened here since we parted on the Gulf?"

13

"What's happened is I haven't seen another woman since we left the coast. Ay, the stillness here, well, if it don't make my skin crawl just to think of it." Molly sighs and rolls her eyes. "Gives me the all-overs, so-o-o quiet it is. You'll hear it, 'specially after the owls screech and the wolves howl."

"The silence hangs heavy, does it?"

"It's not like Missouri, where the Big River was always bringing something new, and you and Green lived down the street. We could visit as much as we wanted and walk up to your aunt's shop on the High Street to buy cloth. Not even like the Gulf coast with the choppy little waves and the boats in the pretty blue water. There we were all together, ye know, lookin' forward. And now we're finally set down here in the real colony, we're spread out. Makes me lonesome like those doves, cooin' for their mates. I hear them saying it over and over again: Coo, coo, coo-roo. Pretty soon I'm jumpy as a cricket, fearin' terrible things. It's the silence here, shivers me to the soul, raises me terror, don't ye know."

Molly's warm voice, despite her fears, pervades the kitchen. As she works at sewing a coat for Creed made from animal pelts he's trapped—raccoon, rabbit, and squirrel, I judge—her words lull me like music. I long to lie down near the fire, roof over my head, and sleep. She goes on, recalling the day a band of Karankawa came to Old Station, where we'd camped by the Gulf before heading north into the Mexican wilderness.

"Those tall Indians, smeared with the alligator grease to ward off mosquitoes, scary a bunch as ever I laid eyes on. And remember the day, with Green gone, when the Karankawa Chief Antoñito and his tribe descended on us?"

The day resides in my memory as the first time I'd dealt with Indians, with Creed helping me to stay calm. "Umm. We didn't know what to think. Friend or foe."

"You took care of the women, laying out blankets in the sand. And we cooked a whole side of venison to feed the hungry lot."

"It was one l-o-o-o-n-g afternoon."

"Aye, you saved us by persuading them we were good, friendly souls. I swear some music plays in you like 'the music of the spheres' we praise in hymns. Or at least we used to praise in hymns when we had a church to go to and hymn books to sing from on Sunday mornings. Whatever it is, you are a godsend to us wayfarers pullin' up stakes and joinin' DeWitt's colony."

Showered with such praise, I vow to keep up my show of calm.

"Wagons and carts do pass on the road. I reckon some are neighbors coming to live in the colony. But on they go, I dunno where, and in the meantime, I've no more than laid eyes on any but me own, the only Irish on Irish Creek."

"Molly, you've got a cabin, a loft, a water well, and a pen for the stock. More than I can say for the DeWitts."

"Well, I'm not faultin' my home, but I declare, I wish we lived a little closer to someone we know. Owning a place with room for stock and all comes with its hazards now, don't ye know, 'cause the Comanche are out there, roaming all over the place. And they're fierce. Some say the Karankawa can be too, but they live on the coast and mostly stay away from these parts. Creed and the empresario put a good face on it. They think we women don't know. But even Creed admits the Comanche will come right up to your front door if they want you or what you've got."

I shudder, knowing the first attempts at building a settlement in Gonzales were foiled by Comanche, who burned it down and attacked the carpenters. I'd heard Green and Will whisper about those days and go silent when I came near. But Green insisted on rebuilding, bringing Will and more men to do it. And on the second try, the Comanche left them alone. Hovered but didn't attack. Maybe because there were more tall white men with long guns. Maybe because they didn't know more were coming. For Green, it was the bargain he'd made with the Mexicans to secure his grant of land. Bring in enough colonists, enough manpower to make the Indians back off, and Mexico could claim the northern wilds for settlement.

Now I hear myself trying to put a good face on it as well: "We'll be your neighbors. Gonzales can't be more than a few miles straight upriver. Just push a boat into the creek, float into the Guadalupe, and paddle straight up to my front door."

Molly stopped stirring the stew to wield her wooden spoon. "Ay, half that distance is too much for me. Being your neighbor out here in the wild is altogether the best idea I've heard in a while, for sure. But it's more than a neighbor you are. You're the closest thing to a sister I'm ever to have out here."

Thinking of my own sisters, I wrap my arms around Molly and hold her close. She wipes away a tear and starts toward the garden to dig out a few late potatoes.

In the quiet, I long for my past life. Closing my eyes, I feel the stillness Molly fears and hear the dark whispers of what lurks out there. What we can't see. A horse in need of blinders, spooked by it all.

From the back door I watch the December light fade. Mistletoe trails from oak branches, a reminder the new year is only a fortnight away. Across the way in the gloaming, the men hobble the oxen and leave them grazing. I hear Will's voice in the crisp air as they near the house. In the knoll down toward Irish Creek, Spanish moss beards the trees, and ball moss nestles in bare branches. Chicken and turkey pens spread out under the post oaks, and newborn calves bawl next to their mothers in the lot. Laughing and splashing in the creek, the children catch rainbow trout, the blue and gold scales catching the late light.

Just as Molly promised before they left the coast, Creed had gone water witching and found a creek and a spring besides: "You know Creed can divine springs," Molly joked as they'd set out from the coast. "If there's a spring in a sweet green meadow in this country, Creed is bound to find it. And I don' mind the idea of groves of big ole moss-hung oaks with the mistletoe draped in them, either."

Taking a look around the corner of the house, I stop and gasp.

Suspended from a pole between trees is a big tawny cat, hanging in the shadows. Its head lolls back on its shoulder, white fangs gleaming. I edge closer to the cat. Creed had slain the animal cleanly with one bullet through its head, leaving the rest as beautiful as if it could slink away on a limb.

I can make out the men's talk now.

"Ay, and when the bright-eyed mornin' comes peepin' over the hill," Creed is saying, "the deer a-feedin' on the rise."

Creed's words flow and trill, especially when he has an audience. I watch the three of them: Creed, motioning with hands and arms; Green, pale and tight-lipped; carrot-topped Will—*El Colorado* to Eugenio—his red hair aflame in the late light.

I stand by the tree, eager to ask Creed about the panther—Mexican lion some call the big cat—when a shriek shatters the silence.

"What in heaven's name?" I call to Molly in the garden.

Molly stands as still as she ever gets. "Sounds human."

I run to the children dashing up the path from the creek.

"Momma, Momma," Naomi calls, with Eveline tugging the boys and the Burns girls close behind. Hustling them all into the cabin, I head back toward the men huddled in the clearing. "Green, no telling where Eugenio has gone. Someone best fetch him. He's swallowed some of that peyote again. He could be in danger."

The peyote button Eugenio downed looks like a green pincushion with tufts of yellow woolly hairs, a small cactus without spines. He calls it medicine, his *mescalito*. And strong medicine it is, transporting him to another world, oblivious to us and to danger. When his green mescalito god takes hold, sweet, retiring Eugenio cries out, talks to spirits, and summons powers we cannot see. What do they say to him? What does he remember?

The screech cuts the silence again, a bloodcurdling sound that now doesn't sound so human. We all turn east, in the direction of the noise, as the men go for their guns propped against the wall.

"You see, it's a terrible silence," Molly says, coming in the door. "And then sounds out of those woods like a banshee's wail." She shudders, rattling dishes onto the table, intent on feeding her guests.

"Come and get it."

I wave Molly's wooden spoon at the children. Molly serves hearty helpings of stew, beans, onions, and cornbread and pours fresh milk into the bottom half of long-necked cymling gourds dried and scoured to a gleaming white. The fire leaps and crackles on the hearth, casting shadows on the opposite wall. Seated around the long plank table, the children have already forgotten the ruckus outside. The girls whisper, while the boys make shadow puppets with their hands on the wall.

Green returns from his search in the woods with no news of Eugenio. He slides into a chair at one end of the table between the boys. With relish, he joins them in making barking-dog puppets with his hands. His hands fly into the shape of a big dog, which quickly chases away a long-snouted threat resembling an alligator. In this rare moment of connection with the children, Green's broad brow is smooth and his shoulders relaxed. His fluid hand motions and energetic barks bring happy yelps from the boys.

Emily Burns, the elder sister, holds herself slightly apart from the younger pairs. Like my Eliza, I muse, thinking again of our eldest. Lillah and Cynthianne Burns sit next to my Naomi and Eveline. They are close enough in age and looks to be sisters. Like sisters, they chatter and confide while Molly and I ferry food around the table, pushing to get the children fed before Will and Creed return with Eugenio.

Green leans back in his chair when the puppet show is over. He is getting the mellow look that tells me he is regarding the two of us as stars in the constellation of womanhood. The whiskey he's been sipping is wearing down his reserve. His feelings flutter like a moth at a lamp, a mood I've not seen in months.

I am sending all the children up the ladder to the loft when Will and Creed return—without Eugenio.

"Sorry to say, Sarah, *el señor no está*," Will reports. "If that was him screaming, he quieted down when we got out there in the woods with him. I wouldn't worry none. He'll be fine if he don't stir up some other wild boar with his song."

"You think the shriek came from him?" I ask, afraid to think why.

"Somehow, a few notes in there sounded like a Mexican love song," Will says. "But I wouldn't swear to it."

"Look at it this way," Creed says. "The fandango that inspired that bleatin' and bellowin' wouldn't attract any self-respectin' natural animal. They'd likely run in t'other direction. And the only red men around here right now are a few strugglin' Karankawa. Comanche took off on their northern route and ain't expected back for a while."

"Sit down and eat." Molly waves me to the table as Will and Creed disappear into the next room with Green. "You're frazzled."

I give in to Molly's orders and collapse into a chair. Thinking about Eugenio's self-described adventures, I eat in silence as the full moon sheds its eerie light through the unshuttered window. The dark woods seem closer now. I wonder where Eugenio goes when he flies "like an eagle." I almost envy him the journey my Presbyterian soul can hardly imagine. Does he travel in visions, the way Green does? Or is he in league with Destiny, Green's guiding light, the subversive spirit who beckons us deeper and deeper into the wild?

MEXICAN LION

I fall into a fitful sleep the moment I stretch out before the dying coals—and wake to the ticking of the mantle clock. Two o'clock. Moonlight crosshatches the room through chinks between the logs.

After tossing for an hour, I venture onto the moonlit porch and listen to the silence, my shawl pulled close. Compared to the uncertainties ahead, the months camping on the Gulf seem safe as a nursery now.

As I become accustomed to the night, the outlines of the cat hanging in the tree take shape around its shining, agate-bright eyes. Then I see something stir close to the house. *Are my eyes deceiving me?* It is curled at the bottom of a tree about a hundred feet from the edge of the knoll. It moves and then moves again, small and compact enough to be Eugenio.

I see a hand and then hear a staccato laugh. It *is* Eugenio, and he seems to be aware of me, too. And then something else moves. Far above him, in the sinuous branch of a huge oak, floats another pair of bright eyes. I watch as Eugenio moves again, and the form above flattens and crouches along the branch.

"Eugenio! *Arriba, mira*, up there." I point, moving toward him and the big cat above him.

My shout brings out the men one after another, carrying lanterns. The panther leaps into another tree and dissolves in the moonlight. On the ground, Eugenio makes a funny little growling noise, speeds around in a circle, and disappears. When Green gets to me at the edge of the knoll, it is quiet as Vespers.

"What are you doing out here in the woods in the middle of the night?"

"I saw Eugenio. There was a panther in the tree. He didn't see it."

"Do you mean to tell me . . . ?"

"I couldn't sleep. Then I saw him—and the wildcat up there in the tree."

While we argue, Will moves onto the moonlit knoll and back out again. He emerges, his shotgun drawn and cocked, suspenders dangling.

"Get some sleep. We're heading for Gonzales first thing in the morning," Green says.

I know that tone. He is tuning up the sternest note he knows how to play with me.

"Well, Sarah," Creed chimes in, "you can't say we didn't sound the trump all around and lay out the welcome mat for ye. At daybreak, we're plannin' a buffalo stampede past the front door. You better get some shuteye to look lively at sunup."

I bed down again, amazed that Molly and the children have slept through the noise. I smooth the quilt and blankets under me. I flop to my back and then roll again. Finally, I rise and stand by the window, gazing into the crescent moon in the dark sky.

Out of the shadows, I see her outline. Moving from limb to limb across a little knoll of oaks, the big cat ventures closer to the house. Finally, she climbs down a big oak headfirst and slinks to the tree where her mate swings. Underneath, she whines and paces, back and forth, as if she were caged. Then she sharpens her claws on the tree and climbs to a branch above the body of the male. She blinks and paws, bats the air, and stretches toward him again and again. At last, she creeps down the tree and disappears.

My heart beats fast. The panther mourning her mate grips me: *Why can I not brave danger so fearlessly for mine?*

I lie down again. Once or twice I hear calls that sound human. What strange powers the button-size peyote cactus holds. I ponder Eugenio's faith in mescalito and wonder why he calls it his ally, his friend.

At first light, Molly begins hauling water from the spring. The clatter of her pans and pitchers floats above me as I catch one fleeting dream. It is morning in my mother's house. My Liza Q, Elizabeth Quick, loving protector through all my years, prepares a warm breakfast of fresh eggs, scones, and honey. Then her mood changes, and she warns me of something I can't make out.

I rouse myself just as Molly disappears out the back door again. The children do not stir. Then the men jostle and shake the floor as they pull on boots and pants, collect shaving mugs, and stride down the path to the creek to wash and shave.

"God grant me good humor and good sense," I pray, "and protect Eugenio's good soul."

I run my comb through my hair and wind my mane around my head, thinking this country is no place for a scalp like mine—considering how Indians might view a head of blonde hair. Plucking hairpins one by one from the pile I left on the mantle, I anchor my hair, gazing into a shard of mirror propped against the chinked wall.

Patches of hyssop and spearmint line the path toward the creek. Plucking a bit to freshen my mouth, I listen to the piping, chirping morning, so promising after the moon's eerie light. Dawn on Irish Creek, just as Creed described it. The fog is burning off, the haze melting into the brilliance of the blue and pink December sky.

Ahead of me, Eugenio wades into the creek next to Creed's boat, bathing his face and hands in the clear, cool water. Elated to see him, I wonder if the cool water soothes the aftermath of a night spent with his peyote dreams. Knowing Eugenio, he would be thanking *Dios* for the beauty of the world and the silky feel of the waters. He has told me more than once how he loves boats and wishes he could travel the soft currents of the Guadalupe instead of the harsh, dusty track of the roads. The stumps distract him, interrupting the pleasure of watching the prairie, which he loves even more than mescalito. As I watch, Eugenio climbs into the boat and sits, bobbing with the current. A heron fishes on the opposite bank.

Not wanting to disturb his morning reverie, I veer to the right, about to head around the bend of the creek for my morning ablutions. Ripples slosh against the bank. I stop and look again. *Something in the rushes? A fish? A beaver?* Then I see her lowering herself onto the bank at the edge of the water. The big cat crushes a four-foot swath of rushes as she flattens her body into a tight crouch.

"Animal . . . *grande* . . . Eugenio . . . big cat!" I scream.

Turning toward me, he sees the cat. Fangs bared, she hisses at him from the bank. "*Grande*," he repeats. Eugenio shifts in the boat as the panther crouches to spring. Crossing himself, he sits on his haunches and gathers his strength. As the panther arches gracefully toward him, Eugenio hops out of the boat in one springing, vaulting motion.

He laughs as he hits the water.

I hear Creed shout from the other side of the hill: "Over yonder. Look! The pan-ter's in the boat. Get my boat! I didn't build it for no pan-ter to sail off in."

I hike my skirts and run. On the bank, Creed is picking up stones and hurling them at the boat while Green and Will pace up and down, looking as helpless as I've ever seen them. At water's edge, a wet, muddy, smiling Eugenio scrambles up the slippery bank.

In the middle of Irish Creek, the sleek female stands with her front paws propped on the flat seat of the boat. Poised and proud, she is a royal Cleopatra sailing down the Nile.

GONZALES

After breakfast, I hurry down the hill to fill the canteens just at the bend of the creek where the big cat appeared earlier this morning. As Irish Creek makes its way into the Guadalupe River, I wonder idly if the current will carry Creed's boat all the way to the Gulf or if a lucky swimmer will claim it. Foremost in my mind, though, are Green's sharp words this morning as we ready for the last leg of the trip: "Buck up, Sarah. All I hear is complaints. It's no way to start."

He is right; I know my duty. But we have been too long getting here to be *starting* anything. It seems like it ought to be just about over by now.

Green, subdued now, finds me next to the spring. "Sarah, it'll be all right. You'll see. Where the road enters the town of Gonzales . . . there'll be a little grove of oaks and the river winding off to the side."

I am prepared for scrub oak and mesquites.

He folds me into his arms and holds me. He wants to soothe my sadness at leaving Molly and Creed. When he's not entirely preoccupied with his mission, his softer side, which appears less and less often, returns to reclaim me. He offers sweet words to quiet my dread. Instead, I hear the pretty speech that inspired me to leave St. Louis against every ounce of my common sense. I listen, weighing his words against what I know is ahead of us.

"Sally, you know you're a true American," he said in that crowd-pleasing tone he could get. "Born in Virginia just as George Washington was inaugurated, raised in Missouri, and traveling to Texas now in the front of the bunch. Yep, the true American seeing the country firsthand and making something of it."

Why had I failed to remind him, then and there, that Texas was *beyond* the country? An altogether foreign country. But then, I always had listened to his speeches and come away inspired. Except for my father and Andrew Jackson, I'd never heard another man say such eye-opening things. But Green doesn't just open eyes. He makes people see the intangible and invisible, oblivious to most every-thing but his highfalutin ideas. He even talks up the sandy track that passes for a road. He doesn't notice the heat or the cold or the flies or scorpions. Or the goodbyes.

Pulling away from his embrace, I peck him on the cheek and gather the canteens. "Yes, I understand."

December turns cold. Even in Mexico, it seems, the wind whips and the temperature drops. In the wagon, I wrap up the children from head to toe, holding C. C. on my lap while Naomi and Eveline bundle Clinton between them. The sky is a dome of deep blue. In the east, the clouds are growing blue black and scudding toward us with alarming speed. Great jagged fingers of lightning reach out to the flat prairie below like some bad-tempered sky king ready to snatch us up. I am no longer sure we will beat the storm, as Green predicts. Nor do I know what to expect of a storm in this wide-open country that leaves us so exposed.

C. C. grasps my hand, then shifts. For a moment, he takes my face in his hands and snuggles against me. Then he squirms and stretches out one hand, testing for raindrops.

"No rain, honey." The sky is ominous, the air dry and charged. Clouds whirl overhead. I feel his anxiety and he mine, as he so often does.

The girls speculate about Gonzales, a word they hear many times a day. They repeat the name of the town the way Eugenio says it, "Gunsallies, Gunsallies." Then we turn down a sloping road and see the river ahead.

"*Señora, la villita de Gonzales. Llegamos, ya.* We . . . here," Eugenio says as if we are arriving at a ball. He has made a rain hat out of his serape. It winds around his head, draping over his shoulders like the seven veils of the biblical Salome. I have to restrain myself from laughing. Eveline and Naomi giggle behind their hands while Eugenio sings to a Mexican beat.

"Why did Poppa give his town such a strange name?" Eveline asks when she gets over her amusement at Eugenio's headgear.

"Señor Rafael Gonzalez was governor of Coahuila y Tejas in 1825 when Poppa got his grant in Mexico," I tell them.

"Co-we-la-ee-tay-hass is the same as Texas," Naomi reassures her sister. "It's a state in Mexico just like Missouri is part of the United States."

"I don't see anything like Missouri," Eveline shoots back.

I glare at her for her need to state the painful truth. The sign announcing Gonzales isn't exactly impressive. Scrawled across a rough plank nailed to a puny mesquite tree, it reads:

"Est. 1825, Gonzales, capital of DeWitt Colny, Green DeWitt, Empersorio."

The sign reminds me it is December 1827. Almost three years of Green's six-year contract already gone, just getting to this point. At least our name is spelled right. On the other side of the road is a lovely grove of live oaks, as Green promised. I close my eyes for a moment. *Thank you, Lord, for getting us here safely and for the live oaks.*

C. C. is looking at me when I finish my split-second prayer. "Is this Gonzales?" he asks and then adds, "I love you, Momma."

I hug him. His empathy, demonstrated since the day he first smiled as an infant, is one of God's gifts. "Look, honey, do you see our name on the sign?"

"Twice," he says, apparently proud of his skill at reading his name. "Once for Poppa and once for Momma."

In the wagon ahead, Green is popping up and down in his seat as if he'd just discovered America. I wave back and beam broadly, hoping he will remember that I smiled as we entered Gonzales. Will faces straight ahead, intent on bringing us into the settlement he's worked hard to snatch from the wilderness.

As the sign disappears behind us, we head straight toward the water, then angle back to the north on a dusty course alongside the Guadalupe River. Even in December, the trees and vines are so thick it is hard to get a good look at the river, except in occasional glimpses through the curtain of green, red, and gold. A rustling amid the vines. I think I see an alligator slither down the bank.

Then a building on the right claims my attention. Looming ahead about a hundred yards east of the river—it's the fort. I'd seen forts at St. Louis and Natchez and garrisons along the Gulf—and this looks like none of them. It looks like an overgrown log cabin, leaning decidedly to the left with a big double door to accommodate horses and wagons. I've heard Will refer to it as the one place safe from Indian attack, so I resolve to keep my opinion to myself. The fort is large as a barn, with openings in the walls for guns to poke out. It looks like many could crowd into it, if there were indeed enough townspeople to make a town, or villagers to make a village. But in the world we've come to, it is just as Molly says. The people are scattered all over the place. They would have to travel a distance to the fort if Indians launched an attack against the town. Here, it seems, even the Comanche don't plan battles. Instead, they appear out of nowhere, strike, and disappear, often with a settler's horse or two tethered behind, or a cabin burned to the ground. Beyond the fort, the wagon ahead veers left into a rutted street and then right along a more traveled path.

We are alone in the deserted landscape. Six tiny cabins line up before us, hardly larger than privies, their backs to the river.

"So these are what they call the log pens," I mutter to myself.

Several have barricades of brush and logs around them. Some have sod roofs, and some shingled log roofs. Smoke drifts from the chimney of the third one. Each sits sadly in a bare little clearing. They remind me of woodcutters' shacks along the Mississippi, where ragged children and gaunt, hopeless women stand and stare from the banks as steamboats and schooners sail by. There is no trace of livestock, pasture, or people. Only the roads, the cleared ground, and the miserable cabins reflect human presence. Beyond the cabins, the river—shrouded by vines, tasseled red buckeye, and blood weeds—cuts a wide horseshoe bend.

The children are quiet as church mice. When the cart rolls to a stop at the last cabin, I meet their wide eyes. "This is Water Street. Stay within my sight at all times. We must unload before it starts to rain. Then we'll have time to settle in."

Leaning up against a corner of the end cabin, Will smiles his wily smile. I drop the hide-seat chair and bundle of quilts right in front of him. "Well, if it ain't Miz Sarah Seely DeWitt, Empresari-ess of Gonzales, pop-u-la-tion fifty. Here we are. The Niña, the Pinta, and the Santa Marie just sailing into the New World," he teases as Green approaches, carrying the big cast-iron cooking pot. "Yep, and right here is ol' Christo Columbo himself." Will gives C. C., trailing behind me, a whirl. He chucks him under the chin for having to bear the name of his father's fantasies.

"While you are jawing, Will, the rain is going to catch us." Green glares at him.

It's clear to me that Will, reliable as he is, is starting to strain at the role of deputy to Green. Life in Texas imposes far different demands than bringing law and order to Missouri. But Will has the hands-on skills Green lacks. Though he has ridden cramped up in a wagon for days and isn't keen on taking on the next task quite so fast, Will goes about opening shutters, getting a fire started, and ordering Eugenio to feed the oxen and secure the wagons.

I look at Green. "I was about to ask about the . . . log pens."

"They are just temporary, Sarah. We'll stay here only long enough to build a house for ourselves. These six cabins are for recent arrivals until something better can be constructed. Settlers live in them briefly. The Lockhart family is just on the other side of us. The Berry family you met on the coast is in the first cabin. They have already built a house on their headright and are about to move to their own place. But now is not the time to discuss the neighborhood. We *got* to unload the dang wagon," Green says again, louder, as another thunderclap breaks above us and the wind picks up. We all snap to.

Green recruits Eugenio and some of the other Tejano drivers to bring up buckets of water from the river and directs them to wash down the walls. Green and I carry another load from the wagon to the little porch at the front of the cabin. He picks out the skillet and hands it to me. Now empty-handed, he hesitates at the door as I confront, at last, this ragged new empire he has claimed. Abruptly he turns on his heel, calling out that he must check on surveyors, and disappears down Water Street.

I stand at the door of the cabin. Behind me, Will waits as I push it open and peer inside. The dirt floor is covered with straw. On one end, there is a chimney and a crude pit for cooking, on the other, a wooden floor for sleeping. Up above the floor, a loft will sleep two or three more.

The dirt floor bothers me most. Camping on the beach in warm weather is one thing. Living in a filthy, bug-infested, dirt-floored cabin through the winter is entirely another. There are no windows, but even in the dim light, I can see the gauze of spiderwebs covering the walls and the pale brown scorpions crawling in the cracks.

Will organizes the children into a line that stretches from the wagons to the front door. We haul in dishes, trunks with clothes, a Dutch oven, a kettle, and a wash pot. While we add to the pile on the porch, the Tejano helpers splash the walls with river water. Hopefully, the water will motivate the army of crawlers in the logs to move out.

Poking under the sleeping platform with a hoe handle, I rake out a solid object. A scaly thing, an armored shell with a halo of hairs slides toward me on four legs. It emerges, snuffling and grunting.

"This here is a traveling meal," Will says. He holds the armadillo in the air revealing four nipples. "I think she'll roast up real nice over a fire."

"No. That's why she hasn't escaped already." I push aside the platform, and tiny pink babies gaze up at us, starting to make surprisingly loud noises. I hastily put back the platform, hoping to silence the screams. "Maybe she and her family will eat their weight in spiders and centipedes. Let her tend her babies."

He sets her down, and she immediately disappears back under the platform; the noise stops.

"Don't tell the boys she's there," I say, then laugh at the notion. "At least until the babies scream for dinner."

"Yup. They ain't exactly quiet, dainty little things." He shakes his head and smiles at me. "Nice to have a woman in this place. Sure *do* make a difference the way the world looks."

For a moment, I look into his eyes.

Eugenio ambles up to tell us that he and the helpers are going into the village to buy supplies. Bare as Gonzales looks, that sounds promising.

Will steps outside to roll a cigarette. I watch from the back door as he follows a trail cut into the embankment behind the cabins. The path, framed by the walls of the bluff, leads down to the river. The children follow him, eager for Will's attention.

They squat beside Will under the overhang of the bluff. Finally, the stormy sky opens up and delivers a downpour. Huddled with Will, protected by the overhang, they watch until the rain stops and the sun comes out. Exploring along the riverbank, the children pry thin, flat-sided stones from the dirt, gather them in a pile, aim low to the water, and skip them two, three, four times across the river. Will taught them that. The children rifle them across the river as Will hunkers down on the sandbar. He puffs on his cigarette, soaking in the scenery as he often does. I share his appreciation of the big trees. And these by the river are the biggest and grandest I've ever seen.

More than once, as we traveled down the Mississippi, Will confided to me that he felt bad about "running out on things," meaning his wife, in Missouri. He'd never considered passing up the chance to go to Texas with Green as he journeyed back and forth to ready Gonzales for colonists. When his wife, Harriet, declined to go, he thought she'd follow him on the next trip. But she flatly refused to leave Missouri, and he was compelled to go. Gradually, he said, worry passed into acceptance. What was done was done.

Will is my oldest friend, and I have a notion of how he's sorted it all out. In truth, not just a notion. I know how he thinks so that he only has to say a few words, and I'm right there with him. Even more tormenting, I understand Will and his thoughts better than I understand Green's. And that understanding only grows deeper the longer

I'm around Will. It's a situation that I'm beginning to fear daily. One that threatens who I am—or was.

Down there under the bluff, I'm fairly sure, Will is considering his philosophy. Even in our youth, Will had a philosophy. He called it his wild card theory, meaning that luck has way too much to do with how things work out. That wild card theory came in the aftermath of our own romance when we were sixteen and seventeen. Our luck in finding one another astounded us both. We paddled my uncle's canoe from Hannibal to St. Louis. We worked in my aunt and uncle's dry goods store. Our dreams were boundless, conspiring. But as well as I knew my own name, I knew Will was an adventurer with a thousand visions, and one day, he told me he was leaving. Crushed as I was, all I could do was let him go. In my heartbreak, I thought he left because he didn't love me. If he had asked, I would have waited for him. In his young heart, he simply believed I knew I was his. When he returned, he found me married to Green and mother of an infant. And in *his* heartbreak, he has never stopped believing that luck rules your life.

After his return, he spoke as the friend he had always been: "Good luck. Be happy. I'll just have to admire you from a distance." It was my first clue of how badly I'd misjudged his feelings. His eyes said even more, a look that has never stopped haunting me. Now, living in close contact for months on end is a cruel twist.

Yet, despite his devotion to his wild card theory, I don't agree with it. Or at least I didn't before now. I have always believed things happen for a reason. That we make choices. Nevertheless, when Harriet refused to come to Texas with him, he was more convinced than ever that luck had once more turned his life around. To be sure, there is one thing I can't dispute. Luck has dealt him—and us—an entirely new hand.

I shake myself out of my reverie as Will gathers up the children by the river. He squares his hat, flicks his cigarette into the water, and starts back up the path. Delivering my brood to me, he starts to his own cabin, sitting fifth in the line of six, next to ours.

In front of our cabin, Green is back and mounting his horse to leave again. "Got to check on the carpenters upriver. Back in an hour or two."

As Green rides off toward the south, Will emerges from his cabin, rifle in hand. "Gonna shoot a squirrel or two for supper. Keep your fire goin'. I'll bring you one too."

WATER STREET

Eveline sits on a trunk on the porch, looking confused. Her soft eyes and mouth, neither smiling nor frowning, make me think of a spotted fawn. Her sunburned nose and freckles glow. Her shoes are crusted with mud, and her skirt is limp and damp. The sun is out again after the rain, but Eveline's mood has not caught up with the weather. She shivers in the late afternoon light.

I perch on the trunk next to her, my arms around her. "You're cold, dear. Why don't we go on in the cabin? By the fire."

"I'm not going in there."

"Naomi and the boys are inside. How about a bite of cornbread before supper?"

Eveline shakes her head. "No. I want to go back to Missouri," she says with sudden clarity.

"And when did you decide that?"

"Just now."

"Just this minute?"

"A little while ago."

"Well, you are one brave woman then. I've wanted to go back to Missouri since we left last April. And all this time I've been homesick, I suppose you've been riding high like a little boat on the waves, weathering every storm."

"Momma," Eveline looks at me in utter amazement, "you've been homesick all this time?"

"Yes, ma'am."

"How come you never cry or anything, then?"

"I cried for two days solid when we left St. Louis."

"I know, but I thought that was because you missed Grandma Liza Q and Grandpa and Eliza and Aunt Susannah and everyone. This is different."

"It is?"

"This isn't about missing people. It's about living *here*."

"And you don't want to?"

"I thought I did. All the way, I thought I did. And when we got to Quaro, it seemed fine. But now it doesn't."

"You mean because of the little chicken coop we have to stay in for a week or two?"

"It's so dark and cold in there. When we camped on the Gulf, it was nicer. There were kids to play with and shells to pick up, and we got to swim in the warm weather."

"Well, it's December, and this is the first cold snap, but Poppa says Texas doesn't have many of these cold spells. Soon, dearest, after New Year's, we're going to pick out a site for a house and have a house-raising and all."

She stares back at me, setting her jaw.

Eveline's struggle to get past the present moment touches my heart. I think she must have a lump in her throat equal to my own.

"My Eveline, you will be a rich woman when you grow up because you save everything, even your tears. Maybe you just need a good cry."

In response, Eveline sputters out a giggle. "Oh, Momma, now you made me laugh."

"Well, if you're going to be so tough, maybe you want to come with me for a little stroll up this street. Water Street, the main street. I'd like to see if this is a town at all, like Goliad, with its big stone church and bell tower in the center, or like Guadalupe Victoria, Empresario De León's town, with its square planted with red flowers. Or just a gap in the road like Quaro."

"Poppa says it's a town, and he's been back and forth here more than we have."

"Well, seeing is believing, Redbird. Let's see who's here. Poppa says people with Texas fever are pouring in all the time. So let's take a look. We might even find somebody we know who came down the Mississippi and then left the coast before we did, like Creed and Molly and the girls."

Eveline's knitted brow smooths out, a faint smile appearing. I smile back. I try to picture a stream of people applying to Green for land they can turn into ranches or farms. Such a stream must cascade into a flood. The story of Jesus turning meager loaves and fishes into food for a multitude crosses my mind. I fear that indeed it will take a miracle to turn a few dozen adventurers into four hundred families in three years.

Eveline goes to get her straw hat while I walk around to the wagon yard, where our wagon stands empty. Underneath the wagon, Eugenio and another Tejano driver from their mission into town lie hat to hat, fast asleep on a bed of grass. I consider why Green has left on his horse so close to suppertime. Probably because, careful as I was to say little, he saw my shock at the log pens.

"Who lives in the other cabins? And why didn't they come out to greet us when we arrived?" Eveline asks.

I reel off the names for her: "The surveyor, Mr. Lockhart; Eugenio and the wagon drivers; Will and some of the single men; the Berry family. The Berrys are building a cabin out on Peach Creek. So they weren't home when we arrived. And the surveyors are out surveying."

Eveline brightens at the prospect of seeing the Berry family. On the coast, she'd followed the older children around, riding double on horseback up and down the beach. She slips her hand in mine as we start up Water Street. I revel in the gesture, knowing that at ten, my youngest daughter will soon move beyond this sweet childish trust.

"Most of the people living in the log pens are men working to help Poppa build and survey the town," I rattle on in explanation. "Some

37

people who were with us on the coast left to get things ready here. Gonzales is a new town without many people yet. Farther out are some families we haven't even met yet who came from Empresario Austin's colony."

Water Street is dry, dusty, and silent, though once or twice I hear voices from up the street, where we see a couple of structures larger than the log pens. The street edges the river, hidden by the curtain of vines and bushes still green in this mild climate. As we move away from the cabins sitting like ducks in a row, the voices grow louder. To the west, the river rushes swiftly along, a new constant in our lives. Overhead, a turkey buzzard drifts, its naked red head sinister between gray wings spread wide. I feel for the sharp knife I've begun to carry in a scabbard in my high-topped shoe. I've told the children they must keep their guard up—always going in groups with an adult close by, taking care before going into the river, and paying attention to the cattle and horses whose sense of danger is often more reliable than ours. I've also reminded them that every poisonous snake in the country is common here and that they are on the Tonkawa and Comanche hunting grounds, albeit at the very edge. I don't dare add that Gonzales sits at the edge of the Anglo-American world—the westernmost settlement of Anglos between the Atlantic and the Pacific.

The first sign of life on Water Street is a wagon next to a lean-to. Propped against the lean-to's entrance is a rough-hewn log with burnt lettering announcing Kimble's Hat Factory. A big, broad-brimmed brown hat hangs from a nail above the sign. We greet the factor, Mr. Kimble, a barrel-chested, exuberant man, intent on attaching a hatband to a new creation. He looks up from his task to tell us he expects a supply wagon filled with fancier hats, including bonnets for us. Three pigs and a skinny dog sniff and root in a weedy path next to the shack, then emerge to trot behind us down the street.

At the center of Water Street, we come to the large, looming wooden fort facing the river. It rises perhaps two stories high in the middle of what town there is. In my mind, it is *La Fortaleza*, as Eugenio identified it on our voyage into town. I marvel again at its perilous tilt to the left, and the crow's nest balanced on flimsy trusses under the roof. The fort's upper timbers are pierced with round holes for gun barrels instead of windows. The gate of La Fortaleza's palisade fence is open to welcome the settlers on Water Street. At the entrance stands a guardhouse without a guard. We peek inside to see carpenters raising walls for an interior room. Others hammer nails into a raised platform that can serve many purposes, including, hopefully, a dance floor. Since we don't have a church bell to toll the end of the workday, I wish for Creed, who loves to play taps on his bugle at sunset.

"The men have built the fort for the safety of the families," I begin and then stop myself, realizing I haven't yet said anything to the children about Indian attacks. Lost in her own thoughts, Eveline isn't listening. I squeeze her hand.

We cross another barren street, hardly wider than a trail, and step into Market Square. It is a grassy, roped-off patch crisscrossed with trails and bounded with stakes at each corner. The red, white, and green Mexican flag ripples above the plaza in the late afternoon breeze. I try to imagine the square filled with market stalls, carts, and people on market day. But I do not share that with Eveline, who is in no mood for cheery visions.

Across another unnamed street east of Market Square stands a lone wooden structure as impressive as a New Orleans gambling house. LUNA is carved in crooked letters over the door and GROCERY in crabbed letters on the front, but it doesn't look like any grocery I know. It looks like what my mother calls a grog shop, a bawdy establishment frequented by vulgar men drinking too much liquor. The loud and discordant voices we heard are coming from inside. Eveline casts a curious look at the door as we walk on.

The two blocks beyond Market Square are of equal size, cut up into six smaller squares, like pieces of a sheet cake. Each is carefully marked with stakes and twine or sometimes rope tied from a tree to the corner. Will houses for new settlers be built here? New businesses? At the corner of the second block, we come to a saddler's shop. Three freshly tanned saddles sit in a row atop a sawhorse, exuding their strong, leathery scent; the proprietor is nowhere in sight. Next door, a trio of men gathers near the blacksmith and his forge. Two tip their hats to us. The smith, Mr. Sowell, shoes a horse. I recognize Mr. Sowell but none of the others.

"Well, Redbird, a booming enterprise."

Eveline watches the efficient Mr. Sowell, who not once looks away from his task as he taps at one metal horseshoe and moves to the next. We continue.

At the end of the block, the town ends. Nothing more is laid out or marked off, and the red land of the prairie closes in again, as endless and unbroken as if this town were a mirage. I am too worried about survival to let my mind linger on the possibilities of the terrifying stretch to the northwest where the Comanche dwell. The Comanche, according to Creed, send war parties back and forth with regularity, on forays for food, deer, buffalo, cattle, horses, trinkets, and the occasional woman or child.

Shuddering, I look at Eveline. "I guess we'll go back now."

Empty as it is, Gonzales seems to me hardly more than one of the play towns my children laid out with rocks back in Missouri, outlining houses and stores and sweeping them with broom weed. Nevertheless, I am heartened by seeing the fort, a few proprietors plying their trades, and lots where surveyors have laid out town blocks. I will my composure back into place and turn to my daughter.

While Eveline is no blithe optimist, she doesn't usually waste time moping when she can find something better to do. A child of purpose and initiative, Eveline likes to understand where things are going. As I contemplate how to engage her, she interrupts my thoughts.

"I know Poppa does important things," Eveline pauses. "But what exactly?"

I struggle with how to put it simply. With Eveline, if you find the right key, she will soon be humming along.

"Well, honey, Gonzales is being laid out as orderly as an anthill. Poppa's job is to create that order, then to bring in the ants."

"That's important!" Eveline grins and almost laughs as we make our way back to the corner where Luna stands. I see the wheels turning. She is trying to understand how she and our family can be part of helping Poppa build his town.

"Let's see what kind of supplies Luna has," I say, feeling timorous as a mouse.

Climbing the rickety steps, we stop at the doorway and peer into the dark interior. A thin border collie lies panting at our feet. Inside, flies buzz over a tray of honeyed pecans, the only edible object in sight. The rough plank floor, stained with splotches of tobacco juice, tilts and heaves like a rutted field. Behind the counter looms a huge barrel of gunpowder and a small bin of corn. A burly man in a dirty apron stands in the shadowy place, talking in low guttural tones to a slatternly woman. Her bulldog bearing indicates she runs the place. She barks orders at a thin girl with lank hair serving drinks to the patrons. A leatherstocking, dressed in animal hide pants, curses at another frontiersman in foul-smelling clothes. Whiffs of dried animal blood, dirt, and tanned leather rise from them; the whole place reeks of whiskey and rum.

Gripping Eveline by the shoulder, I steer her back toward the front door. Then I hear Green's name repeated twice. "Green DeWitt," the man says again, "is the reason." As I strain to listen, he lowers his voice.

Then I grasp snatches of conversation about having to get the crops in the ground for the second time and people being angry about that.

"If DeWitt and that Tejano De León hadn't gotten into a row, we could've stayed a few more months down there and harvested more crops. Pullin' up stakes and planting another crop at the beginning of winter ain't no way to start a colony," one man complains. I stay still, trying to hear more.

Eveline breaks my grip and moves intently toward a dark corner. She stares at two young girls kissing a man hunched over a plate of red beans. At another table, a man strums a guitar.

I move quickly across the uneven floorboards toward Eveline. Catching my heel on one of the rough boards of the puncheon floor, I stumble and lunge forward right into the bartender.

"I beg your pardon," I mutter.

The beefy, bearded man roughly steadies me and then growls, "What the dickens?"

"My daughter there . . . I came in to see about supplies," I stammer.

"Where ya come from?" he demands.

"I'm Sarah DeWitt." I refuse to be cowed by a sour saloonkeeper selling moonshine. "My husband is Green DeWitt, the empresario," I add, seeing he has no notion of what a woman like me is doing in Luna.

The men at the table turn in their chairs and look me up and down.

One of them stands abruptly and says in a penitent voice, "Sorry, ma'am, didn't mean no harm. Just addled about havin' to leave corn for the crows at the coast and start over again up here in December."

I recognize him as a single man who'd lived on the Gulf near the warehouse on the bay. He was one of the small group of early arrivers who trickled in after we did. One of the dozens who heard Green's speeches, saw his newspaper ads, or heard by word of mouth that there was cheap land in DeWitt's colony.

I look straight at him.

"I don't blame you. My husband, of course, is sorry about this mis-understanding between him and Empresario De León. The Mexican authorities left us no choice but to leave the coast before the end of the year. I'm sure he'll do all he can to see there's seed corn available for those hurt by this."

The man tips his hat and sits back down at the table.

I do not like venturing into the uncertain territory of speaking on Green's behalf. Which is about as unnatural to me as carrying a knife. Before I can borrow any more trouble, I grab Eveline's hand and pull her toward the door.

The bartender goes back to his place behind the bar, swats a fly from his dirty face, and grunts something at me. We continue past him and the coarse woman next to him. She stares menacingly at us.

Before we can get much past the door, a pair of men, one tall and one small and bandy-legged, come crashing out in front of us. The tall one is the leatherstocking I'd seen inside. I don't know where the other came from. They roll down the steps past us and wrestle in the dirt.

Eveline tugs at my sleeve. "Momma, the tall one kicked the bow-legged man in the face."

As we watch, the small one rams his head into the big one's stomach, then grabs one foot and jerks the big one's legs out from under him.

On the ground, the leatherstocking picks up a board with nails in it and whacks the other, thrusting the nails at his face and eyes.

"You swine, you'll be sorry," the small man shouts and runs off down the road.

The leatherstocking bends over double, coughing up a foul stream of blood and vomit. Then he sets off after the other man, disappearing into the brush at the edge of the river.

"Well, Redbird, not what I had in mind for our first stroll through town." Eveline peppers me with questions I struggle to answer. Our first view of Gonzales as spoiled as sour milk, we head back along Water Street.

WILD TURKEYS

L ying next to Green, I am unable to sleep. Today is December 21, the darkest day of the year. He stirs but doesn't wake. I dress quickly, wrap in a woolen shawl, step into the darkness outside the cabin, and wait for the sun to rise.

In the stillness of the morning, my sister Susannah talks to me. I talk right back, telling her everything, including that in the town of Gonzales, with a population of fifty, the men outnumber the women ten to one. I start a letter to her:

In December, the northers come on suddenly. October would have been a better month to arrive in Gonzales.

It's no place for women and children. We're in a cabin by the Guadalupe River, which the men refer to as the Warloop (since they can't seem to get their tongues around the pronunciation of Guadalupe). We share the cabin with all manner of creeping things.

The sun moves quickly across the landscape like a ravenous animal. The light spreads, warming me, even on this darkest day of the year. So much sun in December makes being here more bearable.

Composing my letter, I stare across Water Street at the bare post oaks and sycamores white with frost. The sun soon melts the frost. The trees, grass, and vines drip with beads of dew. A red fox emerges from a pile of brush underneath the trees, twitching its bushy tail. It sniffs a trail up a stump and then down again before disappearing.

I begin again, trying to say what is really bothering me:

Green is gone too much, and with his absence, Will is ever more present. Will, who knows what I'm thinking, sometimes before I do. And cares.

No, I can't tell Susannah all that. Now, instead of Susannah answering back, I hear Destiny. Scorning me. Reminding me that Green envisions a new and better life for us. *Green and Empresario Austin see the future*, she says.

And think that it is theirs, I reply. *Which I doubt.*

I want to tell Susannah much more . . . but I don't. *Don't burden her with what you must learn to live with*, I warn myself. Instead, I tell her that there will be no celebration on Christmas Day.

We will miss terribly our traditional carols around the piano and Christmas feast with Liza Q and Father. So I hope to start the new year right with a celebration for us and the other new settlers.

I finish by the time the two-legged world shakes itself awake. I will put my thoughts on paper later and give a letter to Eugenio, who assures me mail boats leave Matagorda Bay every week or two.

Inside, Green and the children are stirring. Over breakfast, I lay out my New Year's plan. "I think we should begin with a celebration. Perhaps a party in the fort on New Year's Day? I can visit the neighbors and issue invitations for a New Year's feast."

Green looks up from his coffee and piles of papers, gratitude playing across his brow. "Yes, Sarah, yes. I haven't stopped long enough to think of such things. Excellent idea."

"I know you have much on your mind, but, yes, here in this new place, we need . . ."

His look stops me. A hard look that softens. He looks at me earnestly for a moment, then stands up to be on his way. At the door, he turns and looks back at the five of us at the table, gazing at him for instructions. He smiles and nods at me. "Excellent idea, Sarah. Thank you."

It is a welcome glimpse of the man I married—kind, considerate, even courtly, before the Texas tide carried him away.

Green heads off to check on the mill, and the children troop up to the Berry cabin to visit their friends. I find Eugenio in the wagon yard and ask him to take me to meet the neighbors. A few miles away we find the cabins of the newly arrived Nash and Taylor families on Peach Creek. I ask the women to bring cornbread dressing, onions, sweet potatoes, preserves, hominy, and whatever else they might scare up. The men are commissioned to kill deer, wild hogs, and birds for barbecuing. Eugenio and the other wagon drivers invite the Tejanos who live in a clump of cabins upriver. I send notes by Eugenio to the McCoys and the Burnses and ask them to spread the word.

When Will appears at our cabin to offer his services, I commandeer him too, to shoot a wild turkey for the New Year's Day meal in the fort. "I guess you know, Sarah, that's a tall order, tracking and shooting a wild turkey. They're faster than a roadrunner and more cunning than Andrew Jackson," he says. "And you know what a tough bird he is."

"I know your gallant efforts will succeed. I was also hoping you might accompany the children and me into the woods to find green boughs and mistletoe. We can put branches up for the festivities. And I don't think it is safe for the children and me to go alone."

Will does not hesitate. "No, you should not go alone."

He and I have planned outings and shared junkets since childhood, when I would fill a picnic basket as my ticket to go exploring with him and my boy cousins. Once, we even got lost for a day before finding our way back.

"I happen to have some ponies penned in a corral behind the fort." He gestures north up Water Street. "Get yourselves ready. I'll be back in a few minutes."

The children are elated.

"Momma," Clinton whispers seriously to me as I ladle stew onto four plates, "I'm going to be a hunter like Will."

I keep a straight face as he confides to C. C. his three-year-old wisdom of "thinking like a man." Listening to them, I feel almost lighthearted. The children eat quickly. Then, zealous as crusaders, they assemble ropes and a gunnysack for bringing back treasures from the woods.

We wait on the front steps of the log pen. Soon Will comes down Water Street, leading his red roan Ruby, followed by a Tejano boy leading two more horses. In front of the cabin, the boy hands the reins to Will and disappears back down the street. The children rush toward Will.

"This here is the best filly I've ever encountered," he tells us, patting Ruby's neck. "Though she's not exactly easy. But we've come to an understanding over the months since I separated her from the wild ones. I can count on her. She never lets me down."

The way he says it makes me feel almost sheepish for being one who has let him down.

"Now these two"—he points to a paint and a palomino— "handpicked for dependability. I call the paint Dandy, and she will be for Naomi and Clinton. She's calm and surefooted. And Naomi will know just how to treat this young animal because she thinks about what she's doing."

Naomi beams as he helps her into the saddle and then sets Clinton up in front of her.

For C. C. and me, he's chosen the palomino. "This one's as pretty as she is smart. Knows how to travel in the woods. I call her Pal.

For her color and because there's no better friend to have in this wild country."

"Before you start scaring the horses," Will tells the children, "I have one thing to tell you. You're going to do exactly what I say. Now you'll all be smarter than me pretty soon, but at present, I still know more about these fillies than you do. So you follow me."

Will knows horses. For as long as I can remember, he has talked and listened to the animals he depends on. We dutifully follow his instructions. Here we straddle a horse. I hitch my skirt up in the middle to my belt, as the girls and I have learned to do. I climb onto Pal, and Will lifts C. C. up to me. We fit snugly into the big western saddle. Will and Eveline lead the way with Naomi and Clinton in between. C. C. and I bring up the rear.

I admire Will's easy slouch in the saddle, his hat knocked back on his head, his grace on horseback. We head south down Water Street toward the low spot in the river. Mockingbirds call in the trees, sounding like squeaky gates. Amazing to me, the December day is mild as spring.

As we head toward the low-water crossing, a covey of bobwhites flutters in an anxious, noisy line. Will takes us past the sign announcing the colony and then to the ford not far beyond. The horses pick their way down a gentle slope across the crystal-clear stream.

Almost immediately, we find ourselves in what seems like a deer park, clumps of live oaks and pecan trees in the open, grassy bottomland next to the river. The beauty of the land surprises me, and I immediately wonder if Will is showing me this as a possible place to build the home Green has promised. I used to be able to read Will's mind, and now I'm doing it again. Absorbing the beauty of the woods, I let myself relax. Today we are in Will's hands.

His maps and sense of direction have guided me for much of my life. In keelboats on the Mississippi, he was the navigator. He sees the country like a bird, from above. His careful map of the route from Matagorda Bay to Gonzales opened my eyes. I bounce along, content in the knowledge that he will scout out generous supplies of mistletoe and guide us to glossy-leaved evergreens decked with berries. He might even shoot a wild turkey.

The forest closes around us for a while. The grapevines and quiet are interrupted only by birdsong. In one field, we stop to watch the rabbits spring straight up in the air and bound off. In full flight, the rabbits seem to be leaping over themselves.

"You boys wanna catch some rabbits?" Will asks. "This is the place to do it. These jackrabbits got the biggest ears and the fastest feet of any rabbit alive. So many of 'em you could catch these 'lopers with your bare hands. Just stand in the field with your paws out and grab one."

C. C. pulls at my sleeve, his enthusiasm rising like a holiday loaf. "Momma, can we come back here and catch some?"

"Dearie, I'm sure you will be back here." I feel certain now that Will is sending messages. He thinks this might be a good site for a house. It is the kind of thing he pays attention to and Green doesn't have time for.

We ride deeper into the woods, and then Will stops his horse before a carving on a live oak tree. "That there is the oldest picture I've ever seen and probably ever will see. Indians carved it a good long time ago."

Gazing at the outline of a buffalo, I follow the cuts in the bark of a huge live oak that has spread its branches over this spot for centuries. Then we are once more on the banks of the Guadalupe, where the narrow, quick-running San Marcos River feeds into the wider Guadalupe just before sweeping back again in a horseshoe bend.

"Why, we're almost exactly opposite the log pens on the other side. They must be behind all those vines over there."

Will gives me a frankly admiring look. "You always know where you are, Eagle Eyes."

In the clear waters below, we see catfish lurking in little pools and some mean-looking gars with long, needlelike noses. "Look at those lazy old catfish draggin' the bank lookin' for a cheap meal. Texas has everything, now, don't it? Catfish with whiskers, and garfish with 'gator snouts."

While he conducts his tour, I squint at a circle of rounded, cone-shaped structures made of tree branches lying close to the confluence of the San Marcos and Guadalupe Rivers. "What's over there?" I ask, pointing far to the west.

"Tonkawa village. But don't worry. Friendly bunch. All you have to do is surrender a few horses and beads from time to time." Will flashes his irreverent grin. "Invite 'em to your New Year's shindy, Sarah. They'll come with bells on and take note of what they might want on the next trip."

We ride down a slope to the river and dismount on a sandbar reaching into the water. I've brought a sack of pecans for a snack. Cracking open the shells and picking out the delicious, meaty pecans, we listen to the rushing river. The swift San Marcos River deposits its load of sand and branches at the bend of the Guadalupe. Willows march from river to land, turtles scramble onto logs, and the children wade and splash while Will and I keep watch in the sun.

"Do you hear anything from Harriet?" I ask when the children are out of earshot. "Or is she still too mad at you to write?"

"Mad at me?" he sputters. "She's the one who refused to come."

"Sometimes I wish I'd been that strong," I confide and then wish I could take back my words.

Will stares at me and then adjusts the conversation to a less dangerous angle. "I never noticed weakness as one of your problems."

"Oh, and what *did* you notice as my problems?"

"I noticed that you never exhibit many," he says cagily.

I feel myself blush. "Well, I think you mean that as a compliment, Will. So thank you."

I want to say more. As I had once. But those days are long gone. I know this is a treacherous path. What worries me is, after all these years, I can't ignore the pull Will exerts on me. Seeing him every day as we sailed down the Mississippi, being around him as we decamped on the Gulf before heading to Gonzales, and now living next door to him. I can't deny that some days, just glimpsing him leaves me giddy and guilty at once.

Will stands and walks to the edge of the sandbar, skipping a few stones across the river, instructing the kids how to make the stones skip farther. One reaches the opposite bank.

When he sits down, I turn the conversation to the girls in Luna. "Whose children are they?"

"I think they're property of Buffalo Belle, a woman with a buffalo hunter's smell and a mug like a wild tusker. She and her dirty old man run our local cantina."

"The woman with the mustache?"

"When did you see her?" Will demands.

"When Eveline and I walked in there."

"Sarah, you and Eveline have no business in Luna. In Presbyterian talk, it's a 'den of iniquity.' Thieves, white slavers, escaped criminals, and that's just the ones I know about. Belle was probably thinking about kidnapping Eveline the minute she saw her."

"Is that what happened to the girls in there?"

"Wouldn't doubt it."

"Will, we can't stand for that."

"You going to walk in and whup Belle single-handed?"

"No. But you and Green could lay down the law to her."

He laughs. "I swear, you sure do have a lot of jobs for me. I'll try to work it in when I'm not stalking wild turkeys. And just what law would you be referring to? Mexican law doesn't cover most of the shady activities you see. Other than trying to force us to buy expensive Mexican cigarettes in their little *estancos* in Béjar and La Bahía. In fact, the *Federalistas* and the *Centralistas* in the capital are so busy trying to sort out their own fights right now, they don't think too much about problems anywhere else."

Will's comment underscores how little I understand. I know what Green has told me: that the Mexican Constitution of 1824 is a liberal, democratic document that many enlightened Mexicans, who call themselves *Federalistas*, support. The *Centralistas* are not so democratically inclined; the tug of war between those factions grows more divisive by the day.

"So that means we must act as if we're following their Constitution and sort out on our own the problems they don't care about? The empresarios' rules are a sort of a local code without much means of enforcement?"

Will gives a slight nod and grows more serious.

"The reason that old Musk Hog hasn't been thrown out of Gonzales before now is that there's a demand for her services. Not only the girls but the liquor. She's got a source *and* a market for all the whiskey and some of the tobacco that comes into this little crossroads. And then everyone dealing under the table can blame it on her. And no one wants to lose *that* advantage."

"Green knows about all of this too?" I shudder. How naïve I am.

Will shrugs, refusing to answer my question.

"Dang, Sarah, I hate the sight of young girls put to work in there too. I'll think about how to accomplish what you want. Makes me cringe every time I go in there. But there is a hitch. Ol' Belle will blow the whistle on me and Eugenio, too, if we make her mad. She's in deep with all the tobacco smugglers, and she surely knows that Eugenio and I have a few stashes ourselves. Tobacco is a big deal to the Mexicans. They don't want us 'importing' it off the ships that bring it from the States. As you might recall, that's one of the issues our Tejano friend Empresario De León was so perturbed about."

"And how did those 'stashes' get there, Will?"

"Señor Eugenio and I stockpile 'em for safekeeping, then sell off a little at a time to anyone whose supply of chewing or smoking tobacco is running low. We're just middlemen taking advantage of an opportunity. But don't tell nobody or we could be in a heap of trouble."

"Where does the tobacco come from?"

"The schooner *Dispatch* that Green uses to bring settlers and goods down the Mississippi picks up cargo from plantations across the South. Or traders buy it in New Orleans, sell it to me, and I sell to any buying customer. The Mexicans call it contraband; I call it business. The Mexicans want us to buy it from them at higher prices. We do have to be careful. I don't want Green to know about our little enterprise because it could get him in trouble with Empresario De León and his ilk. But nobody's watching *me* that close. And Señor Eugenio has a special genius for getting things into and out of places. A quality I admire."

Ignoring the facts about their tobacco dealings, I take the high road. "Will, there's got to be some criminal and civil justice code for living here—for the treatment of children like the girls at Luna, for robberies, for murders. I would imagine Empresario Austin has already thought about issues like this. We must find out what to do. I'm going to bring it up with Green as soon as I can get him to slow down long enough to have a conversation."

"You're right. I'm sure Empresario Austin has an answer for most everything. The simple fact is we're all ruled by Mexican law, but the courts are in Saltillo, seven hundred miles away, and Santa Anna and the rest have decided not to look too close at what we're doing right now. But just remember, Miz DeWitt, folks got their eyes on you, and you don't wanna get too unpopular too fast. Besides, what makes you think the girls in Luna have parents that want them in the first place?"

I nod, knowing he is right. We're living in a place only a tad more civilized than a no-man's-land, and I know far too little about the everyday workings of the colony.

"I'm not going to ignore the abuse of children. But I suppose finding trimmings for the New Year's party is about as much as we can handle today," I admit, trying not to ruin our fine afternoon.

Riding farther into the bottomland upriver, we stop to cut down grapevines. Then I spot the balls of mistletoe I'd been hoping to find.

"Look, Will, way up there." Will shoots down one and then another out of the high oaks. It is a page from our youth. Finding mistletoe in the woods was our winter ritual. It was hard to find in Missouri, and we gloried in bringing armfuls back to my mother for her heartwarming fests. Will even sold it on the street and in my aunt's dry goods store in the holiday season. My mother and aunt insisted that we must honor the birth of our Savior. They marched us to church and planned Christmas dinners that were joyous holiday occasions.

I point, he shoots, and the children run to gather the green balls with white berries. They laugh and climb into lower branches of the oak trees where mistletoe abounds. Midday stretches into midafternoon. Shafts of light stream through the trees. Towering walnuts and giant oaks shelter us. The day wraps around us, encircles us, children of the forest in our protected glade.

When I begin to worry about the lengthening shadows, Will reins in his horse and circles over next to me.

"Look over yonder, Eagle Eyes." On a little rise, three yaupons laden with red berries sit side by side. "You had one of those in your yard in St. Louis, didn't you? You can trim a few branches off and still have a holly bush for your next homestead."

Will helps Naomi and Eveline off the horses, then lifts the younger children down. While I tie up the horses, Will gets a hatchet and tow sack out of the saddlebags. After the options have been thoroughly studied, we choose, for practical purposes, the small yaupon, and Will begins to pull it out of the ground.

When he is almost finished wrapping it up in the sack and tying it behind his saddle, Naomi touches his shoulder and points in the distance.

"Look," she says quietly. Two wild turkeys flutter up into a bare old tree by the river.

"*Je-sús Cris-to,*" Will says. "Those young eyes of yours are something!"

Naomi glows with pride while Will removes his shotgun from his saddle and moves back toward the riverbank. With the sun dropping toward the river, he is able to see the turkeys better than they can see him. With the rest of us frozen in place, he edges back, trying to get the turkeys in his sights.

He is so intent on getting a bead on the turkeys he doesn't see the big hole directly behind him. I imagine a nest of rattlesnakes coiled inside. Three more steps backward, and he will fall into it. A shout would scare the turkeys. I move in front of the hole so he won't edge into it. There is only one step between him and the hole when he backs right into me, taking us both down on the other side of the hole. I grab him around the waist. The shotgun flies up in the air, landing a few feet away. We hit the ground flat on our backs.

Across me, he looks into my eyes and, with a smile, kisses me on the cheek. It is a peck, both friendly and loving, almost as if he were laughing at both of us: star-crossed, thwarted by bad luck, trapped in the twists and turns of his wild card theory, playing another bad hand. After a childhood together and an adulthood apart, I stare back at him, sputtering to explain why I was standing directly in his way.

"Well, Sally Goodin," he says in his leisurely way, softly speaking my childhood nickname. "Like I was sayin', wingin' a wild turkey is serious business."

My cheeks burn as the children pick us up, managing to avoid the treacherous little tunnel that we almost fell into. We see in the distance the turkeys, gobbler and hen, and hear them flapping away toward the river.

Following the arc of the wild turkeys' flight, I look up and across the river. In the far distance, a man is watering his horse. The man stares as if looking straight at me. I can't make him out. The deep shadows on this shortest day of the year make it impossible. But the horse looks like Major, Green's big bay.

A NEW YEAR

eturning from holiday preparations at the fort, I dress in my Sunday best for the New Year's celebration. Down by the river, his shaving mirror propped in the crotch of a post oak, Green lathers his face, then scrapes the blade back and forth. Starting down the path to the river, I hear his voice. He is having a conversation with the face in the mirror.

"You've come a long way," he tells himself.

I have to agree. Three years after securing his grant of nearly four thousand square miles, colonists are finally arriving in Gonzales, the capital of the DeWitt colony. Empowered by the Mexican governor of Coahuila y Tejas, Rafael Gonzales, Empresario DeWitt is the guardian of this vast chunk of territory. It is his to hand over to settlers who will claim and tame it. More than seventy-five thousand acres have been set aside for Green personally. A quarter of the grant will be delivered to him, the empresario, after the first hundred families are settled. I try not to think about the paltry number of families so far. Somewhere around a dozen.

Instead, I think of all he has survived: endless months gaining the confidence of the Mexican government; long trips up and down the Mississippi River; bone-jarring days in the saddle traveling across the Texas prairies; years of preparation to get a trickle of settlers onto a schooner, through New Orleans, and across the wide Gulf of Mexico. Then came the waiting game, the settlers in makeshift cabins on the Gulf while preparations for their arrival continue at Gonzales.

He has to believe it will pay off, I remind myself. And maybe it will. The times are right, as he says. Rising land prices and economic hardship in the States will whet the appetite for cheaper land. In this outpost, he can issue money and sell headrights to every broke settler looking for a homestead. I'd read the words scribbled on scraps of paper he distributed on both sides of the Mississippi: "Redeemable at Land Office in DeWitt's Colony." It serves as the first paper money used in the northern wilds of Mexico, a country without enough people to civilize it. A grant of land "about as big as the state of Rhode Island that will repay us a thousandfold." I've heard that more times than I can count and wonder if it is true.

I continue down the path, calling to him. "We should get over to the fort soon." He splashes water on his face and looks up.

"That red dress . . . you're pretty as a picture," he responds from his post by the river.

The sight of the man watering his horse flickers across my mind again. Was it Green? And what had he seen? I rebuke myself for being distant to my husband, for wanting Will in my life. At forty, as this propitious new year dawns, Green is in the prime of his life. He deserves my full support. I move back up the path, waiting in the door as he collects mug and razor.

He knows who he is, Destiny would say, *a statesman of this new realm taken now as his own.*

Yes, but there is more to it, I protest.

It's not just the simple lure of owning land or of bringing in settlers. It's like gambling. You roll the dice once, it's yours; you roll again and relinquish control. In the casino in New Orleans, it struck me like lightning: taking chances thrills him; the spring prairies of Texas are like the green plush of those tables. It is an affliction that turned a perfectly sensible, prudent man into one obsessed: I will have all this and more, and if I lose, I will regain it twofold next time around.

A terrible revelation. I'd never imagined that teetering on the brink of ruin would so exhilarate him. It galls me to see it. If we'd stayed in Missouri, I never would have realized Green's fascination with gambling. Standing here in the door, I mourn for Missouri and for my piano, my mother's smile, my hollyhocks and sweet peas twining up the chicken-wire trellis, my once-happy marriage. And know, in the back of my mind, that I must try to think of this move, all Green's decisive moves, as courage, not recklessness.

Shaken, I remember my task, my intention to look for candles in the cabin, and I try to bury my fears in the demands of the day. Green comes in and goes outside again. I've forgotten to ask the guests to bring candles. They will know that. But I search anyway and can find only a small store in the trunk, enough to last for an hour or two after dark, along with a rope of red glass beads Naomi might like to wear. I tuck the beads in my pocket and dig into another chest. Despite the brightness of the daytime sky, the sun will set early, long before the festivities end. I hope the dancing will extend late into the evening and buoy the mood, the prospect that 1828 will be a good year for all.

I call to the children and get no response. Instead Green appears at the front door, brimming with confidence. In his boots and duster, he looks every inch the empresario, six-foot-two with sky-high dreams. Yet I know how heavily responsibility sits on his shoulders and that I must try to hearten him from all that weighs him down.

The children come running up Water Street. They appear in descending order: Naomi at the door first, then Eveline and the boys. They've been back and forth to the fort all morning, hanging up mistletoe and yaupon branches with bright red berries in bunches and carrying cornbread and cakes baked on the rough hearth of the cabin.

"Momma, we need help," Eveline reports.

"Yes, my dears, I'm right behind you."

Green strides ahead of us to the fort. We follow, with the boys playing tag and the girls looking for their friends.

Down Water Street, a wagon filled with the Burns family rolls into town. Behind them are three wagons of McCoys, all thirteen of them. North and south along Water Street, the colony's motley bunch comes in wagons and oxcarts and on horseback: Major Kerr, with three of his slaves, Shade, Anise, and their son, Jack; the Nash family, who have just come from Louisiana, with their three tykes under five; the Taylors, from Alabama, with six towheads ranging from toddlers to a grown son. Some walk. Will saunters from his cabin. With him is the legendary Deaf Smith. Trackers and scouts, each considers the other his best audience. The single men arrive in twos and threes: Lockhart's surveying teams; Eugenio and the wagon drivers; other Tejanos who live close by. Then the bartender and his pungent companion, Buffalo Belle, as Will calls her. We are a flow of travelers plagued and pulled together by our improbable dreams.

Following them is Byrd Lockhart. He and his mother, sister, and her children are our new neighbors on Water Street. I wave, my sense of vulnerability diminishing every time Mr. Lockhart appears. Tall, stringy Byrd is a modest, levelheaded presence. He manages survey teams, supervising the cutting and laying out of roads, and it is he who initiated the construction of the fort. I revere the practical skills and dutiful commitment this man devotes to the colony. Will and Mr. Lockhart have provided the roofs over our heads and the roads under our feet. Without them, Green's vision could never have taken shape.

Most of the crowd heads into La Fortaleza, which is hardly a regular fort. It is a mongrel with a ceiling and walls, more like a barn inside a fence. It is a make-do kind of edifice, built to shelter stragglers in the wilderness, one that an architect would spurn for its bastardized, patchwork form. Yet despite its tilt and maverick nature, the structure looms over Gonzales like a cathedral over a Mexican village. Rather than church bells, its upper reaches hold ladders reaching up to lookout posts and embrasures for aiming, sighting, and firing. Below, a big stone hearth and chimney occupy a portion of one side; several rooms line the walls on the opposite side. According to Green, one of these side rooms has cleverly concealed steps that lead under Water Street to a secret tunnel extending to the river. I've never been in it but seriously hope it exists.

The fort's wide double doors let in the noonday sun, lighting up the dark interior. A slab of rough puncheon floor, recently hewn and hammered, rises near the big hearth—a dance floor for our New Year's evening entertainment. Holly boughs and wreaths hang on mantle and doors, balls of mistletoe dangle from rafters, garlands of grapevines loop and trail along the hearth. My little yaupon sits in its own tub near the hearth. Our greenery gives La Fortaleza a holiday glow.

Eugenio drives two wagons into the open area near the hearth. They will serve as sideboard and seating for those congregating inside instead of out by the smoky cooking pits. A wind blows, making the day chillier than the sunny sky promises. Soon people begin to find their places, the women working inside and the men and children heading outside into a winter milder than any other they've experienced, despite the wind.

Next to the fort, the men tend fires for roasting meat, while the women warm food by the fire. Mr. Lockhart and Will provide tables for the crowd. They unhinge the doors leading to the rooms off the big central area and set them on sawhorses. They set up six tables for plenty of elbow room. A bucket brigade to the river carries water into the fort.

As wagons and carts approach, Creed appoints himself wagon master. And Eugenio, who loves anything with wheels, quickly appoints himself the wagon master's aide. Creed directs wagons into a grassy expanse out between the fort and a salt lick.

Creed announces the arrival of the McCoy family wagons, led by John McCoy, who drives his team with his big-boned wife beside him, cradling a shotgun. Everyone accords John McCoy a position of respect. A veteran of the War of 1812, he fought Indians and killed bears with Daniel Boone in Missouri. Eugenio pays polite attention to the history Creed recites, though he understands maybe one in ten words and certainly has never heard of Daniel Boone or the War of 1812. Yet he seems to know Creed pays tribute to his friend John, who saved his life in the war.

The middle of the day is taken up with cooking, roasting, and drinking. Men monitor the blazing fire pits outside. They spit tobacco juice, smoke, and pull out flasks tucked in boots or coats. Green flatters the girls and women, Will charms them, and the Tejanos coax tunes from guitars and banjos.

The noonday meal is served just as the sun starts its journey across the western sky. Creed calls us together with his bugle, a remnant of his military service he keeps handy. Mr. Lockhart and Eugenio—who both hate noise—grimace at the brassy notes. I suspect that at home, with the closest neighbors miles away, Creed bugles to his heart's content. When the crowd assembles, Green delivers the blessing, praising the bounty of the land we've come to and praying for the safety and prosperity of all.

An assortment of competing aromas—venison, chicken, dove, beef, and turkey—fill the fort. At one end, the women line up plates of steaming hominy, roasted corn, mounds of mashed potatoes, yams stacked in a pile, little pearl onions, big garden onions, fleshy carrots, poke salad greens gathered in the wild, cornbread, biscuits, pecans and walnuts, cakes, apple brown betty, and honey. Women and men take opposite sides of the room. The smallest children sit with their mothers, and the young men and women, exchanging flirty looks and talking, fill two crowded tables. Some drift outside because even six tables can't accommodate the whole crowd.

On the women's side, we steal looks at each other's dresses, notice who wears a ringlet hairpiece or powdered her face, and talk about the need for a school. Since, in accord with Mexican law, all the worship has to be Catholic and there are none among us, no one is in a particular hurry to build a church.

With Clinton by my side, I exchange news with Molly Burns, Esther Berry, Margaret Lockhart, and Margaret's mother, the elder Mrs. Lockhart. Several compliment me on my cornbread and cakes, and I, in turn, praise their vegetables, carrots hastily dug up from gardens on the coast and root vegetables lugged all the way from Missouri.

The women tell me that the bins at the front of Luna sometimes hold sugar, salt, flour, and coffee, even shoes and bolts of calico. Thinking liquor is Luna's main offering, I listen carefully, busying myself with three-year-old Clinton because I don't want to say too much. Though the saloon woman, Belle, is some distance away, the women at my table lower their voices to acknowledge that the establishment is indeed a saloon with a back room. But, behind hands, they add that the bartender and Belle are a conduit to those much-needed supplies, which come regularly from New Orleans and from ships docking on the Gulf coast. However the two saloonkeepers are financing the trade, the women are happy to have it.

"Saloons are one thing," I observe. "But what about the young women who seem to be indentured to the proprietors? They are hardly more than children, some no older than my girls."

"*Indentured* is a kind word for it," Esther Berry replies in a firm voice. "It's the same as white slavery. It went on in England in my mother's and grandmother's times, and it goes on here today right under our noses."

"Those poor girls have no home," Margaret Lockhart says. "They're orphans, or they've been taken from people who don't want them."

I don't doubt Margaret's and Esther's assessments of the situation. But I also sense that righting it could bring new woes. I glance at Margaret's daughter's shoes, cut out at the toes. Along with sugar and flour, shoes for growing children are also in short supply. Luna doubles as an emporium where goods can be bargained for and bought on credit. I hold my tongue.

Thinking to enlist the girls' aid in the cleanup, I move outside. Naomi and Eveline lean toward the Burns girls in animated conversation. Next to them, Green and Creed are pointing to a figure advancing from the river on foot: a barrel-chested Indian with three turkey feathers in his headband and a necklace of wildcat claws around his neck. I move toward my girls. At first, I think the Indian is naked but then realize he is wearing a tattered breechcloth. His feet are covered in leather strips bound with thongs. Beside him trails a thin dog.

Regarding the Indian's bald head and brown face speckled with smallpox scars, Creed says, "Well, if it isn't Chief Turkey Egg."

"He's a Tonkawa," Green observes. "There's a Tonk encampment up there by the fork of the river. They're friendly."

Over his shoulder, the Indian has slung a beaver.

"He wants to trade that beaver," Creed says to Green. "What do you think we've got that he wants?"

"Well, they like our horses a lot, but a beaver is not going to get him a horse."

The Indian approaches the curious group that has gathered alongside Creed and Green. He uses some sign language that nobody understands. In response, Creed answers in Spanish and English, "*Amigo*. Friend."

Stepping up, Deaf Smith answers the Indian in sign language, which makes him look much happier.

"What are you telling him?" Creed asks.

"Just what you tried to say."

Then the Indian holds up the beaver. To which Creed replies, "Hell, we don't need sign language to see his prize there. He wants to trade the beaver. But what does he want in return?"

Deaf goes back to signing. After a few more exchanges, while Creed continues commenting on the bald Indian's amazing resemblance to a brown spotted turkey egg, Deaf says, "I think he wants cloth. Something to add to his dress for a war dance. Or maybe for a little squaw."

Looking at the Indian's bare loins and body, Creed says, "Judgin' by what he's wearing, he needs some. Bad."

The Indian is pointing to one of the little pallets of piled-up quilts a few feet away. "The quilt. He likes that quilt," Green says, looking at me.

"It's Molly's quilt. She made it," I respond.

Suddenly, all eyes are on Molly. Without a moment's hesitation, she says, "I'd trade a quilt for a beaver skin any day if it means friendly neighbors over there across the river."

She scoops up the quilt, folds it nicely, and puts it in the Indian's arms. Just as quickly, he hands Molly the beaver skin, which she passes off to Creed.

The Indian turns on his heel and disappears with his dog.

"So, Molly," Creed smiles, "you've got another fine pelt to add to the coat you're making me. One you trapped yourself."

BLUE MOON

The feasting goes on for hours. Nearly everyone returns for seconds and thirds. Before all of the food disappears, Molly throws some of her long tablecloths over the dishes and announces leftovers will be served for supper. That shuts down the eating and leads to more card games inside and a few horse races up and down Water Street.

I busy myself, heating water on the hearth for more coffee and dishwashing. Molly joins me. "I know what you're thinking. You're worried about those girls in Luna, aren't you? And you won't rest until . . . well, I don't know what you'll do, but I know you'll be thinking how to fix it."

I roll my eyes, overwhelmed over how much there is to fix. "Yes, I suppose. But I can't seem to—"

"Can't seem to what?" Will asks from behind me.

"I can't seem to quit worrying about things. The Indians, friendly or not, the mistreated children, the contract with the Mexicans. I know I should be happy about getting here safely and thank goodness for small miracles."

Wherever Will has been, I haven't seen him all morning. Hearing his voice feels like the first easy moment of the day.

"You and Molly come with me, Sarah. I want to show you something that'll cheer you both up."

Molly shrugs. We nod and follow Will.

In the far corner of the fort, Will rolls away a big rock covering a trap door. He opens the door and lights a taper. The circle of light falls on the steps below us.

"This here is the secret tunnel, meant for emergencies: it runs underground straight to the river. You ladies should know about it."

"Ah, the tunnel." Molly and I grope the dirt wall as Will leads us through. I recoil, then reach for his arm, afraid of what I will encounter on that dank cool surface. Molly grasps my other hand.

"If we ever have to hole up here to escape attacks, the tunnel is a protected way in and out."

I follow blindly, trying not to consider the dire event that would make hiding here necessary.

"Some crack planners built this here little secret passage, huh?" he chuckles.

Ahead of us, I see eyes, a coiled thing. "Will, watch out."

He shifts his gaze. "Just a chicken snake. Here, come toward me."

"Not me," Molly says. "Too dark down here for me. And I'm not going a step closer to a coiled-up snake, harmless or not." She turns and goes back, groping her way up the stairs.

I move closer to Will, so close I can feel his breath and smell his fresh air and tobacco scent. I stumble over a rock in the path. He steadies me, his right hand circling my waist.

"I know what you're going through," Will whispers, his words clear as a bell in the dark. He stops and looks at me. "You're not alone."

He looks straight into my eyes, and for the second time in two days, I don't turn away. The taper in his hand lights his face. I step back, and he leads me by the hand, heading toward the steps out of the tunnel.

Arm in arm, we come into the open air. Directly facing us, only a few feet from the tunnel exit near the river, Green stands next to a tall Indian. Both are looking down at the body of the Tonkawa who'd traded for Molly's quilt. The dead man's dog whimpers and growls, lying next to the body.

I quickly let go of Will's arm. Green looks up to see me and Will emerge from the tunnel, my hasty gesture deepening the scowl on his face. To explain to Green that this duo had started out as a trio seems fruitless.

"Sarah, Will," Green says with steely calm. "This is Chief Placido, chief of the Tonkawa. He was riding back from a hunting trip when he spotted this fellow dead here in the brush. One of his boys. He alerted me. Reckons he was killed by Comanches."

"Comanche," the chief said, pointing to the arrow in his chest.

Will nods. "There's a Comanche camp not too far from here. Half a day's ride. Not quite far enough."

Chief Placido says, "Comanche everywhere. Don't like Tonkawa." He motions up and down the river. "Looking for horses. Scalps," he says, eyeing the redhead and blonde before him.

I stare at the dead man. My concerns of dire events that would send us into the tunnel now seem sadly prescient. The chief motions to two other Tonkawa behind him, who gather the body and lift it onto a horse.

On the ground lies Molly's quilt. Before Will or Green can turn back to me, I snatch it up and hurry away as the men gather in clumps around the Indians. Back inside the fort, still clutching the quilt, I try to answer the women asking questions, all too aware of how quickly fear and dread descend.

The dancing begins at dark. The musicians fiddle through several bars before the tune is recognizable. A stocky hunter, encased like a sausage in his animal hide suit, plays fiddle, accompanied by the guitar players. Eugenio, wrapped in his dark, ragged serape, his hair combed and glossy with oil, stands on a chair behind the fiddler and watches.

Green and I lead the dancers onto the floor with "Turkey in the Straw." The older boys and girls lose no time moving onto the floor around us. The dancers include several generations: one McCoy daughter and the McCoy wives and sons, the almost-grown Berry kids, young Emily Burns, the Nashes, the Taylors, some Sowell boys, even Shade and Anise. They dance to the side, enjoying a society much more tolerant than the one they've come from.

The younger ones, babes-in-arms up to adolescents, look on. This set includes Naomi, Lillah, Cynthianne, and others, including one of the forlorn girls from Luna. Wandering into the fort alone, she ate ravenously when I piled her plate with food. Now she sits apart from the others, her eyes roving around the room, darting to the doors. Her hair hangs in thin strands around her small face. Some call her "the mustang girl." She seems scared, untamed. Is that how she's gotten tagged with the strange nickname?

The dignified waltz soon gives way to "Cutting the Pigeon's Wing" and other lively dances. During the first dance with me, Green tries to reassure me we are safe despite the Comanche ambush but makes no comment about my exit from the tunnel with Will. After the dance, Green dances with Molly and others, and I greet latecomers to the party. Gallantly, Creed and Will dance with any female who sits close to the dance floor. Even the Luna bartender and Belle join in. They are joined by two more Tejano families, invited by Deaf Smith and his Tejana wife, who came not to feast but to dance.

I drift back to the small wagon at one end of the fort. The music whines on. There is talk of the dead Indian and shaking of heads. Most of the men seem to think that Indians fighting among themselves is not a great threat. Yet there have been abductions of women or children in San Antonio de Béjar and the surrounding countryside farther west. The men assert there's safety in numbers. I shudder, thinking of all the times the children and I are alone.

Taking in the yaupon holly and the mistletoe hanging from the rafters, I relish my first solitary moment of the day. C. C. and Clinton are asleep in a corner, and the girls are dancing. Awhile ago, I'd seen Will squiring Naomi, Eveline, and the Burns girls around when there weren't enough boys to go around.

Now he is at the punch bowl. When he starts in my direction, I look for Green.

"Stuff is harmless," he says, offering the cup in his hands. "All the liquor in it long since evaporated or guzzled up."

I take a sip. Then he rises and holds out his arms, inviting me to dance. I know I should decline. Before I do, Green appears in front of us.

He doesn't look at me. He fixes his gaze fully on Will as if I weren't there. He motions with his head, tilting it toward the door. Then he jerks his thumb in that direction. The music seems to stop before resuming, a whine turning into a discordant scream inside my head. I watch the two of them stride toward the door and disappear outside. All around, I see stunned faces and eyes drilling into me.

I can't stay seated. Not here. I rise and follow them out the front door.

Green and Will stand toe to toe with the full moon illuminating their movements. I look on, hidden in the shadow of the doors.

In the moonlight, I can see Green's searching look. "We've been through a lot of scrapes together. No one I respect more than you. You know that, don't you?"

Will nods, then smiles. "Why wouldn't I, Green? Glad to hear it. 'Bout time," he jokes. "Since we've been working together for years now. 'Preciate it. Same here."

Green swallows hard. "Well, if that's so, I'd 'preciate it if you acted like it."

"Not sure what ya mean by that."

"I mean just what you think I mean. You can be as sly a fox as you want with everybody else, but it's my wife we're talking about."

I hear Will's easygoing tone, which is exasperating to Green.

"What about your wife, Green?" Will asks.

Green goes silent.

I want to go to Green and say what he saw from the opposite side of the river was not what he thought. I want to explain why Will and I came out of the tunnel together. But I can't force myself out of the shadows.

"Sarah's been acting funny lately. I know it's been a shock getting here and seeing things as they are. The log pen's pretty rough . . . and now the Indian. Not herself."

Will sits down on a stump next to them and rolls a cigarette. "Felled this tree myself," he says, "when we were building the fort."

Green narrows his eyes. "I know how essential you are. Don't switch the subject."

Will looks up. "I wouldn't worry none about Sarah. Whatever happens to any of us, I'd bank on Sarah bein' just fine. Always had good sense, always will."

Green gives Will a long look. His answer only stokes Green's anger, underscoring that he's known me longer and better than Green himself does.

Silence again. But Green refuses to play the same game. "Sense?" Green asks finally. "What's sense got to do with it? No one ever doubted that. We're talking about a place the other side of the moon from sense, and you know it." He turns and goes back inside, leaving Will on the stump.

Standing in the shadows, I am left face-to-face with the gap in my thinking that has widened into a chasm. I have to put things in perspective: Marriage means a world more to me than it ever has to Will. He said it once when we were young, and I still remember how it crushed me: "Marriage is no guarantee of much of anything, far as I can see." The proclamation was accompanied by his impish grin. To my sixteen-year-old ears, that meant he never wanted to marry. Though that wasn't what he'd meant at all. Even so, all these years later, he's walked out on his own marriage. And I'm not planning to walk out on mine.

Will might be able to bluff his way once or twice with Green, but a triangle is intolerable. I need a better way to proceed. But what keeps popping into my mind is the day long ago when I first met Will. The day I turned up with my cousin to help Will bring the keelboat from Hannibal to St. Louis. Even on that first day, we were inseparable.

It wasn't only his red hair, green eyes, and playful ways that attracted me or his skill at handling the boat. We saw eye to eye on everything, laughing at the curious beaver building a home with three exits and three entrances. We cared about the boats on the Mississippi and trees and birds: the big cypresses with knobby knees, the strange anhinga birds that dived and rose out of the river as if walking on water. We fished off the pier and once caught the same number of fish in two hours. That was the day I stood close enough to him that he knew to kiss me. When I reached up and ran my fingers through his red curls, I thought I could stand by him forever. Knew he was the boy for me from that day until he left St. Louis.

For a long while, I thought he'd come back. But when the months stretched into a year, I concluded I was wrong. I started seeing Green. We married, and a year later, Eliza was born.

Then Will returned. When he saw me holding Eliza, the look in his eyes told me how wrong I had been. It was a grim day. Thankfully, Green has never known the whole story. He knows Will and I were childhood friends, even youthful sweethearts. But he seems to have given little thought to a connection beyond that. Or at least he has never acknowledged such thoughts.

But that isn't the worst of it. I honestly loved Green when I married him. I'd moved on, as the young do, thinking my love for Will was unrequited. When he returned, life dealt us a terrible blow. We carried on, of course. A year later, Will married Harriet. We buried our feelings until, once again, wild cards got shuffled into the deck.

I look up at the moon, its light a cold, silvery blue, the lines along its surface running like swift rivers. I shiver. The new year, 1828, stretches before me. Standing behind the doors of the fort, in an alien country, a loneliness I've never known creeps into me. Returning to the celebration inside will not lift my heavy heart. But that is what I must do.

I sit on the bank behind the cabin, watching the children fish, enjoying the day-after quiet. Green has gone with the surveyors. I am grateful for deliverance from the festivities, though this is only a surface calm. Below me, the river's current is especially strong after the recent rains, the river churning, rushing past with considerable force. Downriver, near the cabin where several cart drivers stay, I see Eugenio and his friends cooking up a meal. When he spots me, he waves and then leaves the group. He approaches, looking strangely shy and hesitant.

"*Buenos días, Señora.*" He pulls a paper from his pocket and pushes it into my hands. I recognize the scrawl.

Dearest Sarah,

You're too fine for a mess like this. I'm not going to hang around here crying like a lovesick pup. Heading for San Antonio de Béjar. Figure I can make my way there just as good as here. But I will say one thing: There's a load of pecans in a shed in the bottomland near where your new house will be. I told Eugenio to sell them for you in Béjar, whenever you say. If you want to see me, go along with him, and he'll chaperone our visit. He'll know where to find me.

W.

It is the part about the pecans that gets to me. A silly excuse, refusing to say goodbye. I read the note a second time and then look up at Eugenio. He squints at me with sadness. "*El Colorado* build the fort. Make the road, *el camino a Gonzales.* Draw *los mapas. Es el cartógrafo. El empresario* need him. Very sad to leave."

What sense can Eugenio possibly make out of all this? He looks up the path, and I follow his eyes. Will is standing in his doorway. He motions with two fingers toward our cabin.

I look back at Eugenio. He has seen the whole exchange. "I stay here with *niños* fishing," he says.

I hurry up the hill and station myself on a chair by the back door of the cabin. Will pulls a chair up next to me.

"You feeling as loco as I am?" he asks in a soft voice.

I purse my lips and say nothing.

He moves on to the point. "Not much ink in the inkwell. Didn't want to talk myself into staying. Besides, don't like to push my spelling skills."

I manage a half smile.

"You pretty much know . . . the whole thing doesn't make sense."

I breathe in and out several times and then nod.

He pulls his chair closer and, to my surprise, takes my face in his hands. "Let me see some of that solid-rock calm that's always guided you—me too, for that matter."

I try to assume the look he wants. Then he launches into his speech.

"If you ever need anything, anything at all, Eugenio will know how to find me. I'm going to Béjar. Have to leave, Sarah. For Green. For all three of us. You are the one thing in my life that I take serious. That'll drive me crazy if I hang around here."

My eyes go watery. I turn away.

Will grimaces and scratches his neck. "Gotta get outta here, Sarah, much as I hate to." But he makes no move to go.

I hear in his voice that he needs something from me. A word that will let him go, let him know I see things the way he imagines. I summon a voice as steady as I can make it. "Yes, you have to go. We both know that."

Will leans toward me again and kisses me softly on the eyes and nose. Then he stands up and is gone. I watch him disappear around the cabin toward his horse.

I let the tears come. Everything I thought I knew is turned inside out. I tick off the items: home, country, safety, money, marriage. I consider the trials of Job but don't have the temerity to compare myself to a pillar of the Old Testament. God isn't making me suffer. I made my own suffering.

But all of this, all at the same time? The tears well up again. I fight them back. But I am afraid.

THE MUSTANG GIRL

The oxen drag the last load of logs up the hill. They struggle and lean into the harness, their heavy legs and wide chests straining and heaving. We arrive, just ahead of them, at the crack of dawn.

Green repeats solicitously, "I want you to oversee every part of this, Sarah, so that things are done the way you want. And Lord knows, there's some will be getting here at sunup, looking for coffee and cornbread."

I know what Green is doing and am grateful for it. *You should be overjoyed for the blessing this house will be*, Destiny scolds me. Yet everywhere I look, under the branches of the great elm tree, in the field where the long ears of the jackrabbits pop up regularly, on the trunk of the ancient live oak where the Indians long ago carved the buffalo, I see Will, hear his easy laugh.

I take Green's hand and step down from the wagon as the children tumble out and scatter, disappearing down the embankment to the river. I gather my hair close to my head, tie my bonnet, and follow

Green to the place where the logs for the front and back walls lie stacked, enough logs to build a spacious house.

"It will be forty feet across with dogtrot in the middle, a good twenty-five feet front to back," he tells me proudly for the third time. "The front wall goes in last, after we raise the roof. Those are choice logs, those old eighteen-footers. Trunks eighteen feet up aren't easy to come by, even in a forest as untouched as this one."

We walk into the enclosure afforded by the two end walls and stare into the void where the roof will be. Above us, a long V of geese flaps across the January sky on their way farther south to marshes and coastal feeding grounds. Winter settles in.

A new year. I wonder what more, after an unimaginable beginning, it will bring. If Green notices my strained manner, he doesn't let on. But he has been in a lighter mood since Will left—and has tried hard to get home in the evenings, even though he often rides a long way out.

We walk around inside the standing walls for a few minutes while Green explains that John Murphy from Kentucky, who sold him the lumber, is the best window and door framer around. And the McCoy men will make sure the ridgepoles supporting the house will be pitched in solid under a tight roof. I am about to ask about the loft when we hear the bellow of a vaguely female voice and the crack of a whip.

Up the road comes the woman Will calls Bluebeard or Musk Hog or Buffalo Belle. Standing between two teams of oxen, she tugs them this way and that. John Murphy drives another wagon, bringing up the rear. I remember the gossip. Belle has taken up with a new man and left the bartender for Murphy, the oldest man in the colony. Their place is to the east of us. I wonder if she has walked alongside the oxen the whole way from Murphy's place. However musky she seems inside the walls of Luna, at this moment, I stand in awe of her solid heft, her great legs planted like some female colossus between the oxen.

The wagons and carts roll in before the second pot of coffee is made. The plates, hammered out of old coffeepots and tin Mr. Sowell had lying around his blacksmith shop, worked well for New Year's

Day and are seeing service again today. Those coming to house raisings know to bring their own tin cups. I listen for the clanking of the cups stashed in the carts and wagons when some conveyance rumbles over the ruts. I can usually tell from the jangle of cups if a whole family or just one or two visitors is coming down the road.

What I can't tell on this day is what this crowd, who witnessed the scene on the dance floor on New Year's Day, is going to ask me. Under one of the oak trees in a little clearing of hard-packed dirt, Eveline and C. C. play jacks. They call out the games as they move through the sets–shoot the moon, over the line. My life in the past weeks.

I move through the tasks of getting fires started, coffeepots boiling, and biscuits rising in three Dutch ovens. Five fires blaze in the meadow in front of the house, and on the grassy knolls, logs are rolled under the trees for seating those gathering to build the DeWitt house. Despite my steady activity and better mood, there are times during the day when I feel I would rather be walking over hot coals. Greeting people, I see some hard looks. I know the gossip has traveled rapidly around the colony. "Something going on between the empresario's wife and Will Jones, the men wrangling outside the fort on New Year's Day."

As soon as Molly arrives, she attaches herself to me at the elbow. I understand instantly. After prompts from Molly, a few begin to thank me for planning the New Year's party. I console myself that my fears are mostly unfounded. Moving among groups, pouring coffee, and giving each cup holder a direct look, I see Will's dubious grin and wonder if he is in Béjar now. I know what he'd say. "As for me, oh, they'll wonder, but you'd have to dirty your skirts a good deal more to shock this bunch." True, we had done nothing so terrible. What had Will told me once? "Nobody can shoot you for what you think." Still, what I thought was disastrous enough. I thought I had married the wrong man. And the coward crouched within me was just now admitting it.

Cold puffs of breath rise from every conversation. The wintry day soon prods the men into activity to warm up. They leave the fire to the women and children, and soon the walls, now up on three sides, are surrounded by men organized into groups. Those working on the standing walls begin to notch the next-to-last layer where the loft will be laid in, while others in the group run the foot adze over boards that will become ceiling and floor of the loft.

Finally, the main business of the day can begin. Before the sun, occasionally peeping through the clouds, is directly overhead, the ridge of the house is connected to the ridgepoles on either side and carefully raised. From there, two McCoys, Green, and Creed kick and edge the structure into place. When it stands upright, a shout goes up from those on the ground.

Standing next to me, C. C. presses my hand. "Now, Momma, you'll feel better."

I hug my large-souled child. Yes, I know I will feel better. I will accept that the journey to Texas is changing me. But perhaps the most startling revelation is facing my own buried feelings.

The afternoon seems to go easier, affording some consolation. Rafters are attached to the center ridge of the roof, and the sturdy skeleton of the house grows by the hour. I refill coffee cups on the ground and hand water flasks up to the men on ladders.

I watch the construction from the big meadow in front of the house. The meat, roasted on spits, has been mostly consumed, and the dishes washed in the river. Now there's a lull. A time when women would be quilting and men napping if they'd been at their regular routines. I like these quiet hours in the rhythm of the day, though without church, school, or a real town, nothing seems quite the same.

The men go up and down the ladders, occasionally descending to warm themselves in front of the fire and pick at the roasted meat and cornbread. Many of the women and the youngest children nap near the fires wrapped in quilts and blankets as midday passes into afternoon.

Scanning the scene, I search for the bar girl, the mustang girl, still thinking about why she is called that. It makes sense: she looks wild and seems to belong to no one. This morning she appeared around the same time as old man Murphy and Belle from Luna. The children call her Faye. She is small for her age, maybe eleven or twelve. The buds of breasts show in her threadbare clothes, though she is hardly more than a child, still wanting to play with the ragtag band of girls and boys who dart around with runny noses.

She wore a new coat earlier in the day, perhaps a present from someone who cares about her. More than once, I've seen the bandy-legged man who hangs around Luna talking to Faye and the girl responding as if she knows him. I want to bring her over by the fire, hold her coat up to the fire to warm it, and wrap her small body into it, as I do for my children when they need warming. But maybe Belle, who seems to control Faye's comings and goings, wouldn't like it, and I don't want to make things harder for Faye.

As I ponder, Creed comes down the ladder and sits beside me in front of the fire. He wears the coat Molly made of animal pelts, including the beaver skin from the dead Tonkawa. It makes him look a little like an Indian himself. Our medicine man, I think, thankful for Creed's protective presence and good humor.

"My bonnie lass, how are you farin'?" he asks, patting my hand.

While I figure out how to answer that question directly, the troupe of children, galloping like wild ponies around the fires and up and down the paths, start pointing.

"Faye's out in the bushes," they shout. "She's hollering."

Creed and I jump to our feet, following the children into the woods. A hundred yards distant, movement and sounds—moans—issue from the underbrush. As we hover at the edge of the thicket, Eveline emerges from the group of children, looking terrified.

"Momma, those two men out there. They were hurting Faye."

Creed leads the way, and I follow. In a tangle of thorny mesquite scrub, Faye lies crying, her skirt torn and her underpants bloodied. In the brush, two figures are running away.

"Oh, Creed," I whisper as the full force of what Faye has endured hits me.

Creed shakes his head. "Slimy vermin," he says under his breath. "Probably some of the riffraff that show up in the back room at Luna. I'd go after 'em if I knew who to look for."

Faye whimpers and tugs at her dress to cover her legs. I give her a little hug and raise her to a sitting position. On a bush nearby, her coat hangs from a branch as neatly as if it belonged there. I fold Faye into it.

Glancing up at the men now working on the roof, Creed shouts to them across the distance. "Any of ye see what happened here?" The men stop hammering for a moment, shrug, and go back to work.

"I did, Momma," Eveline says, still standing a few feet away, remaining as the other children ran away.

"What did you see?"

"One of the men was the tall one we saw fighting at Luna the first day we got here. He was hurting Faye."

I draw Eveline next to me and then turn back to Faye. "Let's get you warmed up." Helping her to her feet, I hold her around the waist. On the other side, Eveline holds Faye's hand as we make our way to the fire. I want to apprehend her attackers and punish them. But I know before I even start that if Eveline is the only witness, no one is going to do anything about it, especially on behalf of a girl who has no family to look after her. Couldn't Green do something? The courts may be in Saltillo hundreds of miles away, as Will has said, but that should not stop us. Green is the empresario.

Settling onto a log next to the fire, I try to ease Faye closer as Eveline gathers blankets. Hoping to attract as little attention as possible and to shield Faye from the gawkers, I hold her hand tightly and offer her a little sausage and biscuit we find on a grate by the fire.

Faye takes a tenuous bite and then starts to crouch down. A mountain of flesh looms over us. The strapping, pig-faced woman has a hard glint in her eye.

"Does this child belong to you?" I ask, fearing she will snatch her away.

Belle studies us for a moment. "She stays at Luna, yeah, works for me. But I ain't signin' up to take care of her. Wouldn't call her one of mine. Orphan girl," she adds heartlessly, then moves away back to the wagon she came in.

As we sit by the fire, I decide Faye should remain with us for a few days and that it is reasonable to move into our new house tonight. With all the helpers, a sturdy home rises where this morning there was only a clearing shaded by oak trees. I ask Green to send someone in the wagon before dark to gather our belongings from the Water Street cabin. Relieved that Belle so handily refused to claim Faye, I see no obstacle to caring for the child for a while—as I have wanted to do from the moment I laid eyes on her.

When I return to the fire, Faye sits motionless, hunched down like a little animal trying to hide. Though Molly is wrapping a blanket around her, the girl looks as frightened as ever. At a little distance, the bandy-legged man lingers alone near another fire. I want to question him but decide it is a little late for that. For Faye, the damage is done.

Too late or not, many questions plague me as I settle next to the girl. About Faye. About Green and me. I do not scourge myself for the place in my heart Will occupies. I can suppress my feelings, if not fully deny them. I understand that passions can shift more unpredictably than the sandbars of the Guadalupe River. Some days it seems God is testing me, though I'm not sure God does things like that, whatever the preachers want us to believe.

For now, my life here at the edge of the Anglo world holds more questions than answers. We are surrounded: to the west and north the Indians, to the south and southwest the Mexicans. With riffraff, as Creed put it, preying even on children in DeWitt's colony.

Is the Missouri gentleman I married hard enough to survive the task he set for himself, indeed for all of us? Am I? So far, he's skillfully maneuvering the leap. Destiny, his angel of fortune, leads us on. But unlike Green, who so confidently envisions the future, I can hardly fathom its mysteries. Nor do I believe I must remain here the rest of my days.

RED HAIR

I don't know if Will's departure is responsible for what follows in a matter of weeks.

A rider gallops up to our fence, unlatches the gate, and enters the yard. Tall and handsome with an iron-gray mane of hair, he moves to the house in long, determined strides.

"Martín De León." He reaches out to shake my hand. "Señora DeWitt?"

Despite all I have heard about him, I have never met the empresario whose colony lies directly south of ours. "*Con mucho gusto. El Empresario DeWitt no está.*"

"I'm not looking for your husband," he says in perfect English. "I am looking for *El Colorado*, Will Jones, *para comprar* . . . to buy horses. I have traded with him before. Good stock. At Luna, they said you'd know where to find him."

"In Béjar, I believe, Señor De León. He left some weeks ago."

"So they told me at Luna. But I didn't believe it. Your husband's right-hand man? In Gonzales since the beginning." He pauses. "Why did he . . . ? He just left?" De León stops as if he thought he might be asking too many questions.

I wonder if my face reveals more than I intend. "Yes," I nod. "We were sorry to see him go."

He reaches his hand out and shakes mine again. "It is my pleasure to meet you, Señora. You are welcome in Guadalupe Victoria. Señora De León would be delighted to know you."

Halfway back to his horse, he turns around. "I should warn you. Comanche raids have picked up all along *los ríos*—the Guadalupe, San Marcos, and Lavaca. Mostly stealing horses. But there was one abduction of an Anglo woman and children taken near Béjar. Even some Indian women from rival tribes have been taken by Comanche. Take care, with Will Jones gone. Indians know him, fear him. Think he has magical powers. They've never seen a red-haired Anglo."

It is a shocking prospect. With Will's red-headed protection removed, will the Indians attack? I sit on the porch. This magic seems alarmingly real. And what about my strawberry blond Eveline? Have the Indians seen her? Will her red hair be a charm to protect us? Or a prize to be spirited away?

De León's warning rattles me. I count the weapons inside—two long guns above the fireplace and a large *belduque* knife in a scabbard. Outside, the raw February weather threatens rain. The children are feeding the horses and a newborn calf at the barn. I get them in, inventing ways to keep them in. But how long can I keep this up?

Before sunset, whinnies coming from the bottomland along the river pull us to the back window. At the water's edge, we behold a strange procession. Two braves drag an Indian woman forward by a rope around her neck. Her hands are tied behind her back. One Indian leads her, tethered like an animal, as the other walks their horses to a low place in the bank to water them. The woman is very tall, taller than her captors.

As the horses drink, she moves her hands back and forth as if begging to be allowed to drink as well. One Indian shakes his head, but the other overrules him, unties her hands, and lets her kneel to water with the horses. As she kneels, her creeping motion, or something in the water, frightens one of the horses. The horse jumps to the side, knocking the rope around her neck out of the Indian's hand. In a flash, the woman dives into the cold river and disappears underwater.

Quickly the one who'd held the rope splashes in after her, swims to the middle, treads water looking around, and then returns to the bank. The woman seems to have vanished without a trace. On the other side of the river, cattails, rushes, and reeds hide the bank. And nests of cottonmouths. Is she hiding among them?

"Momma," Eveline whispers, "we should help her."

I go for the double-barreled shotgun hanging above the mantle, entirely unsure of what to do next. Will the Indians come after us now? Smoke from the chimney has told them we are here.

"Not yet," I tell Eveline. "We'll wait and keep quiet."

The Indians—Comanche I fear—search for her for another few minutes before a rainstorm, threatening all day, breaks. Thunder booms and lightning pierces the sky. The two seem to take it as a sign. They swing onto their horses and, hesitating a moment, glance up the hill toward the house before heading in the direction of Gonzales.

I agonize. An Indian woman is out there needing help. Should I leave the children alone in the house while I try to find her? Before I can decide, Naomi points to the river.

"In the water, look." A dark head bobs in the river. She is swimming back across to our side, a water plant clutched in one hand.

"She used that reed as a straw to breathe underwater," I whisper to the children as if the Indians might hear us.

We watch as she swims across and emerges from the river. Hesitating no longer, I lean the gun next to the door and venture just beyond the house. Perched as we are on the hill, I think she will see me. I wave my arms and beckon. Looking up, she stops, then quickens her pace and darts toward me.

The rain pelts down in sheets, the storm raging and zigzagging across the dark sky. She races right up to me, still clutching the reed from the river. I look into her dark frightened eyes; take in the long, coarse, black hair braided with shells and a rattlesnake's rattle; and feel the woman's power. Black rings circle the nipples of her large, exposed breasts bulging from a long deerskin shirt too small to close in front. Barefoot, she wears a torn deer-hide skirt. Her body odor is strongly suggestive of polecat soaked with river water. In the afternoon light, she looks like a goddess. Two small circles of blue tattoo outline each cheekbone.

I pull her into the house. Drenched, I shiver and shake as the children run to find something to dry us off. But we don't have much time to think about the cold.

We hear horses by the river.

She grabs the double-barreled shotgun from behind the door. Motioning for me to get back and keep the children away, the woman steps outside.

The children surround me, clinging as I have never seen them do. I huddle with them in the kitchen for a moment, then lead them toward the bedroom to hide under the beds and return to the kitchen to grab the Kentucky rifle hanging over the fireplace.

The woman kneels outside the door, aims and fires once, aims and fires again, cleanly picking off her two enemy captors. I hope for a lead ball planted in each man and pray they are dead. But she isn't done. Inside, she sets down the smoking gun and grabs the long belduque knife from its scabbard, then creeps out the door toward the bodies on the hill.

She edges toward them, turns one man over, and then the other. Satisfied, she steps back, knife in hand. Then an arm shoots out, catches her ankles, and jerks her to the ground. The knife flies out of her hand. She struggles free and runs, the wounded Indian close on her heels.

She has no weapon now. I don't think; I just clench the rifle, the most unerring weapon we have. At the back door, my position is slightly above the Indian woman and her pursuer, now some thirty yards away. I wait for her to get well ahead of him and then fire. He falls as she bolts up the incline, covered in mud and leaves. Down the hill, the Indian ponies switch their tails and nuzzle the lifeless bodies of the warriors they'd once carried.

This time there is no drying or even shaking off. She squats on the floor and trembles, takes several deep breaths. Too curious to stay away, the children scramble from their hiding places and encircle her. Naomi offers her a dipperful of water as I bring a blanket.

She gulps the water, then reaches for the blanket and wraps herself in it. For a few moments, there on her heels, she looks away from us, out the back window, as if gathering her thoughts, her courage. Squaring her shoulders, she plucks a shovel from the corner of the kitchen. Wielding it, she motions to me to reload the weapons. I hesitate until she points to the shot pouch on the mantle. I load, and she stations me with the Kentucky rifle exactly where I stood when I'd made the lucky shot. Hurrying down the hill, she drags the bodies into a copse of trees and starts digging a wide grave. She makes a high-pitched whining sound as she digs, as if quaking, stricken in the presence of death.

I hand the rifle to Naomi and start toward the woman as she digs. She motions me back into the house, despite the keening sounds escaping her. The wails punctuate the silence, broken only by the sound of the shovel and the scraping sounds as she pushes the bodies into the shallow graves. I've killed one of them; yet I feel only fear, nothing approaching remorse. She covers the bodies with earth while the horses, and the five of us, look on. Above her, the swirling clouds, still angry and dark, let loose another downpour. Once she looks up fearfully as if to ask the rain gods why they are punishing her. Even in the driving rain, the blue tattoos gleam as she turns her face to the heavens.

When she has stamped and packed down the dirt with the shovel and her bare feet, she removes the horses' blankets, ties the reins around their necks, and slaps them on the haunches. They gallop away. Finally, she collects the belduque lying in the leaves.

Returning to us—wet, muddy, lips turning blue—her frenzied breathing slows. In the aftermath of the storm, the temperature is dropping. For the first time, she seems to notice the cold. Teeth chattering, she picks up the blanket dropped on the floor, then thrusts the Comanche horse blankets into the fire.

Now it is my turn to act. I send the children to find warm clothes for her. Alone with her, I lace my hands together in a church steeple shape and press them to my lips, then hers, trying to signal she is safe here.

"Sit. Rest."

I offer cornbread and then dip a tin cup into the bucket of buttermilk sitting by the back door. Exhausted, she eyes me blankly, then tentatively takes the cup, drinking a few sips, stashing the cornbread in her skirt.

Knowing she won't understand, I ask anyway. "Where did they capture you?"

"*Golfo*," she says. And then "*Antoñito*."

I'm not sure if she is answering me or trying to tell me something else. But her words prod my memory. I begin to understand: Was she among the group of Karankawa women at the coast, somehow associated with Chief Antoñito? Green negotiated a treaty with the Karankawa there. She'd seen me there? Was she Antoñito's wife? Sister? Daughter? And now, what?

I gaze at her strong body and long for the help she can provide if I can trust her.

The children come back with a long skirt and a woolen shirt belonging to Green. They stare and then hand the clothes to her. Her vigilant, hawkish look softens, and tears well in her eyes. I wonder if she has lost a child. I'd heard that the ferocious Karankawa are strangely tender with their children. Whatever the reason, the expression on her face seems a good sign. Sweet Naomi soothes her and holds up the clothes for her, while Eveline shows her how she might fit into them.

Focusing on Eveline for the first time, she draws back, almost in a panic. She edges toward the back door as if to leave, making a whining sound. She keeps glancing at Eveline. *Is it her strawberry blonde hair?*

Wanting to keep her there in the kitchen, all I can think of is Chief Antoñito, and I blurt that out: "Antoñito, Antoñita, you Antoñia?"

Something in my tone stops her. But still, she makes the keening sound, a monotonous, high-pitched moan, like a hurt animal or a child fearing punishment.

Frightened by her moans, Clinton starts to cry, running to Naomi. Quickly Naomi takes him from the kitchen. Eveline and C. C. stay with me, trying to help. The tall woman stands perfectly still now, her posture upright and almost frozen. The fleeing children leave her trembling, and her anxiety seems to grow anytime Eveline approaches her.

"Antoñia stay here." I take her hand and lead her to the stool by the hearth, motioning for her to sit. She looks back at me with big, liquid eyes. I don't know if she is sad or glad, but she lowers herself onto the stool, curling her long legs underneath, understanding, at least, that we aren't going to hurt her.

When Green gets home, he finds us gathered in the kitchen where a six-foot-tall Amazon with blue tattoos and dressed in his shirt perches near the hearth. First, we try to explain the smell of gunpowder in the house. When we reveal that the two captors are buried on the hill close to the house, he shakes his head as if he doesn't believe us. Most unimaginable to him is that I killed one of them in one shot. He knows I am a good shot, but he'd never considered I might kill someone. Nor had I. The children and I blurt out the story in bits and pieces.

He stares, then his words drill into me: "God help us, Sarah. You know you shouldn't have done this. The Comanche are nothing to fool with."

I plant myself directly in front of him, between him and Antoñia.

"I was to leave this poor woman with no defense? At the mercy of her captors?"

He fixes me with a fierce glare. "I understand your motives. But it was a dangerous path to take." He thrusts his index finger at me.

I cut him off and glare back at him. "It is the dangerous path *you* put us on." As soon as the words are out of my mouth, I know I've made things worse. But I'm not sorry.

Green's eyes blaze in response. Without a word, he walks through the door and down the hill toward the graves.

Antoñia stares from the corner, watching and listening like a painted bird in a distant tree.

THE SCHOOLROOM

The big mullioned windows, Green's special purchase in New Orleans, let in the bright light of the full moon. The moonlight illuminates the delicate features of my girls, sleeping curled together on the rope bed. Up in the loft, the boys are finally quiet. But it is an eerie quiet. Every time there's a full moon, I fear what the clearly lit night might bring: Indians coming to steal horses or, worse, abduct a child or two. Fear for my children pursues me like a swarm of bees, just as Molly warned. The girls stir, Eveline snuggling closer to Naomi. Stacked back to front, they sleep the untroubled sleep of youth.

Across the dogtrot corridor in the kitchen, Antoñia lies on a cot by the hearth, her breaths regular, her body facing the fire. I cover her feet, hanging off the end of the cot. She shifts but does not wake. I thank Providence for delivering this woman to us. Manna from heaven. With us for weeks now, she hunts with bow and arrows and dresses the deer she slays. She catches big fat fish and never lets the children out of her sight.

But there is more. Antoñia is a grateful soul, aware of our aid in her improbable escape. Like a feral animal, she shies away from contact but returns all kindnesses with heartfelt, if restrained, nods and half smiles. Sometimes she even touches us. With me, she has a habit of grabbing my arm or stroking my face when I praise her. As if she'd known what awaited her among the Comanche. The atrocities, according to those captives who've escaped them, are grim—rape and slavery, to say nothing of torture. I wonder when the Comanche who captured her will come looking for their lost brothers. A new threat to live with, though one offset by all she offers. In the corner, her quiver of arrows and longbow reach halfway up the wall, tall as Antoñia herself. Crafting the bow from mesquite and the arrows from cane were her first tasks in this new life with us.

Despite the threat of Comanche revenge, I feel infinitely safer with her in our lives, especially with Green gone so often, tonight working with the carpenters building the mill upriver, a project plagued by two Indian attacks and one death. And, on this moonlit night, the man Green engaged to stay with us for protection is nowhere to be seen.

Moving to the window to close the shutters, I stop as two figures head toward our gate. They are too far away to recognize, even in the bright moonlight. Then a knock on the door, quickly repeated. Relieved by the civility of a knock, I grab the loaded rifle next to the door and wait a moment, listening.

A deep voice calls out. "Nothin' to be scairt 'bout."

I crack the door.

Before me stand Belle and a big man. "Come like I promised," the man says. "Empersaro sent me." I put down the gun and let them in.

The man looks around and then disappears around the house. I blink a few times and look at Belle.

"Tough ol' coot," she growls. "Nobody'll touch ya with him around."

I recognize him as Ol' Murphy, who sometimes lives with her in a cabin on Peach Creek, owner of the oxen that brought logs to build the house.

"What about you? Don't you need . . . ?"

"Nobody messes with Belle." Looking beyond me, she motions toward Antoñia, asleep in the kitchen. "Kronk girl, huh?" She uses the name that some substitute for the tongue-twisting "Karankawa."

I nod, thinking she probably knows more about Antoñia than I do.

She points at her. "Trouble. Comanche don't abide gettin' robbed."

It is the most civil thing she's ever said to me, but I'm not going to act as if Antoñia is a worthless "Kronk."

"She fought for her life. I helped her."

Belle shakes her head as if to dismiss such foolishness. "'Nother thing. Your little friend Faye. Askin' for ya. Wants to come out here again. Thinks you'll teach her to read."

"Yes, I will. And any of the girls at Luna who want to learn." There is no better time to get my secret hopes out on the table with Belle. Though I can hear Will warning me not to get "too unpopular too fast."

"Is Faye all right?" I venture.

"You're dangerous," she says, staring me down. At that moment, Murphy reenters through the back door.

"All right then," she says, and out the front door into the night she goes.

"Be settin' on the porch and a-makin' rounds. Don't worry none 'bout me," he mutters, shuffling out the back door again.

At last I fall into bed, feeling somehow safer than usual.

At daybreak, Antoñia gathers buckets to tote water from the river. Awakened by the clatter, I dress, stoke the fire, and follow her out. A cold but clear morning, I am alone with my thoughts for at least a few minutes.

With Murphy on duty, I continue around the house. I admire the pitch of the roof and the back gallery and stop to warm myself against the chimney, its heat held and stored in the smooth blue-gray river stones.

From the side of the house, I take in the Guadalupe as it winds in the distance to meet the San Marcos River beyond. The high bluff affords a lookout point, east toward Gonzales and west toward the confluence of the two rivers. Now, with the leaves off the trees, the broad Y where the San Marcos meets the Guadalupe and continues northwesterly shines in the morning light. The arms of the river point to the Camino Real, the long-ago-named Royal Road toward

Béjar. The lay of the land stands out clearly on this bright morning. Across the river sits Gonzales, our little village, not nearly so consequential as her neighbors. Between San Antonio de Béjar, the Tejano stronghold to the west, and San Felipe, Empresario Austin's Anglo colony to the east, Gonzales is the poor sister.

Moving around the house to the front porch, I settle onto the mesquite bench newly carved by Antoñia. The fresh wood still bleeds from its cuts and oozes its amber sap. The rooster crows, and Pal whinnies once or twice in the corral. Time to let her out.

Yet I sit rooted to the spot, last night's events replaying in my head. A double-barreled blast of apprehension and hope. The hope surprises me. *Did I hear her right? Did those words about Faye—"your little friend askin' for ya ... thinks you'll teach her to read"—really come from Belle, queen of the Luna underworld?*

And what does Belle know? Who sent Faye to live in the back room at the saloon? When I try to talk with her at Luna, the girl ducks her head, not daring to oppose Belle's tight control.

I relive the ride into Gonzales a fortnight ago as we delivered Faye back to Luna at Belle's demand, the uneasy quiet settling over the children. The long faces of Naomi and Eveline. Our gazes fixed straight ahead, unable to look at our small friend as the January wind bit into our faces. When she is halfway up the steps, I say, "We'll be back every week to see how you're getting along." Faye blinks and dashes up the steps, into the place where Belle's other "girls," twelve- and thirteen-year-olds, serve whiskey to customers, often sitting on men's laps.

This new year of 1828, just over a month old, washes over me, the blessing of a house meant to be a new beginning, with troubles piling up on the doorstep before the last nail was hammered in: Will's departure; Faye's attackers getting off scot-free because there is no one to bother about an orphan girl; Faye summoned quickly back to Luna after her brutal assault; Green away night and day after the Indian attack at the mill; De León's warning; Antoñia's rescue, a compelling motive for Comanche revenge.

But most of all it is Green. Or rather, the absence of Green, who is consumed by his dream, with time for little else. Incidents such as Faye's attack, that once would have inspired rage and action in this moral man, are now dismissed. His eyes are vague, absent unless focused on his land, his buildings, or the bodies he needs to fill a quota for the colony. Whispering in my ear, Destiny's voice counsels patience. I ignore her murmurs. Through the years, Green has been gone a lot, engaged in causes we both embraced. In the early years of our marriage, he spent months away, fighting with Andrew Jackson's "dirty shirts," as the British called them in the decisive Battle of New Orleans. Days, sometimes weeks away, campaigning for a seat in the Missouri legislature. Now, though not far away in miles, he is curiously out of reach: haunted by Gonzales, this child born of his ambition that he must breathe life into; afraid to look away from his venture for a moment for fear it will collapse. Just as Molly warned, this Texas outpost, carved out of the vast unknown at the edge of Anglo settlement, leaves us isolated, plagued with distance and danger.

I can do little or nothing about any of it. But with Antoñia helping me and Belle at least talking to me, it feels like a small break in the clouds. If Faye and Antoñia can survive, surely I can too.

During one of his few days at home, Green points out a striking fact. There is an empty room on the first floor of Turner's Hotel. It is just the space I need for a schoolroom. I ride into Gonzales a day later, ready to greet all comers. I will sign up three pupils from the DeWitt household, along with Faye and the girls at Luna, for as much time as I can talk Belle into. That would make at least six pupils. Enough to start a school.

Arriving before eight o'clock, I find children playing a game outside Turner's Hotel, including the three towheaded Turners. They streak through a patch of weeds barefoot. The winners are the ones with no cocklebur stickers in their feet after five passes.

News has traveled fast. Up the steps, Mrs. Turner watches the children's game as she waits for me on the porch of the hotel.

"A schoolroom is the best idea I've heard since we got here," she says. "Happy you can use the space. All three of mine need to learn to read and write and do sums."

"Yes. Mine as well. And I think Naomi and Eveline can help me with the children."

"Margaret Lockhart says you're even signing up the saloon girls a few days a week."

"As long as Belle doesn't refuse me. We have to come to terms. Sign up today. School starts tomorrow. And if you have primers or readers in your house, send them along."

Mrs. Taylor signs up her three and also three of the Nash children. I wait in the schoolroom for my next customers. Within the hour, three more families come and go. The tally is up to twelve, fifteen with the DeWitts.

I find a feather duster and dust the room, arrange donated benches and chairs, and find a wobbly, lopsided blackboard on legs. Tucked in the corner, a table that can serve as my desk looks sturdy enough to hold papers and a few thin books.

When the clock strikes noon, I admit to myself that Belle is not coming. I leave the sheet with names of students on the table, with clear instructions for latecomers, and head for Luna.

In the cold light of day, Belle is menacing. Her face, crosshatched with deep wrinkles and a formidable patch of mustache, holds no smile lines. A bruise and a cut under her eye make me wonder about her relationship with Murphy.

"Whaddya want now?" she grunts as if she'd done her duty to me by lending Murphy's protection when Green is gone.

"I want to sign up the girls who work here for school classes. A few days a week. If you can spare them."

"I can't. So don't come sniffin' around here. The girls can come on their own time."

"And when would that be?"

"When I say so."

"That doesn't allow me to plan for lessons. Or space."

"Ain't no never mind to me."

Facing the back room, I spy three heads through the dirty curtain. One of them is Faye's. "Could you allow them three days a week for three hours in the morning?"

"You tryin' to ruin my trade, woman?"

"No, I'm trying to figure out a schedule and start a school."

"Humph. You don't know nothin' 'bout these ninnies. Don't need to read. Be doin' good to find a husband in a year or two."

I narrow my eyes at her. "They won't be ninnies if they can read. And they might learn not to put up with men hitting them in the face."

She looks daggers at me, then steps back as if she has no more to say.

"I'd be prepared to pay you a small fee to cover their hours. But you'll have to come tomorrow morning to the schoolroom and sign a paper. I hope to see you at eight o'clock before school starts." Trying not to look at the girls peeking from behind the curtain, I nod at her, intent on betraying no weakness of resolve.

At eight a.m. Belle follows me up the steps of the hotel. I proceed to the schoolroom, push open the door, pull the paper from my bag, and hold my breath, hoping for resolution.

"Good morning, Belle. Glad to see you. Here's the paper to sign."

"Where's the money?"

I don't flinch. "I'll pay when you sign."

"How much?"

"For three hours, three days a week, $10 for all three for a year. I have a $5 gold piece. Half now. Half in the fall when school begins again."

She looks at me like I'm crazy, her big face breaking into a cross-hatched smile. "Better than selling a heifer." She grabs the paper from me. Sitting down, she carefully signs "Belle of Kintuck."

I had expected an X and try to hide my surprise. "So, you come from Kentucky?" I reach into my bag for the gold piece, hoping the battle is over.

"Last place I pulled up stakes." She exhibits the indifference that seems her most positive emotion.

I hand her the gold coin. She turns it over several times, as if not sure it's real, then rises abruptly.

"Are you going to deliver the girls to me, or do I have to come and get them?"

She snorts. "Feisty, ain't ya?"

She steps to the door and then out to the porch. "Git in here, you hussies," she growls at the three of them sitting on the steps of the front porch. "And back to Luna when I said."

The three girls scoot into the schoolroom as Belle moves down the steps. Once inside, they gaze around as if this were the nicest place they've ever seen. Faye, standing tall, comes forward and hugs me shyly.

"These here are my friends, Lila and Bess." She calls them over: Lila looks ragged in too-tight, wrinkled clothes. Bess wears a thin sweater over a dress with holes in it. "C'mon, meet Miz Sarah. I mean Miz DeWitt. Lila, Bess, you can shake her hand. She's nice; she don't yell."

Faye's transformation from mouse to mother of girls who seem older and more worldly so startles me, I am eager to let her keep talking. But I shake hands as directed and soon have the girls moving benches and washing the blackboard. By the time other students arrive, the girls have formed a reception line at the door, as directed by Faye. The girls greet their fellow students with pats and handshakes until Naomi, Eveline, and C. C. appear. Then Faye, buoyant at seeing them, separates from the line to hug each DeWitt, leaving the greeting to Lila and Bess.

By nine o'clock, I stand before a roomful of two dozen children. The youngest are seven-year-old twins, and the oldest, Lila and Bess, say they are fourteen. I group them by age, the youngest near me in the front, the older group at the back. Alphabet cards go to the youngest, primers filled with stories and writing lessons to the oldest. Ben and Seth, the twins, master the alphabet cards with ease and say they can write all those easy letters, too. I send them to the blackboard. Next, I work with two intermediate groups. Lila and Bess barely know the ABCs. They are bogged down before they get to M. Before I can solve that, Naomi breaks from the advanced group and ushers Lila, Bess, and Faye to the back of the room to learn the alphabet. Eveline follows suit, taking over the intermediate eight- and nine-year-olds. When latecomer Lewis Sowell, a new friend of Eveline's, peeks into the schoolroom midmorning, he takes another group in hand. When we break for recess, Lila, Bess, and Faye disappear, no questions asked.

For arithmetic, I bring out three sets of cards: easy, not so easy, and hard. When it becomes clear that Lewis already knows all his multiplication tables and can do long division, he takes over the hard group, which consists of Naomi and Eveline. But that soon ends; I need all their help with the other three groups.

School is out at two o'clock. When only DeWitts are left in the classroom, I repair to my table with its rickety legs, thankful for the quiet. The children collect books and packets of arithmetic cards and then line up in front of me, regarding me with bright eyes.

"Momma," Eveline says, "Lewis can help us. I knew he was smart that day I met him at the blacksmith shop. He even offered to show me some eagles' nests when it gets warmer."

But it is Naomi who warms my heart. "How did you get Faye and her friends here, Momma? Faye is so pleased. She whispered to me that she prayed for a miracle—to go to school. But she never believed it would happen."

"The miracle will be if anybody learns to read or write before school's out *this* year," Eveline responds, with her usual penchant for truth. "Except Lewis, of course. And maybe you, C. C. You're not too bad at it."

Naomi's revelation about Faye renews me. Naomi Q, named for my mother, Elizabeth Quick, is my devoted, steadfast, sweet-tempered dove of a daughter. More than a year since we left St. Louis, and it's the first day I think I know what I'm doing. The first day I don't desperately wish to return to my old life; the first day I think I can make it for the next three years. My woes are hardly comparable to Antoñia's. Yet in my mind's eye I see her swimming back across the river, keeping her head above water. In that, we are one.

LETTERS

The chilly winds of March whip my skirt. A few wildflowers are pushing up. Fat bees visit the redbuds, the pink blossoms lining slender limbs. My mother calls them Judas trees because Judas is said to have hanged himself on one after betraying Christ. But I love them for the way they stand out in the woods, an unerring announcement of spring.

I want to continue downriver, where a whole copse of redbuds blooms, but I must not stray too far from the house. The trees prompt a long-ago memory: a windy April day walking with Will into a stand of redbuds. Shaken by the wind, the blossoms showered down on us. Pink buds in my hair and his, Will plucked them from each strand and stole a kiss.

A sound behind me jolts me from my daydream. I feel for the knife in my shoe, although I wouldn't even hear the footfall of a Comanche until it was too late. In the distance, a white-tailed deer vanishes into the woods.

The woods do this to me: spark memories and visions—myself at seventeen, Eliza now. It's been more than a year since I've seen her, all the time yearning for her by my side and now wishing for her advice on the beginnings of the schoolroom which lacks just about everything. This thought soon propels me back home to write to her on this Saturday morning.

Our progress such as it is, I begin the letter to Eliza in my head. *We at least do have a space in Turner's Hotel and we have, amazingly enough, twenty-four students ranging in age from six to fourteen. To complicate matters further, none of the pupils seems able to get there two days in a row. Only Naomi, Eveline, and the blacksmith's boy, Lewis Sowell, can read, though C.C. is making very good progress.*

Eliza will have suggestions. She will bring books and paper and pencils and maybe even some reading primers and elementary arithmetic books. Remembering that Eugenio is about to make his next mail run to the coast and fearing calls that sound like no bird I know, I hurry toward the house.

On the porch, Green is poring over a letter. He looks up as I climb the steps. He thrusts it at me, his face a mask of apprehension.

It is from Austin, our guiding spirit in all matters of running a colony, and it means far more than I comprehend. Even after I've read it twice.

"A boundary commission? And why is this commission led by this Mexican general, Mier y Terán, coming to visit us?" I ask Green after the second read-through.

"The Mexicans are anxious. They're trying to assess whether the Anglo settlements in the north are good—or not so good—for Mexico. They've pretty much left us alone until now."

"They asked us here, didn't they? To start settlements where there are none?"

"Yes, but this expedition seeks to find out more about the attitudes and numbers, the 'character of our settlements' as Austin says. They want to know whether we're actually rebels, even revolutionaries, at heart." He sounds more and more worried as he continues. "Whether we're observing the Catholic religion or violating the Mexican Constitution. Far as I can tell, it is a real commission to survey and establish the boundaries between Coahuila y Tejas and the US. But it's a cover as well. They suspect we're crossing other boundaries. Like bringing in slaves forbidden by their Constitution—or plotting to take Coahuila y Tejas away from them."

"And this General Mier y Terán is the leader, head of the expedition?"

"As Austin tells it, he's one of the most powerful and enlightened men in Mexico. Honest as well, Austin says. The general will visit the districts of Béjar, San Felipe, and settlements on the coast to gather census data and make maps. And cast a cold eye on the Anglos."

"When will the meeting take place?"

"The team is already in Béjar, meeting with Señor Músquiz, the *jefe político*. They'll take one more meeting in San Felipe in several weeks. I will join them there."

The news fills me with questions I've never considered. The commission is charged with determining the boundary of Mexico with the United States, surveying the natural resources in this northern reach of Coahuila y Tejas, and observing the Indians and the settlers. Yet, despite its official-sounding name, the real interest of the commissioners is to determine the "numbers and attitudes" of the Anglo-American colonists?

The Mexicans worry that we are a threat, perhaps even rebels plotting to take Coahuila y Tejas away from them? Colonel Austin worries about making the right impression on the evidently very influential General Terán? We're suspected of fomenting revolution before we've even brought in a hundred families? But, of course, there is more going on in this Texas world than just the DeWitt colony. There are thousands in Austin's colony already, including many slaves, and rumors that new empresarios, named McMullen and McGloin, are negotiating with the Mexicans to receive grants on the coast and eastward to bring in more families. Further, the Tejano Empresario De León's colony southeast of us is growing. But one thought nags at me more than the rest.

"Are we supposed to convince Terán of our loyalties? That we are good Mexican citizens?"

Green nods. "That's the view we want him to carry back to Mexico. The report he makes will shape the future relations between the rest of Mexico and us, the newcomers."

I am about to say that we Anglos are all American to the core when I see, from Green's dismay, he needs no greater cause for worry. What will it mean for us to be Mexicans in the long run? The curious General Mier y Terán has a mission to protect his people and look out for Mexico's future. Indeed, the course of these relations is not likely to run smooth.

A letter to Eliza is at least within my powers.

March 25, 1828, Gonzales
Dearest Eliza,

March came in like a lion, to be sure. I have a schoolroom to mind with twenty-four students, and a letter arrived today from Colonel Austin informing us of an upcoming meeting between us and a commission headed by a Mexican general named Terán. We are to convince the Mexicans of our best efforts on behalf of Mexico.

First, my own battles. My schoolroom. We've been at it for a month. Attendance is spotty, but the days full nonetheless. C. C., Eveline, and Naomi are invaluable helpers, along with Lewis Sowell, a new friend of Eveline's. I am teaching some their ABCs; others are learning to read. But we have very few books. More primers like the ones I brought from St. Louis would be a godsend. The lowest level possible, if you can find them. And your suggestions for what Naomi and Eveline can teach children who attend only a few hours a week in one cramped space. We miss you and long for your presence every day!

Though we've been gone from you and St. Louis for more than a year, we are only just digging into the task at hand: namely, populating the colony. Working on settling our first hundred families. Poppa says, though there's no official census record yet, there are about a hundred people living in and around Gonzales. More are coming in every day. Not by scores as in Austin's colony, but dozens of new faces. With a little imagination, I can see the beginnings of a real town. The blacksmith shop, Luna

*(the grocery and grog shop), and Turner's Hotel line the main
street, called Water Street, since the river runs a few hundred
yards to the west. To the east, the fort overlooks our little village.
Of course, there are only a few streets and a square laid out. The
square is empty so far, except for the Mexican flag hoisted up a
rickety pole.*

CONT., late March

*I am sorry to say I missed posting my letter before Eugenio left on
his March mail run. So now I hope to get it into the April packet.
As I wrote earlier, the arrival of the Terán expedition is much on
our minds. Poppa will leave soon to make the trip to San Felipe
to meet with Colonel Austin and his secretary, Mr. Williams.
Together they will welcome the expedition to San Felipe.*

Later, April 16

*My dear Eliza, here is surprising news for you: Eveline and I
have had a most unusual experience. Since I started this letter
this morning, we rode into Gonzales to get supplies at Luna.*

*When we crossed the river, we noticed a new family in the very
cabin where first we stayed on Water Street, and we stopped to
welcome them to the colony. Taking our leave, we saw a wagon
train crossing the river. First, two wagons, and then a gleaming
coach drawn by three horses, and two more wagons following
them. The coach, of prodigious dimensions, perhaps two feet
wider than ordinary, was carved and inlaid with silver! A
strange contraption, the back wheels were big as paddlewheels
and the puny ones at the front hardly wheelbarrow size. The
procession stopped on the riverbank to water their horses, and
then one of the men came up the hill toward us. He bowed
deeply and spoke to us in Spanish I have heard only from the
most educated, each word clear and distinct. He introduced
himself as Señor Sanchez and said he was el cartógrafo, the
expedition's mapmaker, visiting the districts of Coahuila y
Tejas. I introduced myself and Eveline. She picked a bunch
of wildflowers and handed him a little bouquet, saying,*

"Bienvenidos a nuestra villita dc Gonzales." *I had no idea she knew how to say, in Spanish, "Welcome to Gonzales." Señor Sanchez was charmed. And tried to tell us how beautiful our location is here on the Guadalupe. But that was not all.*

General Mier y Terán, walking by the river, joined his draftsman. Señor Sanchez introduced us to the great general, letting him know that we are the family of the Empresario DeWitt. True to Colonel Austin's laudatory descriptions, Terán is a dignified and quite reserved person. A slight frame, dark brown sideburns, and eyes with dark circles beneath, the darkest I have ever seen on any human face. There is a great sadness about him. He was in uniform, epaulets and all. Glancing at the cabin, he asked, incredulously, if the empresario lived there. I told him that we'd built our house on the river a few miles away. He looked relieved, and I didn't bother to reveal that indeed we had stayed in the miserable cabin for several weeks. Some things are better left unsaid! I assured him Empresario DeWitt would soon be on his way to meet him in San Felipe de Austin. The general introduced us to the botanist traveling with him, a Mr. Jean Louis Berlandier, and a mineralogist, Mr. Chovell. Though brief, it was fine to meet these personages. I trust Colonel Austin's insights and opinions entirely, but it was gratifying to have a look firsthand. The encounter ended too soon, and Eveline and I made our way to Luna, of which, more later. It will take another letter to explain.

We miss you terribly,
Momma

SAN FELIPE DE AUSTIN

I did not expect to accompany Green to the meeting of the boundary commission. Nor did I even desire to go until I met General Terán and his distinguished aides. Meeting this Mexican general—depth and capacity apparent in his every move—has shifted something in me. It's as if I've put on eyeglasses, bringing the horizon into focus. Other than my financial support, I've envisioned no essential role for myself in Green's mission. When he has hinted that my judgment could be deployed on behalf of the colony, I've thought it mere flattery. Now at least I'm open, even drawn to the idea.

Green and I have always operated in separate realms and kept out of each other's way throughout our journey and, indeed, our marriage. Separate stars in the constellation of children, siblings, nieces, nephews, and elders, a twining grapevine of family. But now I wonder if it is I who has kept that distance, never venturing far from the bosom and bounty of parents and sisters. Have I ignored Green's confidence in me, his need for my participation in his ventures? Has his need for me always been greater than I allowed or imagined? And why have I held back? How strange that General Terán has inspired me to draw closer to Green and his dreams. Perhaps it is the intensity of the man, his seeming love for Mexico and its people. Indeed, as Austin has observed, he exudes integrity and an extraordinary force. Perhaps I see these same qualities in Green and Austin, which makes them all brothers under the skin and helps me feel the consequence of their vision.

Molly and Creed have offered to stay with the children if I want to make the journey to San Felipe with Green. Naomi, who is learning to exercise authority in the schoolroom, can take charge for a week. And our incomparable giant Karankawa woman, I reassure myself, can handle just about anything at home.

"In just a few months," I tell Molly when she arrives, "Antoñia has gained the children's trust. Little Clinton calls her 'the big woman' and follows her around, staring up at her. Even Naomi's tomcat, Yowl, who complains about everything, purrs happily in Antoñia's lap."

"I won't mind having her grind the corn for me either," Molly says. "She filled that bowl she carved in the oak stump out yonder."

"She turns a pile of corn into cornmeal in short order, using the stone and bowl, a *mano y metate* she calls it, like a mortar and pestle."

"We'll be fine." Molly pats my arm. "Creed and Antoñia could—"

I nod. "Yes, I know, and Naomi and Antoñia are secretly thrilled at the chance to be on their own." Yet leaving them, as Indian raids grow more frequent, my babes all here together—I dare not finish the thought.

"Seeing the country," as Green puts it, is better than I expected. It is the first time we've been alone since leaving Missouri, camping under the stars and staying close to each other. As we leave the Coushatta Trace, after three days in the saddle, the prospect of seeing Colonel Austin, our old friend, revives us. In the distance, in front of his cabin, we catch sight of him waving both arms as if flagging in winners of a race. He welcomes us in his distinctive white broadcloth shirt and deer-hide pants.

A crowd mills around in front of the small cabin, which is divided by its open-air dogtrot passage into living quarters and a land office. Some file in the land office door.

"One side of a cabin in the woods, the hub of immigration to Texas," Green chuckles as we rein in the horses. Humble as it is, who would guess that this is the most important place between the Brazos and the Río Grande? Every civilizing influence in these northern wilds of Mexico has been initiated by the man living inside this cabin. Green's eyes gleam with excitement as he observes the bustle of activity–applications for headrights, acquisitions of plots large and small–filling yard and road.

Austin hustles us into his cabin as his manservant, Simon, waters and feeds the horses. "It's a bachelor's quarters, rougher than I would like. I'm sure you have made a home, Sarah, more comfortable than mine. While you settle in, excuse me briefly, I'll be with you shortly." Ushering us into his living quarters, Austin disappears back into his office.

The large, cluttered room is unmistakably the abode of Empresario Stephen Fuller Austin. It thrills me to be setting foot in the puncheon-floored space, more than if we were entering Andrew Jackson's executive mansion. The racks of antlers on the wall and the gun behind the door might belong to any settler. But the library stacked on three sides of the room–scores of dusty volumes, including *Rees's Cyclopœdia*, Shakespeare's sonnets, *Plutarch's Lives*, *Don Quixote*–and a small, four-key flute by the bedside define the extraordinary man who lives here.

While Green washes his hands and face in the basin near the bed, I step to the door of the land office. At a small desk piled high with papers and books, Austin confers with his secretary and translator, Samuel Williams. They pore over papers set before a family seeking land. I know Austin spends his days there, laboring to establish and maintain a system in which lands are surveyed and allocated to settlers, taking care to avoid any overlap of property lines.

Austin soon reappears. "So, my old friends, this is where I labor in the enterprise we share. I think no man on earth understands better than you, DeWitt, how extensive those labors can be."

"Pleasure to be here," Green says quietly. But the unbridled admiration in his heart is apparent. Standing in the presence of Austin again, I too feel a surge of affection for this slender powerhouse of a man.

The years have worn Austin. His task, which has occupied him for almost a decade now, is unrelenting. He has more lines in his face and more gray in the curly dark hair atop his chiseled features. But his hawk eyes are as bright and penetrating as ever, his energy boundless.

"Can it be three years since we met?" he asks Green. "You were here in spring 1825, just after securing your grant from Mexico," Austin says with characteristic precision. "I received you in San Felipe, and you were off the next day, back to Missouri to bring your fine family and your first group of settlers down the Mississippi. I remember the floor was clay, and I had not even a desk, but plenty of stacks of papers and confusion even then. Yet you have enjoyed a great progress in three years."

Green beams and nods. "I have more than a hundred settlers and a house for my family to put down roots. Modest as it is, it feels like a palace sitting above the Guadalupe, as yours rests here near the Brazos. But settlers are not pouring into Gonzales as they are here."

"We have much to discuss, my dear DeWitts, and a good bit to look back on. So, please, avail yourselves of the spring water in the water barrel. I know you must be thirsty and tired. Then we'll sit down to the venison feast that my dutiful cook, Mary, has prepared for us."

We eat in Austin's living quarters with his manservant Simon attending us from the kitchen. After supper, Austin brings out two bottles, whiskey for the men and sherry for me. Toasting our ventures and the future of this adopted land, he leans across the big red oak table. The table's rough planks, now planed down, are a tacit reminder of the raw land these two have set themselves to smooth and shape. The two, so different in appearance—one tall and diffident, the other wiry and intense—are much alike in character. Possessed by blazing visions of what they must do to transform their rough outposts, they relish each other's company. Touching briefly on their common past in Missouri and at Transylvania University in Kentucky, they soon move on to more pressing matters.

"The biggest change in my life," Austin announces, "is the election of the self-governing council, the *ayuntamiento*. My fear, of course, is a froth of activity and meetings for a few months and then nothing. We must cut roads, establish ferry rates, organize a militia; the list goes on and on."

"It is overwhelming," Green interjects. "But beyond the many tasks, there are bigger worries, such as the court system prescribed to deal with civil and criminal offenses. What will we do when a real crime is committed in our colonies?" he asks urgently. "We have been lucky so far. After Indian depredations against settlers, that is my greatest fear. My days as sheriff in Missouri tell me it will not be long before somebody gets shot. What will we do when one of our settlers turns into a criminal, a murderer? Do you have a jail?"

Green does not mention the assault of Faye. *Wasn't the attack on a child a real crime?* I wonder at Green's concept of crime but hold my tongue. I will continue to pursue the matter with him. Even so, I know neither of them will take it as seriously as I do. As for the capture and rescue of Antoñia, I don't know what Austin would say. He wouldn't condemn her rescue. Yet he could accuse me of bringing down the wrath of the Comanche on the colony. I listen to their concerns, which at least distract me from my own.

"No jail here either, no, and indeed, it is a great worry. The elected ayuntamiento must address that. And in due time, you will elect your own."

"We can manage to deal with drunkards and vagrants, but serious crime in our midst poses a risk," Green agrees.

"True, but the reflective and worthy settlers here adhere to my wishes in most everything, and I thank God for it," Austin says. "The whole lot stuck close with me last year, when we opposed the frontier republicans' upstart rebellion against Mexico in the eastern part of the colony."

Green rises from the table and begins to pace around the room. The good liquor and forthright conversation have set his thoughts racing.

"Of course, the Mexicans describe a process, but the delays in getting the courts in Saltillo to address a criminal case would be a nightmare, which is why we need to set up our own elected councils." His worries find expression in his deep strides and narrowed blue eyes.

Watching my well-spoken husband, I feel his agitation, knowing his fertile mind does not spare him from labyrinths of conscience and despair.

"There is another issue I'd like to discuss with you," Green says in almost hushed tones. "It is a great concern to me. And most urgent. The question of slavery."

"It is indeed urgent," Austin acknowledges, just as a knock comes at the door.

Lucky for Austin, I think, all too aware of their differing views. Austin opens the door to the colony's surveyor, Seth Ingram.

"It's late, sir, and I hate to bother you and Colonel DeWitt," he says, nodding to acknowledge my presence as well.

"No matter, Seth, what is it?" Austin responds patiently.

"The allocation of lands for several families. The survey is not complete. Mr. Sam Williams thought it had been, but I still have days of work to—"

"I thank you for being punctilious, sir. Leave the papers for Sam and me. We will attend to it tomorrow."

With a tip of his hat, Ingram backs out of the room, and the empresarios return to the topic at hand.

Still standing, Green resumes his pacing. "As I'm sure you know, I'm against slavery. I took a stand against it during the run-up to the Missouri Compromise in the Missouri Congress. It is an evil that cannot be tolerated."

Austin gives him a hard look.

I listen carefully, curious as to how Austin's diplomacy will be brought to bear.

"We are men of principle, DeWitt. But we are pushed up against this issue in ways that demand compromise. I know you have few if any slaves in your colony. But among the more than two thousand settlers in this colony, there are now close to four hundred slaves. Settlers from the South come with slaves. Your region, like mine, is ideal for growing cotton crops, which requires slave hands to pick it. Agriculture is the colonists' mainstay, and from it trade will flow."

A ruckus from the back of the cabin distracts me from the conversation, though I'm not sure the men, so intent, even notice.

Before Green can reply, Simon enters to say the ferryman is in the kitchen. "In a terrible fix, Mr. Steben. Hear the sounds comin' from the kitchen?"

"Excuse me a minute. I can't ignore my ferry operator if I ever want to cross the Brazos River again."

"Can I be of help? Of necessity, I've learned to be a nurse."

"Yes, yes, please, Sarah."

We find Jubal Collins with a rag tied around his leg and one of his hip boots beside him. He shakes and trembles with chills and fever. Austin removes the rag and looks at an ulcerous, puffy area on his calf.

"Hmm, a bad sore. Yes, a very bad one," Austin says.

"I've seen this before, Mr. Collins, a spider bite. Have you seen any small brown spiders with a fiddle pattern on the back, on your flatboat?"

The man, doubled over and about to vomit, shakes his head of gray curls. A gap-tooth grimace reveals three front teeth filed to points, making him resemble Beelzebub, though I realize the filed-down teeth are what is left after decay took the rest.

"Naw. No dang lil' ol' spider'd bring a man so low. Got to make 'nother run tonight."

"Well, the bite of the ol' fiddleback, some call it a brown recluse, is serious. I think you're going to have to give up on the ferry run tonight. This sore is nasty. Let me clean it for you. Then you must stay off your feet for a day or two."

"Simon, can you boil up some water and find a little of that lye soap Mary made? And maybe a little draught of whiskey for him?" Austin asks. "Look in the larder. After Mrs. DeWitt cleans his wound, give him a few swigs and put him on a pallet out here. We must check on him later tonight."

"He may smile like the debil, but he's a-quakin' like a leaf," Simon says under his breath.

"Yes, soap and boiling water, if you please, Simon, and I'll see what I can do." I notice a pot in the window and remember Eugenio's remedy for venomous spiders. "Perhaps some cool aloe smeared on the bite would help as well after we clean it up."

Simon nods in approval and goes straight to his task. "Yessum. All right now, Mr. Shoeball, I'm goin' to fix you up like the lady says. The Lord willin', this bad ole place gonna stop festerin' and oozin' soon as I get some coolin' on it."

Returning to the sitting room, we find Green leafing through a copy of *Plutarch's Lives of the Noble Greeks and Romans*. Austin shakes his head.

"This is how my life goes, DeWitt. One thing after another, day and night. No wonder I make such slow progress."

"Your progress looks remarkable from my position behind you."

"Well, now, where were we?" Austin shrugs off the praise.

"I was about to engage in my views about slavery. Your words mollified me, though I cannot turn away from the issue," Green says, placating his host despite himself.

Now it was Austin's turn to unburden himself. "Our problem at the moment, DeWitt, is not the wrongs of slavery. No one could deny its evils. But, as I see it, our focus should be completely in the opposite direction: We must try to persuade the Mexicans to pass legislation to *delay* outlawing slavery in their colonies."

Green keeps quiet as Austin continues.

"As you recall, no doubt, I opposed emancipation in the Mexican Constitution just last year. I will continue to argue that immigrants be allowed to bring enslaved people from the United States."

I see Austin's point, yet I cannot agree. Again, I feel how this land has turned everything I know and believe upside down.

As Green is about to register an objection, Austin continues, "Our colonies are still in their infancy. If they are not to founder, DeWitt, we will have to compromise our principles. I deplore slavery as you do. But I am not ready to sacrifice my years of labors to the cause of slavery just yet."

Without a word, Green gives his friend a look of deep concern.

I cannot keep still. "It is a difficult and dark question. It tears at my conscience to think we are perpetuating it here when the Mexicans want to end it. Who knows how this can be resolved? *¿Quién sabe?*"

"The time will come when, indeed, the question must be resolved. But that time cannot be now in Texas."

"Colonel Austin, I know you bear the scars of years of wrestling such problems to the ground. And you can ill afford to jeopardize all those efforts," I say, hoping he hears the admiration in my voice, despite our disagreement.

Green looks at me and nods, acknowledging my way of bridging this divide.

"Sarah, you have put it perfectly," Austin says, relaxing back into his chair. Then, steering the subject to more practical matters, he brings us back to the present. "The Mexican commission will arrive here in San Felipe soon. We must rise early to plot our course before the meeting."

"Before I retire, I must check on your ferryman. A brown recluse bite is as serious as snakebite."

In Colonel Austin's back room, Jubal Collins is tossing around on the palette Simon has laid for him. The bite actually looks a little less inflamed to me, so I apply a bit more of the aloe salve from Simon's pot in the window.

"Handy plant for bites like this," I tell them both.

"Yes, ma'am," Simon says. "You right about that." After administering a long swig of whiskey to Jubal, Simon assures me that the man will soon be asleep. "I set me up a cot in the next room so I can see to Mr. Shoeball."

"In the morning, Simon, we'll see if our patient is any better."

I consider Simon's devoted service to Austin as I make my way to the bed Austin has provided for us in his quarters. I wonder if Austin has given, or plans to give, Simon his freedom. It is a burning question.

"Strange, that on this antislavery issue, you and I are on the side of the Mexicans," I observe to Green as I climb into bed next to him. Before snuffing the candle, I lean over to kiss Green. "I'm glad you brought up the issue with Austin. You had no choice but to leave it where you did."

"I took my cues from you, my dear. You were right. There was no need to say more. And yes, even without our empresario contracts demanding loyalty to the Mexican Constitution, which prohibits slavery, we are on their side on this issue at least."

"Though it may be our only point of agreement with the Mexicans," I observe, mindful of the commission about to descend on San Felipe. As for loyalty, I believe only Green and Austin take that so seriously. For settlers, the issue is land. Loyalty to the Mexican Constitution is a distant concern.

"Sarah," Green turns to me, speaking softly in the dark, "you can read people. You're the one person I can trust in all of this. More than I trust myself sometimes. I'm glad you came with me. Even if we can't solve the slavery issue tonight," he says, closing his eyes and moving closer.

Green's declaration of need is rare, and I treasure his words so lovingly expressed. As he falls asleep, I nestle against him, feeling a connection returning, the first time since we left St. Louis. I never dreamed of participating in a boundary commission that could determine our future or seal our fate. I am glad to be here.

AT THE WHITESIDE HOTEL

The horses, saddled and waiting, snort with impatience in the April morning. At sunrise, the sky takes on a peach-colored glow above Palmito Creek. In long, loping strides, the horses cover the mile from Austin's cabin on the creek to the village of San Felipe de Austin. Snakes, rabbits, deer, and foxes scatter before us.

San Felipe is silent, except for a dog and a few hogs. Slowing his horse to a trot, Austin points out the names of streets intersecting the main road. Emblazoned on oak posts are Calle Guadalupe Victoria, named for the president of Mexico; Calle Vicente Guerrero, named for a leader of Mexico's struggle for independence from Spain; and most fortuitously, Calle Manuel Mier y Terán, named for our anticipated guest, one of the nation's most respected minds.

"Our Mexican *calles* will do us some good with Terán's commission, I pray," Austin says.

The chinaberry trees lining the main street, Calle Comercio, bloom with sweet-smelling lavender flowers. Inhaling the perfume, I wish for a street so inviting in Gonzales.

We keep the horses to a trot as we pass a string of log houses and stores. The Mexican model for new towns, a grid of avenues and streets dominated by markets and church plazas, is lost in the helter-skelter sprawl. The houses and shops snake back from the Brazos River in two thin lines on either side of the main street. Scores of rough log houses and lean-to stores face this way and that. At the edge of the prairie bluff, we stare at the swift Brazos below.

"*El Río de Los Brazos de Dios*, the arms of God," Austin translates, "was probably named by travelers dying of thirst. No one knows when. A long time ago. Unlike the clear blue waters of your Guadalupe, our brackish Brazos scoops up sediment and mud for a good piece."

The limpid "Warloop" suddenly improves in my estimation as we gaze at the dirty, chocolate-colored water. Austin lingers above the river for a moment and then turns back into town. We follow his lead.

On the journey back, we pass Ingram's General Store, along with Dinsmore's and White's, Peyton's Tavern, and next to it, the only frame building, Cooper and Chieves's saloon and billiard hall. Austin waves to Cooper, whose body is crooked and crippled, bent as barrel staves. Beyond is the one-and-a-half-story Whiteside Hotel and the blacksmith shop of adventurer Noah Smithwick, a young rowdy known for his hair-trigger temper.

I count forty log cabins on the ride back from the river. The town zigs and zags along either side of the road for half a mile. Seeing what Austin has accomplished, I understand that, for Green, this village shines bright as the North Star.

Returning to Austin's cabin, we sit down to a huge breakfast of biscuits, bacon, eggs, and coffee. The biscuits are as solid as sausage but, slathered with honey and sweet butter, their density hardly matters.

When Austin and I check on ferryman Jubal Collins, we find him writhing in pain at the back of the house. His forehead is very hot. As I warm up cloths and apply a hot pack to the leg, Austin calls Simon, tending his vegetable garden.

"You must help him hobble over to Dr. Peebles's house, Simon. The leg looks worse."

Simon comes to him, takes one look, and rolls his eyes. "Mr. Shoeball, dat's bad." Simon hobbles around the room with the man a few times, trying to get him out the door, but that doesn't work. Then Simon disappears, returning with his one-wheel barrow. Unceremoniously, he pushes the sick man into it and rolls off to the doctor with his load.

"Simon gets things done," Austin observes appreciatively.

As the men sit down to work on their agenda at the oak table, we hear the rumble of wagons on the road. Approaching from the direction of the Atascosito Road is a grand coach with silver trimmings. Our Mexican commissioners are arriving. At the window, I am elated to see the strange silver coach again.

Green and Austin join me at the window to watch the procession. The stately arrival of the gleaming silver-inlaid coach with its huge back wheels, a phantasm from another realm, inspires our attention. The silver coach carrying Mier y Terán is like none we have ever seen. Though I have glimpsed it before on the banks of the Guadalupe, it is no less spectacular now. It announces the importance of the man and his mission in a way that words could not. Behind them, a rider veers off, heading toward Austin's cabin. Galloping up to Austin's door, he informs us that the coach and wagon drivers are traveling into San Felipe so that wagon parts can be repaired and conveyances made safe for the continuing trek through the eastern part of the province.

"El General Terán," the messenger announces in perfect English, "requests the presence of Empresarios Austin and DeWitt at noon at the Whiteside Hotel." Then he whirls his horse around and gallops away.

The invitation has a notable effect. It reminds us that we are the guests in Terán's land. "This puts a burr under our saddle," Austin notes, when he finds his voice, though his expression remains dazed. "We must proceed. And you, dear lady, will join us?"

I smile at the broadminded man and Green beside him, nodding approvingly. "I am honored."

Back at the table, Green proposes overwhelming the general with facts. "Your secretary, Mr. Williams, and I can present a mountain of material. And stress our successes here and in Gonzales."

Austin nods enthusiastically. "Yes, yes, including our function as a buffer for the rest of Mexico against the Indians. We have expended considerable energy on quicting the Karankawa, for example. You have negotiated treaties with Kronk Chief Antoñito as well as the Tonkawa chief."

The reference to the Kronks sets my teeth on edge. The "energy" Austin mentions is nothing short of the butchery of Antoñia's tribe. I know only one part of Antoñia's past: the rape and death of her mother at the hands of Anglos, and Antoñia's narrow escape when she was barely fifteen. Which is enough. But I also know that the attacks have continued for years, reducing the Karankawa to a small, sad group. The Mexicans heartily approve, as they hate the Indians more than the Anglos do. While it was the Karankawa who put up more resistance than other tribes in the beginning, their resistance was no match for the whites and their guns. The Comanche and, some say the Tawakana, are now the greater threats. However, it is not clear how great that threat will be, as raids and attacks are random and erratic.

But it is the slavery issue that hangs in the air, and Green's interest puts the matter back on the table. "When we supply census numbers, we must include the number of Negroes living in our colonies. It can't be avoided."

"You are correct, my forthright friend. We must address it straightforwardly and then move on. Terán knows my views. I don't think he'll want to explore them at any greater length. At any rate, I don't expect you to press an issue you oppose."

Green nods gratefully, and despite my feelings about the Karankawa, I mentally praise Austin for his abilities as a negotiator. "But how do we parry the embarrassing fact that few Tejanos live in our colonies?"

"I believe you can deal with that better than I because you can envision the numbers you expect to draw in. Since you have, shall we say, more than a hundred settlers at the moment, the prospect of adding five or six more Tejano families to those already living there will make a much more impressive ratio than my figures will."

It is clear to me that Austin is more willing than Green to stretch the facts to suit his case. A politician's cunning and expedience is required to deal with the Mexicans. Pacifying the Mexican government must be key in this boundary commission meeting.

"I will make my case for needing a cannon from Béjar to defend against the Indians," Green adds. "Mr. Williams and I can talk about the need for militia units."

"Take care," Austin counsels. "Terán does not want to hear about the organization of militia units by Anglos."

"Then the loyalty of our citizens to Mexico and the settlers of good character we bring in should make a better case."

"Agreed," Austin says.

"I have in fact met these gentlemen, Terán and his aides, as they passed through Gonzales," I interject. "They were most cordial. They will remember our encounter. I look forward to seeing them again."

Green regards me with pride, still amazed I met the great Terán before he did.

"We will need your charms," Austin says. Green and I exchange glances. He, at least, knows that I have more than charm to offer. Thinking it will take more than our efforts here to warm Terán's heart, I keep quiet as Green and Austin wrap up their discussion for the night.

As we ride into town in a miserable downpour, I consider the Mexican-style comforts provided to Terán and his expedition during their visit to Béjar. The visitors' stay in Béjar offers a stark contrast to this one. Green has described to me how painstakingly el jefe político ministered to his guests. Dining in dark, formal rooms with heavy furniture and attentive serving women scurrying between tables, the expedition spent their days at the governor's palace in San Antonio de Béjar. They ate Mexican food, slept in big, comfortable beds, and strolled in the patio at the center of the fine house. Canaries in cages sang all day. Bright orange-and-yellow bird-of-paradise plants reached toward the blue sky, and bougainvillea vines laden with masses of magenta blooms drew admiring gazes.

In San Felipe, nothing bespeaks Mexico. Gray skies overhead and the heavy air preoccupy the Mexicans, who are used to the arid climate farther south. The rain falls in sheets, and the Brazos rises. The travelers' anxiety about crossing the river is apparent. As I dismount and hand Pal's reins to the stable boy, General Terán talks to an aide. Terán's rich, flowing voice dramatizes his harsh comment: "*El hotel es como un burdel.*" I understand, "*burdel*" means brothel. Dismounting, the men slip as they hand over their horses to the gray-bearded hostler in a sea of mud.

I follow them in, thinking Terán's standards do not allow for the deprivations of the frontier: Downstairs, the tables are rough, the chairs covered with deer or buffalo hides, the floor splintered and dusty. The piano is so badly out of tune that it doesn't make sense for anyone to play. At the back of the big room furnished with a few tables and chairs, a counter doubles as a bar and a desk for registering guests.

To make matters worse, Berlandier, the expedition's botanist, is reporting to Terán not only the disgusting accommodations but also the ominous rise of the churning Brazos. But the meeting with the empresarios cannot be brushed aside. Seeing my chance, I approach the general and introduce myself. Instantly Terán recognizes me and shakes my hand warmly. In my best Spanish, I commiserate with him over the terrible weather and invite him to a noon meal at Austin's home, which we've hastily arranged with his servants. Grateful for the hospitality, Terán kisses my hand in response, just as the empresarios and Austin's secretary, Sam Williams, approach.

Austin greets Terán with honest regard. Reminded of his letter to Green describing Terán, I know Austin does not have to invent respect for the general. Austin believes him one of the few men with the education, scientific knowledge, and authority necessary to undertake the boundary commission's task.

Terán assembles his group around the only table large enough to accommodate the Mexican guests. The Anglos pull up chairs. Austin speaks first, welcoming the commission members and putting himself at their disposal. Though General Terán speaks English, he shifts the proceedings to Spanish, firmly asking Mr. Williams to translate.

In precise, fluid Spanish, Terán describes the group's mission as primarily scientific, aimed at collecting geographical data and assessing the agricultural and commercial potential of the natural resources in the province. As he speaks, I cannot take my eyes off his face. He gazes out from pools of darkness: The dark circles around his eyes make his white face almost luminous, adding to the general's dramatic air. His perfectly level gold epaulets give him a ramrod-straight severity.

While Sam Williams translates the general's words, I make my own assessment of the proceedings: a call for occupation and defense of the boundaries between the US and Mexico, for checking on the status of the native Indian population, for ending the institution of slavery, and for balancing immigration from the United States with immigration from Europe and the rest of Mexico. Clearly, in the general's eyes, Texas is an idea gone wrong before the ink was dry on the first grant. Too many Anglos are pouring into the area, with the power of Mexico concentrated farther south. I recall one of Austin's succinct comments: "We are indeed a swarm of locusts to them, even if they do need us to settle their wild land."

Terán, with Williams echoing him in English, makes formal introductions of the commission members, who include a military commander, the botanical artist Berlandier, and a cartographer/draftsman. Austin introduces the newly elected mayor, the *alcalde*, of the San Felipe ayuntamiento and turns to Green. He is interrupted by squeals and grunts. A big blue sow, followed by six pink piglets, crashes through the door before Mr. Williams can introduce the empresario from Gonzales. The general, hardly amused by the low lifestyle of the Anglos, looks on in astonishment.

Chairs and commissioners are upended by the sudden appearance of the hotel proprietor, sliding among them and snapping a towel as he chases the family of pigs. When two piglets hop up into a chair, I laugh out loud, breaking the silence among the onlookers. The general cracks a smile and then laughs with me. The meeting resumes under considerably better circumstances, with Green's introduction coming at a more propitious moment.

The meeting unfolds as Austin and Green have planned. The empresarios respond to the commissioners' questions through the translations of Mr. Williams. Questions about Austin's colony come first. Hearing that slaves comprise nearly a fifth of the population among his two thousand colonists leads General Terán to cast a gimlet-eyed gaze at Austin.

I understand the look. Mexico's antislavery stand has been spelled out in the Mexican Constitution of 1824. The constitution, an enlightened document put together by the best minds of Mexico, is one of the few things Terán can point to with pride. And its antislavery tenets are indeed one of the pillars of its wisdom.

A long, awkward exchange of silent looks passes between Austin and Terán. He does not stop the proceedings, and Austin, as planned, does not attempt to explain. They move on to issues the Mexicans have little interest in, though they sit politely. Only the tap-tap-tap of the general's fingers on the table betrays his impatience.

Green and Austin describe the roads, sawmills, and gristmills being built, including their ferry rates. When Green has answered all the questions, Terán's chief aide, Señor Sanchez, warmly recounts his visit with Empresario DeWitt's wife and daughter in the village of Gonzales. He bows to me politely. I listen with satisfaction, noting that Sanchez, with the greatest discretion, implies that Green and his family seem to be *norteamericanos* more tolerable than most.

After the meeting breaks up, the participants mill about before the Mexicans take their leave—their exodus hastened by the treacherous rise of the river Brazos. Wanting to thank Señor Sanchez for his gracious words, I approach him and Terán at the side door of the hotel.

"Señores, we thank you for your visit." Mindful of the Mexicans' protocols and decorum, I struggle to comply. "We bid you safe travels and hope you find all in order," I say, hoping to strike the proper diplomatic tone.

Sanchez gives me an honest look and replies in sonorous, beautifully enunciated Spanish, heavy with formality.

"Señora DeWitt, it has been a great pleasure to meet you and Empresario DeWitt. We are grateful for your efforts for the greater glory of Mexico. I am sure you and your esteemed husband are worthy of our trust. As is apparent in the numbers in *your* colony, we appreciate your opposition to the scourge of slavery banned in our constitution. May all of the Anglo colonies work so diligently *on Mexico's behalf*," he says with emphasis. "We must not, you understand, be lulled into a false sense of security. We are well aware of what we could lose."

He does not mention Austin or disparage anyone, but the import is clear. They think Austin a wolf in sheep's clothing and the Anglos a dangerous bunch.

The general nods gravely, though he does not comment.

I nod in response, smiling as disarmingly as I know how. The men turn to go. Can this chasm be bridged, I wonder, as they disappear across a sea of mud into the stable.

MAY DAY

It is midafternoon when we arrive at our front gate. Pal, wanting to head for the barn, tosses her head with impatience as I dismount and hurry into the house—which is empty.

Creed and Molly have gone, and Antoñia, with Clinton in tow, must have gone to town in the wagon to get supplies. I tell myself that she and the children will soon be home. Three days of hard riding have left me tired, hungry, and jittery. I join Green in the feedlot at the barn. He rubs down Major while I pour a sack of corn into the corncrib. I expect Pal to bury her nose in the rich feast of golden corn kernels, but instead, she lifts her head and whinnies, moves to the fence, and extends her head over the gate.

I follow her gaze. She is looking to the east of the house, where the Indians are buried. Nothing visible from here, but Pal doesn't depend so much on her eyesight as I do. A knot of fear turns my stomach.

"Green, come with me down the hill. Pal has caught a scent."

Hearing the fear in my voice, he doesn't hesitate. Dropping the brush, he follows me down the hill.

Under the hill, where the two Comanche lay buried, we find a shallow ditch. The wide hollow Antoñia slashed into the earth on that terrible February day lies open. Dirt hills mound beside the graves. Both bodies have been removed. Next to one of the graves, a beaded bracelet lies abandoned in the dirt. I turn to Green, speechless. Why had I left my children and Antoñia here?

"Where are they? Where are Molly and Creed?"

Green catches my hand and pulls me to him. "Sarah, calm yourself. There's no reason to fear the worst. The children and Antoñia will be back soon. Molly and Creed have been here with them, and no doubt Creed . . ."

I hear his words but can't take them in. All I'd ever feared circles above me, a harpy settling on my shoulder. I was right all along to be so afraid. And now it has happened, in one crippling, killing moment.

If, at that instant, I hadn't heard the familiar sound of the DeWitt wagon and horses coming up the road, I might have expired and fallen into the open grave. But Green is right; Antoñia and the children are rumbling into view. With gladness in my heart that I cannot possibly explain, I run to greet them.

Gathering in the house, we learn that the bodies have been removed today, in the time Antoñia and Clinton have gone to Gonzales and Molly and Creed have left. The graves, she is sure, were not open when they left in the early afternoon. After supper, with the children asleep, I ponder the situation. Are the Comanche watching and waiting? Choosing their next time carefully? I shudder inwardly, wondering why they didn't attack Antoñia. Was it simply luck that she was not here when they came looking for her? Or did they have another plan?

"We don't know if reclaiming their dead warriors will satisfy them," I worry to Green. "Or if there is more in store."

Antoñia, by the back door, has a strange look on her face. Then she says quietly, "In Quaro . . . capture white woman . . . people go after . . . bring back in few days."

I stare at her. "Comanche captured a woman? Then she was rescued?"

Antoñia nods. "Eugenio come . . . tell me, be careful . . . you gone."

So they are waiting and watching. Avenging their dead? Or simply picking us off when they see a chance? I swallow hard. We don't know, and we won't know until it happens.

"I will investigate this tomorrow, Sarah," Green says, his voice somber. "The hour is late. We are all tired."

I have to think about getting back to my schoolroom. We must all be up at dawn. What passes for sanity and courage but perhaps is resignation takes over. I can't be afraid all the time. Bone tired as I am, I expect to fall asleep as soon as the house is quiet, but my mind keeps spinning. Yet despite all my fears, I'm also tilting in a different direction. The trip has been uplifting and unexpectedly gratifying. Green is happy over the meetings in San Felipe and hopeful that Terán will look favorably upon us and the work of settling Texas. Which, I believe, is impossible. Yet seeing San Felipe and Green and Austin engaged together, seeing their efforts to forge a new era, the enterprise makes more sense to me now. I have covered the ground between the two main colonies. I feel exactly how close, and how far, we are from Austin, his gains a horizon hopefully in reach for us. And Green has brought me into his confidence in ways that touch my heart. Austin and Green are making a new world. Because we are so tied to Austin in his efforts, the enormity of the endeavor dawns on me in ways it hasn't before. I'm beginning to stand in Green's and Austin's shoes, feel their surpassing strength. I pray to be as strong.

It is good to be back. The children are glad to see me, not only my own but their schoolmates Seth, Ben, Lila, Bess, Faye, and the rest. Naomi has new ways of teaching arithmetic, and Lewis and Eveline have devised lessons about the natural world that involve paints and dyes they've concocted from wildflowers and other plants. They have their colors and paints stored in little bottles and cans obtained from Lewis's father's blacksmith shop. They've already shown the class how reds, greens, yellows, and browns can be made out of the blooms of Texas bluebonnets and paintbrushes and other plant parts when mixed with ashes, cow urine, animal fat, and other prairie chemicals. Eveline confides they are planning something special to teach the class more secrets of the wild.

The next few days go smoothly; the week flies by. Each day I promise, "On the first of May, we're going to celebrate. It's a special day." On May Day morning, we march through the lessons quickly. Then, calling for an early recess so the Luna girls can come with us, I announce the excursion. We will go two by two—an older and a younger student in each pair—across the road and down the hill to the river. Then we'll have a pleasant hike along the river before we return to the schoolroom. "Lewis and Eveline have some surprises," Naomi tells them, following instructions Eveline delivered to us in great secrecy.

Mr. Turner, the hotel owner, comes along as a bodyguard. It is a beautiful day, and he promises to ensure the safety of the class strung out behind me like a line of ducklings.

On the river, mallards, teals, and wood ducks dive, and turtles sun on a tiny island in the middle. Lewis points up at the eagles' nests in two cypress trees and out to the beavers building a dam. Then he says, "Now follow me, 'cause we're going to go up a ways and then gather 'round something none of you have ever seen before."

In our slow parade, we arrive at the appointed spot, a secluded stretch where the land levels out into a sandbar. The sun sparkles on the water, and ball moss hangs in the cypress trees. The trees' big roots and knees jut up from the water. The roots, rocks, and boulders covered with soft moss are like stepping stones into the water. A little stand of cypress trees has formed an earthen dam that looks like an island in the middle of the river.

"In a few weeks," Lewis says, "I'm going to wade out there and climb that cypress tree to see what I can see, if the eagles don't run me off. Look at that big old eagle's nest up in that one. Eggs won't be hatched yet. Too early."

Then Lewis kneels down at the edge of the water and begins turning over rocks. Acting as his assistant, Eveline explains, "Lewis is looking for something I've seen only once—'cause he showed it to me. 'Bout the prettiest thing ever lived under a rock. You'll see." Lewis hands Eveline a flour sack filled with bottles and tins, and she disappears behind a tree.

I don't want to interfere with her special project, but I don't like having Eveline out of my sight. I step away from the group as the class edges closer to Lewis. I catch glimpses of her in the woods. She puts the flour sack on the ground. Squatting down, she starts pulling things out of the sack and stirs one and then another with a stick, an alchemist mixing a potion.

The children on the sandbar are entirely focused on Lewis. I hope no one will fall into the water. But the older-child, younger-child partnership is working, with Naomi supervising. Lila is minding Ben, Bess has Seth, and so on. And Mr. Turner is keeping a close eye on the woods around us.

Suddenly Lewis turns over a rock and plunges his hands into the water. He holds up his prize. "Lookee here!" he cries.

Eveline takes her cue. She emerges from the trees with her face painted in the colors of the water creature Lewis has just produced. They have all the flourish of the great magician Louis Comte pulling a rabbit out of a hat. The children gasp and laugh when they see Eveline's face. They point at the red, green, and yellow bands on her face as if she were as glorious as the critter in Lewis's hand.

"Now you might've seen frogs and lizards," she says, "but this here is a salamander, a special one. A tiger salamander. I bet none of you ever did see one like this before."

She points to yellow stripes and spots on the black body as Lewis grasps it firmly in his hand. Then she takes it and holds it up to her face, which makes everyone laugh again.

The children are transfixed. They want to touch and hold the squirming creature. But Lewis is in command.

"Naw, playing with it could hurt it. But lookee here at these red gills around its cheeks like whiskers. And its wide tailfin like a fish. Not grown up yet. Still a baby."

The children teeter at the very edge of the river; some wade in. Gathered around Lewis, they ooh and ah as he spins out more amazing facts about the beauty he's revealed.

Eveline, too, has a treat to share. "Now, if anyone wants to get their face colored like mine, I can do it."

Immediately three children step up and then four more. Big kids help little kids as Eveline directs and organizes. They crowd close to Eveline and Lewis as the smearing of colors begins. Our two naturalists deliver an entertaining show. It goes from admiring the salamander to celebrating themselves as agents of the natural world.

Though I'm as mesmerized as the children, I remind myself that it is past time for the girls to return to Luna. I look around, wondering where our protector, Mr. Taylor, is.

He lies on the ground about fifty yards back; an Indian dashes toward me.

My screams bring the children up the riverbank toward me. Eveline leads the pack, her red hair streaming, her painted face a mask of red and yellow. Close behind, several more painted faces charge up the hill, a mass of arms and legs and sticks and stones and clods of dirt.

The crowd gains courage from their numbers and perhaps from their warlike faces. I can't see how close the Indian is behind me. But, in seconds, fast as a deer, the figure veers away into the woods. Mr. Taylor, with a bloodied head, is close behind me. He fires a shot. We watch as the runner vanishes into a tangle of grapevines and oak trees, the woods closing around him as if he'd never been among us.

He was after me. With Mr. Taylor addled for even a few minutes, standing back from the group by the river, I was an easy mark. He'd planned on a quick ambush with no one watching. What stopped him? My screams? The painted faces, the swarming children converging like evil spirits? Eveline's red hair? They haven't forgotten. The Comanche aren't done with me.

Eveline reaches me first, with Naomi and Lewis close behind. The children cover me with hugs, the younger ones sobbing.

"It's all right. It's all right," I whisper, despite my trembling hands, knowing this is only a reprieve.

16

SAN ANTONIO DE BÉJAR

Green's reaction to the May Day events surprises me. It seems to have jolted him, shattered the idea that the colony must take priority, that increasing our numbers is the only concern. He doesn't lecture me about being careful but instead moves closer to me. As if it pains him to let me out of his sight. That is impossible, of course, but he *has* started getting home four or five days out of seven. He even visited our classroom before school was out and has made more time for the children. He seems to be searching for ways to diminish the distance this last year has put between us. To preserve the cooperation of our days in San Felipe. It's been more than a year since that April day we left St. Louis. Maybe he's beginning to accept that his Rome can neither be built in a day nor by *his* sheer will alone.

A few weeks ago, he announced a trip to San Antonio de Béjar and again invited me to accompany him. "School is out, and you haven't seen the country west to Béjar," he's said more than once.

Green plans to leave at daylight. "Got to meet with the political *jefe* tomorrow," he says.

We are sure to see Will in Béjar.

I hear the enthusiasm in Green's voice and would love to join him on another trip. He wears his optimism in Texas as he wore his sheriff's badge in Missouri, pinning a brave front on most anything. I know he needs my voice to temper his plans, to help him think through all that comes at him. But for me, it is a double-edged sword.

I struggle to share his view of the colony's future. Underneath that bold exterior is a man well aware of the peril of this place. I believe doubt serves a real purpose: to whisper caution in our rush ahead. Green can swing wildly in both directions, his ups and his downs equally frightening. But doubt never begets caution in him. It just makes him fight harder to accomplish what he must.

I admire his ambition, the vision he and Austin hold. There are moments when I believe in the future he dreams for us. "My stars and body," I tell myself, adopting Molly's phrase, "you can't worry all the time." My love for my husband, broken as it somehow seems, is repairing itself, like a bone mending. Wanting to please him and to assess the situation for myself, I've said I'd go. Molly and Creed will arrive in the morning to stay with the children again. But yesterday, I doubted my decision and told Green I must reconsider.

I tick off reasons to make the journey. After the abduction of the woman in Quaro, near the Burns home, there's no sense in sending the children there. Further, there are no better Indian fighters than Creed and Antoñia. But the May Day attack told me eyes are every-where. Since the day Antoñia and I killed the Indians, we have been in constant danger. I hear the whoosh, whoosh of my skirts and the tap-tap of my heels as I try to quiet my worries, as I go back and forth. Should go, shouldn't go. Should go, shouldn't go.

And what of seeing Will in Béjar? My shame, to say nothing of my undeniable longing, has receded. I would like to see Will and resume our longtime friendship. *It is time*, I reason. *We have been friends most of our lives*, I tell myself often, relying on my Presbyterianism for reassurance. I had been in a resentful frame of mind since we left Missouri. It was as if, once he secured his grant, Green and I had been engaged in a battle. But we are getting past it. Now I should be able to reclaim my long friendship with Will—renew our respect and return to normal.

When Green comes home at dark, I meet him with a smile, despite my fractious thoughts. "You're right. I will be ready to leave for Béjar in the morning."

Green hugs me tightly. "Sarah, that's music to my ears. We'll go in the wagon. Eugenio knows the upper road to Béjar well. We'll camp overnight at Walnut Springs or wherever Eugenio figures is the best place. Might even see some of those river lilies you like so much," he says as if bestowing on me a gift comparable to the one just given him.

I spend the evening giving instructions to the children and to Antoñia. She and I use our sign language and our Karankawa-English vocabulary.

"*Calí*," I point to myself, "to Béjar with *saylá*," pointing to Green.

Then Antoñia repeats the message back to me. "Sar-ah Wo-man to Béjar with Husband Man." I smile, and Antoñia puts her head down shyly and then looks up. Her somber face is transformed by my confidence in her.

Throughout the evening, Antoñia and the girls follow me. Her bow stands propped in the corner of the kitchen, next to a basket of arrows. I take comfort knowing the Karankawa are said to be the best with the longbow of all the Indians of North America.

When Eugenio arrives at dawn, I am ready. I creep quietly to the children's beds. I know Naomi, with her cat curled beside her, is only pretending to be asleep, and I kiss her forehead. Yowl, his gimpy leg folded over Naomi's hair, responds with a deep purr. Kneeling on the hearth to stoke the cooking fire in the kitchen, Antoñia raises her head and nods, an acknowledgment that it is good for Sarah Woman to go.

"Molly and Creed will be here soon," I tell her once more. Then Green hurries me out of the house and hands me up to Eugenio in the wagon.

The early dew, so heavy that our clothes hang wet for an hour or better, burns off in the morning sun. I look for the Tonkawa village when we cross the river but see no signs of their cone-shaped tepees. There is only the clearing and ashes of campfires now abandoned, the wild woodland country gradually giving way to expanses of prairie.

The June meadows are abloom: purple verbena; evening primroses with their closed cups, dry, thistle-like flower heads, and prickly leaves suited to the immense heat of the prairie; and the yellow, pink, and orange heads of lantana, which some call the rattlesnake plant. I imagine the dreaded vipers giving birth to their wriggling young and nesting there underneath these thickets of lantana. Already I've seen two rattlers, disturbed by the vibrating motion of the wagon, slithering through the waist-high prairie grass. This land, so beautiful and so perilous, mirrors the differences between Green and me. For him, it is an untamed paradise. For me, underneath the bounty and beauty, danger lurks, even on a brilliant day like today.

I take in the sights of the prairie, reminiscent of Missouri in places but also filled with so much that is new to me. The lush yellow flowers and red tunas of the prickly pear cactus. The bean pods of the mesquite trees. The occasional glimpse of a brown-and-white-flecked roadrunner with a bushy crest, streaking by, long and large as a cat. More familiar, the flocks of red-winged blackbirds nested in clumps of hackberries and chinaberries and wild peach trees, heavy with round fuzzy fruits. Small herds of deer lift their heads and white tails as the wagon nears. The bucks sport the velvet growing on new antlers, and the does nurse their fawns.

About midmorning, we pass a wagonload of three haggard travelers armed with carbine rifles and carrying a few hide-seated chairs and sacks of corn. The men pull up next to us and say they are headed to east Texas, where they hope the Indians will be less hostile than along Salado Creek, where they've been living.

When we set off again, Eugenio looks at Green. "*El agua del Salado no es de sal. Es de sangre* . . . the blood."

Green shoots me a sidelong glance. I look straight ahead, trying to disregard his look.

"Yes, I know that Salado Creek has been the sight of some bloody encounters, that its sweet waters are salty only when they run red."

"Where in the Sam Hill did you pick that up, Mrs. DeWitt?" Green teases, determined to keep things on the lighter side.

"Colonel," I poke fun back at him, "I hate to upset your applecart, but we ladies do know a few things, even if we don't get them first-hand. There were six hungry wayfarers at our door just last week. I get a tale or two out of feeding half the countryside."

"Sarah, my dear," Green looks at me lovingly, "you figure out things better than I do. All the while keeping that egg-smooth face blank as a poker player."

I squeeze his hand and kiss him on the cheek. "A poker player? Yes, if I were allowed to enter a poker game with the men, I'm sure I could be as inscrutable as you say."

Eugenio keeps his oxen, Pablo and Pablito, at a steady pace. He looks like a grasshopper in a serape, thin legs and arms poking out from his wrap. The serape, which he wears in all weathers, protects him from wind, rain, and sun. His watchful brown eyes scour the countryside, alert to movement, danger, and the beauty of the land. He often points up at the young white herons perched in the trees, like huge white *flores*, he says.

Green rests his hand affectionately on mine. He gazes at me from time to time, propped against the side of the wagon, once adjusting the straw sombrero, borrowed from Eugenio, that sits atop my bonnet and unruly hair. I can see his thoughts, frenetic as an insect trapped in a jar, whirring around issues he must discuss with Señor Músquiz, of the district of San Antonio de Béjar.

"If I can get Chief Músquiz to give me a cannon," he says, "the trip will be well worth it. The Tejanos in San Antonio de Béjar are more like us, wanting a degree of independence from Mexico City. They like us better than the Mexicans in the capital do, but they can't look like they like us too much or they'll lose influence with Terán and with the big general Santa Anna, who controls everyone, even the current president, I'm told."

I've heard, mostly from Creed and Will, that Santa Anna is He Who Everyone Fears. He is likely to parlay his general's authority into that of a dictator with no regard for his nation's 1824 constitution. Green contends that he needs us to colonize the wilds as much as we need him to leave us alone. But, in truth, no one knows how much control he will seize.

"Will a cannon in the fort deter Indian raids?" I wonder, leaving Mexico's national politics out of it for the time being.

"Hopefully. But I've got to persuade them to give it to us first."

"And they may not?"

"They don't trust us, Sarah. You saw it firsthand at the meeting with Austin. They think we might use it against them someday. The Tejanos in the north of Mexico have to stay on Terán's good side. I suspect Terán thinks they should have more Mexicans, more military watching what we're doing. He likely would not support the Tejanos giving us cannons."

"And how will you put it to Chief Músquiz?"

"I have to let them know more about the raids happening around the colony, the incident at the river with you and the schoolchildren. I'll tell them my plans for seeding colonization. Groups from Tennessee and Kentucky we can bring down the Mississippi. A cannon in the fort will be a good advertisement for safety and security. News will travel."

"But won't they take a dim view of that too?"

"Umm," he says, no doubt considering the dilemma of populating a colony just reaching a hundred families while simultaneously trying to reassure the Mexicans that growing numbers of norteamericanos aren't a threat. And all before his contract for settling four hundred families—three hundred fifty more families than we have now—expires.

"The thing is, the Tejanos aren't exactly of one mind with the Mexicans, like Terán, in Mexico City. The Tejanos side with us Anglos as much as with the Mexicans. So that's my main hope for getting the cannon. Then there's the situation with some of our own settlers—Count de la Baume, for instance," Green goes on. "He petitioned to regain title to his lands, which were lost in the Mexican revolution. Authorities at Béjar forwarded his request to the Mexican government. They may have a response by now on his suit. I will emphasize the importance of this issue to all of us, Colonel Austin included."

The mention of eighty-year-old Count de la Baume makes me think of my father. He and the count knew each other during the Revolutionary War. They set off about the same time after the Revolution for Missouri, the count coming later to Texas. What courage to push on, start over, pioneer again and again. When I was a child, leaving Virginia for Missouri, unaware of the dangers, it seemed a wonderful adventure, protected as I was by my parents. Now the risks and dangers make me yearn for that settled Missouri life. Or for the courage the count and my father and mother—and Green—have in such abundance.

Through the afternoon, I keep my bearings by watching for the Guadalupe River, snaking away and back into view. Green points out the mileposts, set at intervals, in the boundless, grass-covered prairie. The river courses west toward Béjar until it reaches Walnut Springs, the halfway point on the journey. I look for patches of the Guadalupe glinting in the sun. When it heads more northwesterly, Green says we will be beyond the western boundary of the sixty-mile-wide DeWitt colony.

Soon after, we spot milepost 36 carved on a mesquite tree's gray bark to measure the miles from Gonzales. Eugenio turns the oxen down a lane leading to a cove and a little log hut. Behind it, the river sprawls in a horseshoe bend. Cypresses and hundred-foot-high walnut trees line its banks. We make camp here for the night.

Eugenio waters the oxen and builds a fire as Green and I walk to the river and back. As we come back up the riverbank, I spot a three-sided windbreak, like the one behind our house that Antoñia calls a *ba-ak*. Along its backside, made from willow poles with skins stretched over them, lie gunnysacks under a canvas cover. The gunnysacks are filled with a stash of contraband tobacco, another waystation for Eugenio and Will or their fellow businessmen.

Green walks over to the mound, lifts the cover, and kicks at the sacks. The aroma of tobacco rises from the pile. Close by, Eugenio is feeding the fire.

"Who does this belong to?" Green calls to him. Eugenio shrugs his shoulders, his face blank in response to questions. Green pretends he doesn't know, though I suspect he does, that the inventory of their little enterprise is scattered around in hiding places through-out the colony.

We eat as the sun sets toward Béjar and the moss-draped trees make big shadows on the river. "So, Sarah, so far, so good?"

"Yes, I'm glad I came," I say, answering the question he doesn't want to press on me.

"Tomorrow night in Béjar, Will's house will be a little more comfortable."

Eugenio nods. "*El Colorado vive cerca del Alamo.*"

"He's gotten a place as a storekeeper for the military garrison housed at the Alamo."

"Oh? You've arranged for us to stay with Will?" I had no idea. But of course, he is our main contact there. I try to look uninvolved, hoping my face is indeed poker-player blank.

"Yes," Green jokes. "Músquiz is not going to put us up at his house, and no one offered the Governor's Palace."

Trusting that the snap of interest in my eyes doesn't show, I none-theless feel his eyes searching my face. "That will be convenient for your meetings, then?" I ask.

"Yes, very close," Green says.

Good man that he is, Green spurns jealousy. I am grateful to him, knowing that he sees no reason to push me. He has never known the history Will and I share, the days of our youth that I can never purge from my heart. But there is no reason for Green to think about that. With Will's move to Béjar, the tempests have been calmed. Green and I are building a new life. He is the companion, the life I have chosen. *Don't go there again*, I remind myself. *You married Green. And that is that.*

We spread blankets and quilts near the fire. Though the night is warm, Eugenio folds himself into his serape and falls asleep instantly. Wrapped in a blanket of stars, Green and I search the sky for the Big Dipper and the North Star. And the little bear, Ursa Minor. Despite the heat of the day, breezes off the river turn the evening cool and pleasant. We hear the booming notes of the bullfrogs from the water, the loud, deep *hoo-hoos* of the hoot owls, and the piercing cries of the screech owls flying along the river. Listening to their long trills, I curl into Green. Contented, he holds me close.

"*This* is Mexico," Green says with sudden clarity as we cross Salado Creek and ascend a high ridge of the plain. Below us stretches a commanding view of Béjar, home to several thousand souls.

"Presidio San Antonio de Béjar was a military post, and then a village came up around it," Green says as we look down on the town. "Sort of a dusty place. Been growing here for more than a century. It was the seat of the Spanish government in Texas before Mexicans won independence and moved the provincial capital to Saltillo. Now it's the garrison of a few hundred Mexican soldiers struggling against the Indians. The Indians despise the Mexicans. The Mexicans return the favor."

As we near the town, Eugenio points toward the horizon. Against the bright blue sky stand the bell tower and dome of Mission San José, a mission that rose there a century ago to Christianize and minister to the Indians. This limestone monument to Spanish efforts at colonization in the New World remains strangely solid in the middle of the vast, dusty prairie. A few miles farther ahead, we enter the town. San Fernando Cathedral reaches above us—a tall, dramatic presence among the otherwise low-lying stores and shops. For a moment, I long for the quiet hours and well-known hymns of my Sunday Presbyterian church. But in a colony that allows only Catholics, a Protestant church sits at the bottom of the list for our builder, Mr. Lockhart, and his carpenters.

Eugenio looks toward Béjar with pride—a place rooted here long before the Anglos came, even before the United States rose to the north, a village he has known all his life. We continue west, the upper road verging into streets and paths and more and more people going about their business. Closer in, we come to the serpentine San Antonio River—easily forty feet wide across here—and clatter over a bridge made from a huge hollowed-out tree trunk.

The dusty streets are lined with hovels. "*Jacales*," Eugenio says, pointing to the huts. In front of one of these clay-and-mesquite-stick homes, an old woman in a bright blue dress, which does not cover her ample bosom, combs her thin, gray, waist-long hair. A dog and child play at her feet. Shaded by a thatched roof made of rushes, the woman looks out on the world. A clay jar sits on the table next to her, beside a cone-shaped oven. Alongside the jacal, tall corn plants fill a garden plot. A few blocks farther west, the wagon rattles across a wooden bridge spanning a big ditch filled with water. "*La Acequia San Pedro*," Eugenio says, pointing at the aqueduct bringing river water to irrigate gardens and supply homes.

Along the narrow streets, the Tejano world unfolds, less grand than the first view from the ridge. On one side of the wagon, a boy leads a burro overloaded with gourds and clay water jars. On the other side, a young man in a wide-brimmed black hat hawks torti-llas balanced in a wide tray atop his hat. Eugenio follows my eyes. Everywhere I look, he is quick to explain—"*aguador*," "*panadero*," "*tamalero*"—as we move slowly through the town.

"*Agua*, uh huh, waterbearer. *Pan*, yes, bread seller," I repeat. "*Tamalero?*"

"Sell tamales," Eugenio explains, licking his lips.

When we come to Flores Street, Green leans forward to give Eugenio directions, but he is already turning the wagon south toward the town center. Green leans back, disappearing into his own thoughts again. I try to look everywhere at once. Ahead stretches a big plaza and a grand building with a huge double wooden door and arch. "*Palacio*," Eugenio says. No doubt the Governor's Palace, where Spanish overlords once lived and Terán and his team were recently housed.

The wagon rolls to the corner, where Eugenio pulls up his team in front of a low adobe, flat-roofed house with a carved wooden door. The Spanish-style house with thick, broad walls and few win-dows stretches north along the street. Crudely carved wooden posts, spaced closely enough to keep out man or beast, line three small windows in the wall. On the inside of one window, a big jar of field flowers sits on the sill.

"La Casa Músquiz. Eugenio will take you on to Will's place." Green looks at me earnestly for a moment, then kisses me on the lips and jumps down from the wagon. "Gotta meet Músquiz," he explains unceremoniously. A servant opens the big wooden door, and Green disappears into the dark interior.

Despite my own apprehensions, I smile inwardly at his trust in me. Apparently intent on his mission, he's left me to navigate my own path. But I can read his thoughts. *Enough time has passed*, he is thinking. *Sarah is back to normal, adjusting to life here. She's stopped resenting me for bringing her here. It will be all right.*

I know what he won't think as well. What, thankfully, he can't consider because he's never known how much Will meant to me. Green deals with this black void between us, my feelings for Will, in ways unknown even to me. Is it just denial? Or is it Green's generosity of mind and heart? Or is he so preoccupied with the challenges here that there is little room for much else? I hope it is a generous heart.

It is late afternoon and the shadows cast by the Músquiz house lengthen across the dusty street. "So now we must find Will," I say as much to myself as to Eugenio. I have no idea where he might be.

Eugenio, of course, does. Yet he looks at *me*, awaiting instructions. "*¿Usted sabe dónde vive El Colorado, sí*? Where he lives?"

Eugenio looks wary. "*¿La casa del Colorado? Sí, sí*," Eugenio answers. "*Comprendo*." But the wagon does not move.

I ponder his confusion. Is he considering the reason for Will's departure six months ago? I grasp Eugenio's misgivings but not how to quiet them, and I wish for a commanding soul.

"*A la casa del Colorado. Vámonos*," I say, with all the authority I can muster, climbing from the bed of the wagon up onto the seat with Eugenio.

Hesitating no longer, Eugenio clicks his tongue, and the oxen move us forward, heading east along the main Market Square. Eugenio guides the team through the sleepy streets, crowded with wooden oxcarts, rickety wagons, and overloaded burros. Mexican soldiers sit atop thin, swaybacked horses. We have moved into another century. The creaky wagons look ancient, held together with frayed ropes and cords and rawhide. They travel on wooden axles with oddly shaped wheels and are drawn by oxen in patched harnesses.

The big cathedral sits in the center of the plaza, and on one side, what looks like a jail. Doors mark cell-like rooms with bars at the windows. It is not a market day, but stalls ring the plaza for tomorrow's market. Their cloth awnings flutter in the late afternoon breeze.

Anchored to tumbledown kiosks and occasionally a solid shed made of adobe bricks and plaster, the flimsy roofs cover stands where vendors will sell their wares on Saturday. Gourds and chili peppers, onions and clay pots, ropes, and colorful cloth hang from the poles at the corners of the stalls. Between a row of empty stands, a girl holding a baby, a woman with a basket, a man pulling a cart amble down the lane.

I glance at Eugenio. He looks at me sideways and starts to hum a Mexican tune. I take heart from his song, elated by his great good nature.

As Eugenio guides the oxen along the market square, the church bells of San Fernando Cathedral call worshippers to Mass. I see Eugenio loves the kettle-toned bells tolling for the service, though he grimaces at their surprisingly jarring noise. We watch as the bells give sudden direction to a community of worshippers strolling idly only moments before. People stream from houses across the market square and hurry toward Friday evening Vespers. Even stray dogs and birds swooping for crumbs in the street seem to follow the bells.

While groups of believers file toward the cathedral, we pass the front door of the Alamo, as the Mission San Antonio de Valero is known. The mission looks deserted. A large door with two spiraling columns on each side anchors the front. Three windows sit above the façade. The mission's church needs repair. Around it, long, solid walls punctuated with small doorways enclose the mission, lending it a sturdy look.

A few hundred yards beyond the chapel of the Alamo mission lies a smaller door to a tiny adobe house with a tile roof. A rangy redhead stands in the doorway.

THE ALAMO STOREKEEPER

ugenio sees Will and gives his little laugh, the rapid-fire bursts rising and falling like a whinny. Will leans against his door, his head grazing the frame. As the wagon comes to a standstill, he steps over and reaches out to grasp the yoke of the oxen, stroking their broad noses frothed with spittle. "Water inside *la misión*." Will points to a gate. "*Por allá*."

"Mrs. DeWitt"—he nods and reaches up to help me down—"let me welcome you to El Presidio de San Antonio de Béjar," he says. I stand beside him, looking into his smiling green eyes as Eugenio sets the team toward the gate in the wall.

"Pleasure to lay eyes on you," Will says, standing back and regarding me with a level gaze.

"The same to you, Will."

"'Course I know it's only been six months since I last saw you, but it's a marvel how the rough life of the frontier doesn't wreck that smooth face of yours."

I gaze at him gratefully, happy that his banter—which I can never come up with—is reliable as ever, part of his sunny disposition. For a long moment, I hold my breath, all too aware of how utterly Presbyterian I was created.

Then, gathering my forces, I fold my hands, keep my distance, and relate the news: our trip to San Felipe and the meeting with Terán, the schoolroom started in Turner's Hotel, the entrance of Antoñia into our lives. And the steady, if somewhat slow, stream of settlers into Gonzales. "They're not coming in droves, as in Austin's colony, but Gonzales is beginning to take shape."

He nods and then responds in kind, catching me up on his life. "I'm here to tell you, I've had a few adventures myself since we parted—got me this here post as El Señor storekeeper for the Alamo. Now I've got more stuff than I can count—saddles and blankets, gunpowder and rifles, bins of corn, sugar, even lanterns and oil."

"Oh my, Will, it's like Missouri and your job at the dry goods store."

"Yup, always wanted to have me a store. People in and out all day long. Getting to know so many faces, I could run for office. One problem, though. The Mexicanos, Tejanos, too, don't do too good with 'Will'—in Spanish, it's *Gui-ller-mo*, a mouthful. So, I've up and changed it."

"You've what?"

"You can call me Will, but around here, most everybody knows me now as John, Juan. I just reversed the J and the W. Instead of William J. Jones, now I'm John W."

"You didn't. How could you?"

"Went over to the San Fernando church across the plaza and got rechristened as Juan."

"When did you do that?"

"'Bout a month ago."

"I can't call you Juan."

"Don't have to. I answer to both. Still the same underneath," he says, looking straight into my eyes.

I hear his explanation—that Guillermo for William is a tongue twister, while Juan for John, his middle name, rolls right out. But it's more than that. In his new life, he is becoming someone else. He is no longer the Will I have long known. Which stops me for a moment, disturbs me. But I remind myself: *I am no longer the Sally who adored him. He is no longer central to my life.*

"What does Eugenio call you?" I ask, trying to sound cool and detached as if I don't know that Eugenio calls him by his nickname.

"He calls me *El Colorado*. Ain't that right, Eugene?" Will asks as Eugenio returns, a tamale in each hand, to find us still in the street in front of Will's doorway.

Eugenio gives us a puzzled look.

"Eugenio needs some food. He's wondering why we Anglos like to talk more than we like to eat. So come on in, and I'll feed you some beans and tortillas and some more of them tamales. I buy 'em by the bucket from the *tamalero*, who spends his day walking from the market square to the Alamo and back. Except when he runs back to his *casita* for a fresh batch."

Inside his one-room home, a table and bench, which clearly doubles as a carpenter's bench, occupy the center of the room. He pushes aside a bucket of wood scraps and dusts off a place for me to sit. The fireplace and hearth fill one wall. Scattered around are fishing poles and a hoe, hammers, nails, a chopping ax, an adze, a saw, piles of ropes, an axle, and two wagon wheels.

Will checks the pot hanging in the fireplace and ladles out beans onto three tin plates. From the ashes, he plucks a dozen tamales, shucks, and distributes them. He piles more beans and a tortilla on top and sets the plates on the table.

I eat hungrily as Eugenio wolfs down his food, and Will just keeps talking.

"So Green is off meeting with the bigwig Músquiz? He's head of the council. Probably meet the whole group tomorrow."

"Yes, Green and I have discussed the ayuntamiento. He is at this moment probably going up against a number of strong-minded Mexicans."

"You roll 'ah-YOON-ta-me-in-toe' off your tongue real nice," Will says. "I had to learn to say it before I met with 'em to get hired as keeper of the Alamo's emporium."

Despite his disarming talk, Will speaks Spanish better than I and figures the politics as easily as he pictures the lay of the land in his maps.

"I'm sure you know all five gentlemen on the council. You always know more than you own up to," I protest as he proceeds to describe the town council.

"There's three or four Green will meet with Músquiz, including Señor José Antonio Navarro, and probably the Seguíns, father and son. These señores are all for the rights of the Texians, as they call us. Not of the same mind as General Terán or that egg-suckin' hound dog, Santa Anna, who's always stirring up trouble to grab power for himself. Green won't have trouble with this bunch. Except when they ask permission from the higher-ups in Mexico City."

Talking with his mouth still full of tamales and beans, Will rushes to finish his meal. "Gotta take you to the store before it's too dark to see my wares." His smile crinkles the edges of his face, his green eyes bright in his tanned skin. "I swear, Sarah, I'm like a rich man with all my goods. I don't really like to sell anything because in my mind it's all mine. And if you want to know the truth, some of it is."

I give him a wary look. His schemes and maneuvers have always made me uncomfortable.

"You'll see," he says in response, getting up from the table. Eugenio and I follow him out the door.

Falling in step beside him, with Eugenio a few steps away, I take a deep breath and deliver my message. "I've missed you in Gonzales. I know it's best this way. Still and all, you're my longtime friend, and we can't go on denying our bond . . . of friendship."

The words rush out in such a tumble I wonder if I'd spoken them or just thought them. Knowing Will's aversion to anything too serious, I fear I've said far too much and, simultaneously, far too little.

As always, he rushes to my rescue, seizing the moment as hungrily as I have. He stops and looks at me for a moment. Without the slightest tease in his voice, he responds in kind.

"Sally Goodin', you know what's best. I couldn't do better in this world than claim your friendship. I miss you too." He looks away as his eyes cloud over.

I stare at him, seared by the words spilling out. Stifling my desire to hug him, I tell myself I have done the right thing, what I had to do. Now I can go on, no longer threatened by our past.

"Thank you, Will. I am grateful for everything." We continue past the mission to another tiny door in the wall. Will fishes in his pocket for a key and unlocks the store, sweeping us in with a flourish.

Inside the cool, dark room, the dank smell of the thick adobe walls envelops us. Along the walls, shelves hold every manner of tool and weapon. Will plucks items off the shelves, showing us saddles, tack, stirrups, blankets, canteens, bands for wagon wheels, and the wheels themselves. One whole wall holds tools, a rig for a plow, hammers, hoes, axes; another wall, knives and guns.

"Now here, Sarah, here's one you might know."

I, however, am looking beyond the guns and rifles. Beyond the bins of corn and bags of flour, I see the back room, which holds gunnysacks of tobacco and bottles of whiskey.

Will follows my eyes. "That's another matter," he says. "Like I say, some of the stuff in my little store *is* mine."

I dare not ask more questions. He and Eugenio are carrying on an illegal trade that might not be so bad in Anglo or even Tejano terms, but Green would not look kindly on his friends' enterprise. Judging from the stash at Walnut Springs, I suspect Green knows and chooses to look the other way.

Will reads my mind. "I'll be glad to tell you whatever you want to know, but maybe you'd rather not know, just to keep things simple when it comes to the authorities, both Texian and Mexican. But most people in this town have next to nothing, and the goods we bring in, which ain't just tobacco, help 'em stay alive. They're starved for most everything here. Tradin' goods back and forth between American ports and this here outpost helps a mess of people."

I look him square in the eyes, noticing that his red, sun-bleached hair has grown long and makes him look rugged, more like a frontiersman than a storekeeper, despite his flour-sack shirt. For a moment, I acknowledge to myself what I fear—that Will, now Juan, is already someone other than the person who left Gonzales only six months ago. The thought startles and troubles me. *But Will's life cannot be your concern*, I tell myself sternly.

While we look at each other as if we have something to settle, Eugenio wanders into the back room and returns with a surprised look on his face. "Now *más, mucho más,*" he notes, in reference to what is obviously their growing business as Will steers us out of the back and into the front part of the store.

I think carefully about what to say, not only about the smuggled goods but also about his life here. But Will is two steps ahead. "Sarah, I have used my business contacts to gather some information for you. Something you've wondered about."

"About Faye?" I ask, suddenly animated by Will's remarks. I know he has been mulling over Faye's fate as long as I have.

"Your little friend, Sarah, has an interesting past. It seems she got bartered to Buffalo Belle because her Poppa lost a load of contraband goods promised to the fine, upstanding Luna establishment."

"And who is her Poppa?"

"The bowlegged man. Which explains why Bandy Legs gets into fights with his partner, the leatherstocking. Bandy Legs is mad as hell at his partner, who forced him to sell his daughter to the proprietors of Luna when he couldn't deliver the goods."

I am about to let loose a deluge of questions when the rusty hinges of the door squeak, and in walks Green. The big, floppy tie of his white broadcloth shirt is still tied neatly at his neck, though he carries his long coat over his arm, and his blue eyes are ringed with fatigue.

"Thought I'd find you in the store," Green says, looking at me with affection that Will cannot ignore. Then he turns to Will with leveled eyes, his tone neutral. "Got to hand it to you, Will. This is just about the best job in Béjar for an ol' Missouri trader like you."

Will nods. "Well, you know, I'm good at landing on my feet."

Green gives him a look. Then, carefully polite, he regains his footing. "Good to see you, and good of you to put us up for the night."

"Glad to have you, Green," Will says, shaking his hand. "What's new with our Mexican worthies?"

"Well, we've had a good day of talking. Not sure what we've solved. They understand that I want more protection from the Indians. And they approve of my opposition to slavery in the colony. Sarah, they've made a very hospitable proposal in response to your visit to Béjar. Tomorrow, the wife of El Jefe Músquiz will accompany you to what they call the *ojos de agua*, some limestone pools a few miles north. They say it's real pretty there. Maybe Will and Eugenio can escort the ladies over there in the wagon."

"Yup, happy to. Good idea," Will agrees. "I'd be proud to show off some of Béjar's natural beauty and attractions."

I wonder if Green's easy manner means his Mexican hosts have served more tequila than food. From his hollow-eyed expression, I know he is dead tired. And I don't particularly want Green to see Will's back room.

"My dear, you must be tired and hungry. Will has a pot of beans cooking. Would you like a bite to eat?"

"I would," Green acknowledges gratefully.

Will takes his cue. With a gracious sweep of his hand, he ushers all of us out.

As twilight softens into evening, the streets are transformed. The bright, scorching afternoon turns into a shadowy evening filled with the light of lanterns and candles. Down the street, a phalanx of horses and riders advances toward us, holding candles high. I am first alarmed and then charmed. It is a celebration, part of Tejano night-life in Béjar. The music of guitars drifts toward us, and the streets are aglow, transmuting the harsh realities of day into a magical world. Suddenly, we are swept along in a tide of song and romance.

"Lookee here," Will says, "a Tejano *con-vi-te*. In-vite to a fandango for the young lady in that house on Commerce Street over there." The procession turns down a narrow street, and Eugenio follows, quickly drifting into the gathering crowd while Green, Will, and I keep a little distance apart.

Ten horsemen strong, the party advances to the door of an adobe house. The *caballeros* are dressed in slit-leg trousers buttoned up smartly, their bridles and spurs gleaming in the candlelight. Dogs bark at the horses' heels. When the party reins in their horses in front of the little house, a young woman appears in the door. Three fiddlers on horseback play "*Cielito Lindo*" while the *señorita*, also with a candle in hand, smiles and bows. The serenade lasts only a minute, and then the party moves on to the next house to issue another invitation.

"Looks like we lost Eugenio. He's going to go get slicked up for the dance," Will observes.

"Where will it be?" I ask, growing ever more curious about this world we've so recently entered.

"Perhaps in the courtyard of the Governor's Palace. Or some cantina that's big enough."

I look at Green. "We haven't had a dance to go to in a while."

"Did you bring a dancing dress?"

"I want to go to a fandango. No one is going to be looking at *me*."

Green smiles, steals a glance at Will, and responds with a reply both gracious and calculating. "Sarah, you will not escape notice."

I understand Green is both complimenting and claiming me—while reminding me of my place as the empresario's wife—all at the same time.

Will looks at us both, his eyes opaque. Is he remembering what he learned in Missouri long ago? Not only had he lost out to the dashing Colonel DeWitt, but, as Green's deputy sheriff, he'd seen what forces the man could gather.

As we return to his house, Will informs us of fandango etiquette. "Those young Tejano swains are some of the high-class gents, going to a lot of trouble issuing invitations to the dance. The party would be proud to have the empresario and his wife there, I'm sure. But we do need to get added to the guest list."

"Happy to attend," Green remarks.

"El Jefe Músquiz could wangle you an invite, but I've got a young Tejano friend who will take care of it without bothering Musquiz. Owes me a favor anyway. You two wait here, and I'll just make sure we're welcome at the party."

Watching Will go, I imagine the paths he blazes in Béjar: friends at the highest levels with the men on the ayuntamiento—and the social inroads with señoras and señoritas that follow.

The fandango begins as darkness descends. We arrive shortly thereafter, the dance already in full swing. We have been invited not just into the courtyard but into the ballroom of the governor's mansion.

Perhaps because the honoree is part of an influential family. I barely have time to notice the elegant appointments of the room, with its wall sconces, beamed ceiling, and polished dance floor, before my attention is drawn to the dancers. Willowy young women in white skirts and plunging bodices sway lightly in the arms of men with bead-adorned jackets. They swoop and turn and tease to the intensely rhythmic beat. After a period of supple moves, the music stops, and the couples, still as statues, freeze in place, until fiddles and castanets take up the beat again amid snapping fingers and stamping feet.

"These are the *Isleños*," Will whispers. "Blue bloods. Came from the Canary Islands. Been here for a century. Now they are full-fledged Tejanos. Not the same ones who live in the huts they call jacales by the big ditch. They have their fandangos in the street. This bunch lives in big houses on the west side of the river in La Villita, with more than a peso or two to their well-known names."

As the dancers entreat and pursue, I notice a clutch of young women huddled with their parents near the musicians. One of them, especially elegant, who looks to be about Naomi's age, stands with an older sister perhaps, flourishing a fan and looking in our direction. At once, I see the girl is staring at Will. She smiles and looks shyly away, then coyly peeks at him from behind her fan.

Will's expression does not change. He neither acknowledges nor avoids the girl's gaze, yet I am sure he is aware of her presence. Then a distinguished-looking gentleman who looks to be her father comes toward us. "Welcome, *bienvenidos*," he says.

"*Señor Castellano, con mucho gusto*," Will responds. "*Gracias por invitarnos*. And, Señor, I'd like to acquaint you with my friend Empresario DeWitt and his wife, Sarah."

"*Encantado*," Señor Castellano replies, bowing deeply to me and reaching out to clasp Green's hand. The elegant, black-coated Tejano gentleman with wavy dark hair and trim mustache taps his foot to the music as the dancers whirl around the room, their lively steps executed in rapid triplet rhythms. During another lull in the music, he whispers something to Will, who smiles and shakes his head. "Too fancy for me," he says.

Señor Castellano again swoops his colorfully banded black felt hat below his waist, bowing to me before taking his leave. When the gentleman returns to his group, he whispers to the young girls and then continues to circulate among the guests.

As the hour grows later, the music becomes more insistent and the dancers more daring. Will takes Green into the courtyard to make more introductions, while I sit in the window well and admire the dancers and the dance. Despite Will's prediction, Eugenio does not appear. I conclude this fandango was not for cart drivers. I keep my eye on the sisters eyeing Will, especially the diminutive, fine-featured one who follows Will's every move as she dances.

Around the room, the Tejano men converse amiably, and the women talk behind their fans. I catch a few snatches of conversation about "*la rubia, la esposa del empresario.*" Not one of the gentlemen is bold enough to ask me to dance, but many dark eyes are cast in my direction, and heads nod politely as they pass close to me. I nod back, smiling broadly. One young man offers to bring me a drink of punch, which I accept.

When Will and Green return inside, Green escorts me onto the dance floor. The dance, clearly a nod to their Anglo guests, is a simple American waltz, set to the tune of Mexican fiddlers and violins and emblematic of what a hybrid blend these cultivated citizens are. I feel a part of the evening, if only as an onlooker. Then the fandango dancers return, with their hand clapping and castanets. Though I do not venture among the fandango dancers, I soak up a part of Coahuila y Tejas entirely new to me. An amalgam of Spanish, Mexican, and Tejano as distinctly refined as the Anglo-Tejano-Indian outpost of Gonzales is raw. Drinking it in, I feel abashed. Barely two years ago, I thought Missouri was the whole world.

Looking around, I see Will is dancing with the girl who was making eyes at him. This dance is a modified fandango with guitars and castanets in the background but fewer swooping, dipping moves. I try not to watch them as Green and I float around the floor. But I cannot help searching the dance floor for the outline of Will's back. Then they whirl around, and he looks directly at me. I smile and he smiles back. His red hair shines in the candlelight. Despite myself, I strain to keep him in view.

OJOS DE AGUA

La Señora Músquiz arrives midafternoon to accompany us to the pools. Will takes charge, echoing la señora's expression of the beauty of San Pedro Springs, the ojos de agua, the heart of Béjar, he says. While Green meets for the second day with the strongmen of the city, Eugenio, Will, Señora Músquiz, and I set off from the other side of the square. We follow Acequía Street and then Flores Street and Amaragura Street north in the wagon.

"One of the prettiest spots in the country, Señora DeWitt," Will says. "Where the San Antonio River starts way before it winds around the town and heads south."

Our hostess informs us that Spanish explorer Cabeza de Vaca even camped there some three hundred years ago. Just the swimming hole itself is worth seeing, she says.

"*Es posible nadar*, to take a dip," Will responds. And then aside to me: "Lotta people go in bare as a baby, though you're probably not going to go for that," he teases, watching for my reaction. The old Will.

With these glowing descriptions, I feel as if I am on a grand European tour. Beyond the town center, we follow the path of the viaduct along Acequía Street. On both sides of the water, women kneel by the bank, washing their clothes in pots of water heated over big fires. They boil the clothes in lye soap, turning them over again and again with big sticks, then fishing them out for a rinse in the stream. The *acequia*, stretching for several miles, waters the valley, gardens, and plots of corn and sugar cane as it meanders along. Farther along, as the road climbs into hillocks and descends into vales, we enter a forest of live oak, a cool relief from Béjar's dusty, sun-drenched world.

On the other side of the groves, the landscape is dramatic. Springwater burbles up through round basins, the ojos de agua in the limestone formation at the base of the surrounding hills. On the ledges above, tall cedars emit a clean, light scent. Down below, a noisy scene supplants the quiet of the woods. From the banks of the pools, men, women, and children dangle fishing poles. Scores of bathers jump from the ledges and splash in the clear waters. Most are clothed in their undergarments, though I can see in one of the far pools, as Will predicted, a few with no clothes at all.

Eugenio guides the oxen to a shaded spot, and we four walk down to a blue-green pool. Señora Musquiz makes a little circuit around the pool, while I sit on a limestone ledge enjoying the view. While she's taking her walk, Eugenio peels off shirt, belt, and worn *huaraches* to take a dip as Will does the same.

Will makes a few dives, which I follow intently. The sun gleams on his skin, hair, and shoulders freckled by the Texas sun. Then he bobs up and comes to sit by me on the ledge.

"Deepest pool is up there," Will says, motioning to a basin of rock in the side of the hill. "From here, it starts to get rockier, more hills and springs and caves a few miles out there." As the shadows deepen, we walk toward one of the deeper pools. Shadows flicker among the cedars. La Señora is almost out of sight, at the far edge of the pools, her back toward us. Up among the cedars, there are more picnickers. But at the rim of the biggest pool, there is no one else but us.

Will says, "Beautiful, huh? Another dive or two and we'll head back." He makes several dives and then comes up once with a fistful of squiggling things. "Crawfish," he says.

But he knows better than to offer me one as a snack. He dives down again and disappears in the blue-green water of the deepest pool. I lose track of where he is. Shading my eyes against the sinking sun, I pick him out some distance away. As he swims into closer view, his face changes. His eyes go wide, and he churns the water faster, heading toward me.

"Sarah, jump, jump! Jump into the pool!" he shouts.

"What? Why . . . ?" I laugh as he swims toward me. I hear the snap of twigs behind me too late. I whirl around just as Will scrambles onto the stone ledge and grabs the Indian's wrist. A tomahawk is poised overhead. It falls and clatters across the stone. Two more figures encircle us, forcing Will to his knees. Within seconds, he is overcome.

There is a blow to my head, and I am thrown over the Indian's shoulder as he races for the woods. Another Indian follows. Will grapples with a third. Then Will is lying on the rock.

COMANCHERÍA

I come to around daybreak. My head pounds. My throat is parched. My left eye, hot and swollen, throbs. I ache all over, but the physical misery is nothing compared to the fear in my heart. My body is hunched against the morning chill, my hands lashed to stakes in the ground. I squint at the onlookers circling me. My crystal beads have been pulled from my neck. The women examine them, divide them up, and chatter in singsong voices.

I am an object of fascination. A young Indian with a scar across his cheek cuts swatches from my hair, holding them up to the light. I freeze like a scared rabbit at the glint of cruelty in his eyes. I am where I have never been: among people who will abuse and discard me. Or worse. Torture me? Scalp me and leave me with the top of my head removed, writhing in the hot sun?

I close my eyes and pray. *I know this is my fault, God. Once again, I could not resist being with Will. I didn't intend to hurt anyone, least of all my children and Green. But you don't mete out punishment like this. I know that's not the kind of God you are. Please let me live, let me return to my family, and I'll never be so foolish again.* But I am uncertain God can help me. I know I have brought this on myself. I believe that God is love, but nothing in my life has prepared me for this. I try to pray again. *Show me the way if you can. I am utterly unable.* Tears roll down my cheeks. Thinking of the young Indian who hacked off locks of my hair this morning, I hold my face to the sun to dry the tears.

When I open my eyes again, the Indians have drifted away and left me undisturbed, part of the landscape. My hands are wet in the early morning dew, my lips crusted with blood. I can still taste where I bit my lip. My dress, stained with grass and dirt, hangs in limp tatters. I am confined in a little pit outlined with brambles, a kind of holding pen. I wonder how many have been kept here and how many have died.

Am I in a Comanche village? Since my scalp is still intact, do they intend to keep me as a captive? The Comanche, supreme in their control on the southern plains, trade kidnapped women and children for horses and goods. I've heard of women being traded and then choosing to stay with the Indians. Can I hope to be traded? Will a trade be better or worse than death?

I count fifteen teepees and see more in the distance. Smoke drifts out the tops where the poles come together. In a clearing, a tall frame holds a buffalo skin drying in the sun. On the ground beside it, another skin stretches between pegs in the ground. A woman kneels over it, scraping and smoothing. Women and children mill about.

Time passes, the hours long and short at the same time. I alternate between states of fitful sleep and jittery panic. I try to pray for calm. For a bit of quietude, so I can think. *Grant me, God*, I begin to pray, but the words stick in my throat. If I could calm myself, could I hatch a plan? But a plan seems delusional. I try to move my arms a bit to get some life back in them. Pain sears my shoulders and back, and my thirst is almost as relentless.

Judging from the light, I think it is midmorning. Then a white man, dressed like a frontiersman in buckskin, points at me as he paces back and forth. He's speaking to an Indian with long, flowing hair. They look me over, walking around gesturing. A few words of

Spanish pepper their conversation. I hear a certain phrase several times: "*parte del pago.*" It is about trading for some kind of payment in return. They are planning to trade me. Does that mean they're not going to kill me?

When the sun is high in the sky, an Indian woman brings me beef jerky and water, unties me enough to eat and drink, and then lashes my wrists to the stakes again and hurries away. It appears the tribe is getting ready to move camp. Women and girls tie skins on sled-like travois framed by poles and wrap their babies on little boards they will carry behind the horses.

I close my eyes and remember Will diving into the pool, his sunburnt shoulders, his smile as he surfaced with the squirming crawfish. Thinking of Green and how frantic he must be, I shiver, despite the rapidly warming day. After a while, out of sheer exhaustion, I will myself into a shaky calm. The past months seem entirely trivial compared with the hell I have entered.

My mind dredges up bits and pieces long forgotten. My adolescent romance with Will. Our first kisses in the field behind my house. The summer my beloved Aunt Ellen died, when I went off with Will every day to escape the gloom, my mother too upset to fret about me. Together, inseparable through the next year. Is that deep memory what led me here? Or is it my dutiful Presbyterian soul that blinded me to what I knew? I didn't want to come to Texas and could have said no.

I struggle to regain hope. The world was already upside down. Mixed with my fear is a strange feeling that once away from Missouri, I started to become someone else. On the way to Texas, I'd heard it said that many "left the Sabbath" at the Mississippi River. It makes more sense now. This world is too hard for that Sarah. That Sarah is gone.

But if this one lives? The answer comes to me immediately. I will never let anyone else, not even Green, determine my fate. I'll learn how to protect myself. Anger rises in me and flashes out at Green, at Will, at myself, at my weakness. If I escape alive, I will honor my instincts and my own resolve. Then I sink back into feeling the pain in my arms and the fear in my heart.

The sun, directly overhead, bears down onto the top of my head, down my neck and breasts. My skin burns. Coated with the grit of the plains, I squint into the bright light as moments turn into hours, noon into afternoon. A scorpion crawls onto my dress, up my arm, and back down again without stinging me. Children stare at me. I think again and again of my young ones, scalding thoughts that leave me gasping. What will they do without a mother? Their faces gaze up at me through my delirium, distraught and confused. Their mother vanished into thin air, never coming back from the trip that was to be only a few days. Who will care for them in this cruel country? Eveline was nearly inconsolable on her first day in Gonzales, and now she is facing a fate far worse! Sweet, gentle Naomi trying to care for the little ones when she's just a child herself. Eliza, separated from her family, alone, on her own. The boys, at their tender ages still babies, clinging to me like barnacles. Green facing the struggle of his life with nowhere to turn for comfort. Will lying on the ground beside the green pool. I can't bear to think him dead. My despair turns back into cold fear: no one will know how to find or rescue me.

At dusk, an Indian girl, about the age of Naomi, feeds me beef jerky again. Curiosity plays across her face as she stares at me. She watches while I chew. But in the serious performance of her task, she does not untie my hands as the woman did earlier. The girl lifts a gourd to my lips, spilling much of the water down my dress. Seeing her mistake, she unties me. I chew a little longer and drink again, lifting the gourd to my lips with my own hands. The use of them is a glorious relief. When it is time to lash my hands to the stakes again, I hold my arms rigidly behind me, hoping she will not notice. I pray that this will afford a tiny bit of slack when I relax my arms again. It works. Though she thinks she has tied them tightly, I have ever so slightly more room to move.

It is not much. I start to work my wrists, press against the leather thongs, trying to stretch them. After maybe an hour, there's more slack, and the right thong is a bit looser. The leather cuts into my skin. I stop, continue, stop, continue. I wriggle, pull and press, press and pull.

New waves of fear rise in me. I pray for my dress, still damp from the spilled water, to dry quickly. Wet, it is easy to see through the thin, white cotton batiste.

In what seems only a few minutes, I hear him—the one who is not an Indian, probably a trader, maybe part Indian. He stands over me, looking down at me. He makes a guttural sound that turns his mouth with its yellow, pointed teeth into a leer. He moves closer. He circles, laughing, looking at my breasts. Then he gets in my face, pinches my nipples, cups his hands over my breasts, and squeezes. I close my eyes and he slaps me. I snap them open, fearing my revulsion will turn him meaner.

"¿*Tiene miedo*, huh?" he snarls. "*La rubia* doesn't want me?" He whines the words out with a lecherous laugh.

I instantly decide not to betray that I speak Spanish. The more they underestimate me, the better chance I have. He wants to frighten me. I try to show no emotion. His touch is nauseating. No one has ever touched me that way. Waves of rage and terror alternate in me.

In a little while, the same Indian who'd been with the trader earlier returns and beckons him to follow. "*Regreso, rubia*," the vile one threatens over his shoulder. I take his threat seriously. I'm sure he *will* return, as promised. My body shakes. I try to stuff the fear down, but my body knows better.

I start to work in earnest. What can I do with only one hand free? But it's better than nothing. It takes another long while, then the thong loosens enough for me to slip my hand through. I must not betray that my hand is free.

Have I seen a weapon on him? A knife at his waist? But what if I reach for it and miss? I can't miss.

Evening transforms the pit into shadows and sounds. I can't sleep for fear the monster will return to perform all the horrors I imagine—him clutching, clawing at me. Is he lurking just beyond me in the night? Fear drifts above me, a black buzzard cruising for carrion.

As the Indian camp settles in to sleep, I dare hope the fiend has passed out in the drunken revels at the center of the camp. I am too far away to make out his stealthy form in the dark. But I think he's come close once or twice.

His ugly laugh shatters the darkness. Squatting on the ground next to me, he grabs at me, reaches under my skirt. A scream erupts from me. He slaps me again, harder this time. His drunken breath spills over me. I clamp down the retching response in my throat and hold my breath in gasps. I can't breathe. It is so dark; I can barely see the creature pawing me. But the drink has diminished his strength. As he starts to tear at my clothes, I feel the knife at his waist.

It is too soon. I must wait. He pushes me onto my back and rips at my dress, then at the buttons of my chemise underneath. Now I feel his hard member poking at me as he yanks at his pants. He is drooling and biting at my breasts. It is still too soon. I struggle for air and count.

He writhes against me as he pushes up my skirt and tears off my stockings. Despite his stupor, his lust is strong. His bare flesh is against mine as he pokes and pushes into me. As he moans and pants, I focus on exactly where the knife is. I can feel the buttons of his pants and a scabbard holding the knife. I bring my free arm around slowly and feel for the knife. He is grunting and heaving. I close my hand over the handle of the knife and slip it out of the scabbard. His drunken state makes it difficult for him to maintain his arousal. He pushes and pulls at me.

His face is buried in my neck, sucking like an eel. He bites and slobbers as I imagine exactly where his jugular meets his jaw. Writhing again, he starts to have more success, his arousal compelling him. He squeals like a rutting hog. I take in his rancid, sour breath, his humping body, revulsion mixing with loathing. Strength flows into me.

I plunge the knife into his neck from the side, pushing hard at where, I pray, his jugular might be. His warm blood pours across my face and into my eyes.

Blood spurts, floods over my shoulders, pools into the ground as he stares at me in horror and disbelief. I clutch the knife tightly as he starts to jerk, his blood covering him and me. It seems like a bucket of blood. It seeps into my clothes, into the earth. He arches and goes limp against me with a gurgling, choking sound.

I am drenched in sticky, slippery blood. Silent as the hour, I free my left hand with the knife. I look into his glassy eyes, wriggle out from under him, and leave him prostrate, face down in the dirt.

Wet from head to waist, I wipe salty blood from my mouth. Stashing the knife in my skirt, I roll across the bramble pit to its far edge.

I crawl in the dark, away from the dying embers of the campfire. Dirt and pebbles cling to my wet clothes. Thankful there is no moon to light up my white dress in the night, I avoid the corral, hoping the horses will not betray me. I long with all my heart for Pal to carry me far away.

Running and walking, I judge it to be around midnight. I can't stop trembling, my heart racing. But I can't slow my pace. His blood sloshes in my shoes. I stumble onto a rocky path. I'm in a rocky creek bed. My heart skips a beat; I dare not believe I have escaped. I find the North Star and rejoice. I must be heading west, back in the direction of Béjar, I believe, treasuring, repeating to myself Will's statement that Comanchería lies northeast of Béjar.

They will come after me at dawn, perhaps five hours from now. The creek bed might take me far enough by then. The rocks will conceal my tracks, except where blood sloshes from my shoes.

I try to think what Will would do. A cave. He said there were caves in Comanchería. If I can find a cave, I can hide during the day and keep going at night.

I walk and run on. I hear myself crying sometimes, but mostly moaning and running until gentle fingers of dawn begin to touch my back, confirming my hopes. I am walking west. From my rough sense of the locations of Gonzales and Béjar, I think I am north of Béjar, heading northwest. And I am sure that is where caves dot the limestone hills.

As it grows light, I catch the glint of water trickling in tiny rills in the creek bed. Up ahead, the creek snakes around. Fearing that I might turn back in the direction of the Indian encampment, I stop. Cupping my hands among the rocks, I press my face into the water and drink, dip my skirt in the creek bed, wipe my blood-encrusted face and arms and neck. I try to wash my hair, stiff with dried blood. But there is not enough water. I must go on. Leaving the creek, I follow a little rise as it climbs to something green.

A few hundred yards north, a willow grove extends along the creek. Above, the limestone rises higher in gently sloping ledges and scrubby hills. In a few basins, little pools of water gleam—from springs or maybe from rainwater. Ojos de agua like San Pedro Springs. Circling around to the other side of the hillock, I find in the porous limestone rock a slit, the hole I'd prayed for. I thank God, squeeze through the tiny door in the earth, lower myself onto a small ledge inside, and weep.

As the sun creeps into the cave, I hear the faint sound of a horse's hooves hitting the rocky ground at a regular pace, coming from far away. Daring to peer out, I spot a lone rider far below. I can't stay in full view, so I slip back through the rock and wait, counting the seconds until I dare look out again. This time, flashes of what looks like a red roan appear, then disappear again among the rocks. I hold my breath, pray, and reenter the dark. I count to five hundred before I look again. I still can't make out the rider. Just the red horse partially hidden in a gully. Now I understand why he is staying in the uneven terrain of the rocky ravine. He's hard to see from up here and harder still to get a bead on. He wants to stay out of sight, which means the Comanche are already up here.

An hour or more passes. Then I hear what sounds like hooves striking the limestone outcroppings among the scrub and rock ledges. They are not far away. Looking for me. I am afraid to breathe.

The sounds come closer. Then a figure is in front of me, pulling me out of the cave. There are two of them. I kick, scream, and hope that the rider down there somewhere will hear me and see us up here. A large fist muffles my screams.

The Indians drag me down several ledges. I flail and kick. One slams me against the rock. I feel a gash open on my head, blood seeping into my hair. They pin me down beside a pool of water in the rocks. While one holds me face down against the stone, his knees in my back, the other kneels to drink.

A shot rings out. The Comanche holding me down explodes into the other, tumbling past him into the pool. The other one quickly flattens himself on top of me. Then a hand jerks him away, pushes him onto the rocks, and shoots him point-blank in the chest. He falls alongside the other, his head dropping back into the water. Sitting up, I stare at the bodies almost on top of each other. One headfirst in the pool, the other lolled back alongside him.

I look on in disbelief as Will lays down his shotgun and puts his arms around me. He is quickly covered in the blood dripping from my head. He stares at me as if he's never seen me before, helping me to my feet. My head is bleeding profusely where it hit the stone. I fix him in my gaze as he takes in the welts across my throat and chest, the cut in my head, my dress, red and stiff. With a kerchief, he wipes at my face and head.

"Got to get outta here, Sarah. Can't be found with our friends on the rocks."

Wordless, I nod and slowly find my voice. "It's you. It's you. Will, it's you. Get out. Yes, get out of here." I glance at the two bodies in the red water of the pool and turn back to Will.

Climbing down the rocks behind him, I fall and slide, clutching at him as I careen from rock to rock. Farther down, Ruby waits.

He helps me onto Ruby and climbs into the saddle. Wrapping a saddle blanket around me despite the heat of the day, he grips me around the waist, sitting me firmly in the saddle in front of him, and spurs Ruby into her full, long-legged stride.

"Now, don't worry, Sarah. I know just where we are. Going in a line parallel to the San Marcos River. Bearing southwest a little until we have to camp for the night."

Among all the things I am worried about, now that I'm with Will, our location is not one of them. The gash on my head has stopped bleeding. I touch my head and feel a thin crust forming. The idea that I am on Ruby with Will fills me with wonder, a welter of emotions, and gratitude for this deliverance. I am alive. I will see my children.

"What I can't get into my head, Sarah, is how you got away from them," Will mutters.

"I'll tell you when I can stand to think about it." I wonder at the same time how he found me. Has it been only two days? Did he know about the Comanche encampment? But how did he find me up in the limestone hills?

We ride in silence. I lean back against him, knowing that he knows exactly what to do. He has no doubt traced out the northern boundary of DeWitt colony on his maps more than once, and now we are heading back toward it—fleeing Comanchería.

A hot breeze swipes at us as we gallop among the low, rolling limestone hills. Ruby descends several hundred feet through the cactus and into cedar and scrubby jack-oak. We ride into the glare of the sun. By late afternoon the heat leaves us dry and desperate for water, spitting cotton in dusty mouths. The oppressive humidity of June drains us of whatever energy has not been wrung from us. Deer and rabbits appear, taunting us as we dream of supper and shelter for the night.

Now I see where we are going. The entrance to a large cave appears ahead. I hope I'm not hallucinating.

"Long as we ain't bargin' in on a grizzly, we'll be fine," Will tells me as darkness closes in around us. He dismounts and leads Ruby and me farther into the dark cave. "Our luck is holding," he says, seeing nothing shining back at us. Beyond the first boulder lies a stash of tobacco leaves.

Will pulls the sack closer to the front of the cave and begins spreading out the tobacco leaves like a quilt. He looks at me and touches my hair, still stiff and gummy. He shakes his head, unable to address the moment in words. I must resemble a harpy from hell, I think absently. He smiles at me.

"Sarah, this may be the first picnic you've had on tobacco leaves, but these here big ol' leaves are one of the most useful plants the good Lord ever invented."

He gathers kindling and soon has a fire going inside the cave. I sit on the leaves, clutching at my torn clothes. Angry cuts and scratches crosshatch my face, arms, and breasts; my head feels like it will split open. My hair covers my shoulders and neck like a shawl, but still, I can't keep from grabbing at my torn dress. The events of the last hours begin to rise again in my thoughts.

Will offers me the last bit of water from his canteen. I look at him for a moment.

"Thank God you found me. When I saw you on the rock above the ojos, I thought you were dead." It is still hard to believe that I am in a cave facing him.

"Nah. Just knocked cold. Eugenio brought me around pretty quick. Then I got on Ruby and came after you. Knew where the Comanche camp was. Problem was they were moving it by the time I caught up to them. And you weren't there. Got to hand it to you, Sarah. Escaping from Comanche is a trick. How in the Sam Hill did you do it?" he asks, almost as astonished as I am.

I clutch the saddle blanket. "I killed a man, my second. I'm not sorry."

"Hmm. But what I want to know is how did you get away from the Comanche camp?"

"A Tejano trader attacked me. I got a hand free enough to grab his knife and slit his throat."

"Where were the Indians and the other traders?"

"Drunk by the fire. The trader was drunk too. That's why I could do it."

"But how did you find your way in the dark?"

"Followed a dry creek bed with stones in it. Until dawn. And then found one of those caves you told me about."

Will shakes his head. "Sarah, you always know what you're doing."

"Did what I had to. I would have died anyway if you hadn't found me. It's one more reason why you'll never be out of my life," I blurt, despite myself.

He takes a long, deep breath, starts to say something, and then doesn't. He sits silently for a moment. "Nor you mine," he says almost ruefully, without looking at me, then answers my question. "Finding the Comanche camp was no trick. I knew where their camp was. I'd planned to steal you away from the camp. Except you weren't there."

"How did you know that?"

"I got close to the camp early afternoon of the day after they nabbed you by the pools. I figured you were there, though I couldn't get close enough in daylight. Once it was dark, I was planning to rescue you. Had a plan to get you out of there while they slept. But then I saw they were moving the camp, some already gone. The vermin trader who was hanging around there was dead in the bramble pit. And you were nowhere to be found."

His words, like honey, continue to flow over me as I lie back on the dark leaves.

THE CAVE

Awakening, I float in the darkness of the cave, my emotions as tangled as the bird's nest of my hair. Opening my eyes, I see Will, his back to me, tending the fire. The flame illuminates the entrance of the cave, beyond which is blackness. Closing my eyes again, I see my torn dress, my missing stockings and underclothes, the knife plunged into my assailant's throat.

I feel small, filling only a corner of the bed of tobacco leaves. Some time later, I hear Will's voice. He is talking to Ruby just inside the cave. Listening to that fine voice, I remember my long-ago plan for avoiding heartache. It amounted to "Never put all your eggs in one basket." My solution when my feelings for Will overwhelmed me. When Will went away, I tried to empty myself of grief like pouring rain out of a barrel. Was it then I promised myself never to care so deeply again? A year later, I married Green.

Lightness and heaviness alternate in me, raking through me for unknown stretches of time. In the lightness, my soul expands with joy. I am safe, out of the Indian camp, with Will. I am alive to mother

my children and return to Green. Then the heavy dread of returning to peril and hardship returns. In the heaviness, I dream of the
panther on the limb of the tree. The tawny coat, the paws stretching
toward her mate. Her screams haunt me.

At dawn, Will leaves the cave. He doesn't go on Ruby. He'll come
back . . . take care of me. But will the Indians find me before he
returns? This time I won't be so lucky. Lying still with my eyes closed,
I listen, terrified, until I hear his footsteps.

"Sarah, lookee here what I found. You know what kind of fibers
these old daggers have." His calm voice makes everything seem
normal. He is carrying a thick, curled, dagger-like agave leaf. Sitting
up, I watch as he carefully detaches the spine at the top. As skillfully
as a seamstress threading a needle, he strips the dagger down to a
few long threads.

"Now, move over here," he says, getting me to my feet and leading
me to a spot near the entrance of the cave where he's spread out his
saddle blanket. "Sit here in the light so I can whip this dress back
into shape."

He is trying to save me the humiliation of returning to Gonzales as
a violated woman. After the last few days, a man sewing up my dress
doesn't even feel strange. I stare at the floor of the cave strewn with
arrowheads and flint rocks.

Using the agave spine as a needle, he ties the strong fibers to it
and begins to pull them back and forth through the front of my dress,
closing up the rips in the cloth. I watch with a measure of content-
ment. The slow motion and rhythm of his hands going back and forth
across the front of my dress soothes me into a transitory calm. He
is putting me back together. In the warmth of the cave, I am a little
animal being groomed. I can think of nothing to say that would make
sense as he concentrates on his job.

But he is never silent for long. "You notice the soil in this cave,
Sarah? Pale as weak tea. And home to all sorts of animalcules. So be
careful. There's sand flies and ants and pale-colored scorpions, hard
to see in the soil. If a scorpion stings you, your tongue will get so thick
you can't talk. So don't get off this here blanket or those bags. You'll
see 'em better that way."

"How did the bags of tobacco leaves get here, Will?" I ask blankly as if that were the most pressing question I might ask of him.

"Like I told you before, in our little business venture, Señor Eugenio and I load tobacco into good places for safekeeping. We have a bunch of stashes and sell a little at a time to anyone whose supply of chewing or smoking tobacco is running low."

I think of our conversation on the sandbar by the river months ago when he explained his smuggling enterprise. The tobacco leaves bring me back to the world, to the stash at Walnut Springs, to the back room in the Alamo store. And then to my foolish speech to him about our "friendship" only a few days ago. My words ring in my ears. How had I managed to deceive myself so utterly? I feel ashamed and yet strangely calm at the same time. *Admit it all. At least to yourself. Maybe it will help to stand it.*

When he has closed up the tear in my dress, Will draws back and looks at his handiwork. With one finger, he outlines the shape of the stitches he has made on my dress.

My heart beats wildly.

"Damn good job. Too bad I'm a man. Coulda been a fine seamstress and caused a lot less trouble besides."

I look up at him, unable to voice my pain.

As if reading my thoughts, he takes a deep breath and jumps in. "Sarah, I feel lower than a snake's belly for having gotten you into this situation. Once we were up there by the pools, compliments of Green and La Señora, I should have left well enough alone. Never shoulda taken you up to that isolated pool and put you in danger. Shoulda been watching over you. Keeping you safe with the others. I wanted to get you alone, and that's why I did it. Just like in the tunnel on New Year's Day. Can't deny it."

I watch him gratefully. As always, he addresses my worries, though I speak not one word to acknowledge the tumult inside me.

"I don't know if you know this or not. And if I hadn't been so reckless already, I sure wouldn't put words to all this. But this here's the truth. You know I've loved you since we were kids. Figured I'd marry you if you'd have me. But I thought I wasn't good enough for a girl like you without going off to make some money, so you'd feel like you'd be getting a good deal. Couldn't say all that, though, when we were so young. Didn't feel I could ask you to wait for me when I had so little to offer. So, I just left. You didn't have any sweethearts but me at the time, and knowing your serious nature, I took my chances. When I came back and found you married to Green, it nearly killed me. All I could do was try to make the best of it. So, I found Harriet, as good a woman as St. Louis had to offer, and I tried to be like Green, following him as sheriff in Ralls County. So that kinda worked for a good long while, until Harriet refused to come out here with me. And then, wouldn't you know it, what I buried came floating back up to the surface, just like treasure washing up on the riverbank."

Will's words break the dam in me. It is a dam held for decades. Tears roll down my face. I look away and then back up at him. "You aren't the only one who buried it all, Will."

"Now listen to me, Sarah. I know what you've been through. I thought I'd fixed things when I left Gonzales. But I jumped right back in when the opportunity presented itself. Please forgive me."

I shake with sobs. I will not repeat the past. I am married to Green. I will never again be the Sarah who said goodbye to Will at seventeen. And I have just been raped by a man so vile I don't regret for a moment that I killed him.

But I will allow myself this moment. I will let Will comfort me, hold me as I weep. I will face the truth that part of my heart will always be with him.

I collapse into his arms. For this moment, I don't have to justify anything. I weep and slip into a tortured silence, barely awake but hardly asleep. Then I draw away from him and close my eyes to sleep by the fire. My fears and thoughts are too chaotic for words, my tears still streaming.

When I awaken, Will is roasting a rabbit. I sit up and stare at the fire, the horrors of the past few days coming back. My cold terror when the Indians pulled me out of the cave.

Will glances at me as he turns the rabbit on the fire.

"We need to get some food in you, Sarah, and be on our way. We're still too close to Comanchería."

We eat quickly, urgently, knowing we must be on our way. As the sun's rays reach into the cave, and despite the warmth of June beaming down, the light of morning is cold.

Will saddles Ruby. Then he says, "Sarah, I don't think we're going to meet up with the search party Green has no doubt formed. But if we do, there's nothing to explain. We'll be making our way back to Gonzales. No one needs to know what happened with the trader. I'm thinking the Comanche moving camp will probably throw the search party off, and Green and the rest will head back to Gonzales. It's too dangerous for them to go much farther into Comanchería. Still close to the edge of it now, and we got to get out, quick as we can."

I nod. "Everything will be just as it happened, except the parts we choose not to tell."

"You know what you're doing, Sarah."

"No, not always. Tomorrow will be"—I press my lips together—"hard."

"This time I'll be sure you are safe. Back in Gonzales. Then I'll head back to Béjar."

I bite my lip. I'm back, not just to where I was half a year ago but to where I was half a lifetime ago. But this time I must make the final turn away from him. Looking down, I close my eyes. The hard light of morning.

He swings into the saddle and pulls me up behind him. The light intensifies the pain. I hold onto Will, leaning into his back as we gallop southeast toward Gonzales.

RETURN

I put my best efforts into breathing life back into the woman who'd left Gonzales days earlier. Ahead, I recognize the familiar riverbank of the Guadalupe. But now, after a day of hard riding, a numbness seizes me, and I find it difficult to focus on anything in particular. I look off into the distance, what my mother calls woolgathering. I gather unformed, woolly thoughts, shapes, trying not to settle on what I know I have to do.

I see Naomi first, sitting on the porch, watching the empty road. As we approach, Naomi is transfixed, as if she can't believe her eyes. Her cat leaps from her lap and runs under the cabin.

She races down the hill toward us.

Naomi reaches us about a hundred yards from the house. She grabs at my skirt and, as tears stream down her face, she says over and over. "We were so scared, Momma, so scared."

I pat and smooth her hair. Tears well in my eyes, yet I can hardly bring myself to speak a word. I grasp her hand, give her a vacant stare, a wan smile.

"Will, how did you find her? How did you get her back?" Naomi demands, laughing and crying at the same time.

"Well, Naomi, it wasn't the easiest thing I've ever done," he says, without his usual smile.

Naomi walks up to Ruby, reaches up to the bridle, and hangs on. "Are you all right? Did you have to fight Indians?"

"I'm sure your mother will tell you the whole story," Will says. "But can you tell me, is the search party back?"

"They haven't made it in yet. We were so worried when they didn't come back last night."

"Well, the Comanche moved camp," Will says. "So, your Poppa and the men are probably having a hard time figuring whether to follow them or how far. They'll be back in before night."

I try to pull myself into the moment, imagining that Antoñia and Naomi will feed me broths, cover me with quilts, and organize the household. I cannot remember a time when I was helpless, except for a day or two when the children were born. My mother and aunts did all the caretaking. I will be glad for Antoñia and Naomi to take charge.

A shout, clear as a bell in the quiet of the late afternoon, interrupts my thoughts. The boys, somewhere behind the house. Naomi tries to help me down. Maybe I won't get down, won't return to my old life.

But Naomi, in a sudden fit of maternal instinct, simply wraps her arms around me and pulls me off the horse. Like a rag doll, I slide to the ground. Will holds me up, his arm around my waist. Suddenly Antoñia is there. I hug her close, let her gather me up, and lead me, as if she can keep all my parts together, toward a bench near the front door. She carefully arranges me as Naomi runs to bring the boys from the back.

I watch as Will tethers Ruby to a tree. I pray for courage. Knowing he mustn't, I wish Will would come to me and help me through it. He does meet my eyes, and then with a worried, distracted air, untethers Ruby, shakes his head, and starts toward the barn to water her.

The children run onto the porch. They stare at me as if I were a mirage and then fall upon me, kissing and hugging me from all directions. Will returns. Standing back to let them reclaim me, he gives the children plenty of time with me. C. C. is the first to register something is wrong. I see it in his eyes. His mother is too quiet, different from when he last saw her. Though I hug him back and tears spill from my eyes, I know he understands I am gripped by something he has never seen in me.

He looks to Naomi—and then draws back as if afraid to find out. I hear the little wheels turning. *Something is strange about Momma. Is it better not to say anything?* He watches as Naomi and Will get me into bed while Antoñia goes to fetch Eveline and Molly.

They come quickly, the questions in Molly's face writ large. She stares at the strange way my dress, stiff with dried blood, has been stitched together and notices the long fibrous threads and the stained chemise underneath. But I can't find words for anything. Molly asks Will: "Where did you find her? What happened? Is she all right?"

Ignoring her first question, he says, "She is very tired and needs to sleep. She's going to be all right. Just give her a little time." Then he relents and answers more fully. "She was snatched by the Comanche in Béjar," he says, shaking his head as he seems to realize that they know at least that.

Molly frowns, hesitates, then asks no more questions.

"She's downright peaked," she says half to Will, half to herself, touching the back of her hand to my forehead and then her own. She diagnoses me as feverish and prescribes bed rest.

When they try to get me into a nightgown, Will leaves the room and heads toward the barn. "No," I say, though I know my tattered dress hangs off me in stiff, blood-stained strips.

They try several times to remove the dress, and then Molly settles it without more ado. "You must sleep, Sarah."

"Yes," I nod, grateful to be given permission to withdraw. "Sleep," I say, with what seems a tremendous effort.

I hear Naomi and Eveline trying to help Molly and Antoñia prepare a broth and tea. I hear C. C. take Clinton outside to an armadillo hole they watch. But soon, they are back. With my eyes closed, I feel C. C. sitting by me, staring, touching my hair still tangled with twigs, tiny leaves, and burrs. I let him pick the stuff out of my matted hair and remain next to me, holding my hand for a long while before he goes back outside.

I open my eyes and close them, wondering what will come next. Molly is stationed by the door when Green and the search party ride in toward sundown. Green charges through the door with the breathless air of someone about to both give and receive terrible news. Then he sees me. He squats beside me, grasps my hand, and kisses it. I give him a glassy smile.

Naomi speaks first. "She and Will got back a few hours ago, Poppa."

"She's very tired, Green," Molly says. "We haven't learned much about what happened." And then, to warn him. "She seems sort of dazed."

Then I hear footsteps as Will comes back from the barn. His clothes are covered with dirt, and several days of red stubble bloom on his weathered face. They all stare at Will in silence.

Will looks straight at Green. "She's going to be all right. Comanche grabbed her at the ojos, by the pools. I found their camp. Got her back."

"The camp had moved," Green said, as if he didn't believe him.

"Yes, but not too far. Found them," Will said, explaining nothing.

"You're a sight to behold," Green says in a tone cooler than I'd expected. Where was the heat, the anger? And then it flashed out.

"What the hell! What did you mean leaving, going after Sarah without me?" He stops himself with the children all around. "I'm grateful you brought her back alive." Then he jerks his head toward the road.

Will looks at him as if judging whether to follow his command. Instead, he walks over to Molly and says to her. "She got some pretty rough treatment. But she's strong. Be fine in a few days."

I watch Green start back toward Will. Will's words, implying intimate knowledge that Green does not possess, drive Green beyond his momentary calm. He strides across the floor and grabs Will by the collar. Catching Will by surprise, Green drags him out of the bedroom to the porch, turns him around, and punches him in the face as hard as he can.

"You had no right," Green says, glaring at him.

I watch through the window. I must take hold, reenter the world.

Will rubs his jaw, hitches up on one elbow, starts to say something, then lets it go.

Finally, I manage it. I stumble across the room, out to the front door. "Rights be damned, Green," I shout at him. "No use laying blame. I'm alive, and I wouldn't be without Will. That's an end to it. Life goes on."

I watch as Will picks himself up and heads toward Ruby at the barn. Green goes in the opposite direction around the side of the house. With Molly and the children staring at me, I lie down, vowing to slam the door on the past. A sinner atoning for her sins, I repeat to myself: *I will accept my life here. I will help Green fulfill his contract.*

I thank God for letting me live, come back to my husband and my children. I ask God for forgiveness. But I will not shoulder all the blame. "We've all played our parts," I mumble like a madwoman, too low for Molly and the children to hear, much less understand.

PART II
VALLEY OF THE GUADALUPE

Coahuila y Tejas, DeWitt Colony
1829-1831

They came in twos, fours, scores, in greater and greater numbers, laying claim first to land on the rivers. Along the Guadalupe and the San Marcos and the Lavaca. Farms and ranches like strings of pearls along the streams, amid the rivers, on the creeks. Bits of land that came so cheaply and yet so dearly. Headrights, acreage to call their own—delivered with a deed and a handshake by the empresario—when they'd never owned anything. The dream, the lure of land washed over them, as Green knew it would. With its lush bottomland and winter grass and pecan trees in profusion along the blue river, the valley cast a powerful spell.

I doubted that dream from the beginning, never trusting it, resisting the luster of those pearls. Green believed it every step of the way, the twists and turns of destiny as natural to him as the course of the Guadalupe itself. Mesmerized, he hardly saw the obstacles.

In the end, we both were wrong. His vision turning and turning again, spinning, like the roulette wheel in New Orleans, in a world more deadly and more profound than either of us could know.

VISITOR

The sounds of saws, hammers, and axes ring out in the crisp February air. Mr. Lockhart's energetic team strikes easy rhythms as a new land office rises east of the house. In front, Green watches and waits, pacing back and forth.

"They will be needing guidance out there if they are to finish this week," I call to him from the porch. "How to partition it. You do want two rooms, don't you? Space for a table and chair on one side, a cabinet to hold records on the other side. There is no room in the house. And what—"

"Sarah," Green cuts me off, "I will get it done. I will talk to them. But I should be up the river today, not here. Yes, we've made progress, and we must keep at it. I need a second tally of colonists. Mr. Lockhart left a pile of papers for us to sort—to make some sense of the information he is collecting on the colony. The land office is the logical place to keep records to send to Músquiz, but we'll have to keep them in the house for now."

He is irritable, ready to pounce, still pacing, looking into the middle distance. Seeing his mood and knowing that what he really fears is too few people in that next tally, I pull back from my protestations.

"Yes, I'll manage until you have a better place to store and access the records."

He stops by the porch steps and pulls himself up to his full height, his expression still pinched and worried. The silver cap of his whiskey flask protrudes from the inside pocket of his coat. To steel his nerves, he's told me more than once.

"You are right," he says. "I will talk to the men and then head upriver to check on the sawmill. It should be operating in a matter of weeks." He is trying to mirror my practicality, to reassure me that all is in order.

When Green rides away, the girls and I spread the papers and notes from Mr. Lockhart across quilts spread on the porch floor. Several dozen new families have arrived since January. We spend the morning trying to make sense of dim scrawls on little slips of paper, sometimes x's in a line or a row of single 1's lined up next to the words *dunkee* or *hawgs* or *beeves*. The human figures are no easier than the livestock. Children's names are sometimes unreadable, and most notes have no tallies for the number in the family.

"Momma, look," Naomi says, showing me one piece of crabbed writing. "Baby Jake ded of feaver" with a line drawn through the infant's name.

I look at the paper, realizing I didn't know that this young family, in the colony for some months, had lost a child. The note, written by a grieving mother unwilling to let her babe's short life and death go unacknowledged, tears at my heart.

The first census, completed in mid-1828, only months after we arrived in Gonzales, named 9 families with children, 27 single men (present without wives), 35 able-bodied workers, and 7 slaves, a total of 72 individuals, as well as 58 horses, 372 head of cattle, 12 donkeys, and 276 hogs. Incomplete and inaccurate as I know this early 1829 tally must be, the girls and I manage to get all the information in neat columns on one sheet of paper. It's now ready for Green to send to Chief Músquiz in Béjar. But the numbers are discouraging:

25 families, a total of 115 individuals. We're still 75 families short of that 100-family milestone that will release the first reward of thousands of leagues of land.

After a morning of compiling and recording this disappointing tally, raindrops begin to pepper the front path. Storm clouds scud across a darkening sky; thunder rumbles in the distance. Smelling rain, I carefully fold the paper into my pocket while the girls gather the scraps spread across the quilts. They duck inside as the land office carpenters abandon their work for the day, and I linger on the porch to watch the rainstorm.

Inevitably, my mind goes back to my abduction by the Comanche. It's been the better part of a year since Will brought me home last summer. But still, the grisly details come back to me. Details I have shared with no one. Especially not Green, who abides by our tacit agreement that it is a closed matter. He accepted my words shouted out the front door when I returned: "I'm alive; wouldn't be without Will. That's an end to it." I cannot blame him for not wanting to know more, and I cannot bring myself to tell him more.

Sitting on the front porch, I thank God that after nearly three years in Coahuila y Tejas, my family is healthy, and I've survived the worst experience of my life. Green's sunny view of the future still haunts me, especially in light of the alarmingly low numbers in this tally of families applying for headrights in the colony. I know my darker assessments would never have changed Green's convictions back in Missouri, and they are little consolation to me now; I must remain the person Green needs at his side as he somehow completes this daunting task. I must accept that life is a struggle and that the first two decades of my life were just blessed with good luck. Watching the rain, I let a few of the hard truths crowding in on me overflow into a letter to Eliza and my mother.

Gonzales, March 1829
My dearest Eliza and Liza Q,

I have learned so much in the last year that I feel, with Eliza's approaching journey, I must put it all in some perspective for you. It is a very mixed picture. And as you plan to journey here early in the next year, Eliza, I should give you some idea of what to expect. I certainly did not have such a clear view when we first came down the Mississippi and across the Gulf to Gonzales. I'm getting the lay of the land—by that, I mean I'm beginning to understand what is happening not only in DeWitt's colony but beyond as well.

Immigration to Texas is not lagging, at least in Austin's colonies. (He has grants for more than one.) His is a thriving enterprise, with many colonists coming in almost daily. Population in his colonies has soared into the thousands. Then, of course, Béjar, to the west, is the oldest and largest city in the Texas part of Mexico, though it looks more like a country village by Missouri standards. It is quite a different country there; its Tejano fandango dancers and adobe homes are a world apart from us Anglos of Gonzales, only some seventy miles to the east. The Mexicans of the capital and states of the interior think Béjar a backwater, I am told, but it is nevertheless a place of some two thousand people with a hundred-year history.

With this view of what lies to the east and west of us, Texas is coming into focus for me. Listening to the talk among the men and helping to get out the tally of settlers in our colony, I've begun to understand. The new towns of San Felipe and Nacogdoches and Brazoria to the east in Austin's colonies are growing faster than a prairie fire. While, I'm sorry to say, Gonzales is the laggard.

Our little village is a crossroads between the Tejano settlements to the west and south and the Anglo towns, where so many from the US are arriving daily. Despite its sylvan setting on the Guadalupe and the lush bottomland filled with bountiful game and crops of fleshy pecans and walnuts now falling from the trees, Gonzales is not attracting the droves of people Green is banking on. The Anglo towns in the Austin colony, with populations in the thousands, fill up like a rain bucket in a downpour, while the next Gonzales census this year will likely come to fewer than half the hundred families needed.

(The secret to Austin's success is likely his location. After a long overland journey, settlers come to Austin's well-run colony and travel no farther. And they bring their slaves. Which we do not encourage here.) Still, the numbers in the DeWitt colony have grown considerably since we arrived. At least we have more than a hundred settlers—enough to elect a town council and to require a Mexican commissioner to sign land titles. Yet many fewer than one hundred families must multiply into four hundred (!) in just two years, by 1831, according to the rules of the contract. We are hoping for a wagon train of settlers from Tennessee any day now. That will certainly add to our numbers.

I stop writing, deciding to finish it later. The effect of all this truth-telling leaves me feeling dizzy and nauseous. Besides the discouraging population numbers, Anglo-Mexican relations are deteriorating, and Indian raids are increasing. And then there is the deeper truth I certainly cannot share that I am alive only because Will saved me from the Indians and, in leaving for Béjar, from myself as well.

From the porch, I peer into the forest of scrub brush, blood weeds, tall walnut trees, and spreading oaks. At least, the wild cattle watering at the river are not stealing grass from my little herd. In the meadow in front of the house, my pretty black-and-white milk cow pulls at a few sprigs of winter grass, her calf nosing into her full bag again and again until she lifts a back leg and kicks in protest. The red bull, Curly, tears at his own little patch of skimpy grass.

Tracks in front of the house, left by the carts and horses, have deepened into mud-sucking ruts in recent weeks. Pal grazes in front. She lifts her tender feet, trying to shake off the mud caked on her white stockings. Without hay or a decent hay barn, I hope the fast-growing spring grasses will fatten the cattle and horses. They've survived on the acorns, beechnuts, and mast that sustained hogs and livestock through winter better than I'd expected.

Downpour over, the girls venture outside again in their oilskin capes, off to the garden patch to plant a new crop of winter vegetables and corn. I think they are rushing the season, but they are convinced that the danger of frost is past in this southern clime, so much milder than Missouri winters. If a norther threatens their tiny garden, they will cover it with gunnysacks, they assure me. They know we need the corn.

I listen to their chatter from the kitchen table. Eveline holds the hoe, and Naomi instructs her in how to dig the holes. Naomi carefully doles out the corn and other seeds, dropping them in each little pocket of virgin soil. Naomi shivers as she supervises. Inside the oilskin cape, Naomi is lean and pale next to her rounder, rosier younger sister. Behind them, faithful Yowl gimps along the rows, his clear eyes and hopping gait making him seem more human than feline. I want to be out there with them, but fatigue keeps me rooted to the chair. Though grateful for a Saturday, when we don't have to be at school, I feel worn down by all that requires attention but so far shows little success. Sensing my mood, Antoñia puts the coffee grounds through one more cycle and serves me another cup.

When Antoñia joins the girls in the garden, I crawl back into bed. But instead of the oblivion of a nap, my mind races. Grind more meal from the remaining corn in the barrel. Haul water. Finish the long-overdue letter to Eliza and Liza Q. Talk to Mr. Lockhart about getting started on the much-discussed schoolhouse.

"Momma, Momma," Naomi repeats in an urgent whisper. I open my eyes to Naomi and Eveline huddled by my bed.

"Yes, yes, what is it?"

"Colonel Austin and Poppa are in the kitchen. I thought you'd want to get up."

I sit straight up in bed. "Colonel Austin? Empresario Austin?"

"Yes. He and Poppa came from Gonzales. He has come to pay us a visit on his way to Béjar. He asks how you are. I told him you are not feeling well, but I thought you might want to get up and greet him."

I throw off the covers, then sink back as the bone-tired feeling returns. "Yes, honey, you are so right. Could you get my brown woolen dress out of the trunk? The one with the white collar."

Naomi brings it to me, and I slip it on, buttoning the long row of buttons down the front. She endorses my choice as I get myself

190

together. "This dress looks fine on you, Momma. Colonel Austin will wish he had a wife pretty as you."

A head taller than I am—already a young woman—Naomi takes the horsehair brush brought from Missouri and begins to carefully comb out my rumpled hair. Then she piles it on top of my head and pins it in graceful swoops, trying to replace the frazzled frontier wife with the mother she'd known in Missouri.

Naomi holds the mirror for me to admire her handiwork. "Now, Momma, you're ready to greet Colonel Austin."

"Nice, Momma," Eveline says in her terse way, her eyes reflecting approval.

Austin rises as I enter the kitchen.

"Mrs. DeWitt, a pleasure to see you as always." His eyes sparkle. "Twice in one year, after way too many years. And to my enduring surprise, you look younger every time I lay eyes on you. How the days in Coahuila y Tejas have not taken a heavier toll on you is a wonder. As one of my crusty old colonists put it: 'Texas is a heaven for men and dogs but a hell for women and oxen.' Yet you are the picture of health, even on this chill, gray day. Not one I'd choose for traveling, but duty demands a visit to Béjar to confer with El Jefe Músquiz. More Indian troubles that must be discussed for the good of all of us living near Comanchería."

"You lift my spirits, Colonel Austin, on, as you say, this very gray day." Thankful that my fatigue is not apparent, I wonder if the news of my abduction and rescue reached him in San Felipe. Apparently, only Will knows all that happened in those torturous days. Whatever Green suspects, he says nothing. Whatever Austin knows, I reason, he is simply too discreet to mention. Almost nothing in the colonies, including Indian predation, escapes Austin's attention.

I visit briefly with the men, hungry to hear what the most informed man in Coahuila y Tejas has to say. Though dressed in buckskin, Austin has the air of a lawyer rather than a frontiersman. A man endowed with shrewdness matched by good intentions, he is the one, if there is anyone, who can transform this wilderness into civilization.

"The debtor protection law passed in January," Austin notes with pride, changing the subject from Indians to Mexican politics.

"It has concerned me for years. For if the settlers can be sued for debts in the United States before they can establish themselves here, they can be ruined."

"You have thought through all the dangers likely to befall the colonists." Green nods in approval. "But I must confess I need your guidance on another matter. The number of colonists streaming in here has slowed, the growth in this colony lagging far behind yours. If ever I am to fulfill my contract . . ." His voice trails off. "We're hoping for the addition of a wagon train of settlers from Tennessee, though it may be a few months. I have contracted William Matthews, a young man who came here from Tennessee recently, to be my agent. He's single and settled on a headright up above us on the San Marcos River. He's taken a keen interest in the colony. Jumped at the chance to help bring in more settlers. He'll start for Tennessee soon. I expect his youth and persuasive personality will do much to swell our numbers."

Austin nods, listening attentively. "Truth is, they get to my colonies on the east and just stop, out of fatigue and exhaustion. Bringing them down the Mississippi, into the Gulf, and then upcountry—your initial strategy—is a good one. It's an easier journey. Perhaps we should encourage more travel by ship, though that might necessitate a trip to Missouri to advertise the arrangements. Yes, a good strategy to send an agent back there to round up another contingent of families. There might be others who want to act as your agent to bring families in a group, as Byrd Lockhart and his brother have done. Or just send this Matthews fellow right back out again. My informants in the States say there are many wanting to make the journey."

Listening, I feel the pressure on Green, especially since funds are not as plentiful now as three years ago. And I note that Austin does not acknowledge that his tolerance of slavery helps swell his numbers as well. Naomi moves silently about the kitchen as she makes cornbread and onion pie. I know she is keeping an ear tuned to Austin's responses.

As talk between the men turns to the mysteries of Mexican politics and the fight raging between the Centralists and the Federalists, I can no longer avoid the thought of the midday meal. I excuse myself to confer with Antoñia on what more is on hand to feed our guest. To my consternation, Antoñia is nowhere to be found. I hike the path down the bluff to the river. There, oblivious to the drizzling rain, Antoñia is fishing with Eveline and the boys on the bank. The corn-cob sinks on their fishing poles bob up and down with the currents.

"Cook fish," Antoñia says, motioning beyond us to a clearing among the trees, where the day's catch is already baking in ashes of a campfire. "Ready now."

She and the children pull their lines from the river and follow me single file, bearing the baked fish wrapped in tortillas. The drizzle soaks us as we troop back up the path. I feel as off-kilter as Naomi's gimpy cat.

Inside, Naomi sits at the table with Austin, wanting to know more about his brother's marriage. While I dry myself and the children and take the cornbread muffins and onion pie from the hearth, Antoñia sets the table with my best pewter plates. We have four. Two for the men, and one each for myself and Naomi, who deserves to be treated as an adult today. The talk gives me time to get food on the table and fill my special glasses with apple cider saved for such a visitor.

Naomi shyly accedes to my prodding, takes off her apron, and smiles at me. We bow our heads as Green prays for good fortune for the colonies.

As I inhale the delicious aromas, a wave of nausea sweeps over me. My forehead grows clammy. To keep from gagging, I squeeze the back of my throat so tightly I can barely breathe. Clinton was to be my last. But I can deny it no longer. I am carrying another child.

While Green explores immigration numbers and Austin floods Naomi with information about his younger brother in Brazoria, I slip into another realm. I calculate when this baby will arrive and settle on September/October, some seven months from now. Before Eliza arrives next year. Is this a sign that God is forgiving me for my trans-gressions? No, I cannot think that way. But it is, at least, part of my return to Green and our beginnings in this new world. Despite all the reasons I can enumerate for having no more children, I sit back and smile at my secret. We need all the new souls we can get. I wonder if the wagon train or the baby will arrive first.

IN THE VALLEY OF THE GUADALUPE

The answer comes fairly quickly. In mid-May, we watch from the kitchen window as wagons approach the clearing in front of the house. Escorted from Tennessee by Green's young agent, William A. Matthews, the families in these wagons will add scores of settlers to the citizens of DeWitt colony, bringing us closer to the holy grail of four hundred families.

The blue-eyed Matthews, who has always struck me as a younger, more outspoken version of Green, has been an admirer of Green's since the two met in Missouri some years ago. Adulation aside, Matthews is not only a believer in Green's dream but also a tenacious disciple, evidenced by his dedication in bringing Green what he most wants.

From the window, we watch the fulfillment of Green's fondest desire. Wagons bursting with settlers lurch into the meadow outside the front gate. As settlers roll in, Naomi, Eveline, and I gaze thunderstruck at the long line. The creaking wagons filled with strangers form ruts in the pasture, scare away the cattle, destroy our winter grass, and thoroughly disturb the peace of our oak glade. We've never witnessed a flood like this nor imagined all these people let loose on our doorstep. Worse, Green is gone, having no idea that Matthews and his throng would show up today.

"Momma, why are all these wagons stopping in the meadow?" Naomi asks, wide-eyed, as I head for the gate.

As the wagon drivers seek shelter under the oaks, William Matthews leads the procession to the house. Having spent months getting dozens of families from Tennessee to Texas, he seems more than ready to hand them off. Dismounting, he strides up to me, greets me warmly, and shakes my hand. Spying chestnut-haired Naomi, he rushes over to her.

"Last time I looked, you were about ten years old." Without warning, he grabs her around the waist and kisses her. "You're 'bout the prettiest girl in five states. And I've passed through enough of them to know," he says as I look on, stunned.

"Mr. Matthews, now see here," I say in reaction. Naomi frees herself from his grasp and ducks away from him to stand next to me. Undaunted, the brazen Matthews runs on through the dogtrot of our cabin and out the back, whooping and shedding clothes as he goes. He grabs the rope swing and splashes, bare-assed, into the river as dozens of his weary travelers follow. Antoñia stations herself at the back of the cabin, bow and arrow at the ready.

Within a day, a tent city sprawls in front of the house, campfires scorch the grass where our cattle lately grazed, and Tennessee wayfarers lounge under the trees, tending fires and washing clothes in the river. Antoñia is mad as a hornet. Naomi, however, quickly adjusts, as she acquires several girlfriends who give her lessons in what to do with a young man as pretty as the blue-eyed Matthews.

It takes the rest of May before some of the campers start to disperse to their own acreages. Many remain, each waiting for the surveying teams to drive in stakes at four corners of a plot to mark the site of a new home. Noisy as they are, the Tennesseans who occupy our front meadow add significantly to the count, which soon will be tallied anew. Though I long for the cessation of the clanging of pots and shouts of water haulers, their presence should bring the number close to one hundred families.

In the quiet of a Saturday morning, away from the schoolroom and the busy meadow in front, Naomi and I look for the bee tree Eveline described to us—a hollowed-out red oak, with an upper and lower entrance for the bees, right below the house and before the first bend in the river. The currents of the Guadalupe slap and slosh against the bank. Naomi creeps ahead, down a little-used path of the embankment. In the cattails, a dugout canoe bounces against the reeds.

Naomi lets out a shout that brings Antoñia running from the house, bow on her shoulder. Seeing the canoe, Antoñia breaks into the biggest smile I've yet to see cross her face. In an instant, she hurries ahead of Naomi on the path.

"Boat. Lost. My boat." With perfect balance, she steps in. Pointing to two paddles in the bottom, she beckons Naomi and me into the canoe. With the rest of the family gone to Gonzales, we do not hesitate. We edge down the sandy bank, following Antoñia's lead but with less agility, as she reaches up and guides each of us into the canoe.

Antoñia's wide grin envelops her whole face. The small circles of blue tattooed over each cheekbone grow more visible as she throws back her hair. The sweater Antoñia wears, fastened with short little canes cut and twisted through the coarse yarn, reveals the tops of the circles tattooed around her breasts. Having gone topless for much of her life, Antoñia never makes covering herself a concern. Her dark, coarse hair, lightened by the Texas sun, falls over her shoulders as she paddles the boat into the middle of the river against the current. Knowing Antoñia's strong arms will carry us upriver, I lean back to enjoy the ride.

In these early days of spring, the river is alluring, swollen by rains and overhung with sprouting oaks and the bright green shoots of feathery cypresses. Mud turtles and red-eared sliders sun on logs and rocks. Antoñia eyes them. I know she would rather be bagging them for dinner than watching them bask in the sun. Widening circles appear where fish snap at insects alighting on the water. The dragonflies' blue bodies, bright as the sky overhead, skirt and dart above the circles. I love the quiet of it, the three of us silent in the open air, soaking up the morning with light hearts.

As we glide upstream, Antoñia occasionally beats the water with quick motions from her paddle, making flat circular slaps. After the third time, I look at her quizzically, wondering if this is a technique learned in the shoals and coves of the Gulf. She simply says, "Fish," and in a few minutes, resumes her rowing. Then she stands up in the boat and shoots an arrow into the water. In an instant, a large fat bass, perhaps investigating the tapping sounds, lies atop the water with an arrow in its side. Antoñia plucks the fish from the water, removes her arrow, and trains her eyes again on the clear blue water.

I often wonder about Antoñia's past and worry about the loneliness behind those dark eyes. Her copper-colored, solemn face rarely betrays an emotion. Unless it is for wild things. I think of the day I'd found her in the back shed, clicking her tongue like a cricket and extending her arms in a swaying motion. A harmless black snake slithered off the ledge and onto her arm. The snake moved up one arm, around her neck, and then back the way it came, into the dark recesses of the shed. When Antoñia spied me watching, she'd said simply, "Snake like me. Keep away evil." I understood: for Antoñia, who often sleeps outside at night looking up at the sky, the wild renews her strength.

Today her happiness is a remnant of her days among the fishing people of her birth. I equate Antoñia's joy with my own daydream of boating on the Mississippi.

"Long time since we were in a boat," I observe to Naomi.

"Yes, Momma. But don't make yourself sad thinking about life in Missouri."

"You know me, Naomi Q." I smile at her, my sweet girl so like my loving mother, Liza Quick, for whom she is named. It occurs to me that Antoñia and I aren't so different. I can't imagine what lies ahead for Antoñia—with her deerskin bracelet and tattoos, living apart from her people—any better than I can see the path ahead for myself and Green, separated and apart from our Missouri family.

Antoñia pops up in the boat again and shoots another arrow into the water. This time she manages to get two fish with one arrow.

Laying them carefully in the bottom of the boat, with a flash of teeth, she says, "Antoñia good catch fish."

As we travel upriver, Antoñia sometimes motions for Naomi to stop paddling as she peers into the water. I think this is Antoñia's way of communing with the water spirits, relishing the river's music. Birds call, and a whole flock of young white herons flaps out of a stand of cypress trees. The mockingbirds imitate their feathered fellows along the banks, and Antoñia points out wild turkeys and a tusked javelina trotting on short legs along the shore.

When Antoñia has a stack seven fish high, she sits on the bottom of the boat, leans back, and brings out her pipe made of a shell attached to the hollowed-out leg bone of a deer. She has painted flowers and birds on the long stem. She pulls yaupon holly leaves out of her skirt now and stuffs them into the bowl of the pipe. In the bottom of the pipe, a tiny coal still glows from a smoke earlier in the day. Soon the leaves smolder and Antoñia draws the yaupon aroma deep into her lungs. Flinging her hair over the side of the boat so that it trails in the water, she laughs out loud, a deep, guttural laugh.

"Look," Antoñia says suddenly, pointing into the woods. A man squats on his haunches cooking at a campfire under a huge chinaberry tree. The road to San Antonio, the Camino Real, snakes into view just beyond him.

When he sees us, the man stands and waves his arms. I see no horse tethered nearby.

"He needs help."

Antoñia frowns. Neither she nor Naomi wants to abandon our floating Eden to pick up a man unknown to us. But I insist and motion to paddle closer to the shore so we can talk to him. Dark eyes wary, Antoñia paddles closer to the bank as the man comes toward us, still waving his arms.

"I come in friendship," the man shouts. "Lost my horse," he adds when we get close enough to see his face. He is tall and sturdily built, in buckskin and boots, his sandy hair and eyebrows bleached by the sun. He breaks into a smile when we float right up to the bank. "I've been walking all day," he says. "Got separated from my horse by a pair of Indians on up the river. Fortunately, still have my gun. Headed for Gonzales. Looking for the DeWitt colony. I'm the lead scout for a wagon train heading toward the colony, several days behind me."

"We're from the DeWitt colony," I say. "If you want to get to Gonzales, you can get in the canoe. We're headed back there."

He stamps out his fire and packs cooked meat and his small frying pan into a cotton sack. He scrambles down the bank and into the boat, rifle at his side.

"I'm mighty grateful, I can tell you that. I can offer you some fried-up bacon on the ride back."

Antoñia glares at me as if I'd lost my senses and destroyed her idyll on the river to boot. She repositions her bow and arrows and seizes a paddle as if she might hit the man over the head. "Man stranger," she mutters.

"Toñia, don't worry, don't worry. He's all right," I whisper, thinking not only of him but the number of families in a wagon train behind him. But the black eyes do not soften.

Antoñia does not allow him to paddle. She motions him to the middle where she can keep an eye on him from the back of the canoe and demands that he set his gun behind him as we start downriver.

"I'm J. C. Davis. Pleased to meet ye. In fact, I'm tickled to death," he says with a smile.

"I'm Sarah DeWitt, and this is my daughter Naomi and our friend Antoñia."

Tossing her head, Antoñia gives a scornful glance before turning back to her task of getting the stranger out of the canoe as quickly as she could.

"Did you say DeWitt?" he asks now. "You wouldn't happen to know Green DeWitt, would you?"

"My husband."

"Well, Mrs. DeWitt, this is my lucky day. I am proud to know you and, I hope, your family. I even have something your husband handed out." From his pocket, he pulls scrip in five- and ten-dollar denominations, given him for purchase of land at the other end of his journey.

His laughing brown eyes and broad brow make me wonder if he might be a perfect suitor for Eliza. About her age, he seems like the kind of man she would like. He has dimples, which soften his sunburned face and complement his polite, though confident, manner. And he doesn't have the roughness I've come to expect of most Texas men.

"Where do you come from?" I ask, pursuing this line of reasoning while hoping he's from Missouri.

"Born in Tennessee, grew up in Missouri, been on my own since about the age of your daughter here."

I cannot see my or Antoñia's future, but perhaps I can see Eliza's. I listen carefully to all the questions about the colony the dimpled stranger presses on me.

The day when we found J. C. sits in my mind as one of the most pleasant days of the year. But it is other days, more crowded with events, which make it into a letter to Eliza, some months later.

October 1829
My dear Eliza,

I have been terribly derelict in writing. And now I must make it up to you with several months' worth. When you get to the end, you will appreciate what a year it has been.

In early spring, John Oliver and Nancy Curtis, known to us in Missouri, as you may remember, got married in the glade in front of our cabin. The newlyweds set up housekeeping just across the river from us. They are part of a steady—though small—stream of colonists claiming the choice land near the Guadalupe, Lavaca, and San Marcos Rivers. At mid-year, the population of Poppa's colony had climbed to 158 souls. Many were brought by the indefatigable Mr. Lockhart's brother and by a new agent, William Matthews. (We are getting closer to one hundred families, though still far from the distant goal.) But there is much activity. Settlers line the rivers. Their petitions for headrights bump up against each other now, so that surveyors measure off adjacent tracts as they fill in Mexico's northern wilds.

Pumping information to us is the weekly, if sometimes irregular, Texas Gazette. It has four pages an issue, and three columns per page. The first edition was published in late September in Austin's colony. The paper links us as never before. We are the distributor for the newspaper in Gonzales, so we receive a bundle left by the courier in the land office shed each week. The copies disappear before the week is out. One delivery brought the sad tidings of the death of Colonel Austin's brother, twenty-five-year-old Brown Austin, newly married and launched in life in Brazoria. The young Austin, dear friend to his older brother, arrived in New Orleans during a yellow fever outbreak that claimed his life in a matter of days. Following that tragic loss, Austin learned of Mexico's nationwide abolition of slavery, effective on September 15th. The law could seriously threaten his settlement because of the wide need for slaves for growing cotton crops in the Anglo colonies. The weight of these events, it is rumored, leaves Austin sunk in melancholy. Austin's struggles with depression and illness and the looming 1831 deadline of the contract with the Mexicans leave Poppa dispatching his own duties with a heavy heart. I am concerned about him; his worry sometimes overwhelms even his staunch optimism.

Along with the new souls brought in by the efforts of Poppa and Mr. Lockhart and William Matthews is a brand-new one, delivered on October 18, 1829. She is the largest one I have brought into the world, a healthy eight-pound bundle. Having gotten past my 39th birthday, I fervently intend her to be my last. We are all happy to have our Minerva, as I know you will be to have another sister. Your arrival in January will be the high point of 1830, as her birth was for 1829.

Love,
Momma

ELIZA

ugenio and I stop at Linn's Landing on Lavaca Bay, two days due south of Gonzales. After a night spent with Molly and Creed, we continue toward the Gulf, a journey, in reverse, of the one that brought us to Gonzales three long years ago.

We rest overnight in rooms next to John Linn's warehouse on our way toward Matagorda Bay. I occupy one bedroom of the little rooming house; Eugenio rents a cot in the back. While I knit a blanket for Minerva in my room, he emerges from his lair, drinking mescal and smoking his peyote pipe, memories of his Yaqui Indian grandfather and the northern Sonora desert of his youth erupting regularly. The mescal of Sonora, he says, is the best-flavored mescal in Mexico, its fire bred in the arms of the daggerlike maguey plant of his birthplace.

We await Eliza's arrival on the schooner *Dispatch*, which will arrive tomorrow, according to Eugenio. Waiting is a part of life, he tells me, as enjoyable as any other. He likes to remember his people in the hours so generously given him—"*Gracias a Dios*," he murmurs— and describes to me the Yaqui wisdom, which lies in finding the right way, the way filled with magic in the heart. For those blessed with the courage to find the right way, life will be fruitful. I wish my Anglo world could be sorted out so neatly. *Though I must get credit for fruitfulness*, I muse, thinking of the just-weaned Minerva, cared for at home with Antoñia and her father and sisters and brothers.

I awaken to the loud cries of "*¡arre, arre!*"—soft and then louder and more insistent. Then silence. Out the window, a line of mule-skinners driving perhaps a dozen mules has slowed to a stop outside the rooming house. Eugenio stands between two muleteers, engaged in exchanges. After a few pointed gestures at three mules' packs, the loads are transferred to Eugenio's wagon, and the cries of "*¡arre, arre!*" commence again, the line of mules and drivers winding south toward the Gulf with their loads.

Eugenio has lightened the muleskinners' load by three large bales of tobacco leaves wrapped in heavy cloth. He has also heard from the muleteers that a boat with big sails had arrived in Matagorda Bay. After a skimpy breakfast of bitter coffee and hard biscuits in the dark dining room of the rooming house, we continue on our way south along the bay's wide inlet to the salty waters of the Gulf.

The schooner anchors in the bay, its riggings billowing in the wind. With long-distance vision keen as his sense of direction, Eugenio spots Eliza even before I do. He points out the young woman pacing the deck of the big boat as it rocks gently in the bay. "*Su hija? Sí?*" Eugenio asks. "*Rubia, como la madre.*" He laughs softly to himself.

"Why are you laughing?"

"*Una sorpresa.* No small like *la madre. ¡Muy alta!*"

"Yes, tall. My big, blonde girl."

I follow her movements eagerly now, tears welling—Eliza's coltish, frisky air heartwarming and familiar. I am hungry to see my eldest child after four long years.

"*Anda rápido . . . y como una generalissima.*"

Eugenio detects the air of authority in her bearing. Yes, she's always been that way—playful, but sure of herself.

"*Guapa.* Beautiful. *Pero lo mas importante: Ojalá que . . .* she is . . . self-forgetting *como la madre.*" I understand. External beauty is not a thing to depend on. Eugenio does not judge by outward appearances.

The group of several dozen travelers has sailed down the Mississippi and across the Gulf on the *Dispatch*, the trading schooner Green engaged at the outset to bring settlers to the colony. The big boat also carries a load of corn and cotton along with the coffee, salt, flour, and tobacco Texas settlers wait for and depend on. Eugenio has met the schooner every few months for more than three years now. But this time, he tells me, the boat with sails bigger than clouds brings the most precious cargo: "*la hija mayor de la señora y el empresario.*" He holds up a handful of ripe early dewberries found in a sunny spot along a bluff. *Un regalo.* His gift for Eliza—a taste of her new land.

She and others soon transfer to a flatboat. Eugenio watches like a bird of prey as the boat brings Eliza to us. Eugenio knows the friendly Indians, a few Karankawa and some Tonkawa hanging around on the shore, and arranges for them to unload her belongings from the little boat. The Indians look fierce with panther and bear skins around their waists and coarse hair cut straight across their foreheads. What I notice, though, is the tattoos down their chests. Blue and red stripes. Unlike Antoñia's circles, the men's stripes make a line, diving from neck to navel. I wonder at the differences and wish for Antoñia to explain. I stand next to Eugenio, giddily waving Eliza ashore, as the flatboat runs up onto the sandy beach.

Eliza is the first out. I reach out and fold her into my arms, our tears flowing freely. We embrace as others step around us. I have mentioned Eugenio in letters but never described him. But Eliza registers no surprise at the small, brown man with hunched shoulders wrapped in a ragged serape. "Eliza, my very dear friend Eugenio. We could not find our way in Coahuila y Tejas without him."

Eugenio approaches with arms extended. "*Con mucho gusto, señorita,*" he says, and then in crisp syllables, "I am Eugenio."

"*Con mucho gusto*, I am Eliza," she says as he encloses her in his warm embrace. She smiles happily, if a little warily, at me.

"*Bienvenida*, welcome," he says as he stands back.

Behind Eliza, a young man remains at a respectful distance. Instead of rushing past us, as do the other passengers, he hovers politely, his eyes on Eliza.

Now Eliza motions to him. "This is my friend Thomas Hamilton." He steps forward as Eliza announces him. "He will be coming with us." I realize that in our four years apart, though she has not said so in her letters, Eliza has fallen in love.

We turn to walk up the worn beach path to the wagon. As the ship's passengers quickly disperse, the wilderness swallows us up. Before us, a vast plain of grasses and dunes rises boundlessly from the sea. Nothing like the booming port of St. Louis or the relentless bustle of New Orleans. I wonder if Eliza finds the sweeping view breathtakingly desolate.

Our earnest guide leads us to the wagon, sheltered on the leeward side of a dune, the Indians following with trunk and bags. They hoist the baggage into the wagon and move single file back down the path to the water, their bronze skin glistening with sweat in the sunny morning. Even for the balmy Gulf, the weather is surprisingly warm.

Eugenio points his passengers to their seats, the bales of tobacco under the canvas.

"A soft enough seat." Eliza laughs, looking at Thomas. The young adventurers pile in with little idea of what the journey holds.

"*Muchas gracias*," Eliza murmurs as Eugenio bestows bread, water, beef jerky, and the plump gift of dewberries.

I have prepared for Eliza's arrival for weeks, washing the mattress sacks, baking sweets with my precious supply of sugar, reorganizing sleeping arrangements so that she can have a bed to herself. I had carefully informed Eliza, in letters, of the additions of Antoñia, as well as Minerva, to the family. I also noted the conspicuous absences—no church and only a tiny room used as a schoolroom in the one hotel. But I know none of this will convey the distance, greater than the miles, between St. Louis and Gonzales.

We arrive two days later on a February evening bright with a new moon and a dome of stars overhead. The whole family rushes from the house to greet us. Green holds his daughter close, shaking his head over the years of separation, tears in his eyes. Her sisters and brothers crowd around. Eliza cries more tears of happiness, then steps back and introduces Thomas, whom she calls her "special friend."

The fire glows in the big fireplace, and the starlight shines through the window. Candles burn on the mantle and on the long table Antoñia has set for the DeWitt household and Eugenio, with a place hastily added for Thomas. Eyes deprived of Eliza for almost four years shine with happiness as the children hand out gifts to their beloved elder sister: a shiny mica rock from Clinton; a patterned turtle shell from C. C.; a linen apron that Naomi cut out and sewed with small, even stitches and that Eveline embroidered with Eliza's initials, using my best skeins of blue thread. Antoñia parts with one of her finely crafted reed baskets, and tiny, three-month-old Minerva dispenses bright smiles and gurgling coos.

"And now to table," I announce. The meal has been perfectly prepared by Antoñia, who has been cooking for days. She and I serve generous portions of venison stew with squash, beans, sweet potatoes, and cornbread, topped off with pecan pie. Green sits Eliza next to him and holds her hand, patting it between forkfuls. As we eat, Eliza regales us with stories of the voyage and news of Missouri—when she isn't stealing glances at Thomas or trying to read what her father thinks of him. I like seeing the two of them side by side, Eliza's blue eyes and smile so like her father's. Her face reminds me of the man I married and reflects a softness sorely missed, though slowly returning, to Green's eyes.

Green's dedication to the colony has beset his waking moments and absorbed practically every ounce of his energy. Yet deep within, he yearns for what we both desire: the marriage we once had. The children and I feel the difference. We have all grown to understand that his labors—with the surveyors, the road builders, the carpenters at the mill, the Mexican officials, the agents hired to bring in more settlers, the hours spent in the land office—are not only for his colony but for us, too. For our future. But perhaps it is the birth of Minerva and now the arrival of Eliza that have touched his heart most deeply and brought him back to us. That is what I see, as he sits next to Eliza, his eyes shining tonight.

The days of the new year are unusually mild.

"Come, Green, let's go for a walk in the woods," I call to him. "Poison ivy's not out yet, and I can see the honeysuckle just setting up to bloom." The children are at lessons, Minnie down for her nap, and Antoñia in the kitchen.

Since the trees haven't leafed out yet, the view along the river stretches for miles. It is such a nice day that Green proposes riding to the sawmill upriver and having a picnic on the way back. We are soon on our way.

Green has planned and helped build the water-powered sawmill and suffered through the Indian raid that left one of the carpenters dead. To him, the mill is a monument to civilization, as significant as Rome's Colosseum. We gaze at it from across the river.

"This mill is supplying lumber to settlers not only around Gonzales but in Goliad, Victoria, Quaro, and Mina up the other way"—he proudly motions north—"and in Béjar, too."

We walk the horses through the low-water crossing and then dismount to admire the stone mill. Its waterwheel churns the clear waters of the Guadalupe, powering the big, jagged teeth of the saw. Accompanying us, the carpenter managing the mill hoots with each little revolution of the wheel, "Whoo-hoo, thar she comes, and thar she comes again."

In the warehouse, I breathe in the fresh smell of newly cut lumber.

"Look at those planks, stacked by even lengths and widths so it's easy to find what you need. Pretty as a picture," Green says.

I nod as he basks in the glory of taming the wilderness, as Austin decreed the two of them would.

On the ride back, we find a green spot under the live oaks for our picnic. Pulling the counterpane out of my saddlebag, Green spreads it on the ground, and I set the food in the middle: boiled eggs, some honey cake, watermelon rind pickles, and a cache of shelled pecans. Bundled in two serapes after the chilly ride, I start to shed my wraps in the midday sun.

"I knew there was a woman in there, inside all those blankets."

I smile and start to share a story about little Minnie and her sunny temperament.

He puts a finger to my lips.

"You know, today I'm not thinking about the children. I'm thinking about you."

Plain as that sounds, it is a sentiment that Green rarely voices. It comes from his deepest feelings, and I know there's need couched in that simple message. I think about how hard he works, pushing himself night and day, about how many times he's told me that he feels he must be a thief in the night to make love to me. For the last two decades, we've been surrounded by an army of children. To say nothing of sharing the same sleeping quarters with them for much of the time since Eliza was born.

I move closer to him, responding to the yearning so difficult for him to express.

"I know I've been away a lot. In twenty years together, we've had few days like this," he says. "Let me just look at you, thank my lucky stars for you, and take in this beautiful day on the riverbank."

I smile at his openness and remember the ardor of our earliest days together. Today on this lush bank of the "Warloop" with its soft, plummy soil and velvety grass is God's gift. The thrill I once felt hovers there, always in the shadows.

We lie back in our little bower. When I can get him away from all his ambition and sidetrack him into relaxing like this, I am content. The woods are good for that. Despite all his preoccupations and gentlemanly ways, he sheds them in the woods. I know he has never really slept well, except after being in the woods. In fact, I don't think he's had more than a few good nights' sleep in all the years I've known him, and those after wandering for months in the wilds of Alabama as he returned from the War of 1812.

He kisses me fully and then brings his body next to me in familiar ways. I whisper what he wants to hear, and he moves against me, letting me feel his passion, welcoming the circles of longing that are returning to us. His physical response comes quickly as we lie together under the oaks, and he relaxes into a nap.

Lying beside him, I think about his stuttering as a boy. The stories he told me about practicing his words in the woods of Kentucky while hunting and fishing, stories that made me fall in love with him. Plagued with an unruly tongue, he devoted solitary hours to pushing out the sounds that gave him the most trouble, shouting out the m's and p's and k's in the silence of the forest until he conquered his speech, triumphed over himself. I love him for that perseverance and for his ability to find comfort in the woods.

I doze off for a few minutes and catch a dream of all of us back in Missouri, returning to the life that was once so good for us.

When I wake, wrapped in my dream, he is sitting up looking down at the river. I wonder what he would say if I broached the subject of returning to Missouri. Since Minerva's birth and Eliza's arrival, St. Louis is much on my mind.

I rub his back and hold his hand. "A penny for your thoughts."

"Well, I'm not sure you want to hear them."

He's no doubt thinking about the lagging numbers of settlers to the DeWitt colony and what to do about it. What a pair: he, dedicated to staying, and I, dreaming of leaving. But I will keep my end of the bargain until the contract is fulfilled or not. I remain silent, trying not to lose the comfort of the woods.

Eliza's "special friend," as she calls him, is a godsend. Thomas Hamilton distracts Eliza from the rawness the rest of us have adjusted to over four years. For Eliza, the prospect of riding and hunting in the woods with Thomas is a welcome gift after her cloistered days at a girls' school. What Eveline and Naomi and I feel as privation, Eliza sees as adventure. It takes little time for me to understand that my long-legged, square-shouldered daughter, now so assuredly self-possessed, and the amiable, well-spoken squire from Vermont will not live separately for long.

Her brothers and sisters, however, do not allow Eliza to spend all of her time with Thomas. Naomi and Eveline are especially keen on getting her help in the schoolroom and quickly press her into service. But when Eliza isn't in the classroom, she is out with Thomas. They kill wild turkeys, shoot deer, and explore the paths in and around the town. Gonzales is now nearing twenty structures, including Eggleston's Store with its buckets of buttermilk souring and stinking to high heaven. In the corral behind the fort, Indians and Texians and Tejanos trade horses almost every day. "More horses," Eliza tells us, "than in all of St. Louis." They come home from their hunts at sunset, filled with tales of fleeing antelopes, Mexican lions, and howling wolves. They come home from town with more stories, including how Benjamin Fulcher's donkeys set up such a terrible braying that all the town dogs and pigs tuned up too.

And then one evening, the sun dips toward the west, the sky grows pink, and still, the two have not returned. After watching the road with Minerva on my hip for too long, I hand her off to Naomi and whistle for Pal. Green will not be home from the sawmill tonight, and I cannot wait until pitch dark to go after Eliza.

Several miles northeast, near Peach Creek, Eliza and Thomas, on their horses, loom in the middle distance. They are watching one of Mr. Lockhart's survey crews coming to the end of their workday. The noisy crew yells back and forth among themselves, crashing through the brush hacking and chopping.

About to call to Eliza through the woods, I look up to see a line of warriors on the horizon, heading toward the surveying crew. Green has spoken of a band of the southern Comanche known as the Penateka, the Honey Eaters, who often make raids on the *caballadas* of the cattle-rich Empresario De León, or Capitán Vacas Muchas, as the Penateka call him. But it is the surveyors the Comanche truly hate. For them, the surveyors are the incarnation of evil: grabbing territory, leaving strange symbols on the trunks of trees, wielding the transit eyepiece and the terrible compass. "The thing that steals the land," they call it, an instrument of sorcery from the white men's gods. The Indians, the very band Green has described, ride screaming into the crew of surveyors.

The chainman in front of the crew sees the line of horses and shouts a warning. Eliza and Thomas hunch over on their horses and creep deeper into the brush. I fall over Pal's neck, hardly daring to breathe or make a move. The crew members drop their instruments in the field and run for cover. On foot, they are no match for the warriors, who lash their horses and descend with high-pitched, bone-chilling shrieks, spears and tomahawks raised high. The tomahawk wielders drop the men in the field, their heads split like cracked walnuts. One crew member disappears into the creek. Another is pierced through with arrows from two directions. The warriors even attack the black dog next to him. The creature lies next to its master, a small man trampled face down and covered with dirt, his blood pooling with the dog's.

Then the Indians, with ribbons and yarn in their horses' manes and tails, are gone. So intent are they on whatever lures them farther south, they don't even bother to scalp the hapless victims nor notice the three of us on horses in the brush.

I approach Eliza and Thomas, leading the horses out of the trees.

"Momma," she murmurs, her voice barely audible, her face ashen as they huddle in the brambles a short distance from the creek. She reaches for my hand, as cold as hers. Shaken, we hold onto each other for a long moment before we creep toward the bodies. Deer edging out of the shadows lift their heads. In the fading February light, we can just make out where the bodies lie. We count four dead and hope the man who'd splashed into the creek escaped.

Suddenly, I catch movement out of the corner of my eye. Whirling around, rifle raised, I watch the black dog struggle to its feet. Kneeling before the poor creature as its head oozes blood, I see an arrow has torn a deep track through the fur and taken much of the dog's ear. The hound cowers before me as I try to soothe him. Eliza gives him water from her canteen. He raises his other ear and then trots behind us as we make our way home in the near dark.

In Gonzales, we stop at Mr. Lockhart's cabin to alert him to the sad plight of his crew. "And the Indians did not scalp them or take their horses?"

"No, they kept going south, never looking back. Thankfully, they didn't see us in the thicket." Shaken, he heads for his horse, intent on gathering other crew members to help him collect the bodies.

Antoñia has taken up my post, pacing on the porch with Minerva in her arms. I wave as we near the house. The moonlight shines on the children huddled in the house trying to occupy themselves. Naomi is posted by the window reading to the boys; Eveline plays a solitary game of jacks.

In the light of the kitchen candles guttering down to nubs, Antoñia cares for the wounded dog, while the children stare at the three of us. We hesitantly tell our tale, explaining that the dog seems to have belonged to one of the surveying crew, a small man trampled face down in the dirt, his unrecognizable body pierced by three arrows. Hearing those words, Eveline whirls toward me and clutches my hand.

"The dog's name is Gyp," she says. "He belongs to Faye and her father."

HIGHS AND LOWS

The girls and I are making wedding clothes. Yards of cloth, neatly folded in her trunk, came with Eliza from St. Louis. With less than two months to prepare for a late May ceremony, the seamstresses—when they aren't in the classroom—make patterns, cut them out, and stitch them together. And two days a week, after lessons, Faye, hired away from Luna for those days, helps us with the sewing. Thimbles, needles, and thread, along with swaths of fabric cover beds and tables. Fingers fly, making careful, even stitches in the satin for Eliza and the cambric and batiste for the girls and their brothers who are to stand with the bridal couple.

Such a labor of love, I understand, has no parallel in Faye's life. Now, as she and the girls sew, one-eared Gyp lies contentedly beside Faye. Ever so gently, I begin to coax from her the story only she and Gyp know. The sewing circle listens spellbound as Faye's tale comes out day by day in bits and pieces, the trip to Texas from Tennessee a blur for the girl who was not yet ten years old. The death of her mother in Brazoria, at the mouth of the Brazos River, from yellow fever, awakening the child to the perils of her existence. Her attempts to cook for her father and care for her baby sister, who died soon after. The beatings from her father for not keeping house as well as her mother did. The confusion and fear when he sold her to Belle. The irregular meals at Luna and the men she serves who poke fun at her with names like Mouseface and Foxface and worse. She hesitates and then, blushing, whispers to Naomi that they make fun of her, calling her Tiny Tits.

We listen and comfort and sew, needles never pausing, measuring tapes in hand as bits of Faye's life are laid down one upon the other like cruel lashes from a whip. Quietly we nod, pat her hand, and soothe her when tears stream down her cheeks.

"It is sometimes good to cry, Faye," I say, or "It's all right to tell what happened to you." At times, I put down my sewing and hold Faye as she buries her head in my shoulder.

After a series of days, including times when Faye retreats into her silent self, the young waif gets to the part that troubles her most. "I'm sorry Poppa died," she says soberly, "but I didn't love him like I loved Ma. He was mean to Gyp, too," she says, patting the dog on the earless side of his head.

Knowing of Faye's indenture by her father, I am not surprised by what she divulges. Seeing how far she has come in a few years, I marvel at her progress: learning to read, building friendships with Bess and Lila, working at Luna without complaint. "You are a brave, brave girl," I tell her over and over again.

As Faye's story unfolds, I study Eliza, who does not receive the facts with the composure of her sisters. She winces on hearing the unsettling details that speak volumes about life in this raw outpost. For Eliza, discussing these things is opening Pandora's box. I suspect she takes pains to disguise her misgivings, so as not to upset me. She devotes her time and attention to Thomas and the wedding as would any young bride-to-be. Yet I am sure the forlorn Faye is much on Eliza's mind, as it begins to dawn on her day after day just how far from Missouri we have come.

Eliza is not the only unsettled one. "Ill wind coming from Mexico," Green confides to me on his return from another trip to San Felipe. "The seat of government will be issuing a new law to limit immigration, thanks to our friend Terán. He presented a report to the officials in Mexico City saying Texas was about to be 'delivered to the foreigners' and demanded that the borders close to Americans."

While we escorted Eliza along the road from the Gulf to Gonzales, General Terán, Mexico's watchdog for the northeastern frontier, traveled the La Bahía-Goliad Road to Mexico City. Green is not the only one who's gotten wind of his report. Around the colony, rumors of Terán's assessments hang as heavy as the clouds stacked in the wintry sky.

The news grows worse. I garner from Eugenio what I can. By spring, the news is damning. The new Mexican Congress decrees that no more colonists are to be allowed into Texas. Those already in residence can stay, but even as colonists pour in by the hundreds, immigration is to be halted. Immigrants are turned away by soldiers stationed at the border.

Even Eugenio, for whom politics is as ephemeral as the west wind, senses the gathering storm. The bill, known as the Land Law of 1830, passes the Mexican Congress on April 6, just about the time the number of applications for land in the DeWitt colony reaches 150 families. Whether the newcomers have entered before the passage of the Land Law is impossible to say, as the land applications aren't always accurately dated. We will hope that they all stay. No matter: the milestone is no less bittersweet. This law will make it impossible to meet the quota of four hundred families. Green, positively haggard for the past month, receives confirmation of the law's passage from Austin in mid-April and starts for San Felipe the next day to deal with and possibly head off the crisis.

The law embodies the perils worried over for years—indeed, even before we left St. Louis. The injustice of it is another thing. It is only fair, I reason, that Green receive the premium lands due him for bringing in one hundred families. By now, the tally has grown past one hundred. More than 75,000 acres had been promised to him personally. A quarter of it is to be delivered after the first hundred families are settled. True, his contract to bring in three hundred more families is not yet fulfilled. Nevertheless, the provision to deliver that first portion should be honored. But now, the interpretation of that contract depends solely on the judgments of Terán and the authorities in Mexico City.

The weight of it, the threat of losing everything, grows heavier with each passing day. It feels like a body blow. More than that, it leaves me incensed. Have we not brought settlers down the Mississippi at our own expense? Have we not undergone every privation imaginable? Going without flour for bread, with not even a roof over our heads for months on end. *I personally financed this colony*, I repeat heatedly to Green, in my mind, still furious over the sale of my Missouri land. *The children and I have endured the same fears as you have. Does not Mexican law grant women the privilege of owning land? Have I not acted as loyally as any Mexican citizen to bring civilization to the untamed lands Mexico wants to see colonized?*

My thoughts harden. Why, in fact, should I not receive my own grant in compensation? A grant in my name, a recognition of my contribution to Mexico, and a hedge against the possibility Green might not receive his. I will petition the Mexican government for a land grant in my name, for the entire league surrounding the house and outbuildings.

I look around the room at my children. Yes, for them, as well as myself. I see, with fresh eyes, what is required and what I must do.

As I cook for the wedding, I plan what my petition will say: *I, Sarah Seely, wife of Green DeWitt, with a family of six children, with all due respect, present the following statement. In the year 1826, I arrived in this country with my family from the state of Missouri. Since then, I have dwelt on a sitio of land, chosen by my husband on the Guadalupe River, opposite the town of Gonzales.*

I'm not set, just yet, on how much land to claim for my own in the petition. Nor am I sanguine about the likelihood of receiving an independent grant. First, I must tell Green of my determination to do this. I must do it. But not just yet.

At the beginning of May, Green returns from San Felipe on Major, his remarkable big bay, covering more than thirty miles in a day. He rides in just before dusk. I hear Major's hooves, hear Green water him at the river, and follow Green's energetic motions from the window as he feeds and brushes the horse at the barn. He seems jaunty, despite his long ride and fateful mission.

He bounds through the gate, not bothering to hook it with the leather thong we loop around the fence post to keep cattle from coming into the yard. His step is as springy as if he is about to lead me onto a dance floor. He kisses me, playful and teasing until Naomi joins us. Eagerly he spills his news:

"It's going to be all right," he tells us. "Austin has determined a course to follow in response to the Land Law. With the aid of his translator, Sam Williams, Austin has reviewed the wording of the new law and focused on Article 10 of the new decree. That article states there will be no change to 'colonies already established.' That is key."

"And just how is that?" I ask, not at all convinced we are in the clear.

"In the Land Law," he says, launching into a speech in his salesman's voice. "Article 11 suspends only 'contracts not fulfilled.' Since Austin and I are the only empresarios who have brought significant numbers to Texas and whose colonies are advanced in settlement, we have fulfilled our contracts. Hence, Austin's several colonies and the DeWitt colony should be exempted from the law. That means we should be able to continue expanding. This law makes it tough for any empresarios who follow, but Austin and I should be safe. Austin is preparing just such a letter to Terán and expects he will agree."

Naomi is rolling biscuits. I stir a pot of beans. How much of my disbelief should I voice?

"I expect Austin can turn the situation around and put things right," Green says, almost lightheartedly, making the world into what he wishes.

I listen to his rosy views, thinking that we have circled back to the beginning. He cannot, or will not, see that a crisis is inevitable. Our existence here is still a house of cards about to tumble down. In less than a year, the deadline of April 15, 1831, will be upon us. We have twelve months to bring in more than 250 families. It has taken five years to get close to 150 families here. Even if you discount the time to get started, does he really believe he can bring in nearly double that number in less than a year? Unless he does so, he will never reap the reward the contract bestows: leagues and leagues of land. In the current climate, there is no guarantee that people will arrive or that he will receive even the first few leagues of land.

In my indignation, I stop stirring the pot before me. My gaze falls somewhere out the window into the lofty live oaks. It shouldn't surprise me that Green can put a good face on the uncertainty of this situation. He refuses to recognize the chinks in the armor. He cannot face that this gamble is becoming less and less likely to pay off.

Destiny frowns at me. *It is your job to believe in him.*

Naomi watches me closely, a troubled expression on her young face. Does she, too, understand that, even if this crisis passes, there will be another? Does she, too, dread the road ahead and all it means for us?

I smile at Naomi, guessing she knows instinctively that the future is treacherous. Despite her father's assurances.

"What's the matter, Sarah?" Green asks, looking hurt that I've ignored his good news.

"I'm not so confident as you are. I don't think it's easy to 'put things right,' as you assert."

He gives me a puzzled look as Naomi glances at me and leaves the room.

"Doesn't it occur to you that this could be impossible to recover from?" I ask him.

He starts to speak, shrugs, shovels down some beans, and heads for the land office.

I can almost hear his thoughts with each footfall, out the door, down the steps, thoughts of ruin stuffed once more beneath plans for the future, like bad debts swept under a rug: another crisis averted. Austin's plan for the colonists is already underway. Colonists are entering with special certificates of admittance to the DeWitt or Austin colony.

Austin's diehard credo must be ringing in his head: We will steer our "precious bark through the shoals and quicks," though few will appreciate what we're doing.

But no matter. Destiny is right. I must believe in Green. It is his and Austin's remarkable strength that lets them make this gamble. The rest of us are not made of such unalloyed iron, or brazen belief.

Eliza's wedding brings a respite in the tense spring of 1830. The crowd gathers in a bower of aged live oaks, branches sinuous as they are long. With Green officiating, the boys take their places in their new shirts, little groomsmen next to Thomas. Then bridesmaids Naomi, Eveline, and Faye, daisy chains in their hair, march toward them as fiddles play.

The entrance of the bride is spectacular. Her simple satin gown, embroidered with beads sent from Missouri, complements Eliza's tall, full-breasted figure. While few know Eliza, many know about her. The crowd swells to more than a hundred pairs of eyes before the bride comes floating down the path to the oak glade. Among that crowd are the celebrated and gentlemanly Stephen F. Austin, who has known the bride since childhood; red-haired Will, recently renamed John W. Jones, who brings Eliza an Appaloosa mare with a spotted rump as a wedding present; and the ancient Count de la Baume. The count, our neighbor, comes to pay his respects to the granddaughter of his Revolutionary War compatriot, my father, Jonas Seely. Among the guests are the Burnses, the McCoys, the Lockharts, the Sowells, and many more. The fiddlers play for a good while since the oak grove is a fair way from the house. The minister's slot stands empty while Green moves down the path, his eldest on his arm.

No one minds the wait. The long entrance gives the women and men time to look the bride up and down and the children time to run around before they must be still and silent. It gives Thomas time to appreciate his prize. As one wag in the meadow observes, "That Yankee boy's plucked the highest cherry on the tree." The long march gives Green time to contemplate the wedding present of a league of land we are bestowing on our daughter and her husband, Thomas.

For me, the long entrance is a rare moment to have my entire family together, free from care. It makes me remember my young self at my own wedding just over twenty years ago.

I see that for Eliza, the moment is sublime and bittersweet. Despite the joy of her love for Thomas and the reunion with her immediate family, I know sorrow tugs at my daughter's heart. Bereft of her Missouri grandparents, aunts and uncles and cousins, and all that world means to her, Eliza comes to a home as treacherous as it is alluring.

In late spring, I start a long letter to Liza Q and sister Susannah describing Eliza's glorious wedding and the happy occasion, explaining that Eliza and Thomas have settled happily just upriver on the league of land given to them. But, in the last paragraph, I refuse to mask my concerns for the future:

Eliza and Thomas's marriage was, unfortunately, the only spring celebration in the DeWitt colony. The Land Law, passed in April, has upset everyone. Despite Austin and his editorials in the Texas Gazette, *it is grim news. Almost every settler here has family and friends about to make the journey or on the way. Austin has brought the crisis under control for now. But the uncertainty has spread, slowing immigration and heightening tensions between Texians, as they call us, and Mexicans as if a big fish had leapt up, shattering the calm surface of the River Guadalupe, before diving back beneath the ripples.*

TERROR

It is time. On a clear September morning, I make my move.

I am driven by the deceptive quiet in Coahuila y Tejas. Is it the proverbial calm before the storm? Terán has approved Austin's solution to exempt the DeWitt and Austin colonies from the Land Law. In addition, Austin has been elected to the Coahuila y Tejas state legislature in the provincial capital of Saltillo. For Austin, it means more journeys of hundreds of miles, exhausting but crucial for maintaining relations with the Mexican government. Despite the approval for our two colonies to continue, tensions are mounting with other Americans. Mexican soldiers posted near Galveston Bay are preventing immigrants from entering Texas, in accord with the Land Law.

And that is not all. The colony is experiencing more Indian raids than ever before. With the influx of settlers comes greater encroachment on Comanche territory. More people also mean more cattle and horses, which the Comanche desire. Just this week, in a letter to Chief Músquiz in Béjar, Green explained that we are surrounded by

Indians and repeated his plea for a cannon to protect the town. The fort stands as a monument to the mass attack we all fear.

My petition for a grant has been at the forefront of my thoughts for weeks. I cannot wait any longer. Since Green won't face it, I must. I cannot trust fate or even Austin's clever dealings with the Mexican officials. I have to secure, in my name, some part of the future we came for.

I resolve to approach Green despite his long morning at the land office. People press him for answers about the mostly unmapped and unsurveyed tracts they claim. Married heads of families—tinsmiths, blacksmiths, backwoodsmen, and attorneys, all claiming to be farmers and ranchers—hope to glean the maximum haul: a league, 4,428 acres, and a labor of 177, making a total of 4,605 acres. They stand by the land office under the trees for hours, chewing and spitting tobacco, rolling cigarettes, waiting on Green to call their names. It is an activity he revels in, work sanctioned with official deeds to follow. At last, they disperse, and Green starts inside for his midday meal.

Seeing his bright mood, I hesitate no longer. I set a plate heaped with beans and cornbread before him and launch into the speech that, even after so many days of consideration, nearly sticks in my throat.

"Green, you know how proud I am of all you're doing," I begin, a false cheer in my voice making my Missouri vowels sound raw even to my own ears.

He looks up at me, frowning.

I rush on, thinking that wallowing in bull nettle would be easier. "But I must bring up something that plagues me. Something I have long considered."

From the folds of my skirt, I produce the paper carefully recopied this morning.

Green smiles at me. "Well, I hope you're not divorcing me."

"No, my intent is to make us stronger . . . to secure our family's future."

With that prospect circling like a bird of prey, Green arches his eyebrows, takes the paper carefully from me, and begins to read:

I, Sarah Seely, wife of Green DeWitt, with a family of six children, with all due respect and in the best form of law, present the following statement: In the year 1826 I arrived in this country with my above-mentioned family from the state of Missouri, one of the United States of the North. Since then, I have dwelt on a sitio of land, chosen by my husband on the right bank of the Guadalupe River, opposite the town of Gonzales. My husband, before mentioned, has made improvements such as houses and outbuildings for the family. The family has suffered much in consequence of being in an unpopulated country on the frontier. I, the petitioner, with a view to acquiring and preserving a secure estate for the maintenance of myself and my children, humbly ask that your government grant me and my children the league of land on which I now live.

Green reads the words twice and then looks at me with a wan smile. "Yes, Sarah, I should have pressed you to do this myself. This provides protection for you and the children, should anything happen to me."

Startled by his wilted response, I soften my offensive. "Dear Green, you have given us your life and dreams. This is the only way we can be sure to protect your legacy."

"Yes, you're right. Land in your name would protect you and the children, despite the ambiguous state of my affairs. But I don't want to get on the wrong side of the powers that be in Mexico City. The language has to be right. Let me work it out and return it to you."

"I can—"

He silences me with a look. "It will have to go through both the Gonzales and the San Felipe ayuntamientos once we get the wording we want." Rising, he strides to the barn, saddles Major, and disappears toward Gonzales, leaving his meal untouched.

Minerva and I spend the afternoon alone. Of all my babies, she is the sunniest and least demanding. She smiles and coos and laughs and finds few reasons to cry. Now almost a year old, she walks across the floor so sure-footed and confident, I believe Green's choice of the name Minerva, after the Roman goddess of wisdom, might turn out to be apt. As to the myth of the goddess springing from her father's head, her name is unquestionably emblematic of the colony, which indeed has sprung from his head.

I watch Minerva tottering back and forth across the floor, her joy apparent. The innocent babe, another girl who looks so like her father, brings to mind Green's own guilelessness, a trait I marvel at even after two decades of marriage.

Minnie prattles and plays. We move onto the porch as I contemplate Green's abrupt departure for Gonzales. His opaque expression and stoic response do not fool me. I have wounded him. At the same time, he knows I am right. And I know his strength. He doesn't blame me for my petition but rather approves my initiative. Governed by fair-mindedness, he offers reason and patience; even when I doubt him, he extends his principled code unstintingly to me.

Watching Minnie and enveloped in the joy of Eliza's return, I am grateful to God—and yes, to Green—for my blessings. Green and Destiny have waited for me to shut the door on the past. How long it has taken me to get here!

Green, rather than narrowing my life, as it once seemed, has indeed expanded it. And it is his example that has led me to advance a petition on my own. *Terror has many uses*, I think, turning my thoughts back to Minnie.

She is at the other end of the porch near Yowl, the cat sitting patiently by his water bowl. She is playing with a stick. The cat's eyes are fixed on the stick. At one end of it a red, yellow, and black thing wraps around Minnie's arm. Minnie dangles her fingers in the water as . . . "red and yellow, dangerous fellow" blasts through me. The small venomous coral snake is not prone to bite. Its mouth is only large enough to close around the web of hands and toes. *Or tiny fingers.*

Heading toward her, I trip and rush to her just as the snake's head reaches her hand. Instantly Yowl swats at the snake. It draws back, its head coming up off her hand in a colorful question mark. It opens its mouth, issuing a foul smell that makes the cat draw back.

I must get it off her arm.

Again, it raises its small head toward Minnie, and she points with her other hand, laughing. Yowl arches his back and hisses as the snake turns toward him. A mesquite branch lies on the porch nearby. I grab it and wave it in front of the snake. It starts to bite at the branch and then to wrap around it, advancing toward me now. When it is almost entirely off Minnie's arm, I thrust the branch onto the floor and kick and stamp at the snake. The branch whips this way and that, and I scoop Minnie into my arms. She giggles at my funny dance as I pound the deadly poisonous thing into the floorboards.

Not daring to let go of this adventurous child, I drag a bucket of water to the site and wash off the porch, fearing Yowl or Gyp might decide to feast on the snake's poisonous remains. But I'm not sure what to do with it. With a stick, I pluck the trampled mass from the porch and throw it into the bucket. Then I think better of that and fish it out again. I think I will burn it, despite the heat on this scorching day of late September. I am still clutching Minnie and pacing when horses come up the lane.

Green and Mr. Lockhart find me nearly hysterical. Spotting the rubbery mass of red blood and bright stripes, they both cast a fearful look at me.

"It's all right. It didn't bite anybody," I sob, incapable of explaining myself or controlling my shaking.

Green reaches his arms around us, holding me as I cling to Minnie, and gently takes her from me.

Pushing his hat to the back of his head, my petition in his hand, Mr. Lockhart says, "Sarah, you've had quite a day."

He waits for me to quiet down and puts his arm around my shoulders as Green steps inside with Minnie. "Coral snake's no joke," he says. "Good thing you knew what you were dealing with. Thank God you're both all right."

I bless him for granting me some small degree of sanity in saving my child. When I pull myself together, he says, "I've come with Green to look at the progress the carpenters are making with your barn and to tell you I agree with Green. This petition makes sense."

Hugely relieved, I restrain myself from throwing my arms around him.

He waits a moment, then goes on. "You deserve this land. Our group and the San Felipe ayuntamiento will approve it. Seems like, since this is an entirely separate matter from Green's contract, Colonel Austin ought to be able to persuade the powers that be, if there's any resistance. The Mexicans do it for widows, the only women who receive grants. That makes you an exception. With his election to the state legislature, Austin will have to travel back again to the provincial capital, to Saltillo, by the end of the year. Just make sure the wording in here is flowery enough. Got to get the right words. Austin's man, Sam Williams, can translate it. Put it the way the Mexicans want it."

When Antoñia and the children return from Eliza's the following day, Green rides away. On the mantle lies the envelope with the petition inside. I've been thinking about some lines I want to add. Now I muster the courage to read what Green has added to my draft.

I make this request for these reasons and also because my husband, the said Green DeWitt, finds himself behind in his negotiations on account of the enterprise he has undertaken. The attendant physical dangers and political risks have left the family in an unfortunate financial situation and exposed them to an uncertain future. I, the petitioner, with a view to acquiring and preserving a secure estate for myself and children should any harm come to him, humbly beg your excellency to have the kindness to concede to me and my children in fee simple for myself and my heirs the sitio of land above mentioned on which I now live, with the understanding that all the requirements of the law in the matter will be fulfilled. Therefore, I ask and beg you be so kind as to favor me by doing as above stated.

Reading Green's words twice, set down in my voice, I put aside the paper and let the tears flow. I know what it cost him to put his humiliation in writing for Austin and Mr. Lockhart and the world to see, my petition a death knell to his highest hopes and dreams. His words are an admission, a refusal, for once, to put the best face on things. I feel Destiny eyeing me with deep disapproval.

A TOAST

The red-headed rider is unmistakable, as is the lurch in my heart. Approaching on his red roan, Will rides next to a long-faced man on a Spanish mustang. I stop weeding my vegetable patch to watch the two come up from the river. His spirited Ruby tries to dance sideways, but Will keeps her at a leisurely pace. He takes in the scene, soaking up life on the Warloop. Chickens cluck and flutter out of the way. Leaning on my hoe, I consider Will's familiar slouch in the saddle. Hatless, his carrot-red hair catches the light despite the overcast January morning. When the riders are in shouting distance, I start toward them. They rein in their horses next to my garden.

Combing his fingers through the roan's strawberry blond mane, Will looks down at me, his eyes bright with affection. "This here woman," he says to his companion, "is the one and only Sarah Seely DeWitt."

"And this here dignitary," he says to me, motioning at the man in a vest and duster, "is the most influential Tejano in Coahuila y Tejas, Señor José Antonio Navarro."

I extend my hand to the other rider.

"Welcome to Gonzales. We've waited a long time for a visit from you," I say, acknowledging the importance of the land commissioner in the continuing life of the colony.

"A great pleasure to meet you, Señora DeWitt," Navarro says, his arched, pointed brows moving up and down in an otherwise placid face. I think Will might describe him as horse faced. He makes me think of Old Testament prophets, seeming both kind and inscrutable, clearly a man of composure.

Green comes out of the land office with his shoulders hunched against the chill of the morning. He covers the distance between us in long strides.

The men dismount and tie their horses.

"Señor Navarro, good to see you, good to have you. Will, it's been a while." Green shakes Navarro's hands warmly, avoiding the same with Will. "So much to do," Green says, rubbing his hands together with evident pleasure as he walks ahead toward the land office with Navarro.

Señor Navarro nods calmly, his deliberate demeanor signaling that he does nothing hastily or without knowledge of the consequences. About the same age and height as Green, he nevertheless seems the elder statesman.

Will follows the men with his eyes and then purposefully moves into the garden with me.

"Now, don't stop what you're doin'. I ain't gonna interrupt the noble task of weedin' a garden. Happy to tag along here and see what you're growin'." He smiles broadly and seats himself on the nearest stump.

It has been six months since Eliza's wedding, the last time we laid eyes on each other. I greeted him as one of the guests then. Now I don't have to dissemble. I am happy to have him in my garden.

The corners of his eyes crinkle in lines as familiar to me as the contours of my own face. Will's smile holds a quality of mischief and warmth that never fails to remind me of our youth. Somehow, his features—the boyish grin, his upturned mouth lines, the purse of his lips, and even his lined square brow—work in concert to give him a steadiness I always want to lean on.

Reluctantly, I take my eyes off him. I dig out a few potatoes and carrots, extolling my winter vegetables, and laying out my plans for spring.

"Green beans, squash, spring onions, okra. If I can get the seeds from my sister, or Molly, in the mail." I chatter on, wondering if Will has something on his mind. Uncharacteristically, he is short on words. He listens, follows me for a bit, and then sits again in silence on the stump as I continue my garden chores. When I finish, we go in to have coffee and warm ourselves by the fire.

"I guess you're doing pretty good here, huh?" he asks not once but twice as we talk about nothing in particular. He brings up Eliza's wedding and seems on the brink of divulging something. But he backs away from it, turning to matters of the colony.

After I feed Minerva, Will dandles her on his knee to give her a horsey ride. Minnie screams with delight, and Will plays with her as if he can't think of what else to do. I sit down to shell some pecans. Though this unusual hesitation around me is puzzling, I don't press him. I don't want to squander the goodness of being in his company.

"You know I'm never going to call you John or Juan," I tease as I crush pecans together, picking out the sweetmeats and dropping them into a bowl.

"So I'm going to remain Will to you, no matter what," he says.

"Yes, you are." I smile and offer the pecans I've picked out. "I can't think of what would change you to John in my eyes."

"That's good, Sarah," he says, sitting on the floor and looking at me. His eyes tell me much of what he feels can't be said. Under his warm gaze, I enjoy the open admiration. "I hope you stick to that," he says as Green and Señor Navarro enter the kitchen.

The girls help me with the midday meal as Antoñia puts Minerva down for a nap and takes the boys for a walk to gather pecans. The heavy-laden trees dropped their loads far and wide all fall this year. Even now, in January, industrious gatherers are still finding them.

Seating themselves before the fire, the three men talk about all that needs to be done. Preparing for Gonzales's first election of an ayuntamiento is high on the list. We have passed the 150-families mark, far beyond what is required to elect a council, and a formal governing body is needed. However, the top priority is approval of Mr. Lockhart as an official surveyor. It's a formality but crucial, nonetheless.

"The town must be surveyed according to the rules laid out by the authorities. Gonzales has grown," Señor Navarro says politely, referring to the random score of stores and cabins popping up everywhere like weeds. "We must lay out the town properly, *en una manera* adecuada."

Listening to them as I prepare the meal, I know he is referring to the preliminary survey. It was not fully in accord with Mexican law, since it lacked provisions for the correct number of public squares. The plan for the town tract is to contain several leagues, with public squares and inner and outer towns correctly designated.

"First, however, I must get all the official notices from Saltillo and the capital. Then we can resurvey the town tract," Navarro says.

Green nods in agreement.

This means months more of delay, I realize, but in this case, might it give us more time to bring in settlers, if the Mexican authorities do not hold strictly to the contractual date?

"There are close to five hundred people in the colony now and right at two hundred families with more coming every day. We'll be taking another census next month," Green says.

The number sounds pitifully low now. Am I the only one who thinks it is impossible to get to the magic number of four hundred families by April 15?

"New contingents of families set to arrive any day now," Green informs Navarro again. He is noncommittal about official numbers and doesn't mention the stipulation of four hundred families to be settled in the colony if Green is to reap his full reward. Navarro is clearly performing his obligations with little investment in whether there is room to extend the contractual deadline until official surveys are completed. Glancing at Will, I am sure he sees it simply: Green's success, like most matters, is governed by luck. The Mexicans would take a while to resurvey and get official business completed. During this time, there could be a valuable increase in the number of settlers. But I'm sure Will is aware of the contract's terms and must think that Green's luck is running out.

As the girls put food on the table, our guest unwraps a bottle of wine brought from his fine wine closet in Béjar. Thanking him for his gift, I provide cut-glass tumblers, and we sit down to eat after Green delivers the blessing. Then Navarro, in flawless English, proposes a toast. "I congratulate you, Empresario DeWitt, on the milestone of bringing several hundred families to the colony."

My ears prick up. "Several hundred" means he doesn't know exactly how many families have come into the colony. And indeed, until the next census is done, no one is quite sure.

"I consider it an honor to be your land commissioner. What you have done here is important not only for your personal fortune but for the good fortunes of Coahuila y Tejas."

Green nods gratefully. "To many more celebrations." He holds up his glass.

Looking at Will, Navarro adds, "We also should toast our friend here, Señor Jones, on his good fortune, his recent marriage to Señorita Maria de Jesus Castellano."

Will stares grimly at me. I remember the night of the fandango in Béjar and my introduction to Señor Castellano. And the young woman who gazed after Will with longing.

I glare at Will, the expression on my face visibly unnerving the Tejano.

Only Green raises his glass. He smiles slowly and shakes his head as if amazed at the wiles of Will Jones.

"Dang, Will, that's a surprise." Though not unfamiliar with the code of the West (if you leave one behind, you can take another), Green's incredulity shows for a moment. Then, recovering his composure, he says, "Congratulations are in order. Bring your new wife around to meet us."

Glasses clink. My hand trembles as I touch mine to the others. You're married to Harriet Jones. You can't marry again, I want to shout at him. The jarring tinka-tinka-tinka of the toasts fills the silence. I draw back as if from a hot stove. Naomi's eyes widen. Mine go opaque.

As the food is passed around the table, I excuse myself to check on Minnie, crying in the loft. I force myself back to the table only when the others have almost finished their meal. When I sit down again, Naomi, who continues to tend to the adults, looks searchingly at me. Will remains quiet, his eyes fixed on my face. I will not meet them. I stare beyond him, my mouth set in a line, my face as blank as I can make it.

FATE

Schoolroom demands keep all of us busy. Though Naomi takes her job seriously, Eliza's presence helps relieve her duties of teaching now three dozen students, allowing Naomi to steal time to be with William Matthews. I watch Eliza eyeing the young lovers as she waits for Thomas's return. Gone now for more than a month to attend to legal matters, he sailed on a coasting schooner back across the Gulf to New Orleans with promises to bring gifts and supplies for their new homestead. Her land a morning's ride northwest of us, Eliza lives with us in Thomas's absence. A couple of workmen help tend her growing herd of cattle as she makes regular trips to her place on her mare. Eliza has named the horse Quick, for her speed and for her own beloved grandmother, Liza Quick Seely. Today, as we've planned, the girls give me a free day out of the class-room to attend to tasks at home. As the children head off to Gonzales, I hear a rider coming toward the house.

Noting the slow footfall of a trail mule, I look out to see Eugenio perched on its back. I cannot recall ever seeing him ride a horse or mule. He always arrives in his squeaky, two-wheeled *carreta* or his lopsided, creaky wagon. The big, surefooted mule with Eugenio on his back is an oddly troubling sight. As they plod toward the house, I see not the industrious cart driver and trader but the messenger, wanting to avoid the bustle and noise signaling his arrival.

His face falls as he greets me.

"What is it, Eugenio? What is it?"

Taking my hand, he heads me to a little bench Green carved from fallen walnut limbs. Watching Eugenio's face, I calm myself by accounting, in my head, for my family: Green is in the land office, the children are gone in the wagon, Antoñia and Minnie in the house. I know even before Eugenio speaks that the news is about Thomas.

"*El esposo de la hija rubia*," he says, hanging his head. "*Está muerto.* Dead. The yellow fever. On the ship. *El cuerpo*, the body, *ya está* sleeping in the wave*s, durmiendo en las olas*."

Sadness envelops Eugenio. Today he is shrunken, lost in the folds of his familiar brown serape. For a brief moment, I feel, by its absence, the buoyancy of this man.

I grab his hand and hug him close.

"Oh my, oh my, God help us. Yes, yes, as you say, Eugenio, sleeping among the waves."

Eugenio struggles to make me understand the details. Thomas died on the return trip. Others on the schooner also died from a yellow fever epidemic rampant in New Orleans. The bodies were cast overboard before the ship docked in Matagorda Bay. When Eugenio arrived to bring Thomas home, the ship's captain gave him the news. His eyes redden, and respectfully, he utters his epitaph for the marriage: "*Ni un año*." Nodding, I repeat his sad truth: "Not even a year."

Eugenio's arrival and departure is so quiet, so unobtrusive—as he intends—I am the only one who pauses in my daily activities as he comes and goes. The children are off to school, Antoñia and Green perform their duties, the cattle graze languidly, and the horses look up occasionally in the pasture to see what the humans are doing. I remain on the bluff, staring down at the river. Newly arrived, newly married, newly widowed. My big, beautiful Eliza, who never needed protection, to experience such loss, and barely twenty-one years old.

Grazing nearby, Pal ambles up to me and nuzzles my hand. Feeling the soft velvet of the mare's nose, I weep, telling the horse my sorrow. "Eliza will be home soon, Pal, and I have to tell her today before the sun sets, today before she spends another night looking for her husband's return."

When I turn from the river, Antoñia looms in the doorway, her straight-across bangs emphasizing the thin slash of her mouth. Unlike the others, she has no doubt sensed trouble arriving on the mule. She will know something, a potion, a tea to give Eliza to calm her, something to let her sleep perhaps. We have several hours before her return. As I enter the house and sit down to explain, first to Green, then Antoñia, I keep hearing Eliza's laugh as she went out the door. How long will it be before I hear it again?

Death is no stranger to the people of the DeWitt colony. Yet my family has been spared until now. The days of grief claw through all of us: Eliza spends days asleep and nights awake. Hours prowling the river and moments, along its banks, in utter collapse when Green or I, or both of us, go after her and bring her back. Antoñia's concoctions help, but what I see, as the weeks dull the pain, is Eliza no longer young. At least not twenty-one years young. She ages almost overnight, not in the lines in her face or the stoop of her shoulders but in the sadness of her eyes. The bold Eliza is replaced by another one I do not know so well. She does not lose her strength. Perhaps it is the coltishness that goes out of her. But more than that, a kind of empty, erratic quality overtakes her. She is sour and pale and distracted. And a pale, ashen streak grows into her honey-blonde hair.

Along with the death of Thomas comes another less momentous, yet unprecedented event. In the fall, Green had again petitioned the Mexican authorities in Béjar for a cannon. In March, Músquiz, the political chief at Béjar, approved the request, and a colonist transported the big gun back to Gonzales. I am home alone when he arrives with the cannon. I instruct him to leave it on the porch.

The first full day it rests there, Eliza walks around it several times. "For defense against the Indians," I explain, though it seems singularly unimpressive.

"Umm," Eliza says. "It reminds me of the small one on the schooner *Dispatch* that brought Thomas and me to Texas." Using her sewing tape, she measures it. "Poppa would like it, I'm sure, if we could get it up in the fort. Think I'll ride to the fort and see how we might do that. Come with me?"

Eager to spend time with Eliza when she will talk with me, I quickly agree. We saddle up and ride to Gonzales. We pass through the double doors into the big fort, which Eliza has never entered. Its dirt floor is packed solid from dances, celebrations, and the drills by local men in case of Indian attack.

Weeds grow in a few small patches by the back wall. I sit on a log while Eliza walks around the barnlike edifice, an empty cavern with a few side rooms and a raised dance floor toward the back. Sparrows, robins, mockingbirds, and red-winged blackbirds fly in and out of the open rafters above. Armadillos scurry under the walls. We listen to the birds building their nests and feeding their young. I know she is thinking of Thomas while trying to remind herself why we are here.

Along the high front of the fort is a lookout post. Pointing from just outside the double front door, she says, "There, Momma. That's where the cannon can go, a warning for Indians and all who would threaten the colony. Strong arms can carry it up or hoist it up the stairs to the lookout balcony, and there it will remain."

I join her outside. It looks like there is enough room on the little makeshift crow's nest for a man to stand, load the muzzle, and lay the wick inside. Eliza climbs the stairs and measures the dimensions of the platform. The unassuming little brass six-pounder is just an unmounted tube.

"Yes, it will fit," she says, looking out on Water Street and the ferry, which is running today. Putting her measuring tape back in her pocket, she sighs with relief.

It is the first positive thing she has done since the news of Thomas's death. Today she doesn't seem to be so exhausted by her own emotions. I know how she thinks. If she can do something, once a day, paltry as it might be, then maybe she can get her bearings again. Eliza comes back down and sits on the dance floor with me, feeling its rough boards. She curls her feet under her and looks up in the rafters at the birds. I'd written to her of the celebrations here, though none have taken place since her arrival with Thomas a year ago.

Leaving the fort, we continue riding down Water Street. Beyond the fort is the market square, where people regularly bring produce and eggs and livestock to trade and sell on Saturdays. The Mexican flag waves above the empty square. We ride past the square, Sowell's smithy, and two more houses before stopping at the saddler's shop.

No one is there. Just three saddles on sawhorses, tied down with thick ropes to discourage theft. We dismount and walk among the saddles, smelling the leather.

"Thomas admired these saddles," Eliza says. "I was going to buy one for his birthday." I slip my arm around her before she turns away.

Mounting Quick, as if trying to rejoin life in Gonzales, Eliza continues her tour of the town. I follow on Pal. We ride over to the next street, past three more houses, past Luna, where two men are weaving down the steps with one of Belle's girls between them, then head toward Turner's Hotel. On the front porch of the hotel, Mrs. Turner is shooing away a grunting sow and piglets trying to make their way inside. At the hotel with our familiar schoolroom inside, Gonzales feels almost like a real town. The Turners and their five children are enough to keep things busy. Three children chase on the porch. We keep the horses to a walk past the hotel and Horace Eggleston's store, which now has bolts of cloth and sewing notions for sale.

In the next block, the recently arrived Tennessean, Mr. Almeron Dickinson, negotiates with Mr. Kimble, agent for the hat shop. The close-fitting caps of animal skins—raccoon, rabbit, fox, squirrel, beaver—look as if Mr. Kimble has sewn them together on the spot. Also on display are several country hats with high crowns and wide brims, a flat-brimmed mountain man's hat with feathers in it, and a top hat looking like an upside-down flowerpot.

I'd seen men in Missouri wear those. Most of the hats, I figure, have lived several lives before landing in Mr. Kimble's open-air business establishment. I wonder how he came by these hats and imagine him bartering for his wares with travelers passing through. Perhaps from bereaved relatives bidding goodbye to the possessions of the dearly departed. For a moment, Thomas's wide-brimmed felt hat, as he rode away from us in early February, floats through my thoughts. Then Eliza gives her restless mare her head, and we start back across the river.

On April 13, a Friday, Green comes into the kitchen to tell me what I already know. The last wagon train, at the beginning of April, has brought the total to 531 individuals, with just under two hundred families. Unwittingly, Mr. Lockhart had let that number drop in conversation a few days ago. For me, it is simply confirmation of the inevitable. For Green, it is an unthinkable conclusion after years of unceasing effort.

I am mixing cornbread batter when Green sits down in front of the window. I stop when I hear the finality of Green's words.

"Less than four hundred," he says. "That's the only number that matters, despite all the people we've brought here. Less than four hundred families." Then he says nothing for a good while. I go to him and take his crumpled face in my hands.

"I know, Green. I know. But we'll be all right. We'll survive. And it doesn't mean . . . this venture wasn't wrong. You've already made history. You and Austin, Empresario De León, too, have launched a whole new world."

He grabs me and holds onto me for a moment or two, and then shakes his head. Wordless, the smooth talk stuck in his throat, he leaves me to go out to the land office.

Señor Navarro makes a second appearance on April 16, a date both obviously and carefully chosen. The timing is lost on no one—the day after Green's six-year contract to settle four hundred families expires. Though no one mentions or acknowledges it, the latest census, communicated to Green a day earlier, has made the hard fact official. Fewer than four hundred heads of household have made applications to Empresario DeWitt. Legally, no more lands can be procured from the empresario without the renewal of the contract. Today, the precise Navarro certainly has the date, and the telling number, firmly in mind.

The voices of Green and Navarro on the porch reach me in the kitchen. Navarro's task is to issue land titles to the heads of families in the colony. Green could point with pride to the households now sprawled up and down the rivers and creeks and tributaries to points north and south, east and west-northwest of Gonzales. To the settlers who obtained them, gaining title to their lands is a singular achievement. The leagues and labors, adding up to more than 4,600 acres for some families, are as precious as gemstones strung along the Guadalupe and San Marcos and Lavaca Rivers. But Green's only thought is that he failed to reach his goal. And given the Mexicans' wariness over Anglos seizing their land, he has to know that Navarro will not be advocating a contract renewal.

I follow Eliza into the land office. Navarro rises and greets us with a handshake.

"The resemblance between you, Señora Hamilton, and your dignified father is most striking," Navarro says, his stilted but correct English impressive as ever.

The sensitive Navarro makes no mention of Eliza's widowhood. He quickly examines Eliza's petition in his book and makes no comment about women being granted property rights only as widows. Eliza listens carefully, nodding as he speaks about the league she and Thomas had received as a wedding gift from Green. He reviews with her the full price of a league of land—$61 for 4,428 acres. She will be responsible for paying in thirds with the first installment not due until four years after the title is issued to her today by Navarro.

"Yes, I understand," Eliza says. "I am prepared to pay the $15 fee for your service and the $16 fee for the original stamped paper and copies and the survey. I know, from Poppa, that you and Mr. Lockhart are too seldom paid for such." She lays bills and coins on the table.

Navarro nods appreciatively, looking at the young woman and then at me sitting to the side. "An important moment for you and your mother and father," he says, expressing ever so discreetly his concern for our recently widowed daughter.

Mr. Navarro cannot know how significant this moment is for me. I look at the table as he talks to Eliza. It holds several quill pens, an inkwell, and a pen with a metal nib. A cowhide-bound book, opened to recent entries, records settlers and sizes of grants issued to date, all to be reissued and certified with a seal to become final. Watching Eliza as she receives her copy of the land title, signed by Navarro and embossed with the seal, I take comfort in my daughter's acquisition. I hear Green's Angel of Destiny reminding me this is but one of the rewards Green has secured for us.

I know the moment is more bitter than sweet for Eliza—what Liza Q calls wormwood and gall—to own land she can neither share with Thomas nor even inhabit safely alone. Having learned the truth of the maxim "life is short," Eliza is nevertheless mindful of the dreams of her father. After receiving Navarro's good wishes and her land title, Eliza thanks him warmly, then swallows and clenches her jaw.

He then turns to me. "You, Señora, receive a title for your *es-special* grant. You know, do you not, this is the *only* league granted to a married Anglo woman? For your great contributions to Mexico."

I feel a measure of relief. "The Sarah Seely league," he goes on, "lies on both sides of the river, land to the north and south." I indeed do know my league extends north of the river and about three miles south.

"In time," he says, "el empresario also will receive his premium lands, four leagues for the first one hundred families in his colony."

These words, meant to bestow congratulation, hit in the pit of my stomach. It is many leagues and many thousands of acres short of what was hoped for. As I reflect on the gain and loss, I do not see balanced scales. I consider whether my Presbyterian faith is a bulwark sufficient to this wild land. Advice from my mother appears, as if she were standing next to me: "God doesn't close one door before opening another."

Considering all the closed doors, I find such faith impossible now. But, yes, I am thankful for *these* that have opened. With my grant, I have something to leave to my children. And presumably, Green will receive his titles and more land to leave to the children. But does this mean that we must stay here? Five leagues of land in exchange for all we have lost? It isn't even certain we can keep this land. If relations between Coahuila y Tejas and the rest of Mexico remain dire, the mercurial Santa Anna can take it all away with a wave of the pen or the sword.

PART III
SANTA ANNA'S MOUND

Gonzales and Guadalupe Victoria
1833-35

The hill known as Santa Anna's Mound is clearly visible from the house, a part of my league. In the days leading up to the battle, the Mexicans camped there. Indeed, it sometimes felt as if the shadow of Santa Anna himself loomed over it, waiting for the right time to crush the Anglos' dreams.

The slow march to that first battle started when Austin lost his right-hand man in Mexico, General Mier y Terán, in the summer of 1832. If there was any point that marked the beginning of the end, it was Terán's suicide. Enlightened Terán, second in command in Mexico, was the bulwark against the hothead Santa Anna. Facing a civil war in Mexico and beset by poor health, Terán fell on his sword following a military defeat. With Terán's death came Santa Anna's reckless ascent. Discord and dissension between Texas and Mexico followed, the chasm growing wider by the year. Green and Austin refused to believe that the differences between the colonists wanting greater independence from Mexico and her dictator-general Santa Anna could not be bridged. Ever mindful of diplomatic solutions, the empresarios were loyal to Mexico. Reasonable to the end, Austin once more made the daunting journey to Mexico City to appeal to Santa Anna for a resolution of grievances. Instead, Austin was imprisoned. What followed lit the fuse: not in Mexico City, but on my league of land near the mound.

TEXAS.

By

((DAVID H. BURR.))

SCOURGE

ummer seizes me like a wolf grasping a rabbit in its jaws. In the spring, as Austin was departing on his 1,200-mile journey to Mexico City, he warned us about cholera at the mouth of the Brazos. Seven died in April; then it got worse. In June, seventy Irish settlers, who had survived the treacherous crossing of the Atlantic to start new lives in Texas, perished in the port of New Orleans, victims of another cholera outbreak; dozens more died from cholera upon arrival on the Texas coast. In July, at the meeting of the ayuntamiento, there are reports of the dread disease in Béjar, Victoria, and Goliad.

We hesitate no longer. Green and the children will go by boat to Eliza's league upriver. The farther from town we get, the better chance we have, and the well water at Eliza's is clear and sweet. Antoñia and I will gather supplies and come on horseback.

The next morning, Eugenio arrives with news that Empresario Martín De León has formed a committee in nearby Guadalupe Victoria to clean up the stagnant water and filth in the streets. They hope to eliminate the disease, which is said to lurk in the water. Seeing the fear in my eyes, Eugenio tries to tell me what he's heard on the streets of Béjar. "*No se preocupe, Señora,* no worry."

"*¿Por qué no?* I am very worried. *Muy preocupada.*"

"*Sí, pero* I have *información.* I hear some-theeng good."

I frown, shaking my head. "It all sounds bad to me, Eugenio."

"*Sí, sí, yo entiendo.* You a-fraid. But I have *información, de un médico de Monterrey.*" His eyes light up. He flashes a grin, signaling he knows something I don't. "*Regreso.* I come back. *Rápido, con algo* to protect you."

"To protect me?"

"*Y su familia. Ojalá que si.* Hope it is so."

In my fear, I imagine copper amulets around the neck and potions against *mal aire* to ward off the deadly disease.

Within hours Eugenio's cart once more climbs the hill and arrives at my gate. Waving a paper above his head, he joins me on the porch.

"*Un regalo, Señora,* a gift for you," he whoops, as pleased with himself as I've ever seen. Thrusting a paper into my hands, he says, "For you, in Eng-leesh." Printed in a fine, clear hand that looks familiar, RECIPE FOR CHOLERA CURE BY DR. SENDEJAS covers the paper.

Boil one peyote button in a cup of water. Strain the liquid and add as much slaked lime as can be held on a silver real. Stir and drink. If the symptoms do not abate within a half-hour, repeat the dose. An infusion of tea or orange leaves, with six drops of laudanum, must then be given every two hours. If cramps are experienced, rub parts of the body affected with wool. Until eight hours after the attack, no nourishment shall be given. Until the patient recovers completely, give only a thin mixture of atole (gruel made of ground nixtamal, or corn boiled in lime water, and water or milk). After complete recovery, give soup and tender broiled or stewed meat.

Astonished, I quiz him. "Where did you get this? *¿De dónde? ¿De quién?*"

"*El Colorado*," he answers proudly.

I haven't seen Will in more than two years. "And where did he get it?"

"*El Jefe Músquiz en Béjar, tal vez,* maybe. *¿Quién sabe?*" He hurries back to his cart for a basket. With a flourish, he hands me a basket containing an envelope holding the slaked lime powder and a silver coin. Underneath it, a little cloth contains a small bottle of laudanum and a handful of brownish-white peyote buttons.

I stare blankly.

"*El Colorado,*" he says once again. "He no want you to worr-ee."

My eyes go watery. I look down and back up to Eugenio's.

"I tell him *muchísimas gracias de* Say-rah." He chuckles softly at the pronunciation of my first name and his presumption to use it.

"Yes, yes." I grab Eugenio's hand. "*Muchísimas gracias.*"

"*Me voy a Gonzales.*"

"And return along this road?"

"*Sí, Señora.*"

"Then I'll ride with you." Clutching the recipe and basket, a foolish relief washes over me.

At Luna, I peer into the bins, select the supplies I need, and pay Murphy, who hasn't been in the store for some time. "Where's Belle?"

"Taken sick," he growls.

"When was that?"

"Few days ago. Cholera, they say."

"Who's tending her?"

"Belle don't need no one."

Back in the cart, I do not hesitate. Armed with the cure Will has sent me, I instruct Eugenio. "We must see about Belle. She's sick."

Several miles out of town on the road to Béjar, Belle's little hovel sits a few hundred yards up a rutted lane. In front, three dogs bark at our approach. A milk cow with a full bag bawls.

Making our way past the dogs, we push open a creaking door and find Belle on an iron cot in the middle of her one-room cabin. Awakened by the squeak of the door, Belle pushes up on one elbow. "Don't come no closer," she says. "I've got the danged bloody flux, the cholera, but I ain't dead yet."

From pots around the room, a stench reaches us. We stop just inside the door, inhaling the evidence of the disease and its terrible course.

"When did you get sick?"

"Fell down in the yard two days ago. Dragged myself in like a dang varmint. You smell it, I guess."

"Belle, I'm going to fix something to make you better."

"Don't come one step nearer, woman. You want this pestilence? Get away, or I'll have to shoot you."

"Now, Belle, you're not going to shoot me, and I'm not going to leave you alone like this," I say, trying to match my tone to hers. "I have a potion, something you must drink."

Eugenio goes to the cart, returning with the envelope containing the slaked lime powder and coin. Then he hands me a peyote button. I find a pump at the side of the house, a big tin cup, and a gourd. Quickly I fill the gourd with water. I pour the water into a pot on the hearth where a low fire burns. I drop the button into the water and let it boil. From the envelope, I shake a portion of the lime onto the silver coin and dump the powder in as well.

Eugenio reaches into the pot to extract the boiled peyote button. "*No tome*," he says with a little hiccup of a laugh. "No drink."

I pour the liquid into the tin cup and take it to the patient's bedside, covering my mouth and nose with my sleeve.

"Belle, drink this. It will hasten your recovery," I say, wondering why, like Antoñia with her black snake, I somehow trust in this charm. But in the back of my mind, I know why. It is from Will.

"Now you two git. Git outta here," she says. She drinks from the cup with one hand while motioning us out the door with the other.

Running our hands under the pump, Eugenio and I pump water for each other, hoping our makeshift hand wash will protect us from the terrible dangers lurking in Belle's cabin. On the way home, I give up on traveling to Eliza's today. Eugenio will carry word to them that Antoñia and I will come tomorrow.

Morning brings stifling weather. Trying to get ready to go, I sit down, get up, and sit down again. The day is suffocating. Two hogs come up on the porch; one of them is as big as a four-month-old calf.

They shake the floorboards, adding to my headache. I shoo them away, but with barely enough strength to stay standing. I am so hot I strip down to camisole and petticoat. My hands are clammy, my legs and feet stone cold. In a few minutes, the stomach pains start. I head to the privy in the woods. And then, as soon as I think it's over, I'm running back again. When my stomach seems entirely empty, I stumble back toward the house, vomiting up white mucous several times in the woods.

Lurching into the house, I know Antoñia will return shortly. How can I keep her a safe distance away? My stomach cramps with such force I can think of nothing else. Struggling to the cupboard, I find the basket holding the cholera-fighting ingredients. With shaking hands, I drop a peyote button into a tin cup of water and place it on the coals of the fire. Remembering the dose for Belle, I shake the lime powder into the cup and wait while the mixture simmers. It seems to take hours for the liquid to boil.

Just as the bubbles appear, I hear Antoñia coming up from the river. I have to drink the mixture and get out of the kitchen to avoid spreading this terrible contagion. I look around for a cloth to pick the cup out of the fire and see none. Antoñia has washed everything in the river. In desperation, I fish the hot cup out of the fire with the hem of my petticoat and smell the smoldering cloth.

Stamping out the slow burn, I clutch the cup and drink, feeling with indifferent detachment the husk of the peyote button slide down my throat. Eugenio fished the fibrous pulp of the peyote button out of the cup at Belle's, and I know I should have strained the liquid from the peyote. But I am too sick to care what hallucinations may come. I hope its potency is too diluted to induce anything worse than what I fear already.

Trying to focus on the tea I must prepare, I wander about the kitchen. When Antoñia comes in, I repeat, "Tea, make tea, add drops."

Antoñia stares at me in my undergarments, then listens to my instructions and prepares the tea with six drops of laudanum as I direct. Then I give in, letting her lead me into the bedroom, cover me with blankets, and rub my shoulders. She stations herself by the door.

Doubled over in pain, I retch into the pot by the bed. Again and again. After what seems hours of retching and cramping, I am wet from head to toe. Every pore seems to be gushing liquid. Then the aftermath: my mouth, throat, even my eyelids dry, parched. Antoñia gives me water and more water and bathes my face. When the retching stops, dry heaves start.

After a while, Antoñia seems far away. She looks at me strangely. I begin to stare at the walls. They are crawling. Stumbling into the far corner, I grasp at spiders, centipedes, and other creatures. "Spider, spider," I point to the walls. Antoñia comes to me and says gently, "No, no spider," leading me back to the bed. Everything seems larger than life; there are so many colors in the plain brown daddy longlegs and the scorpion's mouth and bulging eyes. Looking into the small mirror propped by the bed, I gaze at myself. My skin, normally pale, is red and blue and pink and purple, as varied and interesting as a map. My eyes and nose, with many veins and colors, belong to a woman I've never seen before.

Lying back, cradling an elbow in each hand, I hear keening sounds coming from my mouth, similar to the wails Antoñia makes sometimes. I can't stop them.

I see Will plain as day, and I have to tell him what is in my heart. "You save me; you worry about me," I tell him, swaying. "You always worry about me. And I worry about you. Must it be so? Will it always be?" I can't stop repeating this refrain, each time as if it were the first. Will gazes back at me, a long, loving look that says he hears me. When I glance at Antoñia, she smiles knowingly.

Then I see Liza Q. Antoñia nods as I talk. "Don't be sad, my dear one, my beloved mother. We'll spend days together in heaven if not on earth. Don't fret. Days . . . together again."

Liza Q answers me: "Yes, my dear child, we will. We will ever hold each other close."

Behind Liza Q is Green. He is trying to tell me something. But I can't hear what he's saying. He looks devastated to see me so sick. "Sorry, so sorry. I don't want you to suffer."

"I know, Green. I know," I tell him. "I've forgiven you. Have you forgiven me? I am back with you. But are we together? Are we truly

together again?" Green nods, smiling with a sad passion that illuminates his face.

"Husband-man now," Antoñia says, nodding her head, giving
me water.

I go back and forth among the three until the sun sets, communing with them as if they are all seated before me. As the room
darkens, I struggle to sit up and feel like I'm floating across the room,
lighter than air, relieved of almost everything. Then I realize I haven't
moved off the bed.

Exhausted, limp as a rag doll, I drop back onto the bed and close
my eyes. Feeling my forehead, Antoñia says, "Better now."

I nod. Coming back from somewhere. Again, Antoñia administers
the tea and laudanum drops, and I drink. Bending over me, mopping
my brow, Antoñia croons softly, trying to sing me to sleep. "Sarah talk
strong magic," she says after a while.

I see the braves of her Karankawa world, rubbed black with alligator grease, summoning power as they dance around the fire.

When Belle and Eugenio come late the next day, I am sitting up with a
lap robe, weak but taking broth and the corn gruel Antoñia provides.
I ask Eugenio to let my family know I'm sick, but that, under no circumstances, may any one return here.

"So, Belle, we have both wriggled free from the clutches of the
wretched cholera sickness."

"Mercy, woman, if you'd a-died, woulda been on my head. I warned
you not to be in sich an all-fired hurry to play nursemaid," she mutters with energy in her voice, though she remains washed out and
wan. But even the gruff Belle is not without gratitude. She regards
me with real concern in her eyes, then says, "Hain't been for that
stuff tastin' like hog slops you made me drink, I coulda been dead
as a doornail by now. Dang pestilence can wipe out a body in a day
or two. Gonna be a month 'fore I'm back to bootin' riffraff down the
stairs at Luna."

Eugenio wears a wide smile, puffed up over the remedy he'd delivered. "*Mescalito, nuestro amigo*, friend," he says, his conviction laced

with a little surprise. I suppose not even an acolyte of the divine cactus root had expected such dramatic demonstrations of its curative powers. While I think how I must thank him for saving my life and Belle's, I consider whether I will confess soaring into his magical land, traveling the road of enlightenment that stretches forward from his ancestors and his beloved grandfather.

Summer holds more surprises. With Antoñia at my side, I'm almost back to normal. I rest and contemplate the news sent back from upriver in a note from Green. It is about Naomi and William Matthews, the young agent who remains closely allied with Green. Though we don't see him often, he and Naomi have spent time together, taking walks, going on picnics, riding into Gonzales on market days. He disappears for great stretches of time, continuing to act as an agent for Green, attending to his league on the San Marcos River. Then he reappears to talk business with Green and court Naomi in a here-today, gone-tomorrow fashion. But now, Green writes, he has asked for eighteen-year-old Naomi's hand in marriage. I try to figure the difference in their ages and calculate Matthews is in his midtwenties. But it is not his age that bothers me. Nor hers, even. I was married at eighteen. Why object to Naomi getting married at the same age? Naomi has assented, Green writes, and he will grant his permission if I give my blessing as well. They want to marry in August.

I am sure it is a mismatch: the giving, selfless Naomi yoked with the self-absorbed, distant, often absent Matthews, as insensitive as he is handsome. I fear he will overwhelm Naomi's gentle spirit. I recall the first day we met him, almost four years ago, the day he brought the settlers from Tennessee into our front meadow. He was brash then, and brash he continues to be. Full of plans and activity, but short on mindful regard for others.

It distresses me that with all her caring for others, Naomi has little sense of how to care well for herself. Introspective and intuitive, she writes in her diary, tends her younger siblings with devotion, dedicates hours to students in the schoolroom, and revels in the attentions of the handsome Matthews when he is around. His attention flatters the starry-eyed Naomi, of course, but I've never seen him exhibit genuine care for her. Further, he criticizes her for the smallest things. Just a few days ago, he was harsh with her when she forgot to pick up a copy of the only newspaper we have, *Advocate of the People's Rights*. I had to restrain myself from reminding him that Naomi is not his errand girl.

Despite my enjoyment of the solitary days given to my recovery, my peace is shattered. Separated as we are, I am helpless to affect Naomi's decision. It seems part of the evil of this terrible summer: Naomi and I are apart for the first time in our lives, and she receives a proposal of marriage. That Naomi is in love, I don't doubt; I try to console myself with the certainty that a mother's reservations rarely change a daughter's heart. With resignation, I begin to work on Naomi's wedding gown, using leftover satin from Eliza's trunk, cutting and sizing from a nicely fitting dress in Naomi's drawer.

I try to reassure myself with each tiny stitch. Perhaps my fears for Naomi are unfounded. Perhaps I am too judgmental of a man I hardly know. Perhaps I am wary of the disappointments that separations and marriage bring. I await their return home with trepidation. How will I convey my concern? Is there anything I can do?

The political front is quiet again, Austin now in Mexico City. The cholera epidemic, raging again in Mexico, is said to be waning in Texas. Amid all this, the delirious experience of flying and speaking my heart remains, a strange antidote to this dreary July, a dreamlike counterweight to the oppressive summer of 1833.

EMPATHY

Faye, who visits overnight once a week, is turning into a young woman. Regular meals fill out her small face, and she is growing a thicker head of hair. I brush the brittle strands vigorously on each visit, hoping to turn straw into gold. Faye is also growing hips and impossible-to-ignore breasts, the curves showing in the cotton dresses the girls make for her. The camisole we gave her is no longer enough to disguise her fifteen-year-old shape. Along with her physical changes, Faye is learning to read and do sums with Eliza's help, for which I hear Faye give thanks in her prayers. With one-eared Gyp at her side, she also prays that Naomi, now living upriver with her husband, will come to visit. But Faye still lives at Luna, subject to the attentions of whatever man decides to notice her.

When I look at her, Faye no longer shifts her eyes away. Now she looks back directly and even smiles a half smile that says she claims a modicum of space in the world for herself. She also has begun calling me Saree. A mix of Sally and Sarah and Seely? Whatever the reason, I love the special twist Faye gives my name.

On this Sunday, Faye and Gyp wait on the porch for Naomi and William to come up the road from town. Only a month married, after the small August wedding Naomi chose with only family and Faye and Antoñia present, Naomi's new status is hard for me to get used to.

"I miss having Naomi even more than Faye does," I confide to Green in the kitchen. "And she's so young."

"Just the age you were when we married," Green reminds me.

When they arrive, Faye hugs Naomi shyly. Naomi coos her approval as she walks around her, noticing how much taller Faye has grown. Faye basks in the attention. Gentle as a dove, Naomi sits with Faye after the midday meal, bobbing her head as Faye reads. Then Faye and Gyp lure Naomi and me back onto the porch while the rest of the family goes into town. Softly, Faye whispers, "I have a secret." We listen carefully as she explains. "Eliza has a boyfriend named J. C. He comes to see her in the afternoons after lessons, and they go for walks by the river."

Is my years-ago instinct that J. C. Davis might be right for Eliza proving true?

"Oh, Faye, what good news! The new head of the ayuntamiento, no less. Do they hold hands on their walks?" It has been two years. Searing hours, days, in which she has found the strength to mend a broken heart. The news brings tears to my eyes.

Naomi smiles happily. "That is wonderful news. Eliza has borne such a loss. She is brave to open her heart again." As always, Naomi understands the depth of another's sorrow.

Faye nods in agreement, giving Naomi a loving look. Naomi's compassion helps Faye open her heart as well.

In the fall, William Matthews is set to embark on another trip to Tennessee, and he is taking his bride with him. I listen to Naomi's explanation. Acting as Green's agent, he will be arranging for another contingent of settlers. They will travel up the Mississippi on a big schooner. Naomi will spend time in St. Louis with her grandparents, and he will come for her on the way back, after concluding his arrangements.

"Naomi on a ship with cholera still rampant in Mexico," I worry to Green.

"Ships are always a worry. But she wants to visit St. Louis. It's an adventure for her. I don't think we should stand in their way."

Despite the dangers, I betray none of my fears to Naomi. Nor mention my misgivings about her husband. William Matthews is a traveling man. He never stays anywhere long. I fear for Naomi but keep my thoughts to myself.

On the day before the appointed journey, I decide to ride to the coast with them.

"To be able to spend more time with you, Naomi, since the date of your return is uncertain and to remind you of all the letters I'm sending in your trunk. Eugenio will take us in his wagon. We can stop overnight with Molly and Creed." Then Faye, who has come to say goodbye, asks if she can go too.

The real reason I'm tagging along is more dire. The dreaded cholera, on the wane for a bit, is back. San Antonio de Béjar is deserted, and La Bahía, with ninety-one dead, is under quarantine. Naomi and William hear the news, but nothing can deter them from their trip. I will rest easier if I least find out about precautions being taken to protect the travelers.

Eugenio arrives at dawn. Tucked in his serape, he brings another copy of the cholera cure and more slaked lime and peyote buttons.

The long trip to the coast is a punishment. Boarding a ship in a time of cholera is at the very least foolhardy, if not deadly. While the young travelers chatter, I wrestle with myself. Should I pretend to be sick and implore Naomi to stay with me? Should I forbid her to go, insisting her life is in danger? I seize on each tack as it comes to mind and, after a few miles, reject it. When we are almost there, I console myself that I will at least talk to the ship's captain and try to get an answer as to whether my fears are justified.

A flatboat takes us and the trunks toward the schooner, and then a stroke of luck greets me. Dancing in the waves of Matagorda Bay is the schooner *Dispatch*. Captain William Jarvis Russell, the very man who brought us down the Mississippi seven years ago, is at the helm.

As Naomi and William board and arrange their trunks, I slip away to talk with the captain with Faye at my side.

"Captain Russell, I'd know you anywhere. I'm Sarah DeWitt, a passenger on the *Dispatch* almost a decade ago. My husband hired you to bring settlers to our colony for the first few years."

"Mrs. DeWitt," he says, taking my hand. "We meet again. And have you decided to leave this wild land and return to the comforts of St. Louis?"

For a fleeting moment before answering, I pretend that I am going to accompany Naomi to keep her safe.

"No, Captain, I'm only bringing you two passengers, my daughter Naomi and her husband, Mr. William Matthews. I have come aboard because I want to know your opinion of the dangers of the cholera epidemic and the safety measures being taken for those on your ship."

"Indeed, Mrs. DeWitt, cholera is a grave concern, but I assure you our crew are well. The ship's doctor is examining all before they come on board. I supervise our water supply personally."

"Captain, I didn't bring my children to Texas to lose them. So far, I've kept them all safe." Hearing that proclamation, Faye squeezes my hand and nods.

I hold myself in check as we say goodbye, determined not to spoil Naomi's excitement. But it takes all my strength. After a long hug, I hustle Faye onto the flatboat to carry us back to shore. On the return to the wide, sandy beach, Faye slips her hand into mine. No one understands loss better than the small traveler at my side.

Naomi's departure leaves me flattened and empty. The trip only worsens my mood as we near Guadalupe Victoria, Empresario De León's town. The sun high in the sky, the coming months of anxiety before Naomi's return, and the lure of St. Louis—all make me question our presence here. We not only remain in this cholera-ridden land but also brave a tenuous future, given the fragile relations with Mexico. I close my eyes. A new day is coming, like a tide onto the shore. I must hang on.

At the crossroads at Guadalupe Victoria, we are surprised to see a long procession led by a priest and a woman in a long black dress. Behind her follow men, women, and children who seem to be her family and townspeople. The procession crosses the dusty street and continues toward the river where a large cypress grove spreads into the water. As the mourners pass, I get a good look at the woman. She wears a black shawl with red roses—the gift I sent her years ago.

I turn to Eugenio. "It's Señora De León." Without a word, Eugenio reins in the oxen and gets down from the wagon. He seeks out a Tejano at the back of the procession.

Returning, Eugenio nods solemnly. "*Sí, es la familia del Empresario De León. Ayer,* yesterday, he die."

The news hits hard. Empresario De León dead of cholera. The Mexican empresario, with hopes as high as Green's, now laid low in his own land. Why are we still here? We should be on that ship with Naomi. We should be flying from this place, raising a cloud of dust behind us, fleeing like a herd of wild horses.

I sit still, afraid to breathe the cholera-infested air, choked with fear at the sight before us. Our wagon lurches through the streets, creeping along as carts with bodies piled high stop and start before us. At the front of the line of carts walks a big Negro. He stops at each house where a bundle lies in front of the door. Inside each is a body.

"*El hombre se llama Black Daniel,*" Eugenio says in hushed tones.

We watch as the big man picks up each bundle and throws it onto a cart not yet filled. Tossing all the bodies along the street into the carts, he leads them on. At the edge of town, he begins tossing the shrouded dead into a huge gash in the earth lined with lime.

Eugenio drives the oxen past the lime pit. When I find my voice, I ask him about Black Daniel.

"*¿Quién sabe?* He no get the cholera. No get seeck. So, the town pay him to peeck up the bodies."

Holding Faye's hand, I try to explain. "He has some sort of natural protection against the disease."

But Faye doesn't hear me. The girl's pale face has gone ashen, her eyes glued to Black Daniel and the dead. I hug Faye close, aware of all she has suffered in her short life: the death of her mother and baby sister to yellow fever; abuse and indenture; her father slaughtered by Indians. It is too much. I shut my eyes, then open them as Faye murmurs something. She looks at Black Daniel. "He must be very sad."

I spread my cape around her, trying to shield her. She rests there a moment and then wriggles away and motions Eugenio to stop the cart. Hopping down, she runs the distance back to Black Daniel and pulls out her lunch, wrapped in a cloth. Wordlessly, she hands him her little gift. The big man, his forehead dripping, takes it and nods. His eyes are tired, filled with gratitude and pain.

Faye turns and rushes back to the cart.

I squeeze her hand and kiss her cheek, awed at her generosity, her empathy—and the peril she risked offering kindness to a heroic soul. She looks at me, a rare smile playing across her solemn face.

THE LULL

reen puts down the *Advocate of People's Rights* broadsheet and looks at me. "Things are changing. The time is right. I think I could get a new contract now."

I frown at him. "How is that possible?"

"Santa Anna has repealed the ban on immigration decreed by the Land Law of 1830." Then he adds, "Austin's secretary, Mr. Sam Williams, is of the same mind. Said so on my last trip to San Felipe."

I give him a look. "Why would another contract with the Mexicans be to your benefit?"

He frowns back at me as if the answer is all too obvious.

"Green, you know as well as I do, canceling the immigration ban means the Mexicans realize they can't control the border, so they've decided to stop trying. Anglos are coming on their own and claiming land on their own. They don't *need* empresarios anymore. But we all know the Mexicans aren't happy about it. They fear the newcomers are going to take Mexico away from them."

Does he really believe that he can revive the empresario era? That he was just too early, his timing a bit off? This too shall pass, I cajole myself, praying

Green will transform himself from an empresario to a landowner with cattle, crops, and family. I refuse to look at him as he rattles on.

"Sarah, you've got to understand. The Mexicans respect the empresarios, not the *hoi polloi* coming in on their own. The basic situation hasn't changed: The future rests on land and more land. I'll have a few leagues, and you've got a league. We've given Eliza and Naomi one each. But we came here to capitalize on a grant for 75,000 acres. That's still possible. I've got to keep at it."

"Meaning you'll be going south, nearly four hundred miles, to an area likely to be swept up in the civil war raging nearby. Many Mexicans see the Anglos as invaders, thieves stealing their land. Do you and Sam Williams think you can pleasantly negotiate a new contract with the officials in the capital of Coahuila y Tejas when much of Mexico is on the brink of civil war? Avoid the chaos and waltz back home with the blessings of the Mexican government?"

"Yes, I think we can make some headway with the right people. Sam and I are making plans. It'll be a few months before we're ready."

"Green, I am totally opposed to this. You will be dealing with Santa Anna, who can change color faster than a chameleon. First, he wants settlers, then he doesn't. Then he imposes the immigration ban. Now he lets Austin talk him into lifting it. He shifts at a moment's notice and will do so again. Especially when he thinks the Anglos are going to take Texas away from him. How can you be so blind after all that has happened?"

"Austin has gotten the ban on immigration lifted. That means things are changing, getting better. Santa Anna is a Federalist. His fight is with Centralists, the opposing party in Mexico, not with us. He sees us as allies, helping Mexico pave the way for civilization."

I listen and repeat the arguments I have so often made. "Green, that time is over. It's been nearly three years since your contract ended, four years since the immigration ban, and things are going to get worse before they get better. The Mexicans won't let the Anglos overrun Texas. And if the conniving general-turned-president Santa Anna prevails against whoever opposes him in Mexico, he can turn against the opposition in Texas just as quickly. Don't you see?"

"Sarah, you have to believe in the future. It will happen. People are pouring in now, as Austin reminded us on his last visit. We need land to sell. The future is now."

Anger rises in me. After close to a decade, are we back to the beginning? Is he going to wade into a hotbed of unrest in Mexico?

"What I see is the pressure building, about to erupt. The Mexicans are extending their civil war into a war against revolutionaries to the north who want to split Texas off from Mexico. Those fires will envelop us all. I'd dare to hope you would be around to help us through it. Or get us out before it starts."

He stares back at me, shaking his head as if I am an uncomprehending child.

In one terrible moment, I feel the seams of our marriage ripping apart again. *Gambler to the end*, I want to scream at him. *You're going to lose—and us too, along with your precious land.* But I don't. I don't scream or try to change his mind. I just stand up and walk out to the barn, to my horse, shaken to the core. We are as far apart as Texas and Mexico.

When I return after a ride along the river, a horse is tied at the gate. Antoñia marches around in the yard, visibly upset that a visitor has had the audacity to seat himself on the porch with me gone and Green nowhere in sight.

"Man," she says, pointing at the interloper. He stands abruptly as I start up the path.

"I'm Sarah DeWitt. What is your business?"

"Howdy, ma'am. I've come from San Felipe with a message for your husband from Mr. Sam Williams."

He does not say his name but casts apprehensive looks at Antoñia, still indignant over his presence.

When Green appears, coming up from the river, the messenger hands the paper to Green and sits back down, looking darkly at the floorboards, as if the news is somehow his fault. Green nods grimly. I move to his side and read along with him.

San Felipe, February 15, 1834

Austin was arrested by Santa Anna's men in Saltillo, halfway to Béjar, on the way home from Mexico City. They took him back to Mexico City and threw him into prison. They are holding him in solitary confinement. He sends word he's not been charged, though talk is he's guilty of treason. Before leaving Mexico City, he wrote a letter to the Tejanos on the Béjar town council, urging them to unite with Anglos to organize a government independent from the rest of Mexico. The letter got back to Santa Anna. Austin counsels calm, patience, and no revolutionary measures. He says he has committed no crime and, in time, will be released.

Samuel May Williams

After rereading the message, Green walks out by the land office and rolls a cigarette. The rider ducks his head, uncertain what to do next. I feed him a plate of peas, biscuits, and chicken in the kitchen and manage to wrest from him his name, Zeke Smith, and a "thank you, ma'am," several times repeated, for the food. But he seems uncomfortable uttering more than yes and no, accompanied by shy glances. It's as if he feels the bad news he bears renders talk useless. And in a way, it does. A half hour later, Green returns to the porch.

"Coupla more stops to make," Zeke says finally, without prodding. "Best be getting down the road. Much obliged for the eats."

"Thank you for bringing the message. My best to Sam for letting us know," Green says, finally breaking his own bleak silence.

After another stretch of silence on the porch, Green comes inside. Without looking at me, he says, "Got to talk to authorities in Béjar and San Felipe before the ayuntamiento meets at the end of the month. Want to see Sam's correspondence from Austin. Talk about what to do next."

I nod, knowing he must go, seeing the inevitability of our separation once again. Later, when the children come home, I give them the news. They look at me warily, seeming to understand that the chances for fighting just notched up.

Eliza says, "Let us pray for Colonel Austin. No man ever deserved our support more."

LETTERS

I can't bring myself to relay to Naomi the terrible news of Austin's imprisonment. It could be months before news reaches her, if it does at all. I don't want it to spoil her trip. But by late spring, there is too much to hold back.

May 1834
Dearest Naomi,

I know you are happy in St. Louis with Liza Q and Grampa Seely. My heart is with you all. Here, events move like a treacherous river—the surface calm, the undertow perhaps deadly. We have gotten news that Mexico's President Santa Anna has abrogated the Constitution of 1824. Like ours in the United States, this constitution is a fair and judicious document. In the past, Santa Anna has supported it. But now, his true colors—and his dictator's heart—are beginning to show. In a deceitful political play, he won the presidency in November of last year as a Federalist, but he is now allying with the Centralists, who care little for the constitution. Without warning, he placed the landed aristocracy—hombres de bien, he calls them, the good people—in power. He betrayed his vice president and used his Centralist allies to form a new Congress that denies power to the states and has gone so far as to dissolve state legislatures. This could prove disastrous for us in the state of Coahuila y Tejas and in other Mexican states. Up until now, we have been far enough north to escape notice.

We in Gonzales are, of course, consigned to our loyal (I say mealy-mouthed) role. Yet it is common knowledge we could be the front line of attack when that comes—as surely it must. Santa Anna does not intend to lose Texas to the Anglos nor grant us the self-government that we desire and have more or less enjoyed out of neglect up until now.

In Mexico City, the Federalists and Centralists are again too busy fighting each other to fuss with us but not too busy to arrest Colonel Austin and accuse him of inciting rebellion in Texas. Even though he is the most reluctant of revolutionaries, they have not yet released him. A priest who traveled through here recently said Austin has been confined in a solitary cell for three months, with only a mouse to talk to.

Poppa and Mr. Sam are writing letters to all who might appeal to Santa Anna to release Austin, though prevailing against the whims of a dictator seems unlikely. Despite all this, Poppa plans to go south to Coahuila y Tejas to secure another grant. He has delayed his trip twice because of the unrest in Mexico but plans to leave as soon as is reasonable. Mr. Williams, Austin's assistant, will go as well. I call it the height of folly, but I cannot change his mind. It is a sore subject.

Nevertheless, it is still possible to count our blessings. At present, Poppa is busy helping Eliza till the fertile fields around her house. The land there is green and beautiful, and her pecan crop promising. She will hire gatherers to pick up the pecans. And J. C. Davis wastes no time making himself available to help harvest the hay and corn crops. That dimpled smile of his grows

*wider by the week. I think he is smitten. Eliza is hard to read, yet
I feel sure she is pleased by his attentions.*

Your loving Momma

July 1834
Dearest Momma and Family,

*My days here in St. Louis are some of the happiest I've ever
spent. Liza Q is beside herself to have me here. She strokes my
hair and will barely let me out of her sight. I sit and tell her
of our life and all that has happened. We walk down by the
Mississippi every day, as we did when I was a small girl. I am
blessed to be here again.*

*As to the latest from Texas, Liza Q gobbled up the news. She
says you have always been clear in your judgment. If you think a
revolution is coming, you must be right. She also says we should
all come back to St. Louis and leave Texas "to its own rat killing."
(I love her funny phrases.) I told her of your land grant and of
Eliza's and the gift of land to me, carved out of Poppa's leagues,
at the time William and I married. But Liza Q would have none
of it. She said the land would be there after the fighting, and we
can return when bad times are over.*

*Grampa Seely approves of William, saying he is enterprising,
like Poppa. That fills me with pride and makes me understand
how Texas has grabbed us all. Happy as I am here, it is there I
have grown to womanhood, and even now, a part of me yearns
to be in Texas with all of you. Tomorrow night, a ball will be
held at the home of Mrs. Ann Perry to benefit children orphaned
by the cholera epidemic of 1832. Liza Q says we must attend
and is finding a gown for me. She says it is our Christian duty
to contribute to this worthy cause, and it will be a fine evening
for me to see life in St. Louis. I do look forward to it. Our life in
Texas bears little resemblance to the civilized society of St. Louis,
and it is so very interesting to see what your life must have been
like here, Momma, before you forsook it for Texas.*

Your loving Naomi

I read and reread the letter for weeks. I long to be there with every fiber of my being to see my mother's face, to sit with her as Naomi is doing, to walk by the river with the two of them. With the uncertainty here, the pull of Missouri grows ever stronger. Yet the lines from Naomi about Texas . . . and then Eliza shares with me the letter she is sending to Naomi.

August 1834
My dear Naomi,

Your letters make me miss St. Louis and Liza Q and Grampa more than I can say. Yet as you have set down so truly, Texas has taken us over. While fate dug a deep ditch for me in my earliest Texas days, the four years here also have brought me happiness just as profound.

I am sharing my news with you first because you and Momma long ago plucked this man who gives me such joy out of the wilderness. This man will become my husband in a few weeks. Since Mr. J. C. Davis and I met, every day has been happier, each building upon the last and bringing us a better understanding of what this Texas life can be for us. So, I must thank Momma and you, dear sister, for understanding so long ago that this stalwart from Missouri is the man for me. While a sad twist of fate brought death too early to my doorstep, I am thankful for the very good Mr. Davis, who buoys my heart again. We will be married in the Christmas season, as our parents were, and shall hope for a marriage as fruitful as theirs. J. C. joins me in sending cordial best wishes. We look forward to your return.

Your loving sister,
Eliza

I reread the lines from Eliza several times. My children, transplanted to Texas, have put down roots. I fear we will never get back to Missouri, but I dream nonetheless.

A BLOODY SPRING

The ferry is hardly more than an oversized log raft bound and lashed together. But I consider it a floating marvel, an easy way to get across the river with my fifteen-year-old ferryman in charge. C. C. slides down the steep path of the embankment, finds the long pole he keeps in the bushes, helps me aboard, and pushes off from the muddy bank.

"You are following the tradition of your great uncle Jacob Seely, who poled boats up and down the Mississippi." I remind C. C. of his heritage, even though I know the Mississippi River is hardly even a distant memory for him. His father's pride in him for winning the job of assistant ferry operator is more to the point.

As if reading my mind, he asks, "Momma, when will Poppa and Mr. Williams return from their trip?"

"Your guess is as good as mine. Maybe we'll have a letter from him soon." I try to make my tone neutral enough to hide my lingering anger. But I am sure C. C. remembers the terrible rift the trip has opened between his parents. I know he heard my angry words when he walked in on our last argument.

"This will be seen as the work of scheming land speculators, trying to enrich themselves, while Mexicans suffer a civil war and Austin languishes in a prison cell. You and Mr. Williams are heading straight into hell. You will rue the day."

The strength of the current interrupts my thoughts and forces C. C. to pole harder as he guides the ferry to the landing below Water Street. I scramble after him up the bank.

On Water Street we head for Luna to buy much-needed staples from the bins at the front of the store. To our surprise, a crowd in the street looks in the direction of a dust cloud left by horsemen on their way north out of town. Inside, the wife of a townsman holds forth.

"Bloody massacree it was. Dozen of 'em kilt. French and Mexican traders a-comin' from Louisiana on their way south. Stopped in front of our cabin, and John went out to warn them of signs of Indians nearby. Before John could get himself in the door, there they were."

"How many Indians?" comes a voice from behind the counter. Belle moves into the group encircling the woman. Another woman, one of the new people streaming into the colony, moves closer to the group, her eyes full of fear.

"Seemed like scores of 'em, mounted, yellin' and yippin' savage-like, and cutting out all the pack animals first thing. Then they went after the traders. Poor things hardly knew what hit 'em. Made a breastwork of their goods and packs and saddles. Fought bravely with those old cavalry guns the Mexicans call *scopetas*. But they was doomed. Picked off one by one. My John frothed at the mouth to go and help them. But I made him stay in. Outnumbered like that, he would have fallen with the traders and the rest of us along with him."

"All those bodies in front of your cabin now?" Belle asks.

The woman doesn't flinch. "Scalped and mutilated," she says. "Wolves and buzzards having a field day. Indians headed north with all the pack animals loaded. Pans and blankets and trinkets and the like."

"Don't worry none," a man in the group says. "Whole posse of trackers will catch up to them Comanches. Headed back up the river to their camp north of here."

"Indians," Belle grunts, "gettin' worse by the day. Out for everything they can steal. In a mean time with this drought, so they're plaguin' *us*."

She looks at a new woman in the group. "Don't you be goin' anywhere all by yourself. They pick off loners whenever they can."

The woman looks even more frightened than before and rushes to finish her shopping. I want to comfort this new settler to Gonzales. It is clear the traders, with pack animals and a collection of knives and trinkets sold from a slow, rickety wagon, were sitting ducks for an attack. But I'm sure that will not serve to calm the woman's fears. Indeed, it barely calms mine.

I buy flour and coffee, and we start back to the ferry. C. C. searches for words to comfort me. "Don't worry, Momma, I'll protect you. But maybe I ought to ride upriver and let Eliza and J. C. know about the raid."

"Did you hear Belle's warning about traveling alone?"

"Yes, ma'am."

At home, Antoñia is pacing the porch. Heatedly, she relates her distress. Eliza and J. C. had been at the house visiting with the recently returned Naomi and William, home from the yearlong trip to Tennessee and St. Louis. Then Eugenio brought news of the Indian raid on the traders south of town. Eliza proposed that they all retreat to her house, out of Comanche territory. Though she argued against it, Antoñia could not persuade them to stay. Eliza left word that J. C. would return later in the day as an escort for the three of us.

"Eliza and J. C.'s house is no safer than home, Momma," C. C. says, in reaction to Antoñia's story.

I stare at the two of them, not wanting to acknowledge his statement and Antoñia's confirming nod.

"I don't want J. C. to come back alone after us." Despite my misgivings, I'm stuck with Eliza's decision to get out of Comanche territory—a dilemma whether we stay or go.

I recall the words of a man in the crowd at Luna; the trackers were going to head north toward the Comanche camp in pursuit of the attackers.

"We'll head west toward Eliza's and hope we meet J. C. on the way." It takes an hour to care for house and livestock and pack supplies onto the horses. By early afternoon we are on our way.

In single file, we strike a trail deep into the woods where the Guadalupe River turns and veers closer to the San Marcos fork. We hear birds' cries and then the deep silence of the woods broken only by our horses' steady trots. I take the lead with Antoñia riding double behind me, her bow and arrows slung across her back. C. C. follows behind us on Dandy, carrying a gun held down by his side the way J. C. does. We ride for maybe an hour and a half, seeing no sign of the white-tailed deer or wild turkeys so common to these woods.

"Glad to have this gun J. C. gave me," C. C. says, interrupting my anxious thoughts.

"Yes, son, we are lucky to have J. C. in the family."

C. C. looks up to his brother-in-law with unabashed admiration. J. C.'s recent election as head of the ayuntamiento elevates him to new heights. But C. C. knows him best as a skilled woodsman who can bring down a deer in one shot and dress it in record time. He considers J. C. the model of manhood, tall and sturdy, with a broad chest and powerful thighs, and, I suspect, tries to convince himself he is just a slighter, younger version of J. C. His brother-in-law's willingness to share all that he knows cements their bond. With his father so often absent, C. C. turns to his Tonkawa friend Hopping Bird and the Sowell boys, when they will take him, for the lore of the forest. But hunting with J. C. is what he loves best.

A strange cry pierces the air, a birdcall we can't identify. The silence of the woods closes in around us. Usually, the woods are full of sounds and movement. I shudder.

The knot in my stomach tightens. I don't know these woods well. I ready my rifle as we continue on the path by the river in the same direction. I can feel Antoñia's tension as she shifts back and forth behind me, her arms around my waist. Then we hear horses ahead, trotting gaits speeding into gallops. I signal C. C. to stop. Hearts pounding, we listen as the sounds of the horses grow fainter, but then another seems to be coming nearer.

Suddenly J. C.'s horse breaks into view. The horse, his back smeared with blood, rears abruptly when he comes upon us.

I dismount and grab the horse's reins, holding Pal close. The horse wheels, and we follow deeper along the path. In a few hundred yards, we see J. C. on the ground with an arrow in his chest. On his back under a spreading oak tree. Soaked in his own blood. Beside him, fresh tracks of several horses. His glassy brown eyes are open to the sky; he is a color of pale I have never seen.

C. C. falls on him and listens for his heart. I scan the trees frantically for the ambushers, Antoñia clutching my hand. I reason it was the Indians' horses we heard galloping off. Tracks lead away, and J. C.'s gun is gone.

C. C. crouches over the body, his chest heaving. "Not J. C.," he keeps repeating. "Not J. C." Next to him, the horse hangs his head.

I kneel by the two of them and let C. C. sob in my arms, tears rolling down our faces. Keeping guard, Antoñia stands next to us, her eyes darting toward any movement in the forest around us. When C. C. can cry no more, we heave J. C.'s body across his horse, tie it on, and continue our dismal journey to Eliza's cabin.

The horse leads the way, so that we cease to think about anything except J. C. and his lifeless body. It is midafternoon when we arrive. Eliza and the girls come to the door as we near the gate. Then Eliza sees her husband of four months draped over his horse and faints.

Inside, we all bend over Eliza. I bathe her face with a wet cloth, then dispatch Antoñia to the woods to gather herbs for a sedative. But before Antoñia can get out the door, Eliza awakens and stares at the circle of family around her. She sits up. "I wasn't dreaming then. Where did you find him?"

"Back in the woods, near the branch of the San Marcos into the Guadalupe." C. C. chokes out the words and begins to sob again.

Antoñia's herbs and honeysuckle sweeten the air. Then we begin the process of preparing the body for burial. Though rigor mortis has set in, I direct Eliza and Antoñia as we stretch the body out on the long table in the kitchen.

Eliza and I undress the body and wash it. We don't try to pull the arrow out of his chest. Instead, I take a large knife from the hearth and cut it off flush with his chest, so only a terrible little stub sticks up from his heart. We wash away the ants and bugs still crawling over his body. At last, Eliza gently closes his eyes.

Still, she has not cried. Fearing she is in shock, I turn over and over in my mind how to pull Eliza out of her trancelike state. I am not sure Eliza admits to herself this body is her husband. It is as if she is stoically going through the process of preparing a body unknown to her. Yet, from time to time, she looks me full in the face, drawing strength from having me by her side.

When the washing and shrouding are done, Eliza bends over and caresses J. C.'s face, kissing the spot where the dimples flashed in his sweet smile. I have underestimated her. Then Eliza sits down next to him, holding one of his folded hands, and buries her head in his torn chest, the stub of the arrow in her cheek. I smooth her hair for a long while and then leave her alone with her husband. As we watch the sun drop in the sky, I begin to understand Eliza's strength anew. With all her suffering, a part of the adventurous, young Eliza has grown as old as the white streak in her hair, equal to whatever comes her way. Turning back to her, I try to be as brave as my daughter.

Eliza runs her trembling hands down J.C.'s strong, muscled arms and thighs.

"How long will I remember his touch and the sound of his voice? I know from losing Thomas, the tone of his voice will disappear first. I can still hear J. C. telling me about the ayuntamiento and still see his smiling brown eyes. I pray their loss won't haunt me forever."

I pull her close. "The Lord giveth and the Lord taketh away. That is what Liza Q would say to us."

Eliza buries her head on my shoulder. Her sisters encircle us, clinging to her on either side. "Acceptance, perhaps. My heart aches too much to fight it," she says tonelessly. After the first death, there is at least the pith to survive the next. Nevertheless, the pain and desolation will change her forever.

While Eliza sits with the body, I circle the yard, looking for a burial spot. At the edge of the yard, a pomegranate tree is just coming into bloom, its orange-red flowers in clusters at the end of small branches. Liza Q maintains the tree in the Garden of Eden was a pomegranate, not an apple tree. It seems a perfect resting place for J. C. But it is not my choice to make. I am still standing next to the tree when Eliza grabs my hand.

"Yes, Momma, this is the spot. I wish we had a sweet-smelling pine box to put him in."

I wrap my arm around her waist and squeeze her tightly, wishing Will were here to build the pine box. Will would have helped all of us get through this. I allow myself to think of Will and J. C. together, both blessed with the gifts of good humor and a loving heart. I see their tall, lean strides and striking aspects: sandy blond J. C., carrot-topped Will. Did we lose our protection when Will went away, when we lost the magic of Will's red hair?

If Green were here, could he help me through? If only we had all stayed home. Then J. C. wouldn't have come out alone to meet us and would still be alive. His terrible intersection with some Indian hunting party, perhaps the ones who killed the traders, didn't have to happen. *If we'd just stayed home . . .* I keep forcing myself back from that thought. The pain of regret is too powerful. *No, don't think that way. Just stay by Eliza.*

And then, when that horror recedes, another comes at me. The Comanche seem to be coming ever closer. Where can we be safe?

I stand at the spot. C. C. starts digging when Antoñia comes back from the river. Together they make quick work of it.

"Good husband-man," Antoñia says as she throws dirt up out of the hole.

In the moonlight, we gather and lower the body into the grave. I hold Minnie's hand, her five-year-old face as grim as it knows how to get. Through tears, Naomi tells us the story of the first day we met J. C. on the Guadalupe.

"Antoñia didn't want to let him into the canoe. But we soon became friends." Tears flow as Eveline, C. C., and Clinton hold Eliza tightly. Tied just outside the gate, Pal watches with her head over the fence.

THE NEWS FROM MONCLOVA

A week later, on a Saturday, we make our way back to Gonzales. We will have to resume our schoolroom duties on Monday and return to the world for a few weeks before we dismiss for the summer. Eliza rides Quick, trailing her milk cow on a long rope behind. The chickens have feed, and the cattle will be all right with the new grass until we return in the wagon. I ride beside Eliza. Having spent almost every moment of the last days with her, I am not ready to leave her side.

We've hardly arrived home when Eugenio comes in his cart, delivering a letter from Green. We gather in the kitchen.

"The envelope is addressed to Family," Naomi says. "I hope there is something here from William, too." Seeing the first line of the letter, I hand it to C. C.

He takes the four pages tentatively. I nod, and a look passes between us. The first line confirms that Green is still smarting from our misunderstanding. It also says that Green wants C. C. to take his duties seriously, something I agree with, though Green could not know how perilous that duty has grown. C. C. starts to read in a soft voice.

Monclova, April 25, 1835
Dear Son and families—

There is an express expected to leave this place tomorrow, for Gonzales, on other business, which you will learn from the enclosed Directive to our J. C. Davis.

C. C. looks at Eliza, who is biting her lip, and then resumes.

I wrote you by the last Texas mail, which I hope you have received, informing you that I had obtained five sitios of land to be located on any vacant land in the State of Coahuila & Texas, Solely to the use & benefit of my Children. I wish you to Select the land and have it Surveyed as soon as practicable because this will be a great deal of land located so soon as this Congress shall rise.

C. C. glances up at me. Seeing the confusion, I explain, "The state congress has been meeting there in Monclova, responding to Santa Anna's outrageous actions. The governor is trying to raise a militia against the general's forces. He's selling land to finance a militia, which is why your father felt he had to go to Monclova to buy land from the governor." I nod to C. C. to continue.

I also stated that it was my opinion that all the people in DeWitt's colony who had not received titles would be put in possession of their proper quantities of land. The Situation now stands as thus—A petition was drawn up by Capt. Johnson, who carefully consulted the views of all who were residents in Texas—B. Smith. R. Peebles, F.M. Johnson, & Sam

Williams—which sets forth very precise and clear reasons for the passage of a law authorizing these commissioners to be appointed for putting the people in possession of their land. This was presented to Congress and signed by Texas members. It has undergone two readings and will be read again on Monday 27th, and I think pass without much alteration if any.

James C. Davis will be appointed commissioner for the district of DeWitt's colony without doubt & to deed the five leagues of land granted us by law. The office will be very profitable in many respects as the settlers will have to pay a fee perhaps 50 Dollars. I shall remain here until the law finally passes, and until I get the commissioners, the main thing now with me.

I have lived with Mr. Sam Williams and Company since we arrived, and I have found all to be gentlemen active in my interest. I am at this time nearly out of money and shall have to borrow from my companions some $40 or $50 of which I want you and Mr. Davis to be prepared to settle for me when we arrive—I have lived as saving as any decent man could do & my money could go no further. You will not regret this, for you will be paid thousands fold.

The Congress does business very slowly and has not done a great deal. The Regular troops were ordered to this place by Gen. Cos, to stop the selling [of land] by Congress. They stopped nine miles out of Town. The time is too short for me to write to all—I intend this for you all and, therefore, I send my Respect and best wishes to all without name or distinction—and to my old friends in Gonzales. I think I shall leave here in about ten days if I have good luck. Remember me particularly to your mother.

> *I remain your affectionate Father*
> *Green DeWitt William A Matthews, Esq.*

C. C. reads to the end, then looks up. He obviously is wondering why his father should be writing him about arranging money.

"Your father is much worried about money," I say simply. It is clear to me that Green, in his world, cannot see the forest for the trees. He is trying to assert that order will prevail and that colonists will receive their land titles. But farther south, there is a revolution going on; things are falling apart. The echo of "thousands fold," which he has been repeating for nearly a decade now, makes me wonder about his sanity. His letter tears at me in ways I can hardly bear. Though his words, his assurances are so confident, I wonder if the children sense their father's anxiety and concern. Do they hear his despair? Am I the only one who hears his torment, the only one who hears his effort to remove the cloud, the unfulfilled contract for settling four hundred families, that hangs over him?

Naomi takes the letter and pores over the signatures. "I wish my William–" she says and then stops, looking at Eliza. I keep quiet and watch as Eliza takes from C. C. the directive meant for J. C. Davis concerning town business. She abruptly turns and walks out to the porch, leaving C. C. staring after her.

Later, Eliza rides to town. As everyone else occupies themselves, I motion to C. C. from the porch. He sits on the steps beside me, looking out into the lush green May meadow before us.

"My dear, the letter from your father is, of course, good news for us all, if in fact these land sales come to pass. But you mustn't take the weight of the world on your shoulders. Yes, you are the eldest son, but whatever comes in the days ahead, we are all in this together. The loss of J. C. feels unbearable; it makes all of us feel more alone. Still, your status as the man of the family does not have to be taken up so completely and immediately as your father's letter implies. You and I will both see to things. He will be home soon."

C. C. smiles lovingly at me. "I would put you up against any man."

I fear for Green and the panic he's going through. I can't change our quarrels now burned so bright in my memory and, obviously, his as well. I could never have agreed this trip was the right choice. But I should have understood he is doing what he must. If he grasps at straws now, it is because he must spare no effort, even now, to fulfill the dream he dreamed. That it's crazy to me is part of our tragedy. He did not write the letter to me. That saddens me and touches my heart. He is trying not to burden me, trying not to ask for agreement I cannot give.

On a sunny afternoon at the beginning of June, William Matthews gallops up the road, accompanied by a second rider. Naomi sees them coming and shouts with happiness for the first time in weeks.

"It's William and Poppa," she says, clapping her hands and running to me.

From the porch, I follow the riders' approach. At first, I think the second rider isn't Green but Señor Navarro. Briefly, I wonder if the land commissioner could indeed be coming to help us claim and survey the five leagues Green refers to in his letter. The horse looks like Navarro's very distinctive mount, which some praise as the fastest horse in Texas. As they come into the yard, Naomi runs forward to be scooped up in a prolonged hug from her husband.

"Welcome to you both," I greet them, seeing now that it is neither Green nor Navarro at all but Mr. Sam Williams, Green's travel companion. Though it seems strange, I am quite sure that Sam Williams is indeed riding Navarro's horse.

That is the first puzzle. The other is why Green is not with them. The men remove their hats solemnly, and the hair on the back of my neck stands up. Silently, they take long drinks from the dippers in the water barrel. Antoñia tends the horses, while I usher the men inside.

Seated in the kitchen, Mr. Sam says, "Mrs. DeWitt, I am—" He pauses, looks at me, glances away, hesitating, then starts again.

"I am sorry to be," then he looks at the children, "the bearer of bad news. Green, Colonel DeWitt succumbed a few weeks ago, May 18 it was, to cholera. It hit him all at once, and he was overcome in less than a day." He pauses as I start to feel my breath come in short gasps. "I was not with him. but William here was. He can tell you more."

I stare at Sam Williams. I've not heard right. I'm back on the word *succumbed*. I'm not sure I'm listening as Mr. Sam goes on. Now he's stopped talking, and Eliza's hand is on my shoulder. The children are staring at Mr. Sam, then at me. I try to construe what he's said. I heard the cholera part and "William was with him." I stare, stand up, then sit down. Then get back up.

"He was to be back home in ten days. No, that . . . we just had a letter."

Sam Williams speaks again: "I come myself to tell you, as Colonel DeWitt's friend and as Colonel Austin's assistant. Of course, he woulda come himself, but he is still detained in the capital, no longer in prison, but now in a hotel. News is he'll be released soon. He hasn't heard about this, far as I know."

I look to William. "Tell me what happened, William. Cholera? Who was with him?"

Lacking his usual bravado, he shakes his head. "As Mr. Sam said, it was quick."

So close on the heels of J. C.'s death, I see Green in a twisted shroud, the way J. C. was, as we lowered him into the ground, but with no family near. Alone. I stare at Mr. Sam as he rattles on about paperwork that needs to be done. My hands tremble. Then my shoulders. Eliza steps closer to me and holds me tighter. I bury my head in her shoulder and let the tears come. The news is impossible, and yet it's true.

William is holding Naomi's hand, and Eveline, who has Minnie, finds her way to my side. I look up at Sam Williams, who seems far away, by the door. "Mr. Sam, I appreciate . . ." but I can't get it out. I want to say: *You should never have persuaded him to go.*

"I am sorry to say, Mrs. DeWitt, I cannot tarry. I am being pursued. I was arrested at the Río Grande by Santa Anna's forces and then released, only to be detained again in Béjar, because I was in Monclova in talks with the state congress now disbanded by Santa Anna. Colonel Ugartechea's troops are stationed at the Presidio at Béjar and will be after me. I escaped and met William outside of Béjar. He's not in trouble. He can tell you the story."

"So that is why you have Navarro's horse." Tears spill down my face. *And where is Green's horse? Where is Major?*

"An astute observation, Mrs. DeWitt. Yes, you are right. The horse can outrun just about any other animal around. He brought me his horse to help me escape." Without further comment, Sam takes his leave, backing out of the room with his head down.

I sink back into a chair and weep into my hands as the children urge me to lie down. They try to comfort me, hover around me, then withdraw into their own wells of sorrow. I can't focus. I have questions but neither the strength nor the will to ask. Everywhere I look, I see Green. His extra hat on a peg by the hearth. Out the window, the land office. On a sawhorse in the corner, his old saddle and bridle. On the mantle, his box of papers: letters from Austin, Músquiz, Sam Williams, one urging this last trip to Monclova; a copy of the application for my league.

I long to be back in St. Louis—yearn, in fact, to have never left. But that is a different life, not mine.

I wait for a bit of steadiness to return, overwhelmed by a barrage of thoughts. I knew Green would chase down every bit of land he could get his hands on, but I never thought he would die in his pursuit of it. Texas fever. He died of Texas fever. I never even considered that. Nor that his last words to me would be passed, strained, through a letter. A heartfelt message, sent through C. C., through "Son and families": "Remember me particularly to your mother." After twenty-five years, it comes to that.

Eliza is sitting beside me, offering a cup of water. I drink, tasting its bitterness. Antoñia's potion for sleep. I drink it down.

Then William comes back into the room with the girls and pulls out a small slip of paper. "The gravedigger's receipt," he says quietly. Two other papers come with it, all dated May 19, 1835, and addressed to Mr. Sam Williams. I read silently:

Sir

The bearer Victoria Gutierrez was employed in attending on the deceased Colonel DeWitt and has to receive Two Dollars for her service.

Jn Blackaller

Sir

The bearer Salomin Gonzales was employed in digging the grave for the late Colonel DeWitt for which he has to receive one dollar four rials.

Jn Blackaller

Sir

*The bearer Martin Villatrigo was employed in making the coffin for
the late Colonel DeWitt and has to receive six dollars for his services.*
Jn Blackaller

I read each receipt twice and put them down on the table.

"I have questions, William, but not yet." I wonder how we can pay people in Monclova and where the funds for this will come from.

It is not questions but a memory of the picnic on the grass that occurs to me now. I'd hoped to coax Green into a pleasant mood that afternoon—and succeeded. It was one of the times when Green and I got back to enjoying each other as we had before Texas came between us, one of the interludes when we were together despite everything. That day, it felt as if we'd recovered the trust once freely placed in one another. Then I thought of an afternoon, a few months ago, just a day before he left. I'd tried once more to convince him not to return to Mexico in search of another grant. But we ended up in yet another argument. Remembering my words, "you will rue the day," I shudder. Now it is I who will rue the day for many days, for many years to come.

AVENGING ANGELS

Transported by Antoñia's potion, I descend into a heavy sleep. A day later, I wake from a dream about Green's muse.

"Back and forth from Missouri to Texas to Monclova. Beckoning him with a sultry smile. Angel of Destiny, Protectress of Pioneers she was supposed to be."

"Momma, what are you talking about?" Eliza asks gently, from across the room.

"What did I say?" I ask, half asleep.

"Something about an angel and a smile."

"Oh, Eliza, I was thinking about the feverish pace your father set. Pulled across the miles, obsessed. Led by an unlikely muse, his Angel of Destiny."

"Momma, you were his muse. The vision was his; the strength came from you."

I sit up straight in horror. "Me? I tried to protect him and the rest of you."

"And you did. As much as is humanly possible. Just remember this: Poppa died fulfilling his dream. His last letter to us said that: 'Five sitios of land . . . to the use and benefit of my children.' Success was there, just within his grasp, and you helped him to it."

I comb my fingers through my hair. It's just as well Eliza sees things that way. Green made it to the other side with his children all believing in him. Though C. C. knows better. He knows how much I opposed his trip, believing it was a fool's errand. Further, none of them, not even Eliza, appreciate the hard way ahead. Nine years, three deaths. Devastation in the form of the Mexican Army, or the Comanche, or both, all bearing down on us.

I hear William in the kitchen with Naomi, reminiscing, describing Green's final days. I want to hear but can't think about particulars. Green is lying in an unmarked grave in Monclova comes to me over and over, along with the fear of knowing there is more, much more to come.

And much I regret: Green and I found each other after losing each other, only to lose each other again. Nine years in this war with him, and we never really found lasting peace.

I am soothed a bit by Eliza's view that he fulfilled his dream, and I am grateful that she has settled things this way. Yet I feel more alone than ever in my life.

I sit in silence on the bed, thinking of the first time Green kissed me. Really, I kissed him. He was so taken aback he didn't know what to say. So I said it for him: "I think we're going to get married some-day, don't you?" He laughed and said, "Yes, I do." Then he kissed me. That was when I began to envision golden days ahead. A life in St. Louis, settled and stable as my parents, with children adding to our happiness, Liza Q and my sisters nearby. Green would pursue his noble causes, lead us all in the right direction, as a foe of slavery and a champion of Jefferson's enlightened ideas. After the blow of losing Will, I was reclaiming the future. My young life was once again blessed, my world full of promise.

I think, too, of the day he brought me two newspapers carrying ads for the DeWitt colony in Texas. I thought it was a venture he would invest in. But then he told me we would journey there to live, all of us. I tried to take that in. Then I began to play the piano. The more he talked, the more I saw a man obsessed. That was the first day I felt the fear in my throat, the fear that has never left me.

I return to the kitchen and sit down across the table from William.

"I am most anxious to hear about what happened in Monclova and all the news you bring."

William and Naomi stare at me. Disheveled and still groggy from my potion-induced sleep, I imagine the dark circles under my eyes and remember the sad raccoon eyes of General Terán.

"I can only put together bits and pieces from what Mr. Sam said and from our last letter from Green. Can you help me understand what happened? Do not spare the details."

True to form, William Matthews is bursting with news of this treacherous adventure and his role as a companion in Green's final days. Without hesitation, he launches into his tale.

"Yes, ma'am, lots to tell. First news we got was that Santa Anna had dispatched General Cos, his number one general, to Monclova, where the state congress was raising money to pay for a militia to oppose Santa Anna and his troops. That's what drew us there, of course. The congress was selling eleven-league tracts to fund their rebellion."

"But on whose authority? Wasn't that illegal?"

"Most of the rest of the Mexican government thought so. But everybody in Monclova was trying to get away with whatever they could. After all, Santa Anna was attacking his own people."

"The letter we got from Green mentioned five sitios, five leagues of land. That was land sold by the congress to him?"

"Yes, ma'am. And that is part of the reason Santa Anna was calling us thieves. Ladrones was his word for us, stealing his land. But the legislature at Monclova was waging their own war against Santa Anna, so because we were buying land from them, we were kinda like their friends."

I motion for him to slow down for a moment. "It's a lot to ponder."

I get up and pace around the kitchen for a while and then sit down again.

"So, the so-called North American land speculators were enemies of the national government in Mexico City but allies of the state of

Coahuila y Tejas congress at Monclova?" This was the speculator talk I'd heard. But now I begin to see the many parts of the puzzle. A civil war within a civil war? Or corrupt deals that Green and Mr. Sam Williams, blinded by their desire for more land, got drawn into, but worse.

"That wasn't all," he says. "While that was going on, Santa Anna dissolved the national congress in Mexico City and declared himself the sole head of the government. A pure-dee dictator. Plain to all. Mr. Sam said he was 'a danged criminal.' That's about when Santa Anna sent his best general, General Cos, straight to Monclova, and all hell broke loose.

"First, we formed a little band of militia volunteers—Anglos and members of the state congress—in Monclova. Couple hunnert of us, maybe. Good enough to keep General Cos, camped a few miles out of town, from marching right into Monclova. A few of his troops entered, and then the showdown was called off. Rumor was that Santa Anna wasn't too happy about that—he wanted to stop the Monclova rebellion once and for all. About that time he marched his troops south to the state of Zacatecas where he put down another local revolt in favor of the Federalist cause. They were rebels standing up for the Mexican Constitution of 1824 that Santa Anna had abandoned. We heard it was awful bloody, thousands of Mexican civilians slaughtered in the streets. S'posed to be an example to anyone contemplating opposition to the high and mighty Santa Anna."

"Yes, we even heard about it here, from couriers."

"So, the governor of the state of Coahuila y Tejas was pretty dang scared that his capital city of Monclova was going to be the next bloodbath. He disbanded the lawmakers and volunteers and headed toward Béjar, where he has friends. We were all about to head out once the governor deserted. There was people runnin' here and there, and no safe place to get supplies. That was . . . that was when Colonel DeWitt took sick."

William paused and took a long drink of water.

"And then Dr. Peebles ordered everyone out of his room. Said he had cholera. After that, I didn't keep track of the news, you know, I just stayed outside his room until the end. Then for days, we were on the run on account of us 'land pirates,' as Santa Anna called us, being branded as troublemakers and worse."

"Did he suffer? Was he conscious? How long was he sick?"

"He was sick from one night until next evening. I don't rightly know if he was conscious 'cause they wouldn't let me near him. The woman, Señora Gutierrez, who cared for him, covered her mouth and wore gloves. She gave him water and wiped his face. I just sat outside, trying to find out how he was doing. But she couldn't tell me much."

I shut my eyes for a moment, hoping his delirium took him quickly into an unconscious state. Did he know he was dying? Knowing Green, he would think that he would overcome this setback, like all the others. Again, I imagine the winding-sheet drawn around him. To die in a strange place with no loved ones nearby. It was a possibility I never considered, perhaps because it is unthinkable to us still alive, carrying our hopes like shields into what overtakes us.

I press William to go on.

"So Mr. Sam stayed too . . . until Colonel DeWitt passed away. And then he and I rode hard to get out of Monclova, not knowing if General Cos's troops were coming for us or not. Thing is, they sort of recognize Mr. Sam, him being Colonel Austin's secretary. But they don't know me, so I didn't stick real close to Mr. Sam. Easier for me to duck and hide than for him."

Eventually, we get back to yesterday, when Sam Williams arrived and quickly departed, fearing Mexican troops could be close behind. It seems clear now that the revolution is upon us. We in Coahuila y Tejas state have no government at all, and our representatives to the state congress are either on the run or under arrest. Eagerly, we await Austin's return.

"What do you know, William, of Colonel Austin? Is he still confined? Rumor has it he's on his way back to Texas, but Sam said he was still in Mexico City."

"Mr. Sam heard tell that they let Austin loose or were about to. People did say one thing real clear, though: that Austin is saying Texas has got to get free of Mexico."

I look at him with hope and foreboding. Nothing to do but hang on and wait.

"After all this time, it can't be much longer now," I say aloud, realizing I am talking like a sleepwalker.

"There's news of tensions at the port of Anahuac on the Gulf. They say it seems like open rebellion to some, but that most aren't ready to go that far," William says.

"Yes, that's so," I say, in a fog. "Not yet." Naomi and William stare at me. "Oh, yes, William, another thing. Where is Major? What happened to Green's big bay? He is a fine horse. And Green took good care of him."

William looks at me blankly and then a little sheepishly. "I think he might be in Béjar. Mr. Sam had him. In fact, he rode him back from Mexico City. Said Major was a better mount than his own. But then there was a mix-up with the horses. I'm not too sure what happened."

I frown at William. "I want him back. I won't let him go. Unlike the Indians, we don't sacrifice the horse with the warrior."

In September, families unwilling to find the money for school fees with all the uncertainty in the air has forced us to "delay" the opening of the school year. In my heart, I know there is going to be no school, not this month, not this year. Money problems are pressing, but we can hang on. I am sick at heart over how to look out for my Luna girls, Lila and Bess. Though Belle lets me take Faye from Luna two days a week for our reading lessons, she does not allow the other two to leave. And even *my* interest in lessons dissipates with the daily bulletins of conflict and rebellion everywhere.

I have been a widow for four months. Many have expressed their sympathy or sent heartfelt condolences. I expect to hear from Austin any day, following his release and return last month. I hear Green's voice every day, bits of conversation that end with my tears flowing and my regrets piling up. Why didn't I say this when he said that? Why didn't I tell him more often how much he has accomplished? We have a good amount of land, thousands of acres—more than we had in Missouri. What if I'd been able to persuade him not to go? He'd still be here. He'd know what to do next.

Once some resolution comes between Texas and Mexico, a return to Missouri could be possible. But will my children come back with me? Naomi would stay here with William. Can I leave her? Can I sell my land and go back? Not yet. I am beset with questions. Too much hangs in the balance.

Amid all this cataclysm, we live in an eerie quiet waiting for news. Without Green, news from outside the colony does not land right on our doorstep; without school and daily trips into Gonzales, there are fewer exchanges. The land office is locked and abandoned. I have settled into a steady routine of feeding the family and taking care of the livestock with Antoñia and the children. One day follows the next, seemingly uneventful. I think of Molly's first description of Texas to me: the treacherous silence punctuated by unfamiliar animals' screams and fear of what is just beyond.

We know this truly must be the calm before the storm. There is news of unrest over customs duties, of tenacious loyalty to Mexico in some parts and outrage against Mexico in others. We clamor for news of the civil war in Mexico. Finally, there is good news; Austin has returned to Texas by ship, landing at Copano Bay on the Gulf in August.

In mid-September, Andrew Ponton, the current head of the ayuntamiento, brings news of Austin's September 8 speech at the port of Brazoria. Welcomed home after two years by both the War and the Peace parties, representing the main views among the settlers, Austin managed to unite them in common cause in one heady night.

A few days later, even bigger news comes. Riders leave a pile of broadsides at Luna, where C. C. picks one up. San Felipe's Committee of Correspondence and Vigilance has met and elected Austin chairman. The committees of safety across Texas are calling on each district to organize its militia and begin forming volunteer companies. Yesterday Eliza returned from Gonzales to report that local leaders across Texas are calling for a meeting on October 15. Delegates would vote on whether citizens favor independence, a return to the Mexican federalist constitution of 1824, or the status quo.

Alone at the kitchen table, I read Austin's words. He notes that Santa Anna's right-hand man, General Cos, has been sent to put down resistance in Texas. Cos and his troops arrived at Copano on the Gulf on September 19. The real object of Cos's expedition, Austin states, is "to destroy and break up the foreign settlements in Texas." The word *foreign* is encouraging. Until now, Austin has never used the word or admitted it was used in reference to us Anglos.

But it is the last part of his message that brings tears to my eyes. Relief washes over me as I read. No more pretending to be Mexican citizens. No more delaying the inevitable. I wonder if this is how my parents felt at the beginning of the American Revolution. I trumpet Austin's words to the people of Texas aloud to myself in the kitchen:

Conciliatory measures are hopeless. Nothing but the ruin of Texas can be expected from any such measures. War is our only resource. There is no other remedy but to defend our rights, our selves, and our country by force of arms. The delegates of the people must meet, advise every man in Texas to prepare for WAR and lay aside all hope of conciliation.

S. F. Austin

Antoñia bursts into the house. Before she can speak, I hear the hoofbeats. From the bluff above the river, we watch a contingent of a dozen horsemen ride past us and encamp on the mound about a mile to the south. Then a lone horseman breaks from the group and rides toward town, carrying the Mexican flag.

I pull off my apron and start toward the pasture, whistling for Pal. The Mexican officer I follow into town stops in front of the fort and looks up at the small cannon sitting next to the crow's nest. A hundred yards behind him, I rein in Pal at the hotel. Inside the alcalde's office in Turner's Hotel, Andrew Ponton is writing furiously, making multiple copies of the latest news from the Committee of Safety from Bastrop, just up the road.

"Miz DeWitt," he greets me warmly, just as the cavalryman knocks at the door.

"What can I do for you?" Andrew asks as we turn to face the Mexican officer.

The messenger, who speaks no English, introduces himself as a corporal in the Béjar Presidio. He hands Ponton a note written in English and steps back. Andrew reads it and looks up.

"Well, sir, that there would be a hard request to fulfill. Nope. Can't do that without a meeting with the people of Gonzales. No sir," he shakes his head vigorously, "not at this time."

"Andrew, if I might be of help."

I turn to the messenger. "*No es posible*. We cannot give you the cannon. *No podemos*. We must consult . . . *Consultamos con el ayuntamiento, con los jefes del distrito*."

The officer bows slightly and then turns on his heel in good military fashion.

"He and his troops are camped on the mound near my place. I followed him in."

"Looks like we've got a situation here," Andrew says. "Mexican troops in Texas, people protesting all summer 'bout customs duties and the like. A few weeks ago, there was an incident outside Luna. Mexican soldier beat up an Anglo pretty bad. Lotta people hot under the collar about that, too."

I'm surprised. Without Green to keep me informed, I've not heard the latest.

"So, the commander of Mexican troops in Texas, Colonel Ugartechea, has decided he doesn't like our attitude and doesn't trust us to keep our little weapon. Since our poor ol' spiked artillery piece wouldn't scare off even a half-hearted foe, seems to me they're calling our bluff. Looks like we're goin' to need a Texian army pretty damn quick. 'Cause if we don't hand it over, there'll be more troops coming."

I nod.

"If the empresario were here, what do you think he'd suggest?"

"I think he'd say you better ask the people of Gonzales what they think while you continue to send for reinforcements. There can't be more than a dozen or two able-bodied men here at present. We may need volunteers quicker than expected. We need time to assemble volunteers, as Austin has rightly advised."

"Reckon we'd better send a letter to Músquiz in Béjar to boot. Let him know the letter puts us in a tight spot. A matter that requires time and consultation with the ayuntamiento. He will understand."

"Yes, I agree. Músquiz does read English, as you know. Green communicated with him regularly. And, as much as he can be, he's on our side. You might explain that the members of the ayuntamiento are spread out across the colony and will require some time to contact. That will help him explain the delay to his superiors."

"Believe I'll do that," he says, with a little chuckle.

The following day, I receive a copy of Andrew's letter to Músquiz.

Gonzales Sept 26, 1835

Excellent Sir, I received an order purporting to have come from you for a certain piece of Ordnance which is in this place. It happened that I was absent, and so was the remainder part of the Ayuntamto when the dispatch arrived. In consequence, the men who bore said dispatch were necessarily detained untill today for an answer. This is a matter of delicasy to me. I do not know without further information how to act. I have always been informed that this cannon was given in perpetuity to this Town for its defense against the Indians. The dangers which existed at the time we received this cannon still exist, and for the same purposes, it is still needed here—our common enemy is still to be dreaded or prepared against. How or in what manner such arms are appropriated throughout the country I am as yet ignorant but am led to believe that deppositions of this nature should be permanent at least as long as the procuring cause exists.

I can't help but giggle at how Andrew draws out the stall to give the militia time to assemble. On and on, he explains he needs more information and an opportunity to consult the authorities so that, if with more "mature deliberation," he can comply with the demand, he will send the cannon, which, of course, Músquiz knows, will never happen. He signs it, "God & Liberty–ANDREW PONTON, Alcalde." I put the letter down and laugh out loud at Andrew's brilliantly long-winded response.

COME AND TAKE IT

Stationed at my window, I look across a field of wild poppies to the dragoon of Mexican soldiers, now grown to more than a few dozen. I imagine them cooking beans, warming tortillas, roasting squirrels, and engaging in knife-throwing contests. They are playing the waiting game that soldiers play, maybe bored, maybe a little nervous.

Things are finally set in motion, even here in Gonzales. With the town council voting against handing over the cannon, the defense of our land seems more imminent each day. Hard to believe that the puny little cannon has become the symbol of standing our ground. With such resolution coming from the citizens of Gonzales, who have long resisted any rebellion against Mexico, I feel energy returning, as after a long illness. Every day, I look for Green coming up the road on Major before catching myself mid-thought. He would have known what and what not to do. Would have talked to Austin and others to get a clear sense of where things stand. Would have figured out the path ahead. Would have laughed with me that our undersize cannon has assumed such importance.

With the call to arms, the Texian force has grown to more than a hundred; most stay in Gonzales and in cabins near town, some camping out at the fort. I expect Will to be in Gonzales soon, if he isn't there already. I wish I could talk to him. To get a whiff of his optimism and humor. To get an idea of where Tejano loyalties lie and what Navarro and others say about the Mexican strategy.

A month ago, many left Gonzales following the formation of the Committee of Correspondence and Vigilance and the Committee of Safety and news of Mexican troops attacked by Texas troops on the coast. The men headed to San Felipe to support Austin or to the coast to join volunteer forces, taking their families with them. Lila and Bess, the older girls at Luna—perhaps tired of answering to Belle—disappeared as well. Faye says they've gone up the road to Bastrop, where another Luna-type establishment employs young women. With the increased communication between towns, the girls, according to Faye, seized the opportunity.

But now, the call to arms and the encampment of Mexican dragoons on the mound has brought many back to Gonzales. The detachment of dragoons I watch from my window, led by Lt. Francisco Castañeda, is here to demand the surrender of the cannon. With the new arrivals, the Gonzales militia now numbers more than 130 men. They have elected a leader, a Colonel Moore, from the town of Fayette in Austin's colony, farther east. And they have begun to call the mound where the Mexicans have camped—the highest point in the vicinity—Santa Anna's Mound.

Lest the fighting break out in my front yard, I've sent the children and Faye upriver again to Eliza's. But I can't peel myself away from the kitchen window. Besides, the men who come for food, news, and a place to sleep need help. Tomorrow, C. C. and I must leave, I tell myself again today.

In the afternoon, Matthew Caldwell, one of the men recruiting for the Texian force, stops by, back from a run to Bastrop to the north. "Gettin' more men," he tells me, between mouthfuls of venison.

"Our own Paul Revere," I say, serving him seconds.

"Pshaw," he laughs. "Just an old Indian fighter. But I do worry about that squad of cavalry posted up there on the mound. They have to be

302

sending communications back to compadres in Béjar. 'Fore they add to their numbers, I think we're gonna have to do something. Today, 27th of September, Lieutenant Castañeda repeated his request for the cannon. And was again refused."

The look in his eye as he leaves startles me. I haven't allowed myself to think too far ahead. But now, after all the waiting, the moment is upon us. Independence might take years, but in the meantime, a battle, even a small one, will be a step toward it. And it will require a flag.

I ride into Gonzales to affirm my urgency. I buy a yard of black cloth, cornmeal, and coffee. When I get home, the children are waiting, back from Eliza's to collect me.

"Momma, look," Eliza calls from the window. Four riders approach from Gonzales.

"It's some who've been gathering men for the Texians, Bitnose Martin and Jesse McCoy and two others," C. C. says. "They're heading toward that pile of arms the Mexicans propped around the tree."

We all watch as the riders get off their horses and advance toward the camp. After a minute, the four stop, and McCoy shouts something. The Mexicans start toward the tree for their rifles. Then Bitnose levels his Kentucky rifle at the foremost of the Mexicans, but McCoy restrains him. While the other two collect the arms, there is more shouting. Then the Mexicans, with their hands up, gather into a circle. One Mexican, sent after the horses, breaks away and heads for the road to Béjar. They let him go as they round up the others and herd them across the river into Gonzales.

"He's going after help," C. C. announces in a fret from the window.

"Yes, maybe so. It won't be long now. I suppose I should go back with you children. But first, we have to do something,"

"What's that, Momma?"

"We don't have much of a force, but whatever bunch they end up with, the men need to fly a flag."

Eveline smiles. "We can make it, Momma."

"Yes, I've bought black cloth. We can represent the cannon in black—since the Mexicans are making such a fuss over it. With a motto underneath to back up the forces."

"Yeah. We'll say, 'If you want this ol' cannon so bad, you gotta fight us for it,'" Eveline declares.

"That's a little long, dear. We don't have a lot of black cloth for letters."

"Well, then, just 'Come and Get It,'" Eveline says impatiently.

"Sounds like you're inviting them to supper," C. C. says. "And what are we going to put this message on?" he asks, unconvinced we should be taking the matter into our own hands.

"I was thinking about the white satin of Naomi and Eliza's wedding dresses. Eliza, look in the dresser drawer, folded under the nightgowns."

Eliza comes back bearing Naomi's white satin dress like a sacrificial offering.

"I think Naomi will be proud to have our wedding dresses put to such good use," she says, signaling me that her resistance to fighting has died a quiet death.

Sitting on the floor, Eveline outlines a cannon, making a drawing on the broadside newspaper still lying on the table. We smooth the shiny skirt of the wedding dress and measure the large white field big enough to hold Eveline's simple sketch of the cannon.

C. C. watches us work. "Making a flag, Momma, is in the category of fighting a war." I give him a serious look but no response.

My fingers fly over the edges of the white satin rectangle I've cut out. Hemming the rough edges, I feel like singing, maybe even dancing. It is just a day or two now. But I'm not leaving yet, I affirm silently, knowing the children will try to take me back with them. No, not quite yet. I tuck the unfinished flag under my pillow and vow to finish it tomorrow.

At first light C. C. rushes out of the house seeking the latest news from Gonzales. Returning at full gallop, he spews out the news: Spies report about a hundred Mexican soldiers marching toward Gonzales.

"I got there just in time to help the men erect a temporary breastwork below the ferry. I helped them hide the flatboat in the slough just below the house." He motions to the river below. "Then the vanguard coming from the south appeared where the ferry should have been and asked to be carried across the river."

I listen spellbound.

"They were informed that they could not cross. If they had dispatches," C. C. reports breathlessly, "one of the men could swim over unmounted. So that's what happened." His eyes are wide with surprise. "Lieutenant Castañeda swam across. When our men read it, they saw it was an order to deliver up the cannon or the Mexicans would take it by force. So the men said, 'You think you can get it from us, then come on, come and take it.'"

I nod vigorously.

"Then they told Lieutenant Castañeda the mayor was out of town and would not be in before morning. They wanted to stall and hold 'em off some more. So that's when I came on back. But I was thinking, Momma, maybe that's what should go on the flag," C. C. says.

"What, son?"

"What the men said to Lt. Castaneda, 'Come and take it, then.'"

I flash C. C. the smile reserved just for him. "Yes, yes, dear, I think that's it." I watch from the window as scores of Mexican dragoons gather on the mound.

The children and Faye and I work for the next few hours, getting the letters cut out of the black cloth. Then, carefully I line up the letters along the bottom: COME AND TAKE IT. With a black star above and the black cannon centered across the middle of the white satin field, the flag is as handsome—and rousing—as it's going to get. We admire it and consider it a good day's work.

"Tomorrow, my dears, you must go back to Eliza's. C. C. and I will follow close behind."

C. C. looks at me and raises an eyebrow. "Soon, Momma. But first, we've got to deliver this flag to the men."

On October 1, Andrew Ponton tells me action is imminent.

"We've mounted the cannon on a pair of cart wheels and forged slugs for it. Had to repair the pitiful ol' spiked thing so it actually could shoot like a real cannon. Sowell's smithy's been goin' night and day. Men itchin' for a fight now, Miz DeWitt, and I don't want you caught in the crossfire."

"I appreciate that, Andrew, but look out the window there, and you'll see the Mexicans have removed themselves from the mound. C. C. says they've gone a few miles upriver."

Ponton goes to the window. "So I see. A little cat-and-mouse exercise then. Well, now, wherever it happens, we're going to call their bluff tonight. Got close to a hunnerd-forty men ready to fight. Camping out at the fort. This afternoon, there'll be a patriotic address by the Reverend Doctor Smith. In his backyard. So come to the speechifying and the hymn singin' and then get yourself on up to your daughter's place."

I sit down for a moment after Ponton has gone and contemplate his directive to leave. What he counseled is no doubt the thing to do. But not a bone in my body feels like doing it. I am going to be part of this war.

C. C. and I arrive at Reverend Smith's place in town in the late afternoon. There are two women (the preacher's wife and daughter), three grandchildren, and the reverend just starting to deliver a stem-winder to a crowd of a couple of hundred people, almost all men. They fill the house and back porch and spill out into the backyard.

I search the crowd for Will. I haven't laid eyes on him in four years, though I did hear from him in May when he learned of Green's death. It doesn't matter. Time apart has no meaning for us. We both understand a simple truth. We always take up just where we left off.

He is on the porch. I look at him and smile. He nods and smiles back.

Mrs. Smith plays a familiar hymn on the piano, and then the reverend steps up next to the piano to address us. But before he says much, Will ambles up to stand beside him. After the reverend leads us in prayer, he says a few words and then turns to Will.

"I expect John W. Jones here wants to add a few choice words and will likely say it bettern' I can."

Will looks out over the crowd. I listen as his easygoing grace gives way to a tone more intense than even I have ever heard from him.

"As most all of you know, the government of Mexico, in the person of Santa Anna, has sent an army to destroy us. They want us to give up the cannon, surrender our small arms, and become the vassals of the most imbecile and unstable government on earth. Will we do that? NO! No, we will not. That plucky fella Patrick Henry from Virginia said it best about a half century ago. GIVE ME LIBERTY OR GIVE ME DEATH! Now our turn has come. We're ready—and we're not about to hold back!"

The men respond with shouts and huzzahs, and Mrs. Smith plays a few chords. Before the singing can begin, C. C. and I make our way through the men and come to stand by Will. Over the notes of the piano, I address the crowd.

"As you take up the fight, I think you might need this."

I unfurl the flag and hold it in front of me.

"I think this represents our true sentiments. The star on the top is for Texas and the independence she is about to gain." In my heart, I look forward to that star joining the others on Old Glory. "I trust it will wave strong above you as you wage the battle."

I look directly at Colonel Moore, the men's elected leader. Still standing beside me, Will sends me a loving glance, quickly rearranged into a proud one, then moves back to his seat.

Colonel Moore rushes up to take the flag, and then Mrs. Smith, who ventured from the piano stool to peer at the flag, hurries back to her post to pound out "Rock of Ages."

Outside, the army lines up in columns, ready to take up its march toward the Mexicans' camp across the river. I let Colonel Moore know we will follow as far as my place. They move slowly and quietly, intending to surprise the enemy. With the river swollen from recent rains, about half swim their horses downstream from the familiar low-water crossing, now a deep pool. The rest, unmounted, must swim or use hurriedly assembled rafts made from lashed-together logs. The crossing takes hours, slowed by darkness and a thick fog rolling in toward midnight. The celebrated cannon travels on one of the hastily built rafts, poled across by a strong-armed volunteer. C. C. and I follow the cannon across, Pal and Dandy swimming shoulder to shoulder with other mounts.

On orders from Colonel Moore, the army takes up positions at the edge of the timbered river bottom, ready to march toward the Mexican camp several miles upriver. Once on the other side, the cannon goes to the middle of the front line on the riverbank. On its little cart pulled by a soldier, it rolls ahead of us over the rough ground, the "Come and Take It" banner flying.

The plan is to approach and surround the Mexican camp, hiding in the trees until dawn and then launching a surprise attack. But as the army nears the Mexican camp, a stray dog, set off by the howls of wolves, barks loudly. Suddenly, the enemy's picket guard fires on the vanguard, hitting no one. But amid the cloud cover and fog, the Mexicans cannot tell how many surround them and withdraw to the nearby river bluff.

C. C. and I drop back. But instead of returning home, I motion to C. C.

"Come on, we've got a front-row seat."

On Pal and Dandy, we pick our way under a thin crescent moon through the darkness toward the mound, just beyond the trees.

The fog clears around daybreak. Several hundred yards away from the Texians, the Mexican cavalry looms in a triangle formation. At once, the Texians emerge from the trees and start firing. Scores of mounted cavalry charge across the field in a counterattack in quick response. The Texians fall back to the trees and let loose a volley. Two Mexican soldiers shot from their horses fall to the ground, and the Mexicans fall back again to the bluff.

As the sun rises higher in the sky and the last patches of fog dissipate, an emissary strides toward the Texas camp and disappears within. Shortly thereafter Lieutenant Castañeda and Colonel Moore meet in the field between the troop encampments. With the sun glinting off weapons raised on both sides, an interview takes place in full view. After a few minutes, no handshake ensuing, the two turn their backs on each other and stride toward their respective camps. Moments after the Mexican lieutenant disappears among his troops and Colonel Moore among his own, the Texians, with shouts and jeers, hoist high the "Come and Take It" flag. Then they light a taper and hold it to the little cannon's touchhole. Without a cannonball, but armed with bags and bags of metal scraps, the cannon's deadly spray of nails, screws, and scraps of tin and iron flies toward the Mexican camp. Outgunned and outnumbered, the Mexican cavalry turn their horses toward Béjar.

I hold tight to the reins as Pal jerks and snorts at the cannon's report.

"Momma," C. C. says, "I think your revolution has begun."

PART IV
THE PLAIN OF SAINT HYACINTH

The Runaway Scrape, East across Texas
1836

The plain lay alongside a marshy bayou, an unnamed spit of land on a peninsula reaching toward the San Jacinto River. According to legend, Spanish explorers discovered the river on the feast day of Saint Hyacinth, a Dominican missionary and miracle worker. They named the river San Jacinto—Saint Hyacinth in English. Centuries later, in the early 1800s, that grassy plain was turned into a cow pasture.

Through the agonizing spring of 1836, we followed Sam Houston's lead, hundreds of miles, across rivers in the mud and wind and rain. After the horror of the Alamo, we fled the wrath of Santa Anna, trailing behind the soldiers, among the carts and wagons and refugees. We believed Houston would find the right place to turn and fight. Amazingly, it was Santa Anna who found that place for us, and in April 1836, that grassy plain-turned-cow pasture was transformed yet again.

WAR AND RUMORS OF WAR

Fear inhabits me like a sickness. Now that we are almost six months into it, I must keep C. C. out of it. Hourly, I wrestle with the panic rising from my chest. He will be sixteen in another two months; the recruitment age is eighteen.

That first battle, watched from the shadow of the mound, left C. C. determined to be part of the action. I let him go with Will a few months ago when the militia attacked Mexican troops in Béjar, the so-called Siege of Béjar, but only because Will assured me that the dangers were minimal, that he expected hardly more than a skirmish, as the Battle of Gonzales had been. But C. C.'s adventures with Will have, in his mind, prepared him, indeed whetted his appetite for returning to Béjar. What we face now, however, is not a skirmish. It is literally the wrath of Santa Anna, with an invading army of thousands. Many thought the war over after the surrender of Mexican forces at the Siege of Béjar; I think two humiliations in a row mean the biggest battle is ahead.

From the kitchen window, I watch him with the horses. He is brushing Major, talking to him, no doubt. Green's big bay is starting to look like himself again after Will and C. C. found him, ribs and haunches painfully prominent, in a corral full of horses confiscated by the Mexican forces near the Alamo.

C. C. puts a load of corn into the crib for Pal, Major, and his own Dandy, Will's gift to him on the day we first rode out of Gonzales into the woods. Several lifetimes ago, it seems now, though hardly more than eight years have passed.

When Will brought C. C. home from Béjar, I vowed not to let him go again. His excited stories of the men running off the garrison of Mexican troops trying to defend the Alamo ring in my ears. Now our forces hold the crumbling old mission-turned-fort with a score of cannons captured from the Mexican General Cos and his troops. But the December victory, after the rout here in October, was, to my mind, good luck not good news. Rumors fly. General Santa Anna himself crossed the Río Grande weeks ago, arriving in Béjar with his army just last week. He is said to have demanded the surrender of the Anglo forces holding the Alamo the day he arrived.

Will and others gather men up and down the Guadalupe and Lavaca Rivers. He will return to Gonzales soon. While I watch C. C. in the lot with the horses, a plan takes shape in my agitated brain: Get the horses out to another pasture. He can't go without a horse. If the reinforcements are soon leaving Gonzales for Béjar to go to the men at the Alamo, I must do it now—today.

Will's letter to me after Green's death comes back to me often, especially the last line: "If you need anything, you know you can call on me."

It is late when C. C. comes in from the lot. "I'm going into town for supplies," I tell him, getting into my coat.

"I'll go," he says.

"No, son, you stay here with Antoñia. Help her with the milking. The cows are way up the road. I'll be back before dark."

I pray to find Will where he usually stops in Gonzales—in the log pen by the river. I ride Pal hard and tether her in front of the tiny cabin on Water Street. Will's red roan is not in front. I perch on the wobbly cabin steps in the cold February wind. Huddled there, I am still considering my options at dusk when a man staying in the cabin rides up.

"Miz DeWitt. What brings you out in this cold wind?"

"Looking for Will Jones. I have a message for him."

"You mean John W."

"Yes, John W," I grudgingly repeat, still reluctant to utter his other name. I don't want to be reminded that he leads at least two lives. I know the ways he can't be relied on. But I also know he will help me when I need help.

"He just came in from out Peach Creek way. Rounding up men with Lieutenant Martin. They say he and Martin gathered up thirty-two more from Gonzales to go to the aid of Travis at Béjar, at the Alamo. Oughta be coming this way directly. Saw him at Turner's Hotel."

"Much obliged. I'll look for him there."

Down the street, Ruby shifts her feet in front of the hotel. Chilled to the bone, I forget my blue fingers when I see her and then Will, who is coming down the steps.

He breaks into a smile. "Dang, been pushin' myself too hard. Now I'm havin' visions."

Despite the hour and the mission, I can't help but smile.

"Anywhere we can sit down out of the wind?"

"If you don't mind being seen with me, let's head over to Luna. Get something to warm our innards."

Inside, Belle is at our table before we settle into chairs.

"You and me might be the only females left in Gonzales," she says. "Why ain't ya hightailin' it out of here, woman? No respect for the wrath of the Big Meskin?"

I want to ask her where Lila and Bess have gone, but I don't. "I've sent most of my family upriver, Belle. But it's hard to leave the nest."

"Yup. Figger we'll know what to do in a week or so. Don't know where I'll go. Strikin' out for parts unknown."

"Bring coffee to Miz DeWitt and a whiskey for me," Will instructs. "And how about some of those hot roasted pecans I spy over there on the counter? She needs warmin' up."

"I'll wager you'll do that," Belle smirks.

"Now, Belle, I'm the most honorable of men, and you know it."

"Bettern' most," she says, bestowing the highest compliment she gives. Walking away, her dirty skirts sweeping the sagging floor, she grumbles for both of us to hear, "If ya'd just waited a year or two, could have had her."

Will reaches across the table for my hand, and I do not resist. "So, my dear Sarah, what is it? Why haven't you gone upriver with your brood? You've heard the rumors. Santa Anna's been in Béjar since February 23. Has our men holed up in the Alamo. He's bound for glory, expectin' to find it 'round here somewhere."

"Yes, thank goodness, we are finally getting to it." I leave my hand inside his.

"Sarah, we've *got* to it. It's here," he says, looking at me hard. "Cavalry brigade's been spotted from the tower of San Fernando church on the outskirts of Béjar. Most have left Béjar heading out to farms around. Albert Martin and I are riding back there with more men from Gonzales tomorrow. If you hold your ear to the prairie, you can hear the cannons. It's started. And we have a lot less than two hundred men."

"I understand, Will. That's why I'm here—I don't want C. C. to be one of them. It's not just that I need him. He's not even sixteen."

"I know, Sarah, but I've already heard from him. And his friends Galba Fuqua and Johnny Kellogg. They all want to go."

"That's why I'm here, Will," I repeat, raising my voice. "He mustn't go with you and the other men."

"I can't hogtie him."

"Will, you kept him safe in December, when things were just smoldering in Béjar. But you won't be able to do it again. So listen to me. Tonight you must 'steal' our horses. They know you, so they won't resist. No one else could do it. Pal is the leader. The other two will do what she does. In the morning, I'll tell C. C. I turned them out to pasture. You can let me know where you've taken them, and I'll find a way to get them back so that C. C. doesn't see what happened. When you stop at the house, I'll send C. C. to get Dandy in the pasture. And none of them will come when he calls."

"Dang, Sarah, you're a genius. If we had you in our lil' fighting force, we'd beat the Big Meskin right quick."

316

"I'm just protecting my son. I've learned a few things in the last decade."

Will takes my other hand across the table and shakes his head. "No, you've always known what to do, Sarah."

I know the look in his eyes. He is thinking of himself at C. C.'s age, falling in love with me, letting me paddle the canoe, coming into my aunt's shop when I first worked behind the counter. But I won't go there. I look at him in cold fear. "Can you do it, tonight?"

"What do you think?" He smiles, rubbing both of my cold hands.

At dawn, C. C. comes running back from the lot. "Momma, the horses aren't in the lot. They were there last night."

"I let them out when I came back from town."

"Why?"

"Why not?"

"Momma, I know you don't want me to go with the men. To Béjar, to help the men at the Alamo, I mean. But I think I should, don't you understand?"

"No, I do not. The fighting age is eighteen. You're not even sixteen. It's not your time yet."

"I know how you feel, and I don't blame you. But I would be a coward if I didn't go with the rest of them."

"C. C., there will be plenty of time for you to do your duty for Texas. Right now, your family needs you. We don't know what's coming in the days ahead, but it's not going to be easy, whatever it is."

"Momma, it's hard to know what to do."

"Yes, it is. If you were eighteen, I'd say go with the men. But you're not. It's not wrong to stay and help protect your family."

"Momma, you don't need protection. You and the girls—you'll be protecting me."

I reach up and grab his face between my hands. "C. C., listen to me. It's going to take all of us to survive."

He gives me a wan smile and kisses me on top of my head—still strange since I've spent his whole life staring down at him. But growing taller hasn't changed much of anything except making him think he should rush headlong into battle.

I follow him with my gaze as he walks out to the porch and stares into the peaceful winter pasture where cattle graze among venerable trees. If the rumors are true, even if he doesn't go with the men, the two of us must leave here soon. We might never see home again. I want to tell him that he knows nothing about fighting, even though he was with the men in Béjar at Christmas. At that little fight, Will drew detailed maps and planned small-scale attacks, often fighting just house-to-house, routing out Mexican soldiers. They never let C. C. go first. He won't survive without them. But I can't say any of that.

I know his friends Galba and Johnny are telling him anyone who doesn't go to the aid of the men at the Alamo is "yellow," that word, no doubt, spinning in his head now. Hearing a horse coming up the road, I take a double-handled pan of freshly cooked cornbread from the coals in the fireplace and set two plates of eggs and cornbread on the table. When Will comes in the door, I hand him a cup of coffee. C. C. follows behind him.

When Will sits down to eat, C. C. does too. He gobbles his food without looking at me. Still, I do not sit down with them.

Finally, Will breaks the silence. "Got a long ride ahead, C. C. If you're goin' with me, best be saddlin' up. Hard day's ride to get there tonight. Have to sneak through Mexican lines. Can't take much. Coat and gun, a few provisions."

C. C. gets up from the table and runs out the back door to get his horse. Antoñia is coming up the path from the river. "He cry?" she asks as she comes in.

I nod and sit down with Will. "He's mad at me for letting out the horses. Dandy usually comes when he whistles. He's out there whistling in the wind. Then he'll probably rush toward the pasture downriver."

Will drinks coffee at the table while Antoñia cleans a fish.

"So what do I do now, Miz DeWitt?"

"Go."

"All right then. Tell him to meet me or Lieutenant Kimble at Market Square."

I nod and then let myself turn to Will. "Are you . . . ?" I start again. "If only I knew how to keep *you* safe."

"I'll be all right, Sarah. I'll be sneakin' in and back out under the cover of night soon as I deliver these men. Got to catch 'em while they're sleepin'. That's my guiding thought on the Mexicans. Be back in a few days to round up more recruits. Don't know how much time we've got left. Got to give our side a fightin' chance. Mexican army's rumored to be in the thousands."

"Will, take care of yourself. You know I worry about you. From my heart, I bless you and I love you for helping me with C. C." I add the last part, hoping to cover my tracks for loving a married man.

"Sarah, you did the right thing. Anyway, after all these years, C. C.'s part mine."

His words bring the pain of our separate lives back to me, and I pull back—I've heard he and his wife now have two children. He leans across the table and kisses me on the cheek.

"Don't need words, Sarah. I know what you think before you say it. Nothin's ever gonna change that. Remember that in the days ahead."

Then he is up and out the door. In tears, I wait for C. C.

"Calí cry many things," Antoñia says, using the Karankawa name she gave me long ago.

"Evil time," I say, squeezing her hand and moving outside.

I watch from the porch as the men pass by. Tomorrow is March 1. The force defending the Alamo, commanded by Col. William Travis, has been there for weeks. Will is at the head of the long file of thirty-two men from Gonzales. George Kimble and Almeron Dickinson are behind him. I wonder who will tend Kimble and Dickinson's Hat Factory, with the factors gone. Mr. Kimble carries the "Come and Take It" flag, the little cannon waving proudly in the morning sun. His face, rarely somber, is as skeletal and bleak as the winter's day.

MADNESS

On March 11, the rumors start again, each more frenzied than the last. The Alamo has fallen to the Mexicans: total disaster. After a siege of two weeks, all on the Texian side were slaughtered. The small force of defenders garrisoned there, including the thirty-two men from Gonzales, were overwhelmed by the thousand-plus army of Santa Anna. I am mad with fear. Will left Gonzales a week ago to recruit more men, and this time I couldn't keep C. C. from going with him.

The wild reports come from Tejano riders living in outlying areas around Béjar. But none in Gonzales will accept it. Even the Tejano riders cannot verify it is undeniably true. General Houston has arrested them to quash the rumors and sent out his own scouts.

On the morning of March 12, as a rider approaches the house, my knees almost buckle under me. I wait on the porch.

"Miz DeWitt? Message from General Houston."

"Gen. Sam Houston?"

"Yes, ma'am."

I take the envelope with my name on it and open it carefully.

Mrs. Sarah DeWitt,

As you may or may not know, the Texas army, such as it is, is being formed into regiments. We will be marching toward the coast, snowballing in size—it is fervently hoped—until we can muster the troops needed to turn and fight the Mexican forces. But there are several matters on which I would like to engage a female mind. I have been told by more than a few that your wisdom would avail me greatly. Would you be so kind as to meet me at the Luna emporium at noon?

SIGNED Sam Houston.

I reread the broad scrawl of the inimitable Houston and then glance up at the sun almost directly overhead and the messenger awaiting my response.

"I'll get my horse."

Belle's grocery and grog shop, far more central to life in Gonzales than any other establishment, now seems almost a haven to me. I look around the dark, dusty place with more affection than I ever imagined possible. Like Antoñia's friendly black snake sunning itself daily on the porch, yet another sign of our topsy-turvy world.

At the end of the bar stands General Houston. There is no mistaking the man: a sculptured head, definite of feature, a brow broad as it is furrowed. As he strides toward me, the rowels on his silver spurs spin and click. I think of Shakespeare's impulsive warrior, Hotspur. Yet Houston has a careful, calculating nature. Around his hair is a band, a feather stuck behind his ear. I know he has served in the United States Congress and walked away from a political career to live with the Cherokee in the Arkansas Territory. Now he has thrown his lot in with Texas: elected commander-in-chief of the army, and just days ago he led the convention to declare independence from Mexico. Yet he is unpopular with his men for his brazen decisions and haughty ways. He keeps his own

322

counsel, consulting with no one. Even so, he is rumored to be the most skilled among leaders, and he is prepared to fight for Texas independence.

Houston ushers me into Luna's back room, almost as noisy as the front one, with restless recruits everywhere. The dark corner he folds us into is the only pocket not filled with boisterous, agitated men. He sits across from me.

"Mrs. DeWitt, first let me offer my condolences. I know the empresario met an untimely end in Monclova some months ago. Please accept my sympathy for your loss. With Colonel Austin, your husband understood the splendid prospects of Texas. Their vision guides our future."

"Yes, General Houston, thank you for saying so. And have you any word about Colonel Austin?" I ask, wishing to call on the courage and caution of that fine spirit.

"His mission is to gain supporters for the Texas effort in the US. That is all I know. I believe he is in the States enlisting support. We are liable to need it before it can be delivered, though. Of course, many brave souls have already come from the States to help our upstart republic. And rushed to our defense at the Alamo."

"Yes, General."

"Mrs. DeWitt, I will come to the point quickly because we have little time. Even as we sit here, I fear a contingent of Mexican forces speeds toward us, intending to destroy all in their path. In fact, scouts have reported that one of Santa Anna's generals with an army of fifteen hundred has set out for Gonzales and San Felipe."

"Any reliable news of the Alamo, General?" I ask, dreading the answer even more than an invading army.

"I fear the worst. The cannons, audible even at this distance, have been silent for days."

"So the news from the riders a few days ago is true?"

"I am inclined to think so. I have sent Deaf Smith and two other scouts to ascertain the truth of the rumors. I believe the end came on March 6. And that was after weeks of holding off repeated attacks from several Mexican generals and their troops and a weeks-long siege from Santa Anna's forces."

I go over in my mind once more the timetable of Will and C. C.'s departure and the silence of the guns.

"Mrs. DeWitt, you have seen the camps along the Guadalupe, the volunteers coming to fight."

"Yes, General, I've been helping to feed them out of my garden, as have many here. They are not prepared. Pistols and knives, a few on horses, but most afoot."

"Exactly right. And it's my devilish task to make them into an army. At present, I can't even get them to pitch their tents in orderly rows. They will elect field officers, and everyone will belong to a unit. We need a flag as well. I've heard you and your children made the first one, the Come and Take It flag, when the fighting started in Gonzales last October. I think that one got marched into the Alamo. We need another now. I have chosen a star as the Texas government's official seal. Maybe a colored field bearing a lone white star," he says, making a little sketch on a scrap of paper pulled from his pocket. "It doesn't much matter. Something simple to carry. If we win this detestable fight, we'll start anew with one for the Republic of Texas."

"Yes, General, my children and I made the Come and Take It flag from the satin of my daughters' wedding dresses. A seamstress in town may have the cloth required to make another flag, if she's still in Gonzales. Many have left, fearing the wrath of the Mexican army." I wonder how many more flags will be flown in this contest. Would the next one be the red and green Mexican flag with the eagle and the serpent?

"Now then," he continues, "that's the easy part. You've probably guessed it already. Gonzales is going to have to burn," he says flatly.

I'd dared not think so far as scorched earth. I stare and try not to flinch.

"I need to put the word out. We can leave nothing for the marauders coming behind us. Must not give succor or shelter to even one Mexican soldier. Deprive 'em of barns to sleep in and provisions to keep going."

I think of the fort with the cannon mounted on the upper platform, of Dickinson and Kimble's Hat Factory on Water Street. And of all the trees felled and the lumber transported by ships from the Gulf, made in the mill that Green and the carpenters proudly built. The homes on inner town lots, Sowell's blacksmith shop, Turner's Hotel, Luna, where we sit. We must burn these very walls?

"I know Gonzales has been rising for ten years. The sacrifice is great. This village will be the first of the settlements to be torched. It would help if a respected resident will say this must be done. But we must try to avoid a panic. All my positions right now, Mrs. DeWitt, are unpopular ones. Will you stand with me on that?"

I frown and set my jaw.

Houston goes on. "At the General Convention at Washington on the Brazos, I even had to argue against sending reinforcements to the Alamo. The rider who came to us was sent by Travis for help, and he thinks me lower than a rattlesnake. He—"

"Do you recall who?"

"Yes, the scout, John W. Jones, the one who took the volunteers from Gonzales. He's famous for being able to slip in and out of the enemy lines. He slipped out of the Alamo again on March 1, after delivering the men from Gonzales. Showed up at Washington-on-the-Brazos, Travis's last messenger from the Alamo, with a plea for support. Then headed off to gather more men. Need more like him. But as you might imagine, he and I had different ideas about sending more men into the monstrous maw of that damnable fort. And now I fear I've been proven right."

I restrain myself from remarking on the terrible choices that set Will and General Houston against each other. At any rate, I don't have words to encompass it all. I turn back to Houston's question.

"General, the news from the Alamo will be brutal. Almost every family in Gonzales sent someone there. The burning of the town will not be the worst of the suffering."

"I will mobilize the army, perhaps four hundred strong, in Market Square tomorrow at midday. It is time to let people know the town must be set ablaze. Again, we must try to avoid a panic. If you could just stand with me, it might help townspeople see the wisdom of the sacrifice."

"Yes, of course." I nod, trembling, as I see my home, my life turned to ashes.

General Houston walks me to the front of Luna. We look north at two horsemen galloping toward us down Water Street.

The red roan's coat shines in the early afternoon sun. Beside him is a smaller paint.

I run into the road, afraid to believe what I see. C. C. quickly dismounts and wraps his arms around me. Will follows at a slower pace, then dismounts and holds me close as well. For a moment, I share the Indians' belief in his magic. Once more, he has eluded death and seems to have passed along his talent for staying alive to my family.

Houston's and Will's eyes meet. Houston nods at Will.

"Well, if it isn't the red-headed messenger," he mutters as he mounts his fine gray stallion and starts for the army camp.

After midnight, it occurs to me that I can no longer send letters. I dig in my trunk for the diary Liza Q sent me for the year 1836 and begin to write:

March 12th: Met with Gen. Sam Houston. Then, thank God! Will and C. C. came home after leaving a week ago to gather more men. Fate—Will would say luck—intervened. They must have been on their way back to the Alamo on March 7th, a day late to join the battle, if Houston's calculations are correct.

Children arrived from Eliza's tonight. The scout Deaf Smith returned from his mission after midnight and confirmed the worst. With him was Almeron Dickinson's young widow, Susannah, who stayed with her husband in the fort, their baby daughter Angelina, and Colonel Travis's manservant, the only survivors of the massacre at the Alamo.

The terrible news travels with lightning speed in town and into the countryside. The screams and wails of the widows and their fatherless children ebb and flow through the night, carrying across the river. And with the cries, the news that part of the Mexican Army has started toward points east. Following that dire communication, the panic Gen. Houston hoped to avoid is upon us.

RETREAT

Like the rest of the citizens of Gonzales, we must get a head start on the Mexican Army. The girls are getting blankets, quilts, and supplies into the wagon. Antoñia loads the pack mules with ropes, axes, fishing poles, and a store of potions and dried herbs. Eugenio's cart sits in front of the house, though Eugenio is nowhere to be seen. Clinton and Minnie are gathering eggs and packing them in a pillowcase full of ball moss, along with early vegetables from the garden. We will carry as much food as possible.

"Your army here, General," Will says when he finds me at the lot feeding the horses, "is better prepared than the one Big Feather Sam is trying to organize at Market Square."

"What are you doing here?" I ask, though I can't hide that I am glad to see him.

"Trying to stay out of sight before I have to follow that hound dog 'til he's ready to fight."

"General Houston needs your help, Will. The panic has upset everything. Now we must just get out. The town will be put to the torch as soon as the exodus starts."

"I'm 'doing here' what half of the men under his command are doing. Trying to take care of women and children before leaving."

I throw my arms around him and kiss him, then draw back as Naomi and Eveline look up from their task of packing quilts into the wagon.

It is quite a bit more than he expected. He kisses me back discreetly on the cheek and, taking my hand, leads me to a shady spot by the river. Out of the children's sight, he covers me with kisses and moves his body against mine. I surrender to the lovemaking we've each dreamed of for much of our lives.

His love is urgent. "Sally," he whispers again and again.

"Yes, Will, yes," I breathe into his ear, my willingness and desire as great as his. Arching into him, I am as breathless as he is insistent.

Looking at me, he says, "Sally Goodin, you are a beautiful sight."

"You make me forget all but you," I admit. "And the eternal damnation I've earned for what I've just done."

He falls into another round of kisses, but I turn away.

"Now I know what you're thinking. But having a wife or two doesn't come anywhere near how I feel about you. Just remember," he grins, "married love ain't the only kind."

It is an answer that will solve nothing. I cannot take away another woman's husband, a father of two children, even if he comes to me on bended knee. I cannot imagine how our tangled lives will ever disentangle, but I know, if we survive this war, I will have to face it.

While I try putting myself together again, Will lies back, puts his hands behind his head, and squints at the sky. He starts to address my reservations and worries, then stops, and instead turns to me for solace.

"Susannah Dickinson tells a terrible tale," he says, as if hoping to get some of it off his mind.

"'All dead,' she kept saying. 'All dead.' Bodies were thrown in the river. C. C.'s friend Johnny Kellogg came to her at the height of the battle in the Alamo chapel with both jaws broken, pressing his jaws together as he tried to talk.

"The part about the smell of burnt flesh from a funeral pyre of bodies, some of them mutilated—that's what got to me," he groans.

"And the fact that I took some of them *into* the damned fort." He goes silent, then continues, "Susannah Dickinson had a personal audience with Santa Anna himself. The general's men escorted her from the chapel where she was hiding. Scared her good—so she could come tell us Anglos what happens to rebels who resist the might of the Mexican Army."

I can't hold back my tears. "Susannah's just Naomi's age. And young Johnny. Slain like an animal. It might just as easily have been you or C. C."

"Not my time, I guess. On the seventh, when C. C. and I started back with more men, we stopped at Cibolo Creek to water the horses. We knew then we were too late. No gunfire or cannonades coming from Béjar. But Sally, my girl, if I die in this danged campaign, as many have already, I'll die happy," he says, taking my hand and holding it to his cheek.

I lean over and whisper in his ear, "Don't die, my friend, please don't die," the words slipping out in a rush.

Will considers me, smiling. "All right, then," he says, his leathered face breaking into a wily grin, "I won't." Then growing serious, "I'll be with the army. Eugenio knows the way to the east. Stay with him. Now I've got to go take orders from high-hat Houston. And I don't like that part one bit."

"Houston has a terrible task. He needs help."

"Following Grandiose Sam as we run from the Mexicans is just about the worst-smelling proposition I can think of. The man's get-up alone sets me at a steady boil: sword at his side, high-heeled Frenchified boots, to say nothing of his clanking spurs and the fancy cape he drapes over his horse. And that white beaver hat he claps on his locks—makes me want to rub his face in the dirt."

I laugh despite everything. Then regret it. "General Houston is our best hope, Will. And he's as wily as they get. He has a strategy for victory, I'm sure of that."

He frowns, then goes on, "Time is of the essence. So, I won't spend too much on how much I dislike the man. I do admire that gray stallion the old show-off rides. Though I figure that fine creature will meet a sad end if Sam Houston ever does turn and fight."

He kisses me once more and starts back. I watch him go, waiting a few minutes, trying to take in the enormity of this day.

As I come up from the river, I spot Naomi peering from the window inside the house, with the mewing Yowl by her side. Her arms are folded across her pregnant middle, and she looks miserable. For weeks we haven't seen William, off tending his cattle on the San Marcos River while she stays with me. And when he does appear, he isn't as nice to her as she deserves, especially since she has had a difficult pregnancy. Presumably, William will come to tell her goodbye before he marches off with Houston's army. But maybe not. Not much time remains for him to show up. Further proof in my mind that he is not the right one for her.

I wonder what Naomi thinks as she waves at Will from the window. He goes on past the house toward patient Ruby, tied in front. For years, Naomi has been the only one of my children who seems to understand that Will occupies a special place in my heart. The day we were shot at on the way to the Burns place, it was twelve-year-old Naomi who whispered to me that our "dear friend Will" would protect us. It was Naomi's eyes that shone with understanding when Will rescued me from the Comanches. It was fourteen-year-old Naomi who caught my eyes when Navarro toasted Will's marriage, and I could look at no one but her.

I find Eugenio eating a tamale in his cart near the road and talking to Will. "*¡DIOS MIO, EL COLORADO!*" he says to me, his face animated with delight. He too feared Will and C. C. had been swallowed up at the Alamo.

"Yup, close one," Will says. "Think I might have been the last one out. After I took in another contingent of men from Gonzales . . ." He stops short and closes his eyes, unable to utter more.

"*¿El último?*" Eugenio repeats, his squint going wide. "*Dios mio.*"

"Eugenio, stay with Sarah," Will says, suddenly urgent. "She will try to stay with the army, but the pace will be hard. Many miles a day in wagons. Many rivers to cross. Alligators longer than a boat."

Eugenio flinches. "We go together. No worry. *Señora* always knows."

Will nods. "Even for the *Señora*, this one's gonna take the cake," he mumbles to himself.

It has started to rain again as it has throughout the week. Will shakes his head and looks at me. "Shame, isn't it, how fast a fine day can turn to slop, deep as a hog wallow."

I laugh to keep from crying.

INFERNO

There is one task left. Market Square, midday, March 13. A day unlike any I've known.

"I'll be back in a few hours," I tell Eliza and Naomi. "Keep things moving. We have to leave today."

Pal lopes through the bottomland and across the river. At each milestone, I wonder if this is the last time Pal and I will make this ride, the last day there will be a Gonzales.

In Market Square, a small crowd has assembled. The troops practice maneuvers off in the distance, lining up, organizing by regiment, then relaxing away from their group. I head for General Houston pacing in the center of one of the squares. I glance around, scanning faces in the crowd for a tall redhead, but I do not see him.

"Glad to see you, Mrs. DeWitt. I feared you would not come. Thank you, dear lady, I need all the help I can get. Now we shall start." He pumps my hand and then moves toward a large stump at the eastern end of the square, motioning for me to follow.

Houston steps up and looks into the crowd, his eyes shaded by the white hat Will scorned.

"Ladies and gentlemen, fellow soldiers and patriots. I thank you all for gathering here. We live in dire times. Yet we are an essential part of history, a current moving as swiftly and treacherously as our Guadalupe River at flood stage. The Mexican Army races toward us from the west. We dare not tarry. This very day we will start our march, camping tonight at Peach Creek. At dawn tomorrow, March 14, we will officially begin our campaign at the big oak in front of the McClure place. Our numbers are growing by the hour, but the stakes are high. We must choose the place to stand and fight. We must deny the enemy every advantage. We must keep all resources out of the enemy's hands. To that end, I make a terrible request. The town, the houses, the barns: all must burn."

A groan goes up from the crowd, but Houston does not stop.

"We must provide no succor to Santa Anna and his generals. My captains will burn the town that you have spent a decade building. Each of you must burn your own home. It is with a heavy heart I ask this of you. For courage in this task, I have asked Sarah DeWitt to stand with me. She has lost a husband, and her children have lost a father. Like so many of you, she, too, must torch her home and all that is in it."

Turning to me, Houston reaches for my hand and pulls me up to stand beside him on the stump.

"This excellent lady supported the very beginning of this colony. Not only with her finances but also with her lifeblood. Now she will do what each of us here must do. Burn Gonzales to the ground and flee the marauders."

Houston turns to me as if waiting for me to speak. It takes a moment for me to think what to say. I can't promise a rise from the ashes, but I can champion the fight.

"I pray that this flag," I say, unfurling the red rectangle with its lone star, "soon will fly over our own independent land. To that end, we must pledge our support and steel our hearts to what lies ahead."

I hear my voice grow stronger as I think of the years through which we've lived.

"My husband's vision gave birth to Gonzales. It is here in Gonzales that our revolution began. We take the fight to the enemy in pursuit of our rights and our liberty. But what we seek is larger than Gonzales and the other colonies in this wilderness. We fight for an independent republic, hundreds of thousands of leagues, the only Anglo settlement between the United States and the Pacific Ocean. The Revolution of 1776 had its own small beginnings, but consider now the United States of America. Let us pray for courage in the days ahead and for the victory of General Houston and his troops."

A loud shout goes up from the crowd as Houston grabs one end of the flag and waves it.

"Mrs. DeWitt," he says, as the shouts and cries continue, "your brave example will go with us as the flag flies before our army."

A wagon rolls up and stops in front of the house. The Burns family tumbles out. As I greet them and the children fan out among them, Creed proclaims in a loud voice: "Came together, Sarah. Ain't leavin' without ye. Been in scrapes, but this might be the worst so far. Don't despair, my lovely. Wagonmaster Burns knows about wagon wheels and mud."

I grasp Creed's hands and hug Molly for a long while. Then I give orders.

"Get water and a bite to eat, children. Food on the table. Eat fast or bring it with you. We must leave. The army will make its first stop at Peach Creek. We'll catch up to them there."

I can't look at what I am leaving or, despite my words only hours ago, accept that I must be the person to burn it to the ground. And I can't let the children watch. I reason that Houston's men will take care of it, if I don't. Yet I hear his words, loud and clear. "She will do what all of you . . ."

I pile the last of the supplies in the wagon, climb up into it, and flick the reins over the backs of the oxen. As we move forward, I thank God for Creed and Eugenio and follow Eugenio's cart, the pack mules, and the Burns's wagon. We move in a file up the road, crossing the Guadalupe at the low-water ford. Already the rain-swollen river is swirling with muddy, eddying currents, the severe drought of the past months broken by the week's heavy rains. As we cross the river,

I look around at my brood, two to a horse: Clinton and C. C. on Dandy, Faye and Eveline on Pal, with one-eared Gyp following at the heels of the horses. The pregnant Naomi, her cat, and little Minnie ride with me in the wagon. Antoñia rides Major, and Eliza comes behind them on Quick, a Kentucky rifle at her side.

When we reach Water Street, it comes to me: *Belle. I can ask Belle to do it.*

I stop the wagon at Luna. "I'll just be a moment," I motion, pointing inside. Belle is handing out liquor bottles. I approach her, hoping the words won't stick in my throat.

Turning my back to all who might hear, I speak in a hoarse whisper. Belle steps back and puts her hand on my shoulder. She nods.

"I brought the dang logs to build it. Might as well be the one to do it."

But I can't walk away. My feet are like lead. I sit down at one of the tables and try to stop my heart from pounding. *It is not Belle's job.*

Belle watches me for a minute, then goes behind the counter.

"Here," she says, shoving a bag full of matches into my hands. "You c'n do it. I think you need to do it y'self."

I walk down the steps of Luna to Faye and Eveline astride Pal. "I need Pal. Have to go back to the house. Wait in the wagon."

My little army stares at me with dread in their eyes. "Stay with Creed and Molly until I return. I won't be long."

Pal and I fly back along the familiar bottomland path.

I'm glad to have no more time to think about it. I pile up all the rags and brush I can find, filling the dogtrot corridor. A brisk wind is whipping through. Deciding which direction it's coming from, I stand on the other side of the pile. It doesn't take long. Within ten or fifteen minutes, the flames are soaring into the roof. I back out the front, unable to watch. Out at the barn, the cattle are lowing and milling about. The chickens are running in all directions, cackling and clucking in alarm. Some of the cattle are following the bull deeper into the woods. I shake with sobs as Pal and I race back along the river. The mooing and bellowing follow me for miles.

At Luna, I hand off Pal to Eveline and hurriedly climb back into the wagon. Creed and Molly watch in sympathy, deep sadness in their eyes.

"Momma," Eveline says as she swings into the saddle, "you are brave." Standing next to Pal, Faye nods.

We are barely moving again as flames rise all around us. Turner's Hotel is ablaze. The Sowells' house. Dickinson and Kimble's hole-in-the-wall emporium of hats. The fort is a roaring tower of fire, the smoke and flames choking us, burning our throats. Houston's men are everywhere, torching one building after another. It is remarkable that there is so much to burn. Twenty stores and homes along Water Street alone. Twelve more in the inner town. Naomi puts her arm around me and squeezes me, and once more, I find it impossible to stifle my sobs. Holding lightly to the reins, I let the oxen lead, wiping tears with Naomi's handkerchief. Yowl jumps from Naomi's lap into mine and then under the seat.

The wagon creaks toward Peach Creek. As the sky darkens into night, the flames rise from Gonzales in the western sky. Then I mourn: for my blossoming spring garden and my bull, Curly, and the Rhode Island Red hens left behind; for the windowpanes shattering and cracking, shards clattering onto the porch; for the trunk of treasures brought from St. Louis now going up in smoke; for Green, gone from us almost a year now, and the love with which he built the house. Despite this dark road, I no longer lament his vision. I see his life whole, apart from mine, courageous and remarkable. Then, the flames shut the door on the past, like heat cauterizing a wound.

Our army advances under cover of darkness for a reason: Houston believes the Mexicans follow close on our heels. I wonder where Will is. I store the stolen hour with him by the river in a distant part of my mind, to be remembered later, and train every ounce of my strength on the treacherous path ahead.

As Houston marches his men and one lone ammunition wagon ahead of us, the rest of us follow in their muddy ruts. C. C. and Clinton ride up the line and back quickly, for most are on foot, and we all fear a testy foot soldier might try to steal our horses. After the rain, it is pitch dark and chilly. Curses ring through the night among the men ankle-deep in muddy tracks, weighed down with what equipment they can carry.

Refugees flow around us. Wagons and ox-drawn carts laden with women, children, and household goods rattle and lurch forward. Pigs and cattle follow. For now, we are in familiar territory and easily follow the road in the dark. The procession stretches for miles, a stream of the desperate—ill-prepared and ill-fed. Deserters from Houston's ranks among us fan the flames of rumor and fear.

Reaching Peach Creek, a few miles east, the army rests and sleeps under the live oaks. More than four hundred men drop in their tracks beneath the branches. In the army's wake, the wagons stop, too. Creed finds a stopping place near the creek, and then we all settle into the wagons to sleep.

At dawn, under the massive oak in front of what was the McClure home, Houston addresses the army. Near the front of the line, I can see the distant figure that is the general.

Creed comes back with news. "Now, this ain't his exact words. I'll boil it down for you: We don't know where we're goin' and won't know when we've got there. We'll keep falling back 'til we've got enough men to turn around and whip the varmints pressing down on us. And to keep it lively, Sam mentioned deserters will be shot. He did say that Burnham's ferry on the Colorado is several days away."

"*Primero, los ríos,*" Eugenio volunteers from behind Creed, dread in his voice. "*Lavaca y La Navidad.*"

"Yep, at least the first river we cross won't be much of a trial. After that, they keep gettin' bigger and wider. Houston didn't say this, but a few days south along the Colorado, we'll hit the La Bahía Road. So, there'll be a stretch in there as easy as pie. Unless we run into Comanche savages, of course."

Eugenio gets the fire started, and we women pluck eggs from the moss-filled pillowcase and crack them into the pan. Eugenio shares his tamales. Sitting with the two families gathered around, Creed, a veteran of another war, pronounces our good fortune.

"Hellfire, ladies, this is a pure-dee picnic."

Eveline glares at Creed. She looks at Naomi's pregnant belly and pats my sagging shoulders.

"In all the days of watching Momma dig us out of trouble, I never expected a hole as deep as this. More like a bottomless pit, a *pure-dee* hell hole," she says, twisting her mouth and narrowing her eyes.

Creed nods at Eveline's scowl. "Ah, my dear, you could say that. But look around you. A whole troop of badgers is here to do the digging."

Eveline doesn't smile, but Eugenio does. In fact, he gives his hyena laugh. Minnie echoes it just as the sun comes out from behind the clouds.

But it is Eveline's take on things that rings in my ears. Before we get through breakfast and back on the road, the rain starts again, accompanied by hail and lightning. We huddle under the wagons when the lightning gets bad and tie the horses in a sheltered site nearby. When the storm passes, I go with Eliza to find Quick, who bolted in the storm.

"What are you doing with that horse?" I shout as we spy a man trying to swing onto Quick.

"Woman, you don't need a horse. I do," he snarls as he gets himself into the saddle despite Quick's bucks and whinnies.

"Stop, stop," Eliza cries, running after the rider as he kicks the horse repeatedly. "Whoa, Quick, whoa."

Quick rears and kicks, but the man hangs on and pulls his pistol. "Stand back and shut up, or I'll shoot," he shouts.

Instantly a shot rings out, knocking the man to the ground. As he looks up from the mud, a second shot blasts the pistol out of his hands.

"Get it, Eliza," a familiar voice shouts.

Belle stands over the unarmed man with his bloodied shirtsleeve, her heavy legs pinning his arms.

"Get up and get out of here 'fore I shoot you in the other arm. And don't try taking a horse from a woman again. Your ugly face looks vaguely familiar to me. If I remember, you'll be sorrier than you are now."

"You buffalo cow," the man screams as she steps back, and he scrambles to his feet. "I know who *you* are, and I'll gitcha," he shrieks, fleeing into the woods.

"You'll have to find a gun first." Belle snorts and laughs loudly at the disappearing figure.

"Belle, where did you come from?" I cry, coming up behind her as Eliza leads her frightened horse toward us.

"From Gonzales, like the rest of you. Hope you know the way ahead. I don't."

I see her mud-encrusted boots and clothes and think once more of her strength.

"Come with us in the wagon. You've just saved us—"

"Wouldn't mind having a place to set and smoke my pipe," she admits as we return to the group watching from the wagons.

Lines of soldiers move up the road. I set off behind them, following the Burns wagon and Eugenio's cart, grateful I do not have to find my way alone. Naomi quizzes Belle about the burning of Gonzales, and I wish for cotton to stuff in my ears.

"Yeah, watched Luna burn. Explosions yesterday 'cause of gunpowder in the barrels and the liquor blowing up. I poisoned most of it in case the Meskins decide to try it. Hardly a bottle left standing far as I could tell. Now the Warloop's climbin' out of her banks. Might slow down the crowd so anxious to slit our throats."

When we reach the Colorado River, I record the date—March 17—in my diary. But I lack the will to write more than one sentence: *Reached Burnham's ferry on the Colorado.*

The army halts and lets the refugees cross ahead of them. Creed and I watch the first wagons roll onto the ferry, which is barely big enough to accommodate one wagonload with a team of oxen. The crossings go faster when it is only people with packs.

Creed goes ahead to help Jesse Burnham and Houston's men load the ferry. When he returns to us at sundown, he is full of information.

"I'll give this to ol' Sam. His spies are behind us, lettin' him know what's going on. Enemy's travelin' slower than we are. Makes sense. Got more men. And the Guadalupe's flooding. Gives us time to get people across this river. Besides that, our little engine is gathering steam. News is the army's got about six hundred men. More flockin' in all the time. Not too bad, when you think we started off with less than half that. Never mind that the Mexicans have maybe four times as many."

"When will we cross?" I ask.

"First light. See those rain clouds? Gotta cross 'fore Colorado goes on its own rampage."

340

ACROSS THE COLORADO

R ain drips in my face. The tent is soaked through, and building a fire is impossible. Several pairs of eyes are on me as I wake. Eveline speaks first.

"Momma, don't worry about feeding us. Let's just get across the river."

"You're right, Redbird."

"Where are C. C. and Eliza?"

"Stayed outside with the horses most of the night. Can't risk more horse thieves."

Outside, Creed's booming voice precedes him. I rise and move toward the only salvation available.

"Our wagon will go first, Sarah. Then Eugenio's cart and the pack mules. I'll come back with the ferry and load up your wagon." The urgency in his voice, so rare for Creed, leaves me shaken.

The children line up at the water's edge. Their gazes follow the ropes attached to each end of Jesse Burnham's ferry on opposite sides of the river. Burnham tugs on the line from the opposite bank.

All goes well until about halfway across when a huge, uprooted tree lodges under the ferry and threatens to overturn it. From the bank, we look on breathlessly. Then the tree flips up and out of the way; the ferry moves to the opposite bank.

Creed returns on the empty ferry, and Eugenio's trip across goes smoothly. Eugenio helps Burnham tug the pulleys sending the boat back to the other side. With Creed and Belle also working the line from our side of the river, the ferry shoots back.

Creed leads our ox-drawn wagon up the ramp onto the ferry. In the wagon, I hold the reins tightly as the DeWitt wagon rolls onto the boat. Belle and Antoñia stand by the oxen. Creed is in front as the children position themselves around the wagon. Eliza and C. C. prepare to swim the horses across. On the far bank, Eugenio waits with his cart, the pack mules, and the Burns family. The rain comes in torrents as Jesse Burnham starts to tug the ferry across once more.

I keep my eyes on Creed as the oxen shift, their eyes rolling and their bellowing growing louder as the waters churn. In the middle of the river, the stamping of the oxen starts to rock the small ferry and sets it lurching from side to side. As the rocking continues, Burnham, used to the Colorado's slower current, begins to lose ground. The rough waters seem to be turning the ferry at the wrong angle to the current.

Without a word, Belle and Antoñia move to the rear, reach for the line, and take up the tugging with Burnham. Their heaves slowly move the ferry back into place until the water disgorges us safely on the other side.

A little way upstream, the horses struggle in the churning river. In the middle of the crossing, the skittish Dandy starts to panic. As the wagon reaches the shore, I see Dandy break away from Eliza's grip, and the rough waters roll up and over her. Eliza folds herself over Quick as they swim across. Pal carries C. C. onto the bank, and Major follows.

The moment he is on dry land, C. C. sets off on Pal after Dandy. He returns around noon, with a slain deer slung behind his saddle. But without his horse.

I try to console him.

"She may have swum out," I keep saying. Unable to hide his tears, C. C. turns away to join Creed, who is dressing the deer among the trees.

Word soon reaches all camped here on the east bank of the Colorado River. The stay will be brief. The army will slog on toward Beason's ferry, where they will camp. There is more urgency among the men and Houston. As their numbers grow, they become more insistent that they can take the force pursuing them. Many speculate a battle will take place at Burnham's crossing. Some even claim Houston will make his stand on the Colorado.

Our little band watches from the bank at sunset. After all have crossed, a soldier sets fire to Burnham's ferry. I think about Gonzales, once the westernmost Anglo outpost on the continent. Soon there will be no Anglo strongholds west of the Colorado. "Green is turning over in his grave," I say, muttering Liza Q's familiar phrase. The flames from the ferry sputter and hiss. The Mexicans will not cross here.

Jesse Burnham, gnarled as a tree limb, looks on grimly as the wet night descends. He turns to Creed. "I built her in 1824. She's made the trip every day, usually several times."

When I can bear it, I begin to record the days in my diary:

March 20: Got to Beason's crossing farther south on the Colorado. The army is making camp. Must burn the ferry here too, as at Burnham's.

"Our day of reckoning may be coming right up," Creed announces as we find a spot away from the banks of the river. "And then again, it may not," he laughs, mocking Houston.

"What a terrible weight sits on his shoulders," I say, considering his choices.

"And he's not telling anybody what he's about. But we have to remember," Creed says, "more goin' on than right here. Where in this earthly hell is General Fannin? 'Sposed to go to the aid of the men at the Alamo. But his soldiers are nowhere to be found."

March 27: As with his water witching, Creed divines the main issue: Where is Fannin? General Fannin's force at Goliad is reputed to be the best-trained and best-outfitted of the whole army. Yet no reinforcements arrive. Pumped up by Houston's promises to fight, recruits flow into the army camp. On the banks of the Colorado, we feast on the venison C. C. provides. Cornmeal boils on the fire, and cornbread fills our stomachs. C. C. shot another deer for those camped nearby. Beginning to dry out a little. But Minnie and Naomi are breaking out in a rash I can't identify.

Eugenio brings news: Deaf Smith captured a scout who revealed that a part of the Mexican force, 700 strong, had split off from the rest and are camped directly across the Colorado two miles upriver. A few skirmishes took place.

"For the first time, at least with that part of the Mexican force, Houston's men might hold the advantage in numbers," Creed says. "We're coming right up on eight hundred strong."

The girls occupy themselves trying to make Naomi comfortable and questioning her about the baby's kicks and what it feels like to be pregnant. Around noon, Molly and I hear the men shouting.

Creed and C. C. start for the army camp to find out what's happening. They return, scratching their heads. "News is that Fannin is in Goliad with close to five hundred men, and they have suffered a bloody defeat. Houston's men are pacing like tigers, spoilin' for a fight. A refugee from Gonzales rode in with the news. But whaddya think our illustrious leader did?" Creed demands.

Belle sits at a little distance whittling a stick into the shape of a dog. I wonder if she is thinking of her mutts left behind. She looks up and snorts.

"Said it warn't true. Like he did with the rumors about the Alamo 'fore Susannah Dickinson dragged in."

"That's it, Belle. Exactly it. Badmouthed the messenger. Tomorrow we'll be on the run again, exactly because that coyote *knows* it's true," Creed says.

Despite the criticism, I see what Houston faces. News of another defeat might further demoralize his men. He must see the bigger picture and plan ahead; his small force is now the only hope Texas has.

"He has little ammunition, and he's probably not going to get more than one chance. He's trying to maneuver a fight on his own terms."

"All I know," Molly says, "terrible as it is, I'm thankful the weather is keeping the Mexicans on the other side of the river."

NORTH TOWARD THE BRAZOS

The march north toward San Felipe de Austin and Groce's plantation begins in the middle of the night. Fires are left burning to fool the enemy across the river.

C. C., Eliza, and Antoñia swing into their saddles. Belle climbs up next to me. We leave the rest tucked in among the blankets in fitful sleep. Clinton and Faye now join Minnie and Naomi with coughs and the rash. It has to be the measles—which could be hardest on Naomi, even bringing on premature birth. I can barely hear the squeak of Eugenio's wheels. What I hear instead is a steady tramping sound, louder than the plod of the horses and oxen, drowning out everything else.

At daybreak, on the next rise, I understand—behind us, a column of thousands of refugees is snaking along in a winding line. On both sides of the road, the misery spreads out. Women and children, rain-soaked and haggard, hunch against the wind of a new norther, trudging along in the mud. Babies whimper, and small children shiver in the dank cold. I pray for the sun to warm us, which seems unlikely.

"They're coming from Goliad," Belle says, pointing to a group of women and children as she climbs back into the wagon after a walk among them. "All Fannin's men, 'cept the ones that escaped, shut up in an old fort. Mexicans whupped 'em. Penned 'em up there."

Early on the third morning of the march toward San Felipe, a rider flies by, presumably on the way to deliver a message to Houston. But he doesn't get by the Burns wagon.

Creed flags him down, and the messenger disgorges his terrible news: Fannin and his men executed yesterday on orders of Santa Anna. Prisoners marched out of the fortress and gunned down at point-blank range, three hundred ninety men massacred.

The women who hear the news sink onto the cold, muddy ground. The moans and screams are unbroken, a chorus of throbbing pain. The children belonging to these women add to their cries as they wander aimlessly from mothers to sisters, sometimes two widows in the same family. The lamentations spread as more learn the fate of their husbands and sons at Goliad.

When the rider gallops on and the women's cries diminish, Creed walks over to a large group huddled close to his wagon.

"My heart cries out for you and your families," he says. "But we can't tarry on this road, with our enemies gainin' on us like fire-breathin' hellhounds. Pull yourselves together. You're a fine, brave lot, and we got to make it to San Felipe today. Save yourselves and your children."

The women simply stare at him and make no move. One speaks up.

"Nothin' left. Men dead and children sick and dying. Not much use going ahead on. Wore out. Cold and beaten. No better off than hunted animals."

I make my way to the one who has spoken.

"Your loss is terrible. Beyond words," I whisper softly. "I have lost my husband too, as has my daughter there." I look at Eliza nearby. "We have to keep going. The future of Texas lies with the army we are following and the strength we can muster. We're the last hope. You must get to your feet."

A few people struggle to their feet, but seeing the cold blank stare of their sisters, sink back down.

"All right, you weak sows," Belle calls out. "No butcherin' Meskins are gonna have the last word if'n I have any say-so. A mewling, puking kitten's got more gumption than you."

Belle picks up a few sick children and simply throws them over a shoulder, carrying them to the DeWitt wagon, where she crowds them in among the blankets. Predictably, their mothers run after them. And with that, the train moves on.

During the rest of the day, as thousands crowd onto the trail east, the DeWitt and Burns wagons stop several times to help bury children and old people. Eugenio cries out as we pass the carcasses of a team of oxen, sunk in the mud, still yoked. Life without his oxen, Pablo and Pablito, is Eugenio's greatest worry. With the scythes Antoñia has thought to bring, C. C. and Eliza and Antoñia hack at the brush when the trail narrows and closes in on us. And at times, the widows of Goliad join us in widening the road. When children or women fall down on the trail, we pick them up and put them in the wagons or on horses and let them ride a while.

March 28, evening: Among the widows of Goliad.

I can't write more. The hopelessness that pervades them gnaws at me. Even reaching San Felipe behind the army is little comfort. Soon San Felipe, Austin's first town, the hub of Texas settlement, will burn too.

I wake in the field opposite the town of San Felipe in a panic. My fears for Naomi and her baby crowd out all thoughts of armies and mud and defeat. On one side, Yowl licks Naomi's hot face and on the other, Faye, eyes glassy as an owlet in the dark, holds her hand. Naomi jerks and moans. She cries in her sleep, babbling about spiders. Before daybreak, I creep outside, guided by the light of our campfire, toward the other wagon.

"Is that you, Sarah?" Molly whispers.

"Yes, Molly, I need your help."

Instantly she sits up.

"Naomi's fever is high. She's very sick."

"Measles can bring on premature labor," Molly says, in confirmation of my worst fears. The measles epidemic in the wagons is now widespread.

"There's a doctor in San Felipe. If I can find him, maybe he can help her. I'm going to see if Eugenio can get us there."

The scent of chinaberry blossoms fills the air as we ride into town. The heavy, sweet perfume intensifies my anguish, reminding me of spring-blooming gardens and the everyday world left behind. Dr. Robert Peebles's sign sits in a window on the main street.

I feel the warm gush of water spread beneath us as I hold Naomi next to me.

"Her water is breaking," I tell Molly. Given her size, I think Naomi can be no more than seven months along; the baby is weak and small. I jump from the cart and pound on the door, thanking the remaining few stars in the morning sky that the town is still standing.

Dr. Peebles, previously asleep on the cot in his office, opens the door quickly.

"My daughter . . . high fever . . . water broke . . . measles."

Molly looks on in amazement. "Now pull yourself together, Sarah. You're jabbering."

Dr. Peebles gets Naomi onto his examining table to check her. Still out of her head, she begins to writhe and twist, now clearly in labor.

"Baby's small, coming fast," he says as he boils water and washes his hands.

I stand on one side and Molly on the other, holding Naomi's hands.

"She's doing fine," Dr. Peebles says, jaded in the art of delivering babies. "Get this down her." He hands me a draught of whiskey and something else with a sharp smell in a shot glass.

In less than four hours, Naomi delivers a frail baby boy. His little legs are stringy and thin. He tips the scales at five pounds. His weak cry doesn't seem to bother Peebles.

"Lungs are okay. Just keep him warm." Putting the back of his hand to Naomi's face, he pronounces his diagnosis. "Fever's broken. But give her another swig of this." He hands me the shot glass with more of his whiskey concoction. "She needs to sleep. That'll do it."

"There's some color in *your* face now. Hope it's not the measles for you too," Molly says to me as the exhausted Naomi rests quietly. Then Dr. Peebles disappears to change out of his nightshirt.

Almost floating, I cradle the child in the doctor's warm office, where a fire burns and water boils on the hearth. Fleeting as this interlude must be, I am almost giddy to have mother and child beyond the crisis, and the doctor at hand.

"How strange, Molly, in the middle of a war, a blessed little island of peace and serenity."

"Sarah DeWitt, peace follows you. That's been true since I first laid eyes on you. You calm the storm."

I hug Molly with my other arm. "Thank you, my friend, but it feels more like a constant battle to me," I say, wondering how Molly could think such a thing.

Molly nods. "Didn't say there weren't plenty of trouble."

Dr. Peebles turns to me when he hears the name.

"You're Miz DeWitt? I was at Monclova with Green. When he died. He's looking down on his posterity then. The future. The land. He'll live on, in more ways n' one. Died too soon to know that."

I nod, astonished I'd forgotten the good man was there with Green.

"Now I've got a thing or two for you to remember," he says tersely. "Good you brought this young'un here. I take it there's more measles in your camp."

I nod again.

"He doesn't have measles from his mother. She's not contagious any longer. But he's weak. If he's going to survive this epidemic, he's got to be kept away from them that have it. Wouldn't make it. Anywhere you can stash him away from the measles?"

"Our wagon. My children haven't got the measles," Molly volunteers with satisfaction.

"You know," Dr. Peebles says, "your daughter's timing was fortuitous. In another day or two, this town, too, will be ashes, another casualty in the march to wherever the fight leads."

"It was *your* timing, Sarah," Molly says.

"Oh my, Molly, if I can't take care of my own, what can I do?"

"Seen that roiling River Brazos yet?" Dr. Peebles asks, raising an eyebrow at Sarah. "Getting across that river with these two, mother and babe, is a worse hazard than the measles."

I hear the warning. I hold the baby closer, unwilling to relinquish the pride that keeps me thinking I can protect them all.

Molly and I settle Naomi and the as-yet-unnamed baby boy in Eugenio's cart. Naomi opens her eyes once and says, "I was going to name a girl after you, Momma. I think we should name this boy for Poppa and for William."

I kiss her as Molly climbs in next to mother and babe, and I move up by Eugenio.

"Before going back, let's take a look at the Brazos."

The water is a frothing monster, alive with boiling rapids and debris tossed like leaves in the wind. Even the uprooted trees are like sticks in the churning foam. Dead animals, wagons, and parts of wagons float below us. Bodies, too, in the terrible wild water. From the promontory above the town, the Brazos looks twice as wide as the Colorado at Burnham's crossing.

Eugenio whispers as if he were in a cathedral, "*Río loco.*" The oxen give rolling snorts.

Crazy river, indeed. A river too crazy for Pablo and Pablito. But how far ahead of Santa Anna can we possibly be?

"We can't cross this," I pronounce. "We'll stay with our troops and see if they can figure out how to keep us ahead of Santa Anna's forces."

Eugenio nods and turns the oxen back to the edge of town.

UP AND DOWN THE RIVER

Creed has his own eye-opener to deliver when we return in Eugenio's cart late in the day. He and C. C. have been to the army camp. As the children gather around Naomi and the baby, Creed lets loose with the latest.

"Discontent with Houston's the worst it's been. Army's crazier'n a two-headed calf looking opposite ways. Two companies of men refused to fall back and follow Houston. He's heading to a haven for the army at Jared Groce's cotton plantation tomorrow. So, the commander has ordered Baker's company to stay at San Felipe to guard the crossing here. And Wiley Martin's company will march for Fort Bend, twenty miles downriver, to keep the enemy from getting across there."

"And where's C. C.?"

"Stayed at the camp. Back in the morning."

Molly stared at Creed in disbelief. "You let him stay?"

Creed looks at me.

"The boy's got divided loyalties. Couldn't find him when I was ready to go. He'll be back. He's on Pal. Knows better than to steal his mother's horse."

I turn away. I won't go after C. C. He's looking for Will, and when he finds him, he'll get sent back.

Sitting out the rain underneath the wagons, the best shelter we have, we watch as San Felipe burns. Through the night, the baby cries, the children cough, and from the thickets along the Brazos, wolves howl. It is almost April, but the wagons are flecked with frost by morning.

At dawn, C. C. trudges in—with Pal at his side. Covered with mud, he acknowledges Pal's limp.

"She lost a shoe in the mud. One of the men helped me fix it."

"So why is she limping?" I ask, feeding the campfire.

"Sore feet. From the mud."

Taking the reins, I pick up the foot Pal is protecting. It is swollen.

"Antoñia has stuff to put on it, doesn't she?" C. C. asks sheepishly.

I glare at him, considering my words carefully. I want to hug him and tell him it is all right. I want to send him to hug Naomi and the baby. I want to ask if he'd found Will. But first, I must deal with the fact he'd gone off with no real plan in mind, flirting with the idea of joining the army.

"If you're going to run off, don't take my horse." I stare him down.

"Yes, ma'am," he says, staring back at me without flinching. "There's no use in going with the men anyway. They all say Houston's a coward and isn't going to fight."

"Do you believe that?"

"I did, but then I saw him through the night. He went among the men, tending to them in the rain and mud and all, and then spent the night sitting on his saddle near the ammunition wagon. He threw a blanket over his shoulders but didn't go in his tent, with the men out in the rain suffering. He put a piece of wood under his feet and just sat there, sort of dozing in the rain."

"Doesn't sound like a coward to me."

"No."

"I think we should stick with him, following along. What do you say?" I ask, trying to help with his limbo between man and boy.

"Yes, ma'am. I agree."

March 31: At Groce's Pass. The march of twenty miles took two full days along impassable roads slashed with ruts and mired in rain. The dispirited army zigzagged back and forth from west to east—as it has done for two weeks. They march on empty stomachs, some in bare feet, often stopping to push the wagons out of the mud; fatigue is heavy as the air. But the secure position we've reached at Groce's cotton plantation is remarkable with lake and woods nearby.

April 1: Army moved deeper into the Brazos River bottom. The camp occupies its own little island on a rise in a grove of trees, safe from the encroaching waters. A far cry from the plantation's welcome setting nearby, the camp is surrounded by murky, snake-infested sloughs, belly deep in places. But here, the men are safe from a frontal attack. Rumor is they'll be here more than a week. Beyond one of the sloughs, the men drill. Creed is more concerned with the comings and goings of Deaf Smith. Knows how cagey he is—and that his eyesight is failing.

Creed appears at first light and says, "I'm gonna need your boy. Deaf's looking for the enemy 'cause he knows they're looking for us. Needs us in his corps of spies. Not only is he deaf, but he also can't see like he used to. Now that hardly stops him, but I'm taking these young eyes with me," he says, nodding at C. C. "Mine are good, but not good as a spring chicken."

"Be careful." I bite my tongue to keep from saying more.

As I look on from our post past the backwaters and lagoons of the Brazos at the edge of the plantation, I agree with what Houston is doing. He's camped the army here on Groce's property to give them time to rest and recover. Jared Groce is the richest and largest Anglo landowner in Texas, with a plantation of more than ten leagues. He has put his vast resources at Houston's disposal, and Houston will make good use of them. In the meantime, I want to see what the place is like.

Molly and the girls mind Naomi and the baby, and Eliza and Belle are in full control; so I make a foray from camp. What I find is gratifying: Pal and I ride among the livestock and gardens, which feed the sick and exhausted men. Stricken by mumps, measles, pinkeye, diarrhea, and flu, they now have Groce's doctors to treat them. The blacksmith shop is an armory for repairing muskets and forging balls and grapeshot. The dairy turns out milk, cream, and buttermilk by the bucketful. Supplies and reinforcements flow to the army as it stays put for more than a day or two. And Houston has a visitor.

April 8: Yesterday, the so-called Secretary of War of the new republic, Mr. Thomas Rusk, came to camp to deliver a letter from the republic's new president, David Burnet. Both were elected at the convention in March when the delegates declared Texas independent from Mexico. I'd read Burnet's name in the Advocate for People's Rights, *though, amid all the chaos, we've heard little of him. C. C. and Creed reported the letter was a demand from Burnet to Houston to stand and fight. Creed heard from Deaf Smith that the message was mean enough to curl Houston's toenails. But Houston is not one to follow orders. And, for that matter, no one can be sure exactly where the enemy is or where to stand and fight, though rumors are flying that Santa Anna was spotted in San Felipe only days ago. Creed says Houston's replies and rationalizations have won over the Secretary of War, who's decided to stay with the army rather than return to Harrisburg, the seat of the self-proclaimed new Texas government.*

April 11: Amazingly, two cannons arrived from the city of Cincinnati, Ohio. Supporters of the quest for independence sent them to the fighting forces of Texas to aid them in their struggle. The men dubbed them the Twin Sisters and took heart; though, for many, the cannons are not enough to restore their faith in Houston.

I continue to slip away on Pal to explore the great plantation as days at Groce's stretch into a second week. Though she is no longer limping, Pal gets a new shoe in the blacksmith shop. In the big, sweet-smelling dairy, a Negro woman called Aunt Liddy watches over troughs of cool water holding pans of milk covered with muslin. She gives me a glass of sweet buttermilk. Along the Brazos, refugees lash logs together to make rafts for crossing. Women with hand axes fell the trees and cobble together the rough rafts. When I counsel them to stay near the army, they look at me with scorn and damn Houston, calling him chicken-livered and worse.

I've spotted a steamboat called the *Yellowstone* on the river. It is now docked at Groce's Landing. The captain paces the deck as slaves carry huge cotton bales on board. Next to the boat's massive boilers, a cord of firewood sits ready to power the big boat as it bucks the swift waters of the Brazos.

Back at camp, I pump Creed for information.

"Been some talk of using the steamboat to make raids on Mexican positions downstream, but Houston has forbidden this action."

"Why not use it to transport people across the Brazos?"

"That's up to your friend Sam."

Creed is right. Houston's army must move soon. Climbing into the saddle, I urge Pal across one of the stagnant little sloughs into the army camp.

Alarmed to see a horse and rider crossing into their space, several raise their muskets as Pal and I fly by. Outside his tent, Houston rises to greet me.

"Mrs. DeWitt, an unexpected pleasure in the Brazos swamp." He pulls his battered hat from his head and takes my hand as I dismount. "What brings you into our bug-infested lair?"

"In a word, General, the *Yellowstone*. Can the steamboat be used to help the refugees across the wide Brazos?"

Houston smiles at me and motions at the stump he has been sitting on. "Please sit down in my parlor here."

Sweeping my skirt under me, I sit to address him as he squats on his haunches in front of me.

"How far behind us are our pursuers?" I ask. And then despite myself, "When will we take a stand against them? Passions run high."

"Indeed, Mrs. DeWitt. Inevitable, of course. Mind you, I can be as hotheaded as any. But the passions and panic of this campaign do not serve us well. There will be a time for the passions yet. In the meantime, as I've said before, roads and ravines suit us best. I bide my time. I still believe we will succeed."

"I trust you will," I say, feeling both empathy and admiration.

"But you came here to talk of the *Yellowstone*, and I want to hear. And again, I must thank you for the flag you so kindly delivered to me. Since you travel behind the army, you may not know we bear the lone star proudly at the head of the line."

"I am glad to be of some service. But, yes, I am here about the *Yellowstone*. To save the lives of many trying to cross the river. Countless desperate women and children have lost their lives on log rafts already."

"I am advised we should not delay our march east. My men are getting ready to board the boat. But you affirm what must be done. I will let the captain know. The *Yellowstone* will be at the people's service. We will cross families along with the troops. And we will do so farther on down the river as well. Spread the word. I wish you Godspeed across to the other side."

44

FORK IN THE ROAD

Hundreds camp along the river, looking west toward the enemy they fear and east toward the hope of refuge beyond. With the wild Brazos frothing and boiling, C. C. and I, on horseback, spread the word and direct them onto the *Yellowstone* tied at Groce's Landing. We enlist Eugenio and Antoñia as well, along with Creed and his bellowing voice. Together we transport buckets of milk and buttermilk from Jared Groce's dairy to old and young, sick and healthy as they climb aboard the sidewheeler *Yellowstone*, its engine now belching black smoke in a clattering thunder.

Many have never seen a paddle wheeler. Wagons, horses, oxen, and frightened refugees climb aboard, alongside Houston's army of some eight hundred men and two hundred horses. The horde crowds onto the boat, squeezing together like cattle in a stampede. Some sit atop or squat beside the cotton bales the *Yellowstone* is carrying downriver. Amid them come volunteers who walked from Brazoria and Harrisburg and other points, even as far away as

Georgia, to join the forces. The loading takes a day and a half. Mindful of the time and what Houston has divulged to me—that part of Santa Anna's army has been sighted upriver—each second seems longer than the last.

On the seventh and last trip, on the afternoon of April 13, the Burns and DeWitt wagons rumble across the shifting gangplank with Eugenio's cart and oxen in between. We line the railings of the big steamboat and stare into the angry water. The weather has turned rainy and cold again, and I watch Faye pull on her dirty old coat. Threadbare and rain soaked as it is, it seems to bring her comfort, especially now that her bout with the measles keeps her away from Naomi and the baby. I move over next to her and put my arm around her. She looks up at me with a doleful smile, clasping my hand.

At that moment, the captain opens wide the valves, putting steam to the *Yellowstone*'s sidewheeler paddles, and the boat lurches from Groce's Landing. Cold wind adds spray to the muddy turmoil of the Brazos. Faye and I stand together, amazed at the power of the roiling water. Soon we should reach a landing on the east bank a few miles downstream.

The boat lumbers on, crabwise, at an angle to the current and then pulls up to the next landing downriver. A few departing the boat touch my arm, thankful for the milk given on the opposite shore. And then hands grasp my shoulder. I look into the eyes of Lila, Bess, and Juan, the Tejano boy who learned to read alongside Faye. They touch Faye's cheek and hug her close for a moment. Together, they are part of the refugee horde fleeing to an unknown destination. As quickly as they stop, they are gone with the rest, flowing down the gangplank onto the bank.

The army marches southeastward. But still Houston gives no hint where he is heading. I go back and forth between Faye, Eveline, and Eliza in our wagon and Naomi and baby William in the Burns wagon. Belle drives the oxen, and C. C. and Antoñia scout for deer and squirrels to keep us fed. We are part of a column of hundreds trekking along the east bank of the Brazos.

The past decade of my life is narrowing down to the fork in the road ahead. Among the army and those trudging with them, the talk is of nothing but the paths converging ahead. Will Houston head east, straight toward Harrisburg, temporary quarters of the new Texas government? Or will he take the left fork and see the refugees all the way to the US border? Those fleeing the Mexican troops pray for safe conduct to the United States. Most of Houston's troops favor the Harrisburg fork and vow to oust him from his command should he make the wrong choice.

Deaf Smith brings news of Santa Anna in Harrisburg and the government officials who narrowly escaped capture. But the news does not stop the troops from dancing with girls at the home of a settler named Donahoe. Though the man denies the troops a share of his timber for firewood, Donahoe cannot stop them from turning him out of his house to hold a dance.

Bouncing along on the rutted roads, I anguish over the future. If I am going to take my family to the US, back to Missouri, I must talk to them about it now.

Apparently, they neither question my intentions nor face such a possibility themselves. Day to day is so hard, there isn't room for more.

When we leave Donahoe's campsite at dawn, the decision Houston makes is, in a small part, mine as well. But the rain slows us, and we camp again at nightfall, at a settler's place just a mile short of the crossroads.

Still, I have not spoken of my indecision to the children. I leave our wagon to approach Creed and Molly. Pulling them aside, I urge them to follow me on a brief walk beyond the campfire. Out of earshot of the rest, I put the question bluntly.

"Tomorrow, we come to the crossroads. I suppose this is not a question for you two, but I must ask, for it is a grave consideration for me. Do you have any thought of leaving the army at the crossroads and returning home, to the United States, to Missouri? The choice is upon us. Should we just keep going?"

Molly and Creed stare at me. Then Creed speaks.

"Been here too long. Threw in my lot with these rapscallions and Indian fighters long ago. Gonna tan the Meskins' hides, if we ever get around to fighting. And if we don't, hell, we can leave then maybe. Now's not the time."

Molly's answer is simpler. "The children think they belong here now. I couldn't go without them."

"I don't want to press you one way or the other," Creed begins and then stops. "Hellfire, yes, yes, I do. I want you here. You started Texas, you and Green, and I'll give Colonel Austin a little credit too," he chuckles, "and our inscrutable leader at the head of this pack, if he ever turns around and fights."

Tears fill my eyes.

"Thank you, my dear friends." But still, I cannot say what I will do.

I must talk with the children first. I am sure Eliza will agree with Molly and Creed. But I should offer her a chance to say so.

Eliza sits with Eugenio by the fire. Joining them, I waste no time.

"In the morning, we will come to the Harrisburg road. We can, of course, continue with the army. But we could also go where most are going. To safety in the US. Back to Granny Quick and Grampa."

"Why, Momma, I never even thought of that. And I'm surprised you would consider it. Poppa had a vision. And we're fulfilling it. How could it be any other way?"

Eugenio glances at me. I think his look is the only doubtful one he has ever cast in my direction. He shrugs. "I no understand, *no entiendo*."

The next morning, C. C., Eliza, and Creed gallop to the front of the column to see how General Houston will play it. Creed relays it all when the three return.

"No mistaking the place. A man stood with a foot on his gate, waiting for Houston to come along. When he spied the general on his gray stallion, he shouted in a deep voice, 'That right-hand road will carry you to Harrisburg just as straight as a compass.' The general saluted him and sounded out the order: 'Col-umns right.' The words rang out, and the army gave a cheer. Then wails broke out from the civilians in the front ranks. And the general did the right thing. He ordered Wiley Martin and a large company to accompany them all the way to the border, to the Sabine River."

"How many are left in the fighting force?" I ask.

"About a thousand men to do the deed," Creed pronounces.

I nod. "Then we will accompany them. To the very end of the Texas road."

Next to me in the wagon, Faye squeezes my hand.

HIGHER GROUND

We stop on the San Jacinto River.

April 18, morning: Two days and nights of quagmires and ruts. Carried the wagons over bogs too deep to chance getting stuck. More than fifty miles from the fork in the road, Creed figures. Unrelenting rain. Resting some miles from a swamp called Buffalo Bayou. The last month a terrible blur except for the birth of little William Green Matthews.

My attempt to join the family in an afternoon rest is interrupted by the sound of Creed's cry outside the wagon.

"Deaf Smith's swum the bayou and captured two of Santa Anna's boys."

I sit up along with Eliza and C. C.

"One of the Mexican couriers had a saddlebag with red-hot news: Santa Anna is coming toward us. Houston told Deaf he's no more than ten miles away, coming up the Harrisburg road with a small part of his force. He's coming back from the coast where he nearly captured ol' Prez Burnet and the Texas officials in our little makeshift capital."

Quickly, we all gather by the ashes of the noon campfire.

"Need to get some eats and some sleep tonight. Mexican army's gonna be swarmin' thicker than a cloud of grasshoppers by morning. C. C. and I'll kill something to eat pretty quick, and we'll be in shape to move at dawn."

"But Creed," I ask, "hasn't Santa Anna been this close before? What makes this the moment Houston's chosen to attack?"

"Way Deaf tells it, been nothin' but hide and seek up to now. Finally, Houston knows exactly where Santa Anna is, but *he* don't know exactly where *we* are. More'n that, he's separated from most of his army. General Sesma's behind us. And the other two generals, Cos and Filisola, are behind Santa Anna. He's travelin' light, with a force of maybe nine hundred or so looking for us. He's got his men positioned with their backs to the river only a mile or so from Houston's camp in the woods. So now, praise the Lord, Houston has got his spot for a fight."

April 19, dawn: No reveille this morning. It must mean that Houston doesn't want to alert the Mexicans to his position. Now it seems the army is starting to believe in their general. C. C. went up to the front of the line and heard his speech to the men. "Victory is certain! Remember the Alamo!" And the men answered him, shouting back, "Remember the Alamo! Remember Goliad!" We will follow them as far as we can.

April 20, afternoon: Camped in sight of the swamp. Our army crossed the bayou last night, but we can't take the wagons across that marsh. Creed and C. C. are going to cross on horseback. Wanted to go with them, but they left before I said so. Having made it this far, I'd like to see things up close.

At dawn, I listen for the reveille bugle. For the third day in a row, there is silence instead. No crisp staccato notes as we'd come to expect in days of camping near the army. I don't relish a dash across the murky lagoon, but the desire to see for myself is strong, and I decide to head across alone.

"Momma, what are you doing?" Eliza asks as I rise and dress.

"I was about to wake you. I think I'm going to cross the marsh on Pal to see what's happening over there. C. C. and Creed must be right over there on that little spit of land. You and Molly and Belle can hold the fort?"

"If you're going, I'm going with you."

In the darkness of the wagon, I cannot see Eliza's face clearly. "I won't go until there's plenty of daylight. It won't be hard to find them. They're probably just beyond the bayou."

Eliza gets up and speaks to Belle and Antoñia.

"Momma and I are going to get a little closer to the army since our two trusty scouts have not come back. You'll be all right here, won't you?"

Belle grunts an answer. "Sister, don't worry none 'bout this bunch. But you're crazy to cross that snake-infested swamp."

I make the rounds to Molly, Naomi, Faye, Eveline, and Eugenio. When I return, Eliza is saddled up and waiting.

"All right, Momma, ready when you are." The sun is rising, and the swamp reeds wave in the early morning pink light.

We find a narrow crossing about a mile up the shore, spur the horses, and dash across. Water birds scatter in front of us, a water moccasin ripples away, and water lilies thick with blooms scent the close air. The trip across the water takes only minutes, and the murky water is no more than chest deep on the horses. Laughing with relief, we ride toward the woods straight ahead.

C. C. and Creed perch on the slope just at the edge of the woods.

"Dang, ladies," Creed proclaims as we dismount, "welcome to the party."

Below us, the drama unfolds. Creed brings us up to speed.

"A good deal of action yesterday. Santa Anna's boys bunched up over there on the right by the river in four long columns and rolled out some rickety artillery. Started firing at our side, but most of the balls hit the trees, showering the army with leaves. Our boys wheeled out the Twin Sisters cannons and fired a load of grapeshot full of nails and horseshoes—about ten times more effective than the Mexicans' cannonballs. Their bugles blared, but it was pretty much noise and smoke, though those Mexican infantrymen lying dead wouldn't say so."

"So, what's going to happen today?"

"Don't have a crystal ball, my lass. Our commander-in-chief remains a mystery, but he's got things goin' the way he wants. Set it up yesterday with his side hiding in some kind of crazy formation in the woods, the Twin Sisters out in front. Mexicans are goin' to have to fight on his terms. Our sleeping giant didn't show his face until mid-morning. Don't know what to say about him. He's strollin' around under the trees as if he doesn't have a care in the world, while the men are marchin' around with ants in their pants in a total fidget. On the other side of the plain, out yonder, you can see a big tent. That belongs to Santa Anna. He even has thick plush carpets in there, 'cording to the spies Deaf sent out. Seems like Santa Anna has no idea of the size of Houston's army, so he's pretty overconfident. And some say he gets a little hazy from smoking an opium pipe around afternoon siesta time. No one's quite sure why he hasn't made more effort to safeguard his force from attack."

Around noon, we witness what looks like a council of war, which comes to nothing when Houston dismisses the officers arguing among themselves. Right before that, we see Deaf Smith return and then leave again with something in his hands that glints in the sun.

I take this pause in the action to lie back in the bright green meadow grass and close my eyes. I imagine the battle over and Will, somewhere down there in the fray, making it through unscathed. He is coming for a visit to my old house, now rebuilt, but with the same kind of windows. There are grandchildren running in and out. My Rhode Island Red hens scratch in the dirt, and my bull, Curly, grazes in the pasture. My garden is full of fresh vegetables and wildflowers. I dream up a dairy barn, too, clean and fragrant as Aunt Liddy's at the Groce dairy, with shelves lined with pans of buttermilk and cool sweet milk.

"Momma, Momma, wake up," C. C. says, shaking me. "Something's happening!"

I squint at the sun, past the middle of the western sky, and focus on Houston as he raises his sword. Fiddlers scrape out a crude love song called "Will You Come to the Bower?" Then columns of his soldiers emerge onto the green plain between the Twin Sisters cannons and the swamp. They look almost aimless as if they are executing a simple drill. On the right flank of the troops, the cavalry advances, still looking as if they're engaged in a daily exercise. Houston rides up and down in front on his big gray horse, shouting.

A slight ridge in the middle of the plain seems to obscure the Mexicans' view of this advance. Despite the skirmish Creed mentioned, the Mexicans don't seem to have more than a few sentinels on guard duty. Cooks are tending campfires, and soldiers are moving in and out of tents. Then the column passes over the ridge.

A bugle sounds and a line of Mexican infantry scrambles to fire at the troops. The Mexican forces, about three hundred yards distant, come alive. Pandemonium breaks loose in the Mexican camp. Soldiers watering their horses swing onto their mounts bareback. As Mexicans unstack their rifles, Texians, screaming like banshees, overrun the camp. Santa Anna, in his carpeted tent, must have awakened from his siesta in horror. A tall man with a sword, perhaps Santa Anna, runs into the midst of the camp shouting orders, along with one of his generals. Then he disappears. Soldiers run this way and that, with Texians pursuing them. The Mexicans kneel down trying to fire, becoming easy targets for bayonets.

Suddenly Houston's gray stallion goes down under him, and the general leaps onto a cavalryman's mount. Then in ringing tones heard even here on the rise, Deaf Smith shouts from his lathered horse.

"Fight for your lives! Vince's bridge has been cut down!"

"The wily old scout's cut off the Mexicans' retreat!" Creed says. "And cut off any chance for more Mexican soldiers to get through as reinforcements."

The weight of Creed's proclamation sinks in as troops creep through the tall grass pulling the Twin Sisters cannons toward Mexican lines. Some twenty yards in front of the Mexican breastworks,

Houston signals for action, and the Twin Sisters open fire. It is late afternoon. After a single volley from the cannons, the Texas infantry-men break ranks and storm the breastworks. The Mexican barricade melts as if made of spun sugar.

The general standing beside the tall one with the sword rounds up a group of hundreds of soldiers, demanding that they fire. But it is too late. Texians pursue Mexicans, shooting at anything that moves, driving men and horses down a precipitous bank of the San Jacinto River, sending them hurtling to their deaths. The attack seems to be over in a very short time. The general who had tried to mobilize the troops to fight seems to be surrendering. There's no armed defense; the resistance has collapsed. The Mexican general and many soldiers abandon the campsite, fleeing for their lives.

I turn away. Astonishing as it seems, the battle is over. But in iso-lated pockets of twos and threes, the massacre goes on. Vengeful cries of "Remember the Alamo" ring across the plain. I can't watch or even take it in. In a matter of minutes, the Texians have vanquished Santa Anna's troops. Is it over? How would we know? And where is Santa Anna?

Rather than recross the marsh at night, we wait. Our little party of four sleeps on the grassy slope, rotating watch, agog at what morning will bring. The music, drinking, and shouting penetrate the night, on and on.

At sunrise, the drama begins anew. General Houston, wounded in the leg, sits propped against a tree writing notes. Throughout the morn-ing and into the afternoon, we four remain, unable to tear ourselves away. Dare we trust our hope that the war, not just the battle, is won?

Toward evening, as the Texians continue to bring in prisoners, Creed leaves us to find Deaf Smith. While he is gone, a patrol of five men rides close to us on the rise.

"I know one of those fellows," C. C. says as they ride past. "He was with us at Béjar. Name of Robison." Behind him, riding double behind a soldier, is a dejected figure, pale and dark-haired, in a blue smock and red felt slippers.

The patrol goes past. When they reach camp, shouting breaks out. The tall Mexican in the red shoes dismounts on the knoll where prisoners are confined. Some Mexican prisoners bow. "*El General, el General,*" they shout over and over. When an officer rides up, an exchange takes place. Amid cries of "Shoot him! Hang him!" the officer conducts the prisoner toward the tree where Houston sits with his leg elevated on a coil of rope.

While we're trying to figure out what's happening, Creed returns. Striding up to the crest of the slope, he announces, "Ladies and gentlemen, the tall hombre with the funny red shoes is none other than Gen. Antonio López de Santa Anna. Whaddya say to that?"

We watch as a contingent of Texians bring Santa Anna before Houston, propped up in his makeshift headquarters. The tall man, his arms tied behind his back, approaches Houston with an air of complete dejection.

"Houston is not going to be hanging this prisoner," Creed says. "Our esteemed leader has his bargaining chip now. And the first thing he's got to do is have Santa Anna call off the other Mexican generals."

C. C., quiet until now, hugs me and pumps Creed's hand. He dashes down the hill toward the camp.

"Have we won? Is the war over?" Eliza shouts, hugging us all. "We're not just dreaming?!"

"Well, *I* say we've won," Creed says, watching him go. "Deaf said that half a dozen Texians died, with a couple of dozen wounded. Our esteemed General Houston is one of them. Shattered bone above the ankle."

Suddenly Creed stands and shades his eyes against the setting sun.

"Oh, ho, lookee there, lookee there. Santa Anna and Houston are shaking hands. And now Sam is motioning to Deaf. I think he's about to send him out with orders to bring in Cos, Filisola, and the other Mexican generals. We're going to find out here pretty quick that we've got an armistice."

Creed cackles, rubbing his hands together as one who has just hit the jackpot. He savors the moment, slapping his thigh and chortling with glee. Then remembering the rest of us, he returns to earth.

"And another thing. I saw John W. He's as right as rain. Not a scratch on him. I told him we were over here on the hill, and he smiled big, glad to hear it."

"He's all right? He's all right?" I repeat.

"Yes, ma'am. Sends his regards." Creed winks at me.

In concert, Creed and Eliza rise.

"We should get back across the marsh before dark," Creed says. "At the wagons, they can't be sure what's happened in the last two days. Molly will be meaner than a bayou cottonmouth if I don't get back with the latest."

"You stay here, Momma. Tell Will he's a hero." Eliza hugs me again.

I watch them disappear.

"So," I say aloud on the green hill to none but myself, "they think they know all about Will and me."

Of course, they don't know much of anything about Will and me. More than that, they don't know what it has taken me all these years to learn. What my mother tried to tell me, to arm me with, more than once.

"Remember, God doesn't close one door before opening another."

For years, I thought she was talking about her faith. But now I know she meant something else: courage. She'd taught herself to be unafraid of life.

I will have to call him John W. He will have to face the person he has chosen to be. I cannot let him pretend he has no wife—two, in fact—and children. We will not be lovers. We will be star-crossed and separate forever. We will be companions, but I will not be his mistress or his wife.

I go back to my daydream of being in my old house with Will coming to visit. *You don't have to give him up entirely*, I think. *There's nobody in your life who knows you better.* We'll never be weighed down by the travails of marriage nor enjoy its comforts and pleasures. No, we will be what we've always been. He will come and sit with me from time to time. I will wish for him sometimes. We'll keep that place we own in each other's hearts. That is what we have. What we've always had. Like so much in life, a curse and a blessing.

And in this brave world we've come into, I must survive the future shaped by Green's vision, Austin's vision, Houston's vision, suddenly successful now beyond their wildest dreams. The whole greater than the sum of its parts. Texas: a republic separate from Mexico? Can I dare dream of annexation back to the US, as my parents dreamed of the American Revolution and a nation free from Britain?

The light here under a catalpa tree is softer than that below on the plain. Up here, mockingbirds and jays squawk, build nests, and feed babies. The purple and yellow-throated white blossoms of the huge catalpa above me are opening. Down there, the isolated pockets of killing go on, two worlds in sharp upheaval, now on new and changing terms. The plain is littered with dead bodies. Don't they know they can stop fighting? The lines Green and Austin delivered so often about bringing civilization to the wilderness echo in my head like a throbbing headache. Is civilization an idea we've invented to hold the world together? Lifeless men and horses lie on the plain, and civilization appears a poor threadbare garment that keeps ripping open, threads unraveling. The notes of a fiddler reach me, bowing out the strains of "Comin' Thro' the Rye."

Destiny whispers in my ear: *Remember you wanted the war to come.* Yes, I wanted the war to come. It had to be waged, didn't it? And now the godsend of a victory. But not godsend enough to stop the killing. I have no answers for this. Nor for the women, the widows of the Alamo and Goliad, the Mexican camp followers who have lost husbands and sons and lovers, who now bury their men so that the wolves won't eat them. They are trying to keep some thin tissue of civilization alive.

Will approaches from the army camp in the fading light. His hat is knocked back on his red hair, and he leads Ruby. Pal looks up and whinnies. The horses are the innocents, preternatural beings among the chaos. They smell the blood and death, witness it all, sometimes wild-eyed with fear, yet carry on.

As he starts up the hill, I try to think what I will tell Will when he hugs me and tells me he loves me. After I've held him and told him how relieved I am to see him alive. Then I will tell him. "You *are* magic. You *did* catch 'em while they were sleeping. And once again, you have cheated death." But no, I won't say any of that. I'll just say, "You're a hero, John W." and kiss him full on the lips.

EPILOGUE

On April 21, 1836, the battle for Texas independence was won in only eighteen minutes, according to Houston's calculations. Like St. Hyacinth himself, the victory was its own kind of marvel, an unlikely triumph on an innocuous reach of land amid the marshes and inlets of the San Jacinto River.

The battle on the Plain of St. Hyacinth changed everything: the lives of Sarah and her family, the map, the futures of Texas and Mexico; even, in the long run, the borders of the United States. The new republic claimed borders that encompassed an area that included all of the present state of Texas as well as parts of present-day New Mexico, Oklahoma, Kansas, Colorado, and Wyoming. The Republic of Texas was an independent nation from 1836 until 1845, when it joined the Union as the twenty-eighth state.

Sarah and her family returned to Gonzales after the war and rebuilt their home. She lived the rest of her life in Gonzales. She never remarried. She lived to see Texas join the Union in 1845 and died before her beloved country was ripped apart by the Civil War. Her body was placed on a sled drawn by oxen and carried to the hilltop mound not far from her home. She is buried there on Santa Anna's Mound, now the site of the DeWitt cemetery. Generations of her descendants have been laid to rest alongside her.

Green reaped few rewards for his vision and sacrifice. Though hardly financially rewarding to him, his DeWitt colony was considered the second most successful colony in the empresario era, after Austin's. The foundations laid by the empresarios and those who fought in the Texas Revolution led to the modern state of Texas.

Will (aka John W. Jones) is based on the life of John W. Smith. Believed to be the last messenger out of the Alamo, Smith was the first Anglo mayor of San Antonio. Elected in 1837, he served a one-year term. He was twice reelected, serving from 1840 to 1844. He was a leading landowner and state senator. He died in 1845, the year Texas joined the Union.

Eliza remarried in 1837. Her third husband, Thomas Jones Hardeman, fought at San Jacinto and was a member of the Texas Congress. At his suggestion, the capital of Texas was named Austin. They lived in Bastrop and had three children. Eliza died in 1863. She and her husband were buried near their home. Later their remains were moved to the state cemetery in Austin.

Naomi and her husband, William Matthews, had one son. Naomi apparently died young, in 1837. (Records conflict on her date of death.) Her son is mentioned in Sarah's will.

C. C. remained in Gonzales his entire life. He married Parmelia Barrow, raised a family of six children, and became a judge. He lived in his mother's rebuilt home. He was known as "a walking history of his section." He fought in the Civil War, died in 1890, and is buried near his mother in the DeWitt family plot.

Eveline married in 1838. Her husband also fought at San Jacinto and later became a judge in Gonzales. They had three sons. She died in 1891 and is buried with her husband, Charles Mason, in the Masonic Cemetery in Gonzales.

Clinton married Elizabeth Frazier, and they had four children. A sheriff in Gonzales, he died in a shootout with his wife's brother in 1860.

Minerva married Isham Jones in 1845. They lived in Gonzales and had five children. She died in 1902.

Stephen F. Austin returned to Texas in August 1835. He ran against Sam Houston for president of the Republic in September 1836 and was defeated. He died in late 1836. He is known as the Father of Texas. The state capital is named for him.

Sam Houston, after leading the surprise attack that defeated the Mexicans at San Jacinto, was elected the first president of the Republic in 1836. He was reelected in 1841. After Texas joined the Union in 1845, he served in the US Senate from 1846 to 1859. He opposed the secession of Texas from the Union and died in 1863. The city of Houston is named for him.

José Antonio Navarro, like Austin and DeWitt, was one of the founding fathers of Texas. One of the biggest Tejano landowners in Texas at that time, he also represented Texas in the legislature of the State of Coahuila y Tejas and in Mexico City. A signer of the Texas Declaration of Independence, he was a leader of the Texas Revolution.

Antonio López de Santa Anna, sometimes called the Napoleon of the West, greatly influenced the early days of Mexico. Though he served as general and president several times during a forty-year career, he is remembered as one who lost more than half of Mexico to Texas in 1836 and to the Mexican Cession in 1848.

Martín and Patricia De León, founders of the Tejano colony Guadalupe Victoria, between Anglo Texas and Mexican Texas, established the only predominantly Mexican colony in Texas. Among the largest Tejano landowners in Texas, with a 22,000-acre ranch, Empresario Martín De León and his wife, Patricia, were passionately involved with the Texas cause. Nevertheless, they were victims of prejudice against citizens of Mexican descent after the victory at San Jacinto.

Jared Groce, plantation owner of ten leagues (some 44,280 acres) of land and wealthiest landowner in Austin's colony, came to Texas in 1822 with fifty wagons and ninety slaves. Known for his hospitality and generosity, he supplied and tended his friend Sam Houston's forces in April 1836, helping them to gain strength to meet the Mexicans in the coming days at San Jacinto.

GLOSSARY

acequía   aqueduct, irrigation ditch

adecuada   appropriate

alcalde   magistrate, mayor

ayuntamiento   town council

belduque   large sharp knife with pointed blade (possible precursor to Bowie knife)

burdel   house of prostitution, brothel

El Colorado   redhead; nickname for redheaded character Will Jones

empresario   land agent in early Mexican Texas (then Coahuila y Tejas)

escopeta   rifle, shotgun

esposa   wife, spouse

estanco   government-licensed shop selling tobacco products; tobacconist

Isleños   islanders; in particular, residents of San Antonio de Béjar area who immigrated to Coahuila y Tejas from Canary Islands in the early 1700s

jacal   shack; hut

jefe politico   political chief of district in early Mexican Texas (then Coahuila y Tejas)

ladrones   thieves

mescalito   peyote button derived from peyote cactus, containing hallucinogens, particularly mescaline

nadar   to swim

ojos de agua   natural spring, bubbling up in limestone or other porous rock, forming a kind of pond or swimming hole

rubia   blond

sal   salt

sangre   blood

sitio   parcel of land; commonly used in Mexican Texas for land grant, the equivalent of 4,428 acres (called a league in English)

tuna   red bulb-like fruit of *Opuntia*, or prickly pear cactus, also called nopales

counterpane   bed cover, bedspread

dogtrot   an open-ended passage running through the center of a house, flanked by living spaces on each side; style of house, also known as a breezeway house or dog-run, used throughout the southern United States during the nineteenth and early twentieth centuries and common in Mexican Texas in the early 1800s

dragoon   mounted infantry using horses for mobility but dismounting to fight on foot; used throughout Europe from early seventeenth century and common in Mexican Texas in early nineteenth century

headright   a grant (of land) formerly given one who fulfilled certain conditions relating to settling and developing land (as in Mexican Texas in the 1820s and 1830s)

league   league of land in Mexican Texas in 1831 contained 4,428 acres

puncheon   heavy slab of timber, roughly dressed, for use as a floorboard

REFERENCES

PRIMARY SOURCES

Green DeWitt letters
Sarah Seely proposal for grant to a league of land
Anecdotes from oral histories, family documents,
    newspaper records
The Gonzales Inquirer

BIBLIOGRAPHY

Barker, Eugene. *The Life of Stephen F. Austin.* Austin: University of
    Texas Press, 1926.
Bedichek, Roy. *Karánkaway Country.* Austin: University of Texas
    Press, 1950.
Brown, John Henry. *Indian Wars and Pioneers of Texas.* Austin:
    L.E. Daniel, 1880.
DeWitt, Edna. "Lest We Forget." *The Gonzales Inquirer.* n.d.
Frenzel, Victoria Eberle. *Hope, Heartbreak, Heroes.* Gonzales, TX:
    self-published, 2008.
Gonzales County History. Gonzales, TX: The Gonzales County
    Historical Commission, 1986.
Harrigan, Stephen. *The Gates of the Alamo.* New York:
    Alfred A. Knopf, 2000.
James, Marquis. *The Raven.* Austin: University of Texas Press, 1929.
Kendall, Dorothy Steinbomer, Carmen Perry, and Theodore Gentilz.
    Gentilz: Artist of the Old Southwest. The Elma Dill Russell Spencer
    Foundation, No. 6. Austin: University of Texas Press, 1974.
Lindley, Thomas. *Alamo Traces.* Lanham, MD: Republic of
    Texas Press, 2003.

Lukes, Edward A. *DeWitt Colony of Texas*. Austin: Pemberton Press, 1976.

Moehring, Sharon Anne Dobyns, and John A. Moehring. *The Gonzales Connection: The History and Genealogy of the DeWitt and Jones Families*. Victoria, B.C., Canada: Trafford Publishing, 2004.

Rather, Ethel Zivley. "DeWitt's Colony." *The Quarterly of the Texas State Historical Society* 8, no. 2 (October 1904). (Since 1912, known as *The Southwestern Historical Quarterly*.)

WEBSITES

McKeehan, W. (n.d.). *Sons of DeWitt colony*. Sonsofdewittcolony.org. http://www.sonsofdewittcolony.org/.

Texas State Historical Association. (1999). *Handbook of Texas*. TSHA. https://www.tshaonline.org/handbook.

QUESTIONS FOR DISCUSSION

1. There are many conflicts throughout *The Empresario's Wife*. Which do you see as the major and minor tensions?
2. How would you describe Sarah?
3. How would you describe Green DeWitt? What drove him?
4. Why do you think Sarah wanted a land grant from Mexico in her own name?
5. Sarah and her children created the Come and Take It flag, the first declaration of Texas's independence from Mexico. Why do you think that flag is still remembered today?
6. Have you seen modern references to the Come and Take It flag? Do they reflect its original purpose?
7. How would you describe Will's role in the story?
8. What in Sarah's character shapes how she related to Will?
9. Does Sarah's history with Will threaten her marriage to Green? Why? Why not?
10. There is a diverse cast of characters in Sarah's world. Which character(s) did you like best?
11. How do Eugenio and Antoñia play indispensable roles in Sarah's life and throughout the book?
12. How do Eugenio and Antoñia navigate the opportunities and dangers of the Anglo world?
13. Why is Belle's role central to understanding life in Gonzales, the capital of DeWitt's colony?
14. What other characters help to paint a picture of survival in early Texas?
15. What did you learn about Texas and American history that you didn't know?

16. Geography plays a large role in the novel. How are the land and the environment central to Sarah's struggles?
17. How would you describe Sarah's legacy in Texas and American history?
18. Sarah Seely DeWitt is the narrator of the book. At the beginning of Parts 1, 2, 3, and 4, Sarah reflects on her past. How did those brief overviews affect your view of her story?
19. How did the Texas Revolution lead to US expansion and the fulfillment of Manifest Destiny?
20. Did this story of a great-grandmother's legacy make you reflect on your own ancestry and your relationship to your family's history?

ACKNOWLEDGMENTS

I first want to thank three people who helped me through the beginning, middle, and end of this story: my history-loving aunt and Gonzales resident, Mary Ella Hurt; my National Geographic Society colleague and champion editor, Barbara Brownell Grogan; and my loving and brilliant communicator son, Jason Molin, who buoyed me all the way through to finding a publisher. Another essential part of this team was Carl Mehler, cartographer *par excellence*, who went far beyond his professional duties in researching and crafting the 1836 Texas and Gonzales maps. Along the way, there were so many more who helped. To name a few: Joan Mitric, generous writer, reader, and editor; David Beacom, sharp-eyed reader and editor; Amy Jane Lynch, historical novelist and insightful reader; Turner Houston and Michelle Bushneff, design mavens; Susan Leon, NYC independent editor pro; Liz Reilly and Louise Millikan, bilingual speakers who cast expert eyes on the novel's Spanish passages and conversation and offered brilliant bibliographic and copy edits; and my husband, Al Seeber, who tirelessly read and reprinted copies for edits, re-edits, and perusal, scores of times. Finally, to all my friends who provided inspiration, support, and time, and Bold Story Press, my publisher, I am forever grateful.

ABOUT THE AUTHOR

Barbara H. Seeber is a Texas native and graduate of the University of Texas at Austin and Columbia University. With more than 30 years of experience in the publishing industry, she is an award-winning feature writer and former National Geographic writer and editor. In addition to articles in *Science '80-86*, *Horticulture*, *Garden Design*, and many National Geographic publications, she has authored books on health and on the gardens of Washington, DC.

The Empresario's Wife is the author's debut novel. Set in 1826-36 Texas, the novel follows Sarah Seely DeWitt during the era of Mexican land grants and colonization efforts led by figures like Stephen F. Austin and Green DeWitt. Drawing on contemporary documentation and extensive primary and secondary sources, the novel recounts the saga of an ancestor, Sarah Seely DeWitt, and the events that change her—and the nation—forever.

The author resides in Washington, DC, with her husband and two dogs and two cats.

ABOUT BOLD STORY PRESS

Bold Story Press is a curated, woman-owned hybrid publishing company with a mission of publishing well-written stories by women. If your book is chosen for publication, our team of expert editors and designers will work with you to publish a professionally edited and designed book. Every woman has a story to tell. If you have written yours and want to explore publishing with Bold Story Press, contact us at https://boldstorypress.com.

The Bold Story Press logo, designed by Grace Arsenault, was inspired by the nom de plume, or pen name, a sad necessity at one time for female authors who wanted to publish. The woman's face hidden in the quill is the profile of Virginia Woolf, who, in addition to being an early feminist writer, founded and ran her own publishing company, Hogarth Press.

Made in the USA
Middletown, DE
14 October 2024

62620039R00243